Where Wild Hearts Dance

Copyright © 2025 by Victoria Holliday

All rights reserved.

No part of this book may be reproduced in any form or by any electronic or mechanical means, including information storage and retrieval systems, without written permission from the author, except for the use of brief quotations in a book review.

This is a work of fiction. Names, characters, businesses, places, events and incidents are either the products of the author's imagination, or used in a fictitious manner.

NO AI TRAINING: Without in any way limiting the author's [and publisher's] exclusive rights under copyright, any use of this publication to "train" generative artificial intelligence (AI) technologies to generate text is expressly prohibited. The author reserves all rights to license uses of this work for generative AI training and development of machine learning language models.

*To all the girls who keep their wild in the dark.
Your shadows are what make you beautiful.
Wear them with pride.*

Where WILD Hearts DANCE

PLAYLIST

Innocent (Taylor's version) ~ Taylor Swift
You left me alone ~ Up the Rivals
Fell in love with a girl ~ White Stripes
Paint it Black ~ Rolling Stones
Hotel Sayre ~ Craig Armstrong, Lana Del Rey
Cosmic Love ~ Florence + The Machine
Chemtrails over the Country Club ~ Lana Del Rey
Dreams ~ Fleetwood Mac
Hurts like Hell ~ Fleurie, Tommee Profitt
White Wedding ~ Billy Idol
Kiss Me ~ Ed Sheeran

PROLOGUE

enito

If my eyes were bullets, the back of Savero's head would be leaking blood like a fucking sieve.

Each step I take along the church aisle chimes with the sound of my teeth gnashing together.

I shouldn't be here. None of us should be here. This funeral was never meant to happen. Not yet. Not so damn fucking soon.

Gianni DiSanto was young for a don. Exceptionally young for a don who had the whole of New York at his feet. The man wasn't even sixty. And he was the fittest fifty-something fucker I know. I'm half his age and he could run rings around me, literally. He ran ten miles every morning and lifted weights every day. Had to, he said. Not every war could be won with a gun, he said.

Sometimes, good old-fashioned fist fights were not only called for, but good *for the soul*, he said.

The steel in my waistband presses firmly against my back, reminding me of threats that are never far away in this world. I wonder if I'd feel any better had it been a gun that took Gianni's life in the end, and not the heart attack that *none* of us were prepared for.

My heart cracks a little wider the closer my footsteps take me to the final goodbye. Gianni treated me like a son. Way more than my own father did. Not that my own father deserved the title. Gianni recognised something in me when I was in my late teens. Potential, perhaps. Or maybe it was the insatiable hunger I felt to destroy anything that crossed my path with little to no empathy. I guess it was better to have someone like that on side as opposed to against.

My eyes bore into Savero like it's his fault his father died. I know this is how grief works – I've watched enough men die in my line of work. Hell, most of them died at my own hands. Very few I actually cared about, but those I did, the process was the same: get angry, kick a few things, blame the person closest. When I learned of Gianni's passing, I screamed at the sky. I punched a few walls. And now I'm blaming Savero.

One minute Gianni is here, commanding his capos from the quiet of his office, moving money and assets around the city like pawns on a chess board. The next, he's gone.

One minute Savero's a nobody – a capo by name, an incendiary fucker by nature – the next he's the king of

New York. Sure, he was Gianni's first born, but we all know he isn't don material. He's too unpredictable and unhinged to be a mafia kingpin. Locked and loaded soldier, maybe. Don of the biggest crime family this side of Chicago? Fuck no.

Yet, here we are, following the loosest of cannons into a church where we're to bury the greatest Italian leader that ever lived. Coincidence? I'm not convinced.

The anger tastes bitter as I swallow it, then my eyes catch on something to my left. My chest hardens in recognition. Only capos and their families were given access to the church service – not associates, nor even soldiers, were granted that privilege. So why the hell is Tony Castellano – a mere *associate* – and his entire fucking family taking up a whole pew?

I watch for any change in Savero's manner that might suggest a huge mistake has been made. Maybe I can prevent someone from getting their neck snapped in two for this oversight. I breathe a sigh of relief when he walks past Castellano, his sister and four daughters without so much as a pause.

Beppe lowers his voice when I arrive at the capo's side. "What are *they* doing here?"

I stroke a hand down the tie I reserve for funerals and only the most fruitful of legal negotiations. "I was going to ask you the same thing."

I glance to my right and my annoyance lifts at the sight of Cristiano, Gianni's second – and substantially more pleasant – son. He has his head bent, scrolling through his phone while ignoring the mafia charade unfolding around him.

"Must be something to do with the port," Beppe mutters under his breath.

My eyes narrow. Gianni and Tony Castellano had a good arrangement. Tony let Gianni ship a few illegal consignments through his port and Gianni paid him handsomely for it. Savero had always been vocal about wanting more – a majority share in fact – though none of us really know why. This must be why Castellano is here; it's the only explanation. And since Savero's inherited me as his new consigliere, it pisses me off that he hasn't kept me in the fucking loop.

"Yeah, you're probably right," I concede. *Though it doesn't explain why the entire family is here.*

The church begins to quieten and I turn to see the priest walking our way, his head bowed. I'm about to do the same when I feel a hostile pair of eyes burning into the side of my face. It's not an unusual sensation; most people despise me. But it is one I wasn't expecting at Gianni's funeral of all places.

I search for the culprit and have to do a double take. That is not what I was expecting. Not what I was expecting *at all*.

One of the younger Castellano girls is *glaring* at me as though she wants to rip me apart with a blunt blade. I indulge the urge to stare back, which seems to incense her even more. Her lips are full but pursed and her arms are folded firmly across her chest, long black-nailed fingers drumming against smooth alabaster skin. I slowly stroke my gaze over her, enjoying her obvious fury. She has one leg crossed over the other and is wearing a floor length black satin dress that falls open midway up her thigh.

My gaze crawls back up her body to her eyes. I can't confirm the color because they're narrowed to slits, but I catch a flash of green when she blinks. Her hair is jet black, long, and pinned to one side. It's the sort of hair I would normally wrap around my fist.

She's catastrophically beautiful, which is irritating, because the least I can do today is give my full focus to remembering Gianni, a man who practically raised me as his own. Not to a seething beauty who's sticking metaphorical pins into me for some unknown reason.

I feel a sharp elbow in my ribs signaling the service is about to start. A corner of my mouth ticks up, narrowing the girl's eyes even further. Then, with an inhuman amount of willpower, I turn back to the priest.

My attention is feigned though. I can't shake the image of those cat-like eyes burning shards into my skin, making even my tailored suit feel scratchy and uncomfortable. What was her problem?

I piss off a lot of people in my line of work. Very few of them have the guts to show it. But I have a feeling this one might just give me a run for my money…

CHAPTER ONE

Contessa

Three years earlier

Fed's talking to me but I'm not listening. I'm watching Nike-clad feet move effortlessly across the screen, each beat funneling a wave of energy up the dancers' legs, where it embraces strong thighs and loose hips, glides along graceful arms and seeps into liquid eyes.

There it is. That feeling of being one with the music —with the beat.

When I see that kind of harmony, I can't focus on anything else. Not even the voice of my best friend, whom I expect is recounting the story of his second cousin's dice with death in the classroom, for the millionth time this afternoon.

The pause icon fills the screen and I bite my tongue before panning my gaze to Federico.

"You didn't hear a word of that, did you?" he says, in a monotone drawl.

I arch a brow. "You were saying that Raff was hit by a chair, but the other kid only got a half hour detention, so his papa stormed into school, threatened the kid and his family, and put the teacher out of a job." I hold my breath and pray he agrees because, sure, I hadn't heard a word of it.

He curls a lip and flicks the remote toward the screen sending the dancing feet in motion once again.

I pull my ankles into my butt to stop them from jiggling. This always happens. Whenever I'm sitting or standing around, if even the slightest sound of music filters through my ears, I cannot for the life of me keep still. But I'm sitting high up by the breakfast bar in Federico's kitchen, with my legs crossed on the seat, and I'm too interested in the dancers on TV to tolerate sliding off the stool.

The sound of rustling draws my attention from the TV screen.

"Contessa! Buongiorno!"

I spin around to see Federico's mama, Mrs. Falconi, drift into the kitchen in a vision of fur and shopping bags. She drops the bags to the floor and walks over with her arms wide open. She wraps them around me, swallowing my small frame.

"Hi Mrs. Falconi," I squeak, as the life force is squeezed from my lungs.

"So good to see you, Tess. I didn't know you were coming around today." There's a slight edge to her tone that makes me tense. Beneath the shield of her winter sweater, I feel her questioning gaze dart toward Fed.

I normally have dance class on a Thursday but Antonio, my dance teacher, has some family stuff going on, so it's been canceled. I can't think why it would be a problem though. Ever since my mama was murdered in the crossfire of the underworld violence that has colored my life, the Falconi's have always let me treat this place like a second home.

Fed's expression darkens a touch before a glint of mischief appears in his eyes. "We'll get out from under your feet, Ma. Come on Tess, we'll go to my room…"

I arch a brow knowing Fed's pushing his luck.

"Ha ha." Mrs. Falconi releases me, walks around the island and opens the refrigerator. "Nice try Federico, but you know the rules. No girls in your room." She turns to flash me a wink. "Not even girls who are just *friends*."

I smile. Fed and me, we'll only ever be *just friends*. We've known each other since kindergarten. I've witnessed some of his most embarrassing moments, like the time he was staring too hard at Kelly Richards, the prom queen, and face-planted a post, and the time he climbed a tree in the back yard, got stuck and peed himself while waiting to be rescued.

He's always just been 'Fed' to me—my best friend Fed.

Admittedly, since he turned fifteen a few months ago, gotten a little buff and developed a moody attitude that other girls in our school seem to find attractive for some reason, my gaze on him has lingered a little longer than usual. But that's only because he's changing and it's intriguing to watch, not because I'm attracted to him in like a wannabe girlfriend kinda way.

I don't look at any boy in that way. There's no point. None of them would want me.

I'm just the kid who dresses in black and sits at the back of class not talking to anyone, barely able to see through my overgrown bangs. I don't remember ever having a girlfriend, not even before Mama died and everyone my age started avoiding me.

I was twelve years old when it happened. I guess it was a time when hormones were starting to do weird things and all my classmates cared about was fitting in, being 'normal,' being the same as everyone else. Having a mama shot dead by a member of the mafia we all pretended didn't exist wasn't 'normal,' so in their eyes, neither was I.

Still, as uncomfortable as it was to continue dragging my boots into school, it was preferable to being at home, where I was wrapped in cotton and treated like a baby who didn't understand the world.

I'll tell you something, there's nothing like losing a mother to gang violence before you've even hit puberty to make you grow up and understand the world fast.

Trilby, our oldest sister, was in the car when Mama was shot. She needed space after that, I guess. She coped by moving almost immediately into the apartment next door, severing any relationship I had with her at a time when I probably needed her the most.

Aunt Allegra and my older sister Sera, however, more than made up for Trilby's absence by insisting I must never be left alone, I must be shielded from the TV news reports, and always chaperoned whenever I left the house. It's only in the last six months I've convinced them to let me go to dance class alone, and to Fed's house down the street—which is lucky for me since he's the only kid from school who gives me the time of day.

My gaze is drawn back to the screen when I should be thinking about making my excuses to leave. It's clear Mrs. Falconi wasn't expecting me, and for the first time ever, I feel as though I'm not welcome here.

"You wanna stay for some cannelloni, Tess?" I can tell from the way Mrs. Falconi rushes out the words without looking at me, she's only being polite.

My stomach groans, but I know a hint when I hear one.

"I would love to, Mrs. Falconi, but I was just stopping by. My aunt has dinner prepared. Thanks so much though."

Fed's body wilts from the other side of the kitchen island, sending an anxious skip down my spine. A year ago he wouldn't have cared whether I left or stayed—we'd just agree to meet up again the next day, no big deal. These days though, not getting his way when it comes to our friendship seems to bother him.

"No problem." Mrs. Falconi shoots me a smile and I don't miss the way the outer edges of her eyes have relaxed now I've declined the offer. She starts laying out plates and setting cutlery on the table, making my brows draw together. It's not even five p.m. and she's serving dinner already?

"In fact," I say, sliding off the stool, "I better get going."

"What… now?" Fed hops off his stool, plants his palms on the island and glares at his mom.

"Um…" I glance at Mrs. Falconi but she has her back turned to us both. "Yeah. I'll see you tomorrow. I have a free period after lunch. Meet you outside the sports hall?"

Fed's mouth opens and he's about to reply, but a door slams out in the hall and the sound of tense conversation filters through the wall to the kitchen.

I hear several male voices. I identify one voice as that of Fed's papa, Enzo Falconi. But the other two voices are unfamiliar. They're talking low and deep, but not hushed. I can't make out the words but the obviously tense atmosphere makes the hairs along my arms rise up.

"Why don't you two go upstairs?"

I turn around and see Fed looking at his mother, his gaze searching for an explanation. When I look across at her, my breath stills. Her usual impeccably rouged cheeks have drained of color.

I start to decline, because I know I shouldn't be here. "Thanks but I thought we couldn't—"

But before I can finish my sentence, Fed is at my

side, wrapping his fingers around my hand and pulling me toward the staircase. "Let's go, Tess."

I can't drag my eyes from his mom's face as she watches us leave the room. Any other time, she'd be stopping us. There's only one thing she's ever been super-strict about and that's letting Fed take me—or any other girl—up the stairs to his room. But while her voice is calm and measured, her fingers are vibrating against the countertop.

My heart thumps against the wall of my chest. Fed pulls my arm with an urgency that feels more like a need to get me alone in his room than a need to get away from the male voices that are sounding more and more agitated with every step we take.

The landing at the top of the stairs wraps around the entrance hall granting a view of the doors to the kitchen, living areas and the main entrance. My eyes catch on a movement to the right, behind the door to the dining room.

"Wait—" I pull Fed to a standstill. "What's going on down there?"

Fed joins me as I press my back to the wall. Where I am as tense as a wound spring, he lets out a bored sigh. "Oh, who the hell knows? Papa probably forgot to pay the lease on time and you know what those Di Santo assholes are like. They'll be here to inform him of the increased interest. Or the rise in protection fees."

"The *Di Santo's* are here?"

My throat has dried up. The Di Santo's *rule* this city. They've ruled it for so long, it feels like they're almost legit running the east coast. Everyone knows they have every governor, every official, even the FBI in their pocket. No one has been able to stop them, and now? No one dares to try.

"It wouldn't be the first time," Fed grumbles.

I tense further at his nonchalance, which feels even more dangerous considering Di Santo men are in his house right now. "It doesn't sound like a routine visit, Fed. It sounds a little intense."

He scratches at the emerging bristles on his chin. "They'll be gone in a minute. C'mon, let's go to my room."

I resist his pull and press my back harder into the wall. I can hear clipped commands now, and words spoken in a pleading tone. Fed might be unconcerned about what's going on below us but I'm not. A flash of long chestnut hair catches in the corner of my eye. Fed's mama is standing outside the dining room, holding onto the wall, and her fingers are trembling.

I pull away from the wall and lower my gaze to the gap in the door, trying to see through. A man dressed in a sharp, tailored suit shifts into view. My breath scratches the back of my throat. His height and build are nothing short of menacing, and his high cheekbones and full lips are the sort that lure in women like prey.

Everything about him is dark. Dark clothes, dark hair, dark brow.

I shudder. The Di Santos carry darkness with them everywhere they go. It only got blacker after Mama died, and I still blame them for her death, even though the bullet was fired by a member of a rival mob—a Marchesi.

Thanks to my father's port, we've always managed to stay on the good side of Gianni Di Santo and his men, but I can't say the same for other folk in this city. And despite the mutual respect Gianni and Papa seem to have for one another, I know the don of New York can turn on a dime. I've seen it happen too many times and the thought of it releases a sick sense of dread in the pit of my stomach.

The front door bangs open and a man with hair thinning on the top of his head bursts into the entrance hall. Fed steps forward to look over the rail. Then he grips my hand again and whispers, "*Zio*."

It's been a while since I last saw Fed's uncle but I recognize the resemblance to his father in the pattern balding, jerky gait and long fingers that flex as he approaches the dining room door.

"Mario, no—"

Mrs. Falconi reaches out to stop him from going any further, but her plea falls on deaf ears when Fed's uncle ignores her, presses two flat hands to the door and pushes it roughly. It swings inward revealing the full, rich profile of the man in black. He turns slowly to look at Mario but, no matter how hard I strain, I can't see the details of his face from this angle.

"Shit," Fed whispers beside me and we both lower our knees to the carpet to get a closer look. Fear pulses beneath my skin.

Two more figures come into view. They have their backs to the door but swing around when Mario enters.

My gaze narrows on them. I recognize one as Augusto Zanotti, Gianni Di Santo's second-in-command. He owns Alphabet City, near Mr. Falconi's offices. I don't recognize the other man. Their gazes don't dwell on Mario for long—if he thought he'd pose a threat to them, he couldn't have been more wrong. They've given him as much attention as they would the shit on their shoes.

I hear Fed's papa stutter something incomprehensible, then Mario pulls out *a gun*.

A gasp tears from my throat before Fed claps his hand over my mouth and I realize my mistake. The man in black takes a step backward and lifts his gaze to the landing. His hand rests on black metal at his waistband. Time stops as I take in his narrowed bronze eyes and tan skin marred by a scar that runs the length of one side of his face. Everything about him is calm, controlled, *unaffected*. Like the worst type of predator—deadly and carnivorous, as though he has the power to draw people to him like a magnet before gnashing his teeth around their limbs and eating them alive.

A hot flush coasts from my cheeks down my spine to my pelvis. This is what pure terror must feel like.

In fateful synchronicity, the sound of a gun cock fills the house, the bronze eyes dart away and Mario's arm flies up, sending a bullet through the ceiling.

"Fuck—" Fed wraps an arm around my torso and pulls me backward. I always thought I was strong for my build but Fed's muscles seem to have burst out of nowhere in the last few months. He manages to drag my stunned limbs a few feet along the landing. "Tess, come *on*!" he hisses in my ear.

I can't take my eyes off the dining room door. Flashes of black move past the opening in quick succession. There's a fight. There are guns. Mrs. Falconi screams. More bullets are fired, yet I still can't move.

Mario's form appears in the gap; a tan hand is holding his neck tightly from the back. Then a gun is pressed up to his forehead. I can't see who's holding it.

"No—" The word floats from my lips like a puff of air.

I don't hear a sound over the ringing in my ears but I watch as Mario's body falls limply to the ground.

Fed chokes out a gasp and pulls me harder. This time, I move. I move faster than I've ever moved in my life. I scramble to my feet and pull Fed to his, then he grabs my hand and turns, hauling me down the landing toward his room. I twist back once to check there isn't a gun pointed in our direction and there isn't.

There's something else.

A pair of hazel eyes, a heated glance, and most terrifying of all, a man *unaffected*.

I stumble to a bed in the center of the room while Fed shuts the door and bolts it. When I turn around, he's pressed his back against the door as if to protect us against anyone entering. The man I just saw downstairs could snap Federico between his finger and thumb. The door would be a mere annoyance.

We stare at each other, our chests heaving with adrenaline, shock pulling at every nerve ending. The shouting below has quieted to barked commands and stuttered apologies. I jump when another door bangs closed, and only relax when the sound of tires on gravel rises up to the window.

Fed puts his hands over his face and that's when I notice how large they've become. He's starting to look like some college football player. The shake of his shoulders makes me stand and walk across the room, pulling him into me. He cries silent, wretched tears while I hold him tightly, stroking the back of his neck with my palm.

He just saw his uncle being murdered in cold blood.

The thought feels strangely distant, as though I'm having an out of body experience. I should be able to relate to how he's feeling but I'm numb. I feel nothing.

It feels like hours have passed by the time he takes in a long breath and pulls out of my arms. His eyes are raw, his heartbreak written across them in bright red ink.

"I'm so sorry, Fed," I whisper.

He simply nods, closes his eyes and shakes his head.

When his lids lift, he looks off to the side and his mouth ticks up in one corner. The cheeky, mischievous Fed I know is back in the room.

"What?" I ask, confused as to how he can find something funny right now.

His lips then twist into a bitter line. "When I thought about getting you in my room, this is not quite what I'd imagined."

A combustion of nervous relief makes me laugh, then his smile falls soberly.

A light tap at the door makes me jump. I take a step back, suddenly aware of how close we're standing.

"Federico…" Mrs. Falconi's voice is trembling. "Are you okay?"

Fed unlocks the door, and his mama pushes through it and collapses onto him. "Oh baby. Are you okay?" She holds his face tightly, moving it this way and that, inspecting him for damage.

When she's satisfied he doesn't have a scratch on him, the whites of her eyes take me in. "C'mere Tess…"

I walk into her arms for the second time this evening. My movements are mechanical. It's like my limbs have shifted into autopilot. My brain has shut down but my body is still going through the motions.

Mrs. Falconi sobs into Fed's shoulder and I press my forehead into his chest. It solidifies against my skin and something shifts in the air.

His voice is low and filled with conviction. "Papa…"

"He's okay, Federico. He's just dealing with—" A choked breath halts her words.

"I know Uncle Mario's dead," Fed confirms. "We saw it happen."

She looks up, her eyes wide. "H-how? You should have been here, in your room."

"It doesn't matter. What happened?"

She closes her eyes and shakes her head. "Mario was stupid. He was so stupid…"

"Why were the Di Santos here?" There's a bitter clip to Federico's tone.

Mrs. Falconi falls quiet.

"Mama," Fed's voice is uncharacteristically deep and firm. "Tell me the truth. Why were they here?"

A long pause is filled with stuttered breaths before Mrs. Falconi responds. "Your papa is behind on the lease for the offices and the storage facility."

Fed's throat bobs against my hair. "Why?"

"We had a theft. One of the warehouses was broken into and half our equipment was stolen. Your papa had to buy more urgently, so he wouldn't lose the contracts—it's become so competitive out there. He didn't have enough left over for the lease. He hoped they'd understand, give him some grace."

"And did they?"

"I don't know, Federico. Your papa... He's cleaning up his brother's *corpse*. I can't ask him yet."

"Why did they kill my uncle?"

Mrs. Falconi lifts her head and gaze flits between me and Fed. "Because he was *stupid*." When neither of us responds, she continues. "Who the hell walks into a room of Di Santos and pulls out a gun, Federico? Let alone pulls the trigger." She shakes her head and tears roll down her face. "Only Mario Falconi," she finishes, her voice cracking.

I stay in their embrace for a few minutes longer, the tension in my body making me rigid, then say the words I should have said an hour ago.

"I should really head home."

Mrs. Falconi releases a shuddering sigh and tips my face toward her. "I'm so sorry Contessa. After everything you've been through…"

"It's okay," I reply, with a small, hopefully reassuring smile. In truth, I just want to get out of here. While I haven't personally witnessed bullets being fired until now, I live every day with the aftereffects of murder, and the stark reality of it is threatening to singe my skin.

"I'm really sorry about your uncle." My tone takes a sharp dip. "And for what the Di Santo's have done." Bronze eyes and a heated glance flash across my lids but I blink the image away. "They all deserve to go to hell."

Mrs. Falconi's eyes widen. It's practically unheard of in this city to say a word against the Di Santos. They're supposed to be our saviors, maintaining law and order in the city and keeping crime at bay. But they're nothing but criminals themselves. Criminals and murderers. Barely even human beings. They're the same breed as the Marchesi's, who killed my mother. They all deserve to die slow, painful deaths.

I don't care how that heated glance pumped something effervescent into my veins, or infused my bones with a moreish warmth. It was just a look. And I live for the day I can show the owner of those bronze eyes he's worth nothing, to anyone.

"Please accept my condolences." I shake my head sadly, then I walk out of Fed's room, down the stairs and out of the Falconi residence, unbeknown to me for the very last time.

CHAPTER TWO

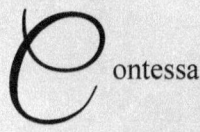
ontessa

My head is full of dark memories as I leave the dance studio the next evening. My bones and muscles ache from trying to get the routine right. Antonio made me repeat the moves over and over for what felt like a hundred times.

It's no secret he thinks I'm a loose cannon on the dance floor. If I got a dollar every time he told me I "simply won't be taught," I certainly won't need to dance for the money.

I've always been this way. Expressing myself in normal ways—talking to friends or having a good cry—doesn't come easily to me. Instead, I bottle it all up then release it through the movements of my body. Antonio says I'm "too wild," that I'm "untrainable."

It's become a part of my identity, for better or for worse.

These days, he accepts the way I come alive in all the inconvenient, unconventional ways, but tonight, he said I was "unhinged."

That's a new one.

I wonder if the reason I was unhinged in this evening's class is because I couldn't hear the music over the ringing of gun shots in my ears. Or because I couldn't sleep last night. My mind seemed to prefer replaying footage of the Di Santo's entering Fed's home and killing his uncle.

I hate that the Di Santos are *everywhere*. It's not often they are seen but my God they are felt. Their presence penetrates everything. New York seems to be in a permanent state of collective anxiety.

I'm certain *that's* the reason I haven't slept and not the bronze eyes that saw me watching as the Di Santo's shot Mario Falconi, an innocent man. What if the owner of those eyes tracks me down? What if me witnessing the killing is inconvenient for them?

A tremble vibrates down my spine until I remember that I'm a complete nobody. A shadow who lives in dark corners. They won't care that I saw anything. I don't matter, and that's just the way I like it.

The street is quiet. It's tucked away in the heart of Alphabet City, just a few blocks across from Mr. Falconi's offices. I'm about halfway down it when I hear the sound of footsteps not far behind.

Slow, deliberate, measured.

My heart sticks to my chest, making its beats reverberate through my torso. Maybe I do matter after all.

I walk faster, focusing all my attention on the sound of the footsteps.

They're still behind me, inching closer.

I dare not look around, but pick up speed until I'm almost jogging. The footsteps quicken slightly but they sound like they might belong to a much taller person who can take longer strides, moving faster without taking more steps like I have to.

I pull my house keys from my pocket, shove one of them through my fingers, the jagged edge pointing outward, and curl my fist around the rest. The end of the street where cabs usually pass is still a few hundred yards away. My breaths quicken with adrenaline.

A long thin shadow stretches across the road. Whoever is following me isn't far behind. I pull out my phone and dial Allegra. Even without the speaker switched on I can hear the dial tone.

It just rings and rings.

Shit.

A quick flick of my gaze across the street again and the shadow is even closer.

I end the call and break into a jog. I just did three hours straight dancing and I'm exhausted, but I force my feet to move quicker, harder. Blood thumps through my dormant muscles making them ache.

I'm breathless when I finally round the corner. A couple of cabs are heading my way, only one with its light glowing. I run out into the road, my lungs burning. Thankfully, the cab stops and I jump in the back, breathlessly announcing my address.

As I squint in the direction of where I've just run from, I can't see any movement. Whoever was behind me didn't turn the corner.

When we near the end of the block I glance sideways and see the same shadow stretching across the street. There's a man standing on the corner, just out of sight. I jerk my focus back to the road.

It's only when the cab is over the Brooklyn Bridge that I properly exhale, and the reality of what happened makes my blood run cold.

I've just been followed.

In the heart of Alphabet City under a thin veil of darkness.

My cell buzzes in my fingers and my aunt's name flashes up. Now that I'm out of immediate harm's way, I debate whether or not I should tell her what just happened for all of five seconds. Allegra became a surrogate mother to four spirited, strong-willed girls just three years ago when Mama was killed. We are a daily cause of anxiety to her. The guy who just followed me… it could be nothing, and I don't want to give my poor aunt any more reason to worry about us.

I press the speaker. "Hey Allegra."

"Hi Tess. I got a missed call from you. Is everything okay?"

"Oh yeah, everything's fine. I'm sorry, I must have butt-called you when I got in the cab. I'm on my way home."

"Okay, honey. There's some lasagna on the side if you want it, just help yourself."

"Thanks Allegra. I'll be there soon." I hang up and push the guilt of lying deep into my gut. The further we get from Manhattan and the closer we get to my home, the more I realize the guy might not have been following me. It's late, I'm tired, and I'm still processing what Antonio meant when he called me 'unhinged.'

I slide my phone into my bag. I'm probably just being paranoid.

As the cab pulls up to the house, there's a familiar vehicle blocking the drive. I pay the driver and make my way to the car. A door opens and I slide into the passenger seat, lifting my gaze to meet Federico's.

"Hey," I say softly. "How are you doing?"

News of his uncle's murder has spread quickly. I've only had to eavesdrop on Papa's calls a couple of times today to know that people are already cutting ties with Mr. Falconi and his business.

Fed leans forward until his eyes are lit by the glow of the street lamps. I gasp at what I see. Rings of fire, swollen skin, a hard, bitter jaw.

"Wha—?"

His forefinger presses against my lips. "I can't stay long, Tess." His voice has thinned, like fragile glass, sharp enough to cut through flesh. "I shouldn't even be here. If my father finds out I've left the house, he'll go crazy."

"What are you talking about?" I whisper round his finger.

His gaze roams my face erratically, and his eyes are filled with more than pure panic. There's a kind of desperation there… almost like hunger.

"We're leaving…"

I go to speak but he presses his finger to my lips harder.

"Tomorrow night. No one knows. And you cannot tell anyone, Tess. Do you understand?"

I swallow a large knot in my throat. Then I nod.

Federico sighs heavily. "The Di Santo's have shut us down…"

"What?"

"According to Papa they've been chipping away at him for months, taking clients away and shutting down premises so he loses business. He's been struggling to pay the lease on the warehouse and he missed one month. *One month*, Tess. And that's all they needed. It isn't enough that they've killed my uncle—they want to *ruin* us. So, we're leaving."

Bitterness clenches its fist around my heart.

Fed's lip curls in disgust. "The don couldn't even grace us with his presence yesterday. He sent his fucking *consigliere*…"

My eyes narrow.

"Benito Bernadi," Fed clarifies.

I realize who he means. The man in black, with the

bronze eyes and heated gaze. The man who saw me through the gap in the door. I try to mask the shiver that coasts down my spine at the memory.

Fed blinks down then lifts his lids revealing soft, sad eyes. "I thought I had forever to do this."

The air inside the vehicle shifts, taking away a little bit of oxygen. His finger slides down my lips and a short smile teases his mouth when he glances over my shoulder into the distance. "I don't know when it happened."

I somehow find my voice again. "When what happened?"

His Adam's apple moves and his expression turns somber before his eyes fall back to mine. "When I fell for you."

I swear my heart stops beating.

Federico *fell* for me?

I can't decipher which emotion wants to rise to the surface first—shock, because I had no idea anyone *could* fall for me; guilt, because I've never thought of Federico that way; or despair, because breaking someone's heart was *not* on my to-do list this evening.

I swallow all of them down.

"I had so many plans for us…"

For *us*? Shock roots me to the seat.

"Starting with this…"

I don't have time to take a breath before his lips are on mine.

Cold, bitter, fragile.

I suddenly feel so remorseful and so guilty and so

broken for him, I only pause for a second before I kiss him back.

At first he seems surprised that I've responded, but he loosens slightly and his lips part. It feels clumsy and unnatural, but I've never kissed anyone before. Maybe it's supposed to feel this way.

I jump when his tongue probes at my mouth. Nerves dance across my skin at the unfamiliarity of it, then I let him in. I'm not sure I like having someone's tongue inside my mouth, but somehow I know that barfing or spitting it out isn't the most encouraging reaction, so I hold my breath and let him do it.

In all honesty, my head is reeling with the thought of him leaving town. I might not have fallen for him, but he's still my best friend. He's still the one I go to when I'm sick of being treated like a baby by my aunt and sisters, which is most days. He's still the one I call when I'm so exhausted by the punishing dance routines I question whether I want to continue with the only thing I'm passionate about. And he's still the one I can laugh with until my stomach feels like it's splitting in half. These memories are what keep my lips parted, my mouth open and my throat from gagging as he swipes his tongue across mine.

Despite not being as into the kiss as Federico is, I still feel a strange sensation unfurling between my thighs, like I'm opening up, liquifying. I kind of like it, but it also feels strange. I'm relieved when he pulls away and I look up.

His eyes are no longer red. They're dark and

strangely un-sated. My heart thumps a little harder as I drift my fingers across my lips.

"Fuck, Tess. That was amazing." The ice in his voice has thawed some, but his knuckles are like cold shards when they brush against my skin. He must have been sitting in the darkness with the engine cut for an hour at least.

He lifts his hand to my cheek and just as he pushes an escaped strand of hair behind my ear, someone else's face flashes across my lids.

Bronze eyes, heated gaze. *Unaffected.*

The contrast between the hard man in black and the soft boy sitting before me makes my breath stutter.

Darkness and light, heat and ice.

And a question so big I can't comprehend it. Why, did my brain pick this moment to recall that beast of a man?

He's the reason Federico has to leave, and he's the reason I now have a terrible feeling in my gut.

"I need to ask you something, Tess."

My pulse thumps through my ears.

"I was hoping I'd have plucked up the courage to make you my girlfriend before asking this of you, but I don't have any more time."

My head feels light.

"But there's something I've always wanted to do and this is my only chance."

I swallow. "What is it?"

He smiles and for a moment looks

uncharacteristically bashful. "I want to make love to you, Tess."

That's it. My heart has actually stopped and if I weren't already sitting, I would be passing out on the passenger seat. It isn't unheard of. I have freakishly low blood pressure and fainting is a fairly regular occurrence.

"I— um…" I swallow again. "I'm a virgin, Fed."

He strokes my hair again and smiles. "I know."

"You, um…" Oh God, I feel *really* faint. "You want to take my virginity?"

He drops his hands to mine and squeezes them. "I've never wanted anything more."

When I don't respond, a look of panic slants across his brow. "This one thing. It's all I'm asking. I have to leave tomorrow, Tess. For good. *Forever*."

I can't do anything but stare back at him. I thought I was going to die a virgin, or I'd have to pay someone to take it from me. I'm just weird Tess, *wild* Tess, *unhinged* Tess.

The thought of someone wanting my virginity, and that person being Federico, has stunned me into silence. Maybe I should feel grateful that someone has seen through my emo aesthetic and liked what they've seen. Maybe this is the only chance I'll get to rid myself of the innocence that the underworld surrounding us seems to prize so highly.

"Please Tess." He's begging. "Just this one thing. Please. For me. For our decade of friendship. *Please*."

He leans forward and presses erratic kisses to my

temple and cheeks. "It's all I dream about, Tess. This is our last chance. Please let me give us something to remember."

His kisses are fervent, scattered.

And so desperate he almost doesn't hear my reply.

"Yes."

CHAPTER THREE

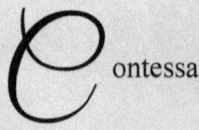
Contessa

There's an empty space above the dance studio. I think it's supposed to be an office but there's no furniture—only wooden boards and a couple rugs. There's a small kitchenette off to the side and another small room which is also empty. And with it being the middle of winter, it's also *freezing*. But this is the only place I could think of where Federico and I could be together away from the prying eyes of our families.

It's mid-morning on a Sunday—not a time I'd ordinarily have chosen to lose my virginity, but then again, it's not something I'd planned on doing any time soon.

The studio is closed on a Sunday so no one's around, and—thankfully—no one else seems to be aware the lock on this upstairs office has been broken for weeks.

Fed takes the stairs cautiously and presses an ear to the door before pushing it open, then I follow him inside. I hug my arms around myself and walk to the window, half conscious of Fed behind me unpacking a couple of bags he brought with him. The street is quiet with only the occasional yellow cab crawling through on a shortcut to somewhere more interesting. For one of the most monumental moments in my life, this day sure feels mundane.

"Did you bring the, um…?" I ask without looking around. I can't seem to form the word 'condom'—it sounds so foreign in my head, but Fed understands.

"Yeah, Tess. Of course I did."

I watch the street for another five minutes and when the shuffling behind me stops, I turn around and swallow.

Federico has laid out comforters, pillows and blankets and surrounded them with candles. Flames flicker gently in the darkened room and a bottle of vodka stands by the wall. Fed's gaze follows mine. "I thought, you know, it might help." He shrugs. "I want it to be good."

My legs tremble as I close the gap between us. I lower to my knees. The blankets make the room warmer somehow. Softer.

He reaches for the bottle and twists off the cap, then holds it out to me. "Want some?"

My fingers brush his when I take it from him and a shiver darts through my arm and across my shoulders. I never used to have this reaction to my best friend. He was always just… Fed. But he's about to become something a whole lot more. He's going to be written into my history—a part of the fabric of who I am.

I take a long swig of the vodka and stifle the urge to choke on it. The most I've ever drunk is the occasional glass of wine at family dinners, and even then it's come with a side of scrutiny from my aunt.

The heat of the alcohol works its way into my stomach and it doesn't take long for it to loosen my limbs and soften my inhibitions.

I look up from beneath nervous lashes. "So, how do we do this?"

His expression sobers. "I want you to feel comfortable."

I'm not sure what that means so, with trembling fingers, I cross my arms, grip the hem of my sweater and pull it over my head. When my gaze drops to Fed he's staring at my bra, his eyes wide, the rest of him unmoving.

"O-okay… Fuck," he says, quietly.

It seemed to be the right move, so I stand shakily and push my leather-look leggings over my hips, knees and ankles, then kick them to the side. Fed's gaze drops to my bare stomach, then slides down to the apex of my thighs. He swallows loudly. "You are fucking beautiful, Tess."

When he looks up, there's something indecipherable behind his eyes. It's a heartbreaking combination of hunger and despair.

"Come here." His voice is hoarse.

I crawl across the comforter until our knees are touching, then he lifts one of the blankets. "Get underneath. I don't want you to be cold."

His tenderness warms my heart against the chilling temperature of the room.

I settle in beside him and we rest our heads against the pillows.

"Can I touch you?"

My heart race like the wings of a hummingbird, but amidst the chaos of my nervous system, I realize there's maybe a chance I'm okay with this.

I mean, it's *Federico*. The boy from school who the older girls have started to take notice of. The same boy I spent a significant chunk of my childhood playing pranks on. And who, despite his changing form—his thicker muscle and growing height—is still my best friend. A best friend who's about to leave New York, maybe for good.

As the seconds tick by, I no longer feel like I'm giving my best friend a parting gift—I'm giving us both something to honor our friendship with. I didn't think I'd ever find someone who'd want to do this with me, and I'm grateful I suppose. Plus, this could be the one chance I get to connect with the closest thing I might ever have to a soulmate.

I nod and he rests a palm on my shoulder then slides it down my arm to my hip. His gaze follows and his teeth bite down on his bottom lip.

I feel warm under the comforter, but when his fingers trace the outline of my underwear, I shiver. His breaths grow ragged the closer his thumb crawls to the space between my thighs.

It feels as though all my blood has raced to the top of my legs and I break out in a light sweat all over my body. Instinctively, I reach down and press his fingers to my panties, and when he sucks in a breath I close in on his lips, a little too eagerly.

He applies pressure with his fingers but it's clumsy. They don't stay in one place long enough for me to feel the right friction. I'm no expert at this, but I'm better at getting myself off than he is.

I silently scold myself. *Give the guy a break, Tess. Maybe it's his first time too.* Then my scattered thoughts take over. *Has he done this before? Who with? Is he keeping secrets from me? It shouldn't matter,* I argue with myself. *He's not my boyfriend.*

I can't focus. His fingers grate against my panties, and he pulls back for second. "Are you okay?"

I nod hesitantly, then push my fingers through his. "Here. This usually works."

His gaze drops to where my fingers are circling the flesh beneath my underwear and I take the respite from his focus to let myself go—let myself *feel*.

"Oh my God," he breathes.

"What?" My body starts to rock of its own accord.

"You're really wet down there."

I close my eyes, breathing heavily. "Is that bad?"

His breaths start to match my own. "No. Fuck, no, Tess. It means you want this."

My fingers slide through wetness, lubricating the tips, and a quiet whimper escapes me. He continues to stare down at what I'm doing, while I bite down on my lip.

Out of nowhere, a white heat unfurls across my pelvis and floods my core. "*Oh!*"

Blinding pleasure mutes the sound of Federico's curses and the sight of his stiffened jaw. Stars fly behind my eyes and my body jerks uncontrollably.

As I relax, shame floods through me. I just masturbated in front of my best friend. I just got myself off instead of giving him more of a chance to do it, or to get some enjoyment out of trying.

I shake my head in despair.

I'm a *freak*.

When I eventually wrench my eyes open, Fed looks *ravenous*.

He pushes me to my back and settles between my legs.

There's a rustling sound at the side of my ear, then Fed pulls back and rests back on his knees. "Here…" He offers me the vodka again. "Have some more. It'll help."

I half-sit and swig a few mouthfuls then wince at my burning throat. He does the same then fumbles with a condom. I glance down at his dick. I've never seen one before—not in real life anyway. I swallow, not expecting it to be so… *sizeable*.

Fed catches me looking. "Try not to think about it too much. Just relax."

I uncurl to my back and bend my knees as he aims himself at my opening. My lids squeeze shut.

"Open your eyes," he says softly. "Don't tense."

I exhale a long breath and he pushes his way in. When he pauses, I know it's because he's reached my hymen and this is going to really hurt.

"Are you okay?" he asks again.

I breathe slowly and whisper, "Yes."

It all happens so fast, yet too slowly. Fed thrusts forward and pain bursts through my core. My eyes snap shut but as soon as the darkness fades, someone else is looking back at me.

Bronze eyes, heated gaze. *Unaffected.*

I cry out like a wounded animal and feel Fed's lips on the side of my face.

He moves.

In, out, in, out.

I feel like I'm crumbling in pain.

I shake my head but the vision just won't leave.

Benito Bernadi is staring up at me through a gap in the door. His whole body is solid, like stone, his eyes possessive, as though he only needs to look at something once to make it his.

Lips slide down my cheek and the heaviness on top of me moves faster, driving a hard length in and out of my body.

Fed reaches for my fingers and shoves them between us. He wants me to take care of myself again. I don't think I can focus on that while my insides bleed, but I'm willing to try anything to lessen the pain. I'm still wet so my fingers move easily, stoking the embers still burning.

Benito turns a fraction so his suited body blocks out the rest of the room. That dark gaze consumes me. His chiseled jaw grinds left to right and his hooded brow darkens. He licks his bottom lip leaving a lick of saliva in its wake. The hand he raises to wipe it away is gripping something with a casual prowess. I narrow my eyes, suddenly desperate to know what it is.

Black metal, a loaded chamber, a calloused finger pressing softly on the trigger.

Fuck.

A bolt of fire erupts across my pelvis and I arch my back, letting my head drop back against the comforter. I can barely hear Fed's words as he moves faster through my slickened heat, driving more tremors through my core. Tears stream down my cheeks. I know I'm crying out but I don't recognize my own voice. It sounds *wanton*.

I'm still shaking when Fed's weight covers me and the sound of his heavy breaths invades my ears.

"Are you okay?" I ask in a throaty voice.

He swallows twice before he replies and keeps his face buried in my shoulder when he does.

"I've never been worse." His words vibrate against my collarbone and I instantly stiffen.

"What?" I whisper.

When he lifts his head, his irises are doused in flames. "I finally got what I've wanted for *years*, Tess. And it won't ever be enough."

I pull his head into my chest and stare up at the ceiling, a heated gaze warming the periphery of my vision.

Then the realization sears me more than the tear in my hymen: My best friend is the person I lost my virginity to, but his face wasn't the one I saw when I came.

It's late afternoon when Fed drops me at the end of my street. He cuts the engine and we stare out of the windshield, not speaking. Only the sound of our breathing fills the car.

Finally, Federico breaks the silence. "Will you write me?"

I turn slowly and take in his profile. "Where would I send mail to?"

Fed reaches into the back pocket of his jeans and pulls out a card. "Ma's friend runs a business in So-Cal. She uses this PO Box address. You can reach me this way."

"Is that where you're going? California?"

He sighs and clicks his tongue. "I don't know where we'll settle, but I don't think Ma's friend is moving any time soon. This is the most reliable address I can give you."

I fold the note between my fingers and turn to face out the windshield again. "In that case, I'll write you there." I don't know what else to say. I feel numb, as though my body has shut down.

Suddenly, Fed takes my face and turns it toward him. His fingers dig a little too deeply into my jaw.

"I'm going to come back for you Tess, I promise. I'm going to make those bastards pay for what they've done."

His anguished expression shocks me out of my numbness and I swallow a hard lump in my throat. Feelings start to tumble over themselves in my stomach and I feel an unbridled urge to dance, to get them out.

"I'm going to kill that fucker Bernadi and take you far away from here so you don't have to live with the constant reminders of what happened to your mama."

A tear starts to form in the corner of my eye. I stare back at him, feeling his fingers fall from my face to my hands.

"I love you, Tess. You know that, don't you?"

I blink at him, suddenly overwhelmed.

"You're mine now and I'm going to come back for you. I promise."

I nod and grope around for the door handle, then step out of the car, drawing in a lungful of air. It isn't enough—I still feel like I'm suffocating.

Without any warning, Fed leans over the passenger seat, yanks the door closed and accelerates off down the street without a backward glance.

I look through the gates to my home, acutely aware of the growing dampness in my underwear. Without looking, I know it's blood.

I turn my back to the gates and make my way to the beach nearby. It's not much of a beach—more a sandy clearing sheltered by oversized dunes and thickly planted palms. With any luck it will be deserted. I don't 'people' well at the best of times, and right now I could live with the idea of never speaking to another human again.

Thankfully, the coast is clear, and I stand at the edge of the sea staring out into a vast expanse of nothing. Just a pink sky, a vague horizon and never-ending depths. I don't think before I strip off my clothes, scattering them on the shore as I stride into the waves. They draw me in without words, without reason. They seem to know what I need.

The floor drops away and I dip beneath the surface. All sound disappears and finally, there's quiet.

My eyes sting but I open them anyway. I swim deeper, further, freer. With each stroke, a nerve unravels and a muscle releases. I can breathe again.

After a few minutes, I turn back to the shore. The wind has picked up and the waves crash against me as I stride out of the water. At the edge I stop and stare at my clothes. As the realization I just skinny-dipped for the first time in my life dawns on me, I scoop up the clothes and race to the trees, pulling them over my wet limbs.

My heart is racing but, for the first time in forever, I feel free.

CHAPTER FOUR

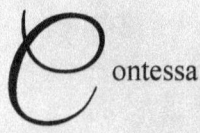ontessa

Three years later

I look up at the enormous house my sister now calls home and wonder, not for the first time, how fate can be so cruel.

Three years after my best friend was sent away, my sister goes and falls in love with the new don of the Di Santo family, Cristiano.

Don't get me wrong, I don't have anything against Cristiano—he makes Trilby the happiest I've ever seen her—but I have *everything* against the organization he's just taken over and the company he keeps. Most notably, Benito Bernadi, the man who ruined my life.

I've had a lot of time to reflect on what happened in the final days of my friendship with Federico. I rushed into losing my virginity without giving it proper thought. If there hadn't been the pressure of Fed leaving town, I would have at least spent time considering it before turning him down. I simply didn't think of Federico in that way. But I felt sorry for him in that moment. And for that, Benito Bernadi is entirely to blame.

I didn't think I'd ever need to see the Di Santo's consigliere again, but the day we attended Gianni's funeral was the day I realized that as long as Trilby is involved with the Di Santo's (which, having seen the way she and Cristiano can't be apart for more than a minute, is likely to be forever,) I'm not going to escape the sight of him.

My youngest sister, Bambi, slips her hand into mine. "Come on! This place is huge, and there's no scary Savero here anymore. We can explore to our hearts' content."

Her mention of Cristiano's late brother—the man Trilby was supposed to marry to save our father's business—sends a shudder down my spine. I knew the first time I laid eyes on him at Gianni's funeral he wasn't the man for Trilby, and that was before I found out he'd sliced a knife through a soldier's throat and ripped out his jugular a foot away from her, and planned to use our father's port for trafficking humans, *and* for poisoning my sister. Then again, it also dawned on me that day, none of us would likely ever be able to choose a man for ourselves. Not with our now-close connection to the Di Santos. It was only because Cristiano killed his own brother and took up the role of don himself that Trilby got the man she actually wanted.

Unbeknown to us all, Trilby and Cristiano had gotten close since that day. So close in fact, he's already moved her into his home, marriage-be-damned. I mean, it's on the cards, obviously. He's a don with a reputation to uphold—he needs that proof of purchase. But it seems he can't wait one minute longer to have her under his roof.

Bambi pulls me up the steps to the porch where the sound of Sera's squeals echo round the entrance hall. She has Trilby in some sort of semi-affectionate headlock. Even Allegra looks half-prepared to call the emergency services.

Bambi skips past them toward the back of the house so I follow her, craning my neck to take in every inch of whitewashed opulence. Cristiano's late mother had beautiful taste. It's not *my* taste but I can appreciate it at least. As we walk beneath high ceilings and mid-century shades, across pale wood floors and through softly furnished rooms, I put my imaginary stamp on them.

Walls and ceilings would be matt steel with heavily detailed cornices, black crystals hanging from glass chandeliers. Furnishings would be dark, old, shadowy, filled with candles, books, gothic ornaments. Ostrich feathers would fill the corners, real logs would burn in the fireplaces and enormous mirrors would reflect the flames. The house would feature every shade of black and my heart and soul would feel perfectly at home.

After we've explored nearly every inch of the house, familiar voices draw us to the terrace. A large pool glitters beneath the sun and crystal glasses ting with a note of celebration. I settle onto a lounger and watch the sun dance through swaying branches.

I have one earpiece in so I can listen half to the White Stripes and half to the chatter going on across the terrace. The sound of my stomach rumbling threatens to obliterate both, but I can't face Allegra's death glare for asking about food again. She doesn't understand that dancing for five hours a day requires a little more fuel than sitting around in bars getting drunk, which is what most people my age seem to do. For a short second, my chest tightens, but I know it's from a feeling of not wanting to be left out than a genuine desire to do the same.

I stretch my arms above my head and rest them over the back of the lounger. At odds as I am with some aspects of my sister's new life, this terrace is hard to fault. Cool blue water laps at the edge of the pool and the sun kisses every inch of my skin. Being the palest of four sisters, I'm conscious I have about ten more minutes before I have to re-coat myself in factor fifty. I lift a knee lazily and arch my spine giving it a good stretch. The hem of my tight dress rises up my thighs but I can't summon the effort to pull it back down. Besides, my limbs are *loving* this heat.

The volume on the terrace has turned up a touch and male voices infiltrate my head. I recognize one as Cristiano's. The second I'm not familiar with, but it sounds mature and friendly enough. Not worth opening my eyes for just yet. I lose myself to the lyrics of *Fell in love with a girl* and try to forget how damn hungry I am.

When the words 'Let's sit' work their way past the guitar riffs, I'm up. Those words mean food is probably imminent and I realize I should probably say hello to my future brother-in-law rather than appear rude.

My heels click along the stone terrace then I slide into a seat beside Bambi. I've had my eyes closed to the blinding sun for so long I can only see shadows. Someone fills my glass with water and I gulp it down gratefully.

Bambi has her head buried in a Taylor Swift magazine. Allegra compliments Cristiano on the house. Sera quizzes him on the casino business and I can hear Trilby laughing softly at something the other guy has said.

I wring my hands beneath the white lace tablecloth and wait for the food to appear, while wondering why, when I'm now sitting in the shade, I can still feel the burning sun on the side of my face.

The sound of footsteps from the house makes my mouth water. I turn to see what kind of delicious feast is heading our way, and just like that, my appetite is gone.

Benito Bernadi is leaning back in a chair at the end of the table, his elbow resting on the arm, a finger stroking back and forth over his top lip. His gaze rests on me. It is heavy, palpable and intrusive, and I feel it in my bones.

I quickly look away as hatred leaks into my bloodstream. When did *that man* get here?

I lift my chin and fold my arms across my chest. But even as I distract myself with the now-unappetizing food being laid out on literal silver platters, I can still feel his bronze eyes on my skin.

"What's his deal?" Bambi's whisper makes me jump. Her magazine lies open across her plate setting but she's taking a break from her version of the bible to observe her surroundings. I don't need to follow her gaze to know who she's talking about. "And why is he staring at you like that?"

"Because he's an asshole," I murmur. I reach for a serving spoon and start helping myself to pasta. I need carbs. Only when my plate is full do I hasten a glance in his direction. I'm relieved to see his attention is now on Papa. His position hasn't changed though. His body is still angled toward me and he still looks like a nonchalant piece of shit who's too big for his chair.

"Do you know him, Tess?" Bambi presses.

I shovel an enormous forkful of pasta into my mouth as I haven't quite worked out how to answer this question. And I hadn't expected Bambi to be the one to ask it. She was only thirteen when Fed left town. I have to figure out the PG-rated version, and fast.

"Do you?" she presses.

"I don't *know* him. I know *of* him."

"And?"

"He's just an asshole."

"An asshole who seems pretty close to our sister's fiancé."

It's an unfortunate, but valid, point. I shovel another forkful of pasta in my mouth to prevent me from cursing aloud in front of my present and future family.

"How do you know *of* him?" She closes her magazine and helps herself to antipasti.

I glance sideways to check he's still preoccupied with Papa, then I take a long sip of water and look into my sweet younger sister's eyes. "You remember Federico?"

Her nose wrinkles for a second. "Falconi? Sure I do. He used to come around a lot. I miss him."

"You do?" Her confession surprises me. I hadn't realized Fed's departure had affected anyone else. Which only gives me more reason to despise the man at the head of the table.

"Yeah. He always said I could call him 'bro. You know, because we don't have any brothers of our own."

My heart squeezes painfully. Hearing nice things about Fed only makes me feel more sad that in three years of writing him, I haven't had one reply.

"That's nice," I say, taking another sip of water.

"Anyway, what does Federico have to do with Cristiano's friend?"

I lower my voice and try to conceal the grit in my tone. "Cristiano's 'friend' is called Benito Bernadi, and he is the reason the Falconis had to leave the city."

Bambi's eyes narrow. "Why?"

I swallow the lump in my throat. "He shut down their family business all because of one month's missed lease payment." I pan my gaze to Bambi's. "He *ruined* them."

Her jaw drops open. This is why I shouldn't have told my little sister—she can't conceal horror like the rest of us have learned to. Though even I'm still a work in progress.

"But… how?"

"He took away their biggest contracts, spread false rumors about them. They lost all their clients, suppliers didn't want to know, insurers wouldn't go near them. In the end, Bernadi took their premises and left them with nothing. Fed's mama has connections in California. As far as I know, they moved out that way, but I don't know if they stayed or moved on."

I have to take a breath to cut through the fury I feel at telling the story that changed not just Fed's life but mine too. I'm no longer a virgin because of it, which makes me practically worthless in the community we now find ourselves at the heart of.

"Bernadi didn't just take everything from them," I say, the loathing in my voice undisguised. "He left them with the one thing an honest, hardworking man can't shake: a reputation for pissing off New York's biggest mafia family."

A puff of air leaves Bambi's lips as she flops back against her chair. "Wow. What an asshole."

I arch a resigned brow and pick up my fork. "Yeah. Like I said."

After a few minutes, she dips toward my ear. "Does he know you hate him?"

The question makes me pause. "I've no idea," I shrug. "Why do you ask?"

"Because he can't seem to stop looking at you."

I growl under my breath. "He's probably just wondering why I scowl at him all the time."

She chuckles and spears her fork into a slice of mozzarella.

Not until my stomach is full do I turn a fraction to glance sidelong at my nemesis. His face is angled towards Papa who is telling him a story that must be entertaining because there's a smile on Bernadi's face. Then, as if he can sense I'm watching him, his eyes flick to mine. My breath stills and the sound of my throbbing pulse floods my ears. He nods along with Papa's story but doesn't remove his gaze from me, and the longer it lingers, the heavier I feel on my seat.

"Tess, you have a show coming up, I hear."

Cristiano's question snaps my attention his way and I breathe out, mentally shaking myself. "That's right. In a few months."

"She's rehearsing constantly, but if you ask me, she's perfect already," Trilby says, shooting me a wink.

"Thanks but…" I jab my fork in her direction, "you're biased."

Cristiano laughs and Trilby's eyes light up like the Vegas strip. "I am biased, yes. But I can also be objective." She dabs the corner of her mouth with a napkin. "And, *objectively*, you are perfect already."

"Yeah, well, try telling that to Antonio."

Cristiano's tone nosedives. "Who's Antonio?"

I look at Trilby with a thread of alarm. She places a hand on Cristiano's forearm. "No one you need to take care of, darling," she says sweetly, and I half wonder if she's being serious. "He's Tess's dance tutor. They have a kind of love-hate relationship. He sees her potential and works her hard."

I turn back to Cristiano. "He thinks I'm unhinged," I smile sweetly. "You can take care of him if you want."

I glance sideways and Bernadi has his hands clasped, both forearms leaning on the table, his focus exclusively on our conversation. My gaze drops to his shirt sleeves which have been rolled up revealing thick, corded arms heavily inked all over. I catch what looks like an image of barbed wire curling around his wrists.

I swallow in surprise. I've only met Bernadi once—although 'met' isn't perhaps the right word. But, because I've unwittingly recalled that memory more times than I'd like to admit, I picture him as a walking suit. So, I'm slightly shocked to see he has actual skin under there. Actual *inked* skin. A shiver ghosts down my spine and I turn away quickly to catch my breath. Hatred sure works in funny ways.

Out of habit, I swipe open my phone and check through my social feeds. I never post anything myself and I rarely take notice of anyone else's feed to be honest. I hate to admit it to myself but I half-hope I see something from Fed. I don't know how I'd feel if I did see a post from him—it would only confirm I don't mean anything to him—but I do want to know he's okay.

Nothing appears in my feed. I check his accounts. Still nothing. My chest weakens so I make my excuses and return to the lounger by the pool.

I manage to avoid Bernadi for the rest of the evening, but when it's time to head home, my aunt, Sera and I are confronted with the problem of getting my dead-to-the-world younger sister into the waiting car. Usually, between us, we manage to carry her, and tonight I don't see any reason why we can't again. Until Bernadi steps in like the rude, presumptuous asshole he is.

"I'll carry her."

He strides toward us, pushing his already rolled sleeves even further up his biceps. The urge to stare forces me to look away as I snap, "We would have managed just fine."

He lifts Bambi like she's a puff of air and turns slowly to rest his gaze on me. And now I can't look away. It's the same expression as the one I recall during those restless evenings lying alone in bed that I would never recount to another living soul.

Bronze eyes, heated gaze, *unaffected*.

Then he drags his gaze over me from the corners of my eyes to the painted nails of my toes and bites out, "You of all people shouldn't be settling for 'fine.'"

I'm too angry at his mere existence to decipher any meaning behind his words, but shamefully, they cause a ball of heat to bloom in my stomach before descending to a point between my legs.

I straighten my back and flatten my shoulders. There's really only one thing for it. I need to stay as far away from this man as is humanly possible. Otherwise the only way out from beneath his dark stare is to murder him myself.

CHAPTER FIVE

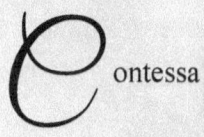
ontessa

Six months later

I smile triumphantly as the studio comes into view. I took a different route this morning. I've gotten used to the guy who follows me, but some days I don't desire the company, and I also kind of like outwitting him.

I still haven't seen his face. He always keeps enough of a distance that I can't make out any defining characteristics, other than that he's maybe six feet tall and skinny.

Some might say three years is a long time to be followed by a stranger but he's never come too close or given me a grave reason to fear him. There are just some days I would like a little privacy on my walk to the studio.

My eyes narrow as I get closer because something about the street seems different. I'm almost opposite the studio, standing outside what used to be an empty retail unit. It isn't empty anymore. It's a barbershop. And it's already buzzing at eleven a.m.

I pause for a few seconds. It's nice to see a little more life on this street, and having more people around when I come and go might make it feel safer. Before crossing the road, I turn my head to check for traffic—it would be a damn shame to survive a stalker for three years only to get run over by a bus.

There are no vehicles heading my way, but a tall, thin figure catches the corner of my eye, making my stomach drop. Before I have a chance to stop and verify that it is indeed my stalker, I hit a wall.

I spin around and instantly forget the skinny man strolling toward me from about two hundred yards behind, because it isn't a wall I just walked into, it is something with harsher edges and potentially even less character.

Damn Benito Bernadi.

It was only a few months ago I stood on Cristiano's terrace and watched Bernadi carry my little sister out to the waiting car—the day I resolved to stay well away from this man—so I'm beyond annoyed that he's ruined my run of avoidance.

I reluctantly lift my lids and glide a bored gaze up to his. "You did that on purpose."

He looks down at me as though he doesn't care a dime what I think he just did.

"You weren't standing there a second ago," I continue, accusingly. "You stepped in front of me."

His left brow twitches. "You weren't standing in that spot on the sidewalk a second ago. *You* stepped in front of *me*." He strokes a thumb across his bottom lip. "*And* you were looking the other way."

Something heats up inside my chest so fast I feel like a pot about to boil over. How is it possible a person can get me so riled up in just a few breaths?

My lip curls into a sneer. "What are you doing here, anyway? Come to shut down *another* business?"

Just a year ago I wouldn't have dreamed of speaking to any man in this way, let alone the consigliere to New York's ruling family. But now that my sister is the most important person in the world to the city's don—who just happens to be Bernadi's boss—I know I can get away with it.

His brows draw together a fraction—perhaps he doesn't get my reference to the fact he closed down the Falconis, the reason I will always despise him—and he slowly shakes his head. "I came to open one, actually."

Italian opera music and the deep baritone of male banter draws my gaze to the right. Every chair inside the barbershop has been filled and the waiting seats are spilling over with wrinkled suits, errant stubble and cigar-ravaged laughter.

I can't conceal my grimace. "This place is *yours*?"

He shrugs and a conceited smile dances across his lips. "Sure."

Footsteps approaching on the sidewalk draw my attention from the window. I roll my eyes, about to walk past Bernadi, when his arm whips out to the side and a loud pop makes my ears ring and my head spin.

The force of the gunshot makes me stumble into the road but Bernadi's hand wraps around my arm, keeping me from falling.

The Italian banter stops instantly and footsteps emerge from inside the barbershop. It takes a few seconds to catch my breath before I can right myself and turn my gaze to the ground.

And there he is.

My stalker.

Long, thin, younger than I thought. Eyes wide open, whites gleaming. Hands splayed at a contorted angle. Blood running from his open mouth.

Then the world carousels and my legs give out.

I open my eyes stiffly and look up at a mirrored ceiling decorated with branding from the fifties. It's clear from my reflection that I've been deposited on a reclined chair in the barbershop and it looks like everything around me is business as usual.

How utterly embarrassing.

My first thought as I come round is, "This chair is so comfortable I could get used to it."

I wiggle a little, then remember why I'm lying here, then a combination of fear, disgust and relief mingle at the base of my throat. Bernadi just shot a guy dead on the street, right in front of me. The audacity! Wait until I tell Cristiano about this. Maybe he'll fire Bernadi. Better yet, maybe he'll send Bernadi off to the west coast, never to be seen again.

My thoughts are quickly drowned out when the back of the chair rises slowly upright and a face moves into my field of view, and it's one I've hated for exactly three years, six months and eight days.

"What the fuck thinking were you?" I spit.

His lip curls up at one corner. "Have some of this, then try again."

I frown and drop my gaze to the glass of water he's holding out. "Arsenic?" I deadpan.

His face is serious. "One hundred per cent."

I end up gulping half the glass.

"What the *fuck* were you thinking?" I repeat.

He straightens and puts his hands to the back of his head. Then he barks out a short laugh. It sounds like relief.

"Fuck me, Contessa. I would have given you a warning if I'd known you were going to pass out."

"Given me a warning for what? That you were about to shoot a passerby in the neck? You were about to murder a civilian for no reason at all?"

Not only am I still lightheaded from the shock of seeing a dead body at my feet, I am *furious* Bernadi did that to my *innocent* stalker.

He narrows his eyes. "First of all, I didn't shoot him in the neck. I would never shoot someone in the neck. I shot him in the skull."

He shrugs like it was the kind of move that in school would've got him a half hour detention.

"Second, what do you mean 'civilian'? This is New York, not the front line."

"Could've fooled me," I mumble, knowing with some irritation he heard me clearly.

He cocks his head and looks genuinely perplexed. "Anyway…" It's hard to tell with his face being so damn chiseled but I'm detecting an affronted scowl. "I thought you'd be pleased."

"You, um, *what*?" I tip an ear in his direction. "You thought I'd be *pleased* you just shot someone to death two feet to my right, for no apparent reason? Are you insane?"

I pause for less than two seconds. "Actually, don't answer that."

In a beat I like the barber chair a lot less than I did a few minutes ago. Bernadi plants his hands either side of me on each arm rest and brings his face close to mine. In a bid to not stare at the ragged scar down the left side of his face I focus on his eyes—dark olive pools dancing with annoyance. They're almost disarming.

"What were you doing?" I say in a scheming whisper. "Showing off?"

"Yeah." His voice is playful. "Flowers and chocolates don't do the trick anymore. Seems only a bullet can get a girl's attention these days."

The longer he stares at me, the shorter my breaths become. I can feel sweat surfacing through my pores. I'm protected against this man but somehow he still manages to make me feel afraid.

He pushes his weight off the chair and folds his arms across his chest. I notice he's removed his jacket and his sleeves are rolled up. Ink upon ink upon ink. He doesn't look like a law-literate advisor to me; he looks like a *mobster*. I need to swallow.

His jaw works from side to side. "He was stalking you."

I tip my chin slightly. "Yes, I know."

He lowers his glare. "You *know*? Did you know he's been stalking you for six months?"

I fold my own arms in front of my chest, noticing his gaze dip then quickly return to my face. "Try *three years*, actually."

His head ticks to one side like he must have misheard or something, but he doesn't respond.

"He was harmless," I say with a sigh. "Sure, he would hang out in the shadows and follow me when it got dark—"

Bernadi flings a hand toward the window and his voice pitches. "He was following you today and it's broad *daylight*."

"Well, yeah. I guess he's become a bit more bold the last few months—"

"Three *years*?" Bernadi runs a distractingly large hand through his thick, black hair. "Why didn't you tell someone? Your father? Cristiano?"

I wriggle off the seat in the manner of a toddler who can't reach the floor, and stand, wobbling only slightly. Then I glare at him.

"Where have you been, Bernadi? You know what my family has been through. First, my mama's murder, then my sister's engagement to that trigger-happy, child-trafficking *freak*. And the mess Papa had to unwind once Savero was gone…" I throw a glance to the window and back. "That guy out there was harmless. What would have been the point in making my aunt and Papa worry when they really could do with a break?"

He seems to recoil slightly without moving a muscle. "What about your safety, Contessa? Your future."

That makes me laugh. "Like you care about anyone's future."

His brow furrows in confusion but I'm not going to waste my time educating him on what exactly has formed my immovable view of his outlook on life. "I have a dance class to get to."

I'm about to turn when his fingers sear into my upper arm.

"Don't I at least get a thank you?"

The look of confusion has slid from his face and it's been replaced by a devious glint in his eye. Well, I don't care how bordering-on-handsome that glint makes him look, I'm not entertaining him a second longer.

"For what? Shooting a guy in the head or introducing me to perhaps the comfiest chair known to man?" I punctuate with a sweet smile.

He ignores my question. "Like it or not, Contessa. I probably just saved you."

A thread of dark hatred wraps itself around my spine and lowers my voice to the level of vindictive. "Well, in future, don't bother, Bernadi. I don't need saving. Least of all from you."

Then I walk straight out of the barbershop to the sound of a razor being rinsed, a comb tapping against a metal dish and a couple jaws dropping.

CHAPTER SIX

$\mathcal{B}$enito

"This is the place."

I'm standing at the foot of some grand steps leading to an even grander brownstone in the lower east village. Cristiano's cousin, Nicolò, is back by our side in New York where he belongs, and not out in Vegas running casino hotels, which is where Cristiano had sent him. He lasted all of ten days before he got bored out of his mind and begged Cristiano to let him come home. Our don replaced him with some straighter-laced guys with a view to maintaining at least some sort of legitimacy within his newly-acquired Di Santo empire.

"Well, this is a surprise," I say, taking in the neat paintwork and tidy stoop.

The scrawny guy I shot in the head looked like he

didn't have two cents to rub together, let alone enough money to afford a place in a smart brownstone.

Nicolò shoots me a morbid glance over his shoulder. "Not so much."

Instead of walking up the steps, he leads me to a stairwell I'd completely missed that heads down into the bowels of the building's foundations. I loosen my tie and follow Nicolò to the bottom where he sticks a knife into a lock. I don't bother looking around to check no one is witnessing us breaking and entering. We own this part of the city, and every other part will follow soon if Cristiano continues the way he's begun. If the cops found us here they'd *help*. They'd know if they didn't they'd find a family member tied by the neck to the branch of a very tall tree in Central Park.

The door creaks inward and I follow Nicolò inside. We're both instantly hit by the stale stench of rotting food. I glance sideways at a kitchenette which reveals overflowing trash cans, cockroaches and rat feces.

Jesus, this place should be condemned.

"How did you find it? Social security?"

Nicolò steps gingerly over a pile of dirty laundry. If I know anything about this capo, it's that he does not like to get his shoes dirty. Hands? Sure. Shoes? Absolutely fucking not.

"No. The guy had a diary in his pocket with his address written up front."

"A diary? How old was this guy—twelve?"

When Nicolò looks back over his shoulder, his gaze darkens. "It wasn't that kind of a diary." He stops and turns to face me, his hands stuck in his pockets and his arms rigid. "Are you sure you want to see this?"

"How the fuck should I know?" I throw my arms out. "You haven't told me what we're going to see, just that I would probably want to see it…"

Nicolò's gaze shoots sideways as though he's recalling the conversation, then he nods. "Yeah. Yeah, I think you would."

I follow him down a dingy corridor that smells of mold, then Nicolò pushes on the last door to the left. I'm still eyeing the floor for live vermin when I realize the carpet has changed color and I look up.

The room has been painted black. The floor—the *carpet*—has been *painted* black. The window—the only source of light in the entire place, which even then faces a wall rising up to ground level—is painted black.

Nicolò flicks a switch, casting the room in a cheap yellow light, and I take it all in.

It's not often in my line of work that I feel sick, and I see perhaps a million times more blood and weeping flesh than the average person. But right now I want to hurl into a fucking basin.

Contessa Castellano's face is plastered to every damn surface a thousand times over. Photographs, college magazine articles, family fucking portraits. Newspaper clippings where she and her sisters feature beside photographs of Cristiano and his late father and brother. Contessa from every possible angle.

I take two steps toward the longest wall and absorb the details. He's tacked notes to each picture, detailing his thoughts and intentions for each one. They range from a desire to hold her hand to *way* more graphic and disgusting actions. And to think she knew nothing of them. To think she thought he was *harmless*.

"I've never known you to regret anything," Nicolò says, watching me carefully. "But if you were in any doubt as to whether your guy deserved that bullet, read this."

He points to a note below what appears to be the most recent photograph of my boss's sister-in-law. At first I'm gripped by the visual. She's emerging from the studio, dressed in black, as always, in figure-hugging gym gear that makes me need to swallow a few times. Her long black hair has just been freed from a ponytail —as evidenced by the scrunchie she's tying around her wrist. And her eyes are wide and bright, the way they always seem to be after she's danced for several hours.

I force my gaze to the note tacked to the image.

You looked at me today, it reads. *Now I know it isn't all in my head. We're going to be together. You won't walk away from me anymore. You won't run like you did the other day. You'll let me wrap my hands around your neck and squeeze until you beg me for air. I will be your air, Tess. I will be everything you need. Not long now, my love. I'm coming for you.*

I inhale tightly. "He was planning to abduct her."

Nicolò snorts. "That wasn't all he was planning."

He hands me a small pile of notes and I flick through them. Scattered sentences, drawings, random words. "What's this?" I look up at him.

"He was detailing every single vile thing he could do to her once he got her in this shithole," Nicolò says, matter of fact. "It's a little jumbled. One word of advice: don't read it while you're eating."

He solemnly reaches out and takes the notes from my hand. "It was just a matter of time, Benny. It was a good thing you shot him when you did."

Reading the notes and looking around the walls… If I hadn't already killed the guy I would be torturing him toenail by fucking toenail. How the hell had he gotten away with this? Why hadn't she said something? I don't know who I'm most angry at right now—a dead man… or *her*.

"The stalking wasn't why I killed him," I say, distractedly.

Nicolò spins around. "What? Then why?"

I shrug. "He was standing less than two feet from her and he smelled her hair."

Nicolò's eyes pop. "You gonna kill every guy that stands within two feet of her and takes a breath?"

I shrug again. "She's a Di Santo now. She's my responsibility."

Nicolò arches a brow. "She was still a Castellano last time I checked."

My blood heats.

"What?" He holds his hands up. "Why are you glaring at me like you want to put metal to my head and fire it?"

"Last time you *checked*?" My voice is unusually low.

His shoulders drop. "It's a saying, Benny. Of course I'm not actually checking on her. My point is, don't you have enough on your plate? She's not a Di Santo."

"Don't let Cristiano hear you say that," I warn. "She's his fiancée's sister. Di Santo or not, she's a part of the family."

Nicolò shakes his head. "Does she know she's under your surveillance?"

Until now, I hadn't realized she was, but there's no point denying I've had my eye on her ever since that day on Cristiano's terrace. "There's nothing to be gained from her knowing I now have my eye on every man who comes within a half mile radius of her." I turn and walk back to the door.

Nicolò's words follow me. "Just her?"

"What?" I reach for the gun in my waistband.

"What about the other two sisters?"

I frown at the question. "The second is in the Hamptons—not my jurisdiction. The fourth is practically held captive by the aunt. Contessa is foolish enough to let a psychopath stalk her for three years—clearly no one's keeping a close enough eye on her."

"Except you." Nicolò grins as he brushes past me.

I shoot him a glare, then I turn to face the room one last time. Those photographs don't belong here. Her face doesn't belong in this basement dive alongside psychotic musings and rising mold. I aim my gun into the room and imagine he's standing in the center of it so I can kill him all over again.

Then I dump an entire chamber of lead in the walls.

The heavy notes of a piano followed by a sweeping symphony rise up through the floorboards. After the day I've had, I welcome the soothing effect the music below has on me.

I nudge an empty vodka bottle with the toe of my shoe then turn to the realtor. "When was it last occupied?"

"Four, maybe five, years ago." There's an apologetic note to his tone. "It hasn't been too popular a neighborhood. But, you know, with the barbershop on the street opposite, things might pick up."

As I walk to the window, a silver wrapper in the corner of the room catches my eye. I really hope that isn't what it looks like.

I watch a client leave the barbershop, manila envelope tucked beneath his arm, then turn my head to the side. "It'll need a deep clean."

"Of course, sir." The realtor scrambles in his bag for the papers.

"And you can cut fifty percent off the lease," I snap. "Consider it a tax for showing me a place that hasn't been swept first for condom wrappers."

He gulps and his gaze darts around, eventually settling on the silver wrapper I'd spotted. "I... um... of course, sir. My apologies, sir."

"If the owner gives you a hard time, give them my number."

He coughs. "I…er… don't think that will be necessary."

He strikes a line through the total and hands me the pen. I scribble down the new lease amount and sign.

A base kicks in beneath our feet and a male voice barks out instructions somewhere below.

My lip curls in amusement at the thought of Contessa Castellano, the girl who can't seem to stand the sight of me, discovering I've just leased the office above her studio.

"I'll be in first thing tomorrow," I say as I walk past the realtor, dismissing him. "Make sure it's clean."

CHAPTER SEVEN

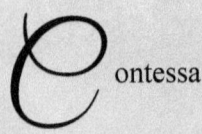ontessa

"Do you promise?" I repeat.

Trilby rolls her eyes in the phone screen. "I *promise*. Benito Bernadi won't be here. I swear."

I see more of Trilby now she's moved in with Cristiano than I ever did when she lived at home. It's probably because Sera has moved to the Hamptons and Bambi's still a little too young to be flitting between the two properties. Still, I'm not complaining. Since Federico left, it's nice to have at least one other person besides Allegra to talk to. It helps, too, that we're a part of the same world. The girls at my dance class have no connection at all to New York's underworld. I wish that I didn't, but now that Trilby's engaged to the don of the city's biggest crime family, I don't really have a say.

"You know, you said this last time and the guy was

perched on a stool in the kitchen like it was his second home."

"I wasn't expecting him that day, and neither was Cristiano. But, this is kind of their second home. Those guys are always coming and going. You know how it is."

No, I don't actually. But it didn't take long for Trilby to get the mafia-shaped memo. I always knew she was cut out for more than art school; I just hadn't expected her to become prime crime wife material. But, as itchy and uneasy as it makes me, the life seems to suit her. I suppose having an unrealistically handsome and unfeasibly powerful man for a fiancé oils the wheels a little, as it were.

"So you can't swear he won't be there, can you?" I challenge.

She purses her lips then lets out a sigh. "I can because I know where he's going to be instead."

"And where's that?"

She closes her eyes and shakes her head. "You don't want to know, Tess. And I'm not going to put you in any danger by telling you. Just believe me when I say Benny is going to be otherwise engaged this evening, okay?"

Benny. That name makes me want to puke more than Benito or Bernadi.

"Fine," I say, straightening my shoulders. Then I grin. "I'll be there in twenty."

A few hours later, I'm lying on a sun lounger staring up at the stars, feeling pleasantly tipsy. Trilby has gone to refill our glasses when I decide I need to pee.

Instead of going through the house I take the garden route to the restroom. After relieving myself I decide to walk back through the property in search of Trilby. The kitchen is deserted but some plates of food have been laid out, presumably for me and my sister, and possibly Cristiano, because there's no one else here.

I help myself to a bruschetta and carry it through the kitchen. Just as I'm about to pass into the hallway I hear hushed voices. Hushed *male* voices. I pause and peer through a gap in a door. It's a room I haven't seen before. Some sort of laundry room filled with closets and cleaning equipment.

I recognize one of the voices as Cristiano's but I can't make out what he's saying, then a shadow leans over a faucet, releasing a shard of light from the window. It shines over the man as he washes his hands, illuminating them.

Quiet, commanding voices utter vindictive words.

Glistening red water runs onto porcelain.

Then a head turns.

Bronze eyes. Heated gaze. *Unaffected.*

I spin away and walk as quickly as I can back to the terrace.

Trilby is standing over my lounger, a frown buttoning her brows together. "Where did you go?"

Um, hell?

"The restroom," I say, gathering up my things.

"What are you doing?"

"Leaving," I snap, clutching my jacket and purse to my chest.

"What? Why?"

"You swore he wouldn't be here."

"Who, Benny?"

I hate the way she says his name, like he's a favorite close cousin or something. "Yes, *Benny*," I reply in a patronizing tone.

"He only just got here," she says, throwing out her arms like it's no big deal. "And he won't be staying…" Her voice tapers off.

"So, he only came back here to wash off the blood?"

Her face pales.

"Then he's going to go back home to his wife, girlfriend, whatever, and they're none the wiser he's just murdered someone with his *bare hands*?"

"We don't know what happened." Her voice carries a warning note.

I laugh, darkly. "Oh, we know exactly what happened. He just brutally murdered someone. No one gets that much blood on their hands unless there's death involved."

She puts a hand on my shoulder to stop me walking away. "C'mon, Tess. Please don't make this harder for me than it already is."

I twist toward her with a slight frown. "What are you talking about?"

She glances around at the property. "*This*. This is what I'm talking about. Being part of the Di Santo family." She rests a weary gaze on me. "A crime family."

When I don't respond she sits on one of the pool chairs with a thud. "This was never in my plans, you know." She looks up at me, guiltily.

I fold my arms because it's going to take more than a confession to compensate for the fact I'm having to share fresh air with that specific *murderer*.

"I hated being told this was my destiny—that I had to marry a don."

I pout. "You don't seem to hate it all that much now."

Her eyelids drop and she shakes her head. "There are two reasons why I don't *hate* it," she says quietly. "One of them is obvious. Another… less so." She glances up at me.

The way she and Cristiano seem to absolutely adore one another is the first. "What's the other reason?"

"If I tell you this, you have to keep it to yourself, okay? I don't want Papa, or anyone else for that matter, to feel worried or even responsible."

"Responsible for what?"

She stares at me.

"Okay, I promise."

"Cristiano didn't have to become don. He could've returned to Vegas."

I sit down in the chair beside her and tuck one of my ankles beneath my thigh. "So, why didn't he?"

"Because Papa is an easy target," she says, sadly.

"When Savero worked his way into the business to use it for his own selfish purposes, he proved it was possible. Cristiano is worried that other organized groups or opportunists might try to do the same. The only way Papa's business will remain absolutely safe is if Cristiano himself, as don, protects it—everyone else just sees dollar signs."

I blow out a long breath. "Oh."

"Yeah, *oh*." She shrugs. "Cristiano didn't want to become the don of this family, you know. Not in the beginning anyway."

"And now?" I ask in a quiet voice.

"He... I don't know. He *fits*." Guilt returns to her features. "Augie told me Cristiano was born to do it, and I can see what he means. He leads well and his men respect him."

I pan my gaze to the house, absorbing Trilby's words. While I won't ever fully support the work of this crime family, I do feel slightly less hateful toward it, knowing it's protecting my family's livelihood and future.

"So, yeah. I can't promise you'll come over here and not see any of his men or advisors, and I can't promise you won't ever see blood being washed off their hands. But I can promise you that while Cristiano is the boss of *this* family, *our* family is safe."

She takes one of my hands and squeezes it. "So now I've given you a truth, can I ask one of you?"

I glance sideways at her, my tone wary. "Okay."

"Why do you hate Benny so much?"

Crap. I should've seen that one coming. I grit my teeth and glue my lips shut.

"Come on, Tess. Tell me."

I take a deep breath and exhale slowly.

"Fine. He is the reason Federico had to move to the west coast."

"Federico Falconi?"

"Yeah." I twist the cotton of my dress in my fingers. "Bernadi closed down the family business, ruined their reputation. They had to leave the city for good."

"I'm sure he had good reason—" she starts.

"His father fell back on the lease payments by one month, Trilby," I cut in. "*One month*."

"Okay, well that does sound a little extreme," she concedes.

"And that's not all." I look away because I haven't told anyone this before.

"Go on."

"I lost my virginity to Federico the night before he left."

Trilby is quiet for so long I have to turn to check she's still there. I'm relieved to see she isn't looking back at me like I've made a catastrophic mistake.

"Is that bad?" she says, quietly.

"I wasn't particularly ready to give it up," I say with a shrug. "But he asked me to do that one last thing for him. I felt so bad he was having to leave."

"But… you liked him, right?"

"Of course I did. I still do, even though I haven't heard from him since he left. But if Bernadi hadn't forced Fed and his family out of the city, I wouldn't have felt pressured into sleeping with him."

She rubs a hand over her face. "Well, it makes a little more sense now why you don't like the guy. I'll do my best to keep him away from you but, like I said, I can't promise he won't ever be here."

"I know." I sigh, then remember the other reason I sometimes lay awake at night. "Is this going to be a problem? Now that you're marrying into the Italian mafia, isn't the fact I'm no longer a virgin going to bring shame on the family or something?"

She laughs, then stops herself when she sees the terror on my face. "I doubt it, Tess. Spoiler alert: I'm not a virgin either." She winks and I grin.

"Cristiano?"

She arches a brow. "Who else?" She goes to stand. "I need to go to the bathroom. I'll be right back."

I glance at our empty glasses. We drank the refills pretty quickly without me even noticing. "Do you think it's safe to go inside?"

Trilby smiles. "Just head straight for the kitchen. If Benny's still around, he'll probably be in Cristiano's office."

I'm still wary as I walk into the deserted kitchen and pour out two vodkas. The place is silent, so when I turn towards the refrigerator and find a huge shadow standing between me and the door to the sodas, I scream.

Immediately, a hand covers my mouth, sending my

heart up my throat and into my ear canal. "What the fuck, Tess? It's me."

The sound of Bernadi's voice makes me want to scream even louder. When he doesn't move his hand, despite my weak attempts to push him off, I bite it.

That works.

"Ow! Jesus Christ." He yanks his hand away and stares disbelieving at the blood seeping out of his finger. "You bit me."

I take two steps backward and hit the island. "Of course I did," I snap. "What did you expect? You loom over me in the darkness then try to cut off my oxygen. Of course you're going to get bitten."

The room is dark except for the light of the full moon streaming through the garden doors but I can still see an annoyed frown covering his face.

"What were you trying to do? Kidnap me?"

He straightens and blocks out the small amount of light illuminating his features.

"Now why would I want to do that?" His tone falls somewhere between exasperated and bored.

"You had your hand over my mouth," I say, accusingly.

"You were screaming and I didn't want four of Cristiano's capos to barge in here pointing their guns in our direction. I've seen what happens when someone wields a firearm near you."

I plant my hands on my hips. "Why did you sneak up on me? You could have said something so I knew you were there."

He scrubs a hand down his face. "I didn't see you."

I laugh but his sudden glare shuts that down.

"You're dressed in black and your hair is black. It's not unfeasible that you blend into the shadows."

"I'm as white as a blanket of snow," I counter and pull the hem of my dress up my thighs to demonstrate the point. His gaze drops to my legs and he's suddenly quiet. I wait for his sharp retort but it doesn't come. Instead, the room seems to heat up by several degrees and his gaze moves slowly up my body, back to my face. A hot shiver skates down my spine and I try to cover it up by talking.

"Can I get to the refrigerator, please? I need sodas for these shots, otherwise you might find me and my sister at the bottom of the pool come morning—"

A bottle of coke lands on the counter beside me, making me jump.

"Right." I stare at it. "Thanks."

He takes a step forward so I have to tip my chin up to look at him. "Do me a favor, Contessa…"

I catch a drop of blood on the sleeve of his shirt in the corner of my eye and swallow.

"Next time you acquire your own personal stalker, tell me."

I grip the counter behind me. "I would but I don't have any plans to enter that dive of a barbershop ever again." I smile sweetly.

In the dim light I see one corner of his mouth twitch as though he's amused but trying his darndest not to show it.

"You won't need to go into the barbershop to see me. Just head upstairs."

A strained gasp leaves my throat. "I'm sorry, what?"

His voice is low and gravely. "Just come upstairs to the office above your dance studio."

My lungs drain of oxygen.

"What?" I repeat, the word a whisper. He can't know what I did up there—what Fed and I did. Oh God… If Bernadi knows, Cristiano will know, and… I don't care what Trilby might say otherwise, but this is the *Italian Mafia* we're talking about. If they find out I'm not a virgin, God knows what they'll do.

I force my voice out through my mouth. "Why would I find you above my dance studio? You gonna try and shut that down too?"

He pauses before his brow dips into a frown. "No, I'm not shutting anything down. I have a new office."

My chest tightens as his words sink in. "In the space above my studio?"

He takes a step back, not needing to reply for me to know the answer.

"Of all the empty spaces in the city, why would you choose that one?" I hold on to the counter to steady myself.

His expression hardens. "Because it's convenient."

I turn my face away so he can't see the relief flood through it. "It's not convenient for me," I mutter.

In a beat, he's right up to me again, and I'm not sure how. It's like he has some twisted superpower. Sometimes, he moves too fast for my vision to keep up.

"You think spending my days less than six feet above your head is convenient *for me*?"

The sudden descent of darkness over his entire body takes my breath away.

"I—"

"You think having to keep an eye on you twenty-four-seven so you don't end up making nice with some other stalking rapist is *convenient* for me?"

"He was not a r—"

"YES. He was." Bernadi's sharp response stops my heart. "I was going to spare you the details but you're starting to piss me off." He pulls out a sheath of papers from an inside pocket of his jacket.

The angle of the light catches the curved lines of his chest, and the combination of that and his suggestion I could have been *raped*, has made my throat go dry.

"Here." He shoves the papers at me. "Some bedtime reading."

I snatch the papers from his hand. I refuse to show him how weak and powerless his words are making me feel.

"Next time you think having a fucking paid assassin holed up in the same building as you is *inconvenient*, I suggest you take a look at those."

Then moonlight falls between us as he turns away. Then he stalks out of the kitchen as silently as when he arrived.

CHAPTER EIGHT

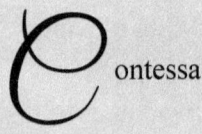
Contessa

I'm now sitting on the floor of a guest bedroom in Cristiano's house reading a bunch of police reports and trying not to throw up all over the pristine white carpet.

When I returned to Trilby, having left the two vodkas on the kitchen counter, unmixed, she took one look at my blood-drained face and steered me in the direction of a guest room in the east wing of the house. She told me to get some rest and we'd have breakfast together in the morning. She didn't ask what had caused my sudden decline; I assume she thought I'd run into "Benny" again and decided I'd had enough of him for one night.

She would not have been wrong.

I'm still reeling over the fact he's going to be permanently based in the office above my dance studio, supposedly "keeping an eye" on me. And to make matters worse, I really don't like having the impression he too doesn't seem very happy about it. Has someone forced him to be some sort of bodyguard? Could it be Cristiano? Or Papa?

I'm determined to find out, as soon as I've recovered from the trauma of reading these frankly grotesque police reports.

My stalker's name was Ronnie J. Smythe and he was a three-time-convicted felon. He was older than he looked—thirty-nine—and he'd spent in total twelve years in jail for crimes ranging from drug abuse, to sexual assault, to attempted abduction. It was clear from the reports he wasn't a reformed character; he was dangerous. And I let him follow me without breathing a word about it for *three years*.

I look down and realize I'm pressing a curled fist against my heart. I'll never know how close I came to being hurt, but I do know in my gut it was imminent. If Bernadi hadn't killed him when he had…

My gaze is drawn to the window. The full moon illuminates one half of the guestroom and the lawns outside. I'm reminded of when I stood opposite Bernadi in the kitchen only an hour ago and the feelings colliding in my chest are confused. I hate him, so I have to assume it's possible to hate someone yet still feel grateful to them.

And maybe it's not unusual to *shiver* beneath a heated gaze.

My vision softens and I rub my eyes. Dragging my

heavy limbs into the enormous bed, I pull the comforter up to my ears. And when Bernadi's burning gaze as he coasts it up my thighs enters my head, I'm too tired to bat it away, so I don't. I let it linger until sleep consumes me.

I tiptoe past Trilby and Cristiano's bedroom as quietly as I can. It was a well-kept secret in our family that Trilby hadn't slept a full night ever since Mama was killed. This is only the second time I've stayed at this house, and both times it seems, Trilby is out for the count. Still, I don't want to risk it. I tiptoe so I don't wake her—she deserves all the sleep she now gets.

I clutch a towel around me with one hand and grip the handrail with the other and make my way quietly downstairs to the pool. It's not even seven a.m. so the terrace is deserted. There's some bustling coming from the direction of the kitchen but I expect Cristiano's housekeeper is up and about.

I reach a lounger and let my towel fall onto it, then I sit by the edge of the pool and lower my feet. Warmth crawls up my calves and I let out a relieved sigh. It's too early for the sun to have warmed the water so the pool must be heated.

I close my eyes and slip beneath the surface, letting weightlessness wrap around me. When my toes touch the floor I push off and swim underwater to the far end of the pool. I come up for air and push the wet strands from my face.

God, this is nice.

I'd say it's worth the risk of running into Bernadi last night just to get a few lengths in his boss's pool.

I dive under again and swim a couple of lengths back and forth. After punishing my limbs for weeks to perfect my current dance routine, my body is relishing the way the water supports it and pushes me along.

I pop up again in the same place I'd slipped into the water and take a few moments to look around. It's so quiet and peaceful I can almost hear the waves a few miles away.

But I can't fully relax. Just like the moments after I lost my virginity to Federico, I feel tight everywhere, and even the water isn't helping me fully unwind. I need to feel *free*—unhindered and uninhibited. Since that first time I swam naked, having felt how freeing it is, I do it quite often. Sometimes, nothing else can unwind me better than feeling the cool water against every part of me.

It's a Sunday so I'm pretty certain no one will be awake, let alone out on the terrace, until at least eight, and even that time is for regular churchgoers, which I suspect Cristiano *isn't*.

With adrenaline thumping through my veins, I peel off the top of my two-piece bathing suit and drop it onto the edge of the pool. Then I roll the bottoms down my legs until I'm completely naked. The release is instant. My breaths loosen and a long sigh escapes my lips. I drop my head back onto the edge and let my legs float up to the surface.

This is exactly what I needed. Now, I feel like I'm back in control. Reading those reports made me feel like I can't trust myself—that I'm not capable of being the independent woman I so want to be. But now, as my whole self, embraced by the water, I know I wasn't to blame. Smythe was the crazy one, not me.

After a few minutes I duck down again and swim a few more lengths, loving the way the water hugs and glides along every inch of me. My long black hair swishes over the arc of my bottom with each stroke, sailing along behind me like a sheet.

When I pop up at the other end I arch my back and let the sun warm my face. Then the sound of metal on metal makes me jump half out of the water. Droplets spray around me as I spin my head to the right, then my cheeks *burn*.

Benito Bernadi is sitting on the edge of a lounger about fifteen feet away with a gun in one hand and a cloth in the other. I grip the side of the pool and hold my breath. There's no way he *couldn't* have seen me and I feel hollow with embarrassment.

I silently watch him as he turns the gun this way and that, using the cloth to polish it. His dark hair gleams beneath the early morning rays and the inked muscles in his forearms move like a ballet with each twist and turn.

He doesn't look up once. It's as if I'm not even there.

And something about that irritates me.

I continue to watch as he lovingly polishes the metal. I watch his large, thick hands twist it about. He takes off a part and places it gently on the lounger beside him, then inspects the cavity in the pistol. After more twisting and polishing, he replaces the part. It makes a *click* sound that fills the terrace.

On the few occasions I've recalled Bernadi's form, I've viewed him as a brute. Yet there's something about the way he handles the gun—with such gentleness and care—I almost yearn for someone to touch me in that way.

My breaths are ragged and deepening to the point my chest lifts out of the water with each one. My glare is hot and prickly.

I hate him, I remind myself.

I *hate* him.

So why am I treading water and willing him to turn his gaze in my direction?

Minutes pass slowly.

My fists clench at my sides. Well, that's just about ruined my morning dip.

Pissed, I duck beneath the water and swim to the steps at the opposite end of the pool, then I reach out and grip the handrails. Pulling myself up, slowly, I place a foot on one step. Then I shake my hair down my back. Despite its length, it doesn't cover my naked bottom. Water runs down my upper thighs, droplets roll down my back. Another step. My entire body is on display and I don't care that if Bernadi looked up from his spot on the lounger, he would see all of me.

I *want* him to see it.

Want him to see what I gave away to someone else, because of *him*.

I saunter slowly to where I left my towel. A small puddle forms at my feet as I take my time bending to lift it, then leisurely wrap it round my body. Only when I've secured the towel in a knot above my breasts do I dart my gaze to the figure at the other end of the terrace.

He's still staring at the piece of metal in his hand. He hasn't moved. His body is still angled slightly away, just as it was five minutes ago. My lips tighten over my teeth and I turn sharply and walk back to the house.

CHAPTER NINE

*B*enito

I wait until I hear the terrace doors close, then I lift my head and lower my gun to the lounger. I only cleaned it two days ago but I needed *something* to focus on.

Ripples still roll softly to the outer edges from where Contessa Castellano exited the pool. I breathe steadily and watch them settle until the sun rays reflect off a sheen of stillness.

I've been sitting out here since six having lain awake all night. I tried convincing myself it was down to the adrenaline generated by the hit we made on the Marchesis' drug drop. It was a close call and I shouldn't have been in the center of it all but I can't help myself. Call me a psychopath but I get a total hard on for annihilating my enemies. Whether that's by blowing up their fortune, blowing off their head with a round of ammo or squeezing the life out of them with my bare hands.

I've never been the kind to pay someone to do my dirty work. I prefer that blood to be on *my* hands, not some paid help's.

But I'm not convinced that is the reason. I have a shady and unwanted feeling my inability to sleep was caused, equally as much as and perhaps more than the hit, by a certain dark-haired Castellano sister showing me the full length of her leg in Cristiano's kitchen.

She's been nothing but petulant towards me, and I don't care for petulance, no matter how long it's legs are or how fucking *pretty* it is.

When I saw her at Gianni's funeral, I thought I was up for a bit of fun taunting, but there's only so much teenage button-pushing I can be bothered with, and I thought I'd hit my limit last night. Feeling the softness of her skin before she gnashed her teeth into my hand lit a fire in my belly, but her petulant reaction to the news I've moved my office above her studio put that fire right out, and it pissed me off. I hadn't planned on giving her those police reports but she needs to know this isn't a mere *duel*.

Her safety is *not* a fucking game.

But when she sauntered onto the terrace this morning, completely unaware she wasn't alone, I was struck by the pure, unguarded truth of her. I couldn't tear my gaze away when she lifted her face to the sun, warming it in the early morning rays. When she swam a few lengths she looked so graceful and liberated. And when she stripped off her two-piece, *holy fuck*, she came alive.

My gaze wasn't glued to her because she looked so disturbingly attractive, it was sucked in by the way she looked so *free*.

It was a surprise to see her devoid of black, and not just in clothing. The shadows beneath her eyes were gone, the darkness in her usually tight shoulders seemed to have washed off in the water. She'd shed her armor along with her two-piece and she'd never looked more beautiful.

I permitted myself a long look as she swam away from me, then averted my eyes when she turned to face in my direction. Forcing my gaze to stick to my gun was almost distressing but there was another surprising development. She knew I was there.

Sure, she didn't see me at first, but I heard her sharp intake of breath when she spun around. I pretended to be absorbed in polishing my pistol, thinking she might be embarrassed. I wanted to save her from that horrible feeling, but knowing I was there didn't stop her from flaunting herself freely in the water.

She swam three, four more lengths of the pool and took her goddamn time climbing out. I physically couldn't extract my gaze at that point—the scene looked like something from a Bond movie. Her rounded hips were practically moaning at me, her slim waspish waist glistened beneath droplets of pool water sliding down her back. My dick groaned against the tightness of my pants, the crown feeling outright sore. When she turned, I caught a small triangle of dark hair between her legs before I looked away, causing me to painfully swallow a primal growl.

Then, to my combined regret and relief, she wrapped a towel around her, darted an obvious glare in my direction and stomped off into the house.

Only a few minutes later, while I'm still reeling from the sight of Contessa *naked*, Nicolò saunters onto the terrace. The thought that if he'd been only ten minutes earlier, he too would've been privy to that tight white body gliding through the water with only a sheath of black hair for coverage, makes my blood heat.

I've been planning to speak to Cristiano about his future sister-in-law at some point over the next few weeks, and she just pushed up my timeline. I know her family pretty much leaves her to her own devices, but I didn't know she was naiveté personified until I had to explain why I'd killed her stalker friend, or stubbornly defiant, as evidenced by that naked swimming exhibition.

She should be thankful it was only me who saw. If it had been anyone outside of the crime family, they'd have met a bullet between the eyes.

Nicolò walks around the pool and settles beside me on a chair. "Did you get the papers I left for you?"

"The cop reports? Yeah. I gave them to Contessa last night."

Nicolò's brows rise a touch. "Wow. You *trying* to traumatize her?"

My eyes narrow on the door as if willing her to re-emerge any second now. "She wasn't taking the threat seriously enough."

Is that why I shoved the papers at her? Or was it because she wasn't taking *me* seriously enough?

Having Benito Bernadi move in right above where you hang out most days should be a relief. It'd be a fucking *privilege* for most people. But instead of looking grateful, she looked like she'd just been caught out in something. I know it was dark in the kitchen but I swear the blood drained from her face.

A voice in the back of my head says it had nothing to do with me providing a layer of protection—even Contessa isn't naïve enough to believe that wouldn't be an advantage right now. The voice thinks there's another reason why Contessa freaked at the thought of me being in that space. And it isn't going to fucking shut up until I find out what that reason is.

"Fair enough." Nicolò's voice in the distance draws me back to the terrace. "Any word on Fury?"

Fazio 'Fury' Marchesi is—*was*—the boss of our biggest rival gang in New York. He stepped down as don in the early hours of this morning following our hit on his latest cocaine smuggling operation last night.

"No. They still haven't announced his successor."

"His son's in a bad way. Broke both arms, his collarbone and three ribs in the collision."

I interlock my fingers and stretch, the knuckles

cracking in unison. "Yeah, well, Frankie wasn't destined to take over from his father. He's always been too weak."

"Well, whoever it is won't stand a chance against Cristiano. Not in New York. We own it now."

"Almost." I cock a brow and glance sideways at him. "They still have influence upstate."

"True, but minimal," he scoffs. "You know, I can't believe I'm saying this but Cristiano is as much a mob man as my uncle was. He took north Jersey like it was already his."

A small smile crosses my lips. "The shooting on the day of Gio's funeral provided more than enough motivation."

Especially now we know Trilby Castellano was in the car that was attacked, and Cristiano will blithely torture any man who threatens her existence.

"If you asked me, he relished it." I hear Cristiano talking on the phone just inside the house. I stand and brush my palms down my thighs. "And he deserved to."

Nicolò's chin tips upward as his gaze follows me. "What's the plan now? We just wait it out, see if they retaliate? Or do we hit them again?"

"Cristiano will have the final say, but it's my counsel that we step back, at least for a few days and watch for their next move. They might panic; they might retreat. They might surprise us."

"Surprise us, how?"

"I don't know, but Fury isn't stupid. He'll have something up his sleeve."

I leave Nicolò mulling that over while I follow the sound of Cristiano's voice. There are still drops of water on the steps from where Tess walked barefoot into the house. An image flashes in front of me of her slim, strong limbs wrapped in a white cotton towel, but I shove my hands in my pockets and blink it away.

Cristiano is leaning back against the kitchen island, an espresso in one hand and a phone in the other. He nods when I enter. There's no sign of anyone else. Not Trilby, nor her sister. I turn on the faucet and pour a glass of water then wait for him to finish the call.

"Nothing," he replies to my unvoiced question, as he puts his cell on the island. "We do nothing now. We lie low."

"That was going to be my recommendation. What do they know about the hit?"

Cristiano takes a slow sip of espresso. "Well, they know it was us. Or, more specifically, they know it was *you*."

I shrug. "I wasn't the only one there. I had three capos and a couple of soldiers."

"But you were front and center Benny. You might not have pulled the trigger but you were the one who snapped their necks."

"They were already half dead. I was putting them out of their misery," I reply. "Plus, if you'd seen their internet browsing histories, you'd have snapped their necks too."

Cristiano shakes his head and tries to bite down on a smile. "I know you love being… *hands on*. And you're good at it. But you're no use to me dead. I don't need you at the front; I need you to be my advisor—my *consigliere*."

"I can't advise you properly unless I'm in the thick of it," I reply. Being on the frontline of our operation gives me oxygen. Gianni never had a problem with me getting my hands dirty.

Cristiano pushes himself off the island. "Then you're just going to have to practice."

His answer annoys me. Like I need to practice doing the *admin*. I want to be a mob man, not a pen pusher. My tone turns exasperated. "And what will I do for pleasure?"

His lips turn up into a wicked grin. "You'll just have to get yourself a woman."

"I already have plenty," I say with a huff. "And they're fucking boring."

"Then you haven't found the right one."

I refrain from rolling my eyes, which only creates space for the vision of Contessa in a towel to flash across my lids *again*.

And she's not that woman.

She's the *last* thing I need.

"Speaking of women…" Cristiano folds his arms across his chest pushing the Di Santo crest inked to his skin through the white cotton. "What's this I hear about you putting a bullet in some guy's head because he sniffed Contessa's hair?"

I know another son of a bitch who's going to get a bullet in the head.

My tone throbs with impatience. "That's not what happened."

Cristiano smiles like a cat that got the fucking cream. "You want to elaborate?"

"Make whatever you want of it but the fact is, she's part of our family now, and she's a liability. I've been keeping an eye on her ever since you moved Trilby into the house."

"So, six months then?" Cristiano's brow dips like he's working overtime to take me seriously, which only pisses me off more.

"I happened to notice during that time she was being followed."

Cristiano's smug grin falls. "Followed?"

I fold my own arms across my chest. This is *my* game now. "Yeah, *followed*."

"Who was he?" Cristiano bites out.

"A nobody," I assure him. "A low-life criminal. But he was sick. He'd been convicted of sexual assault. Jailed for it. He'd been stalking Contessa for three years, obsessing over her, documenting every move she made." I take a heavy breath in. "He planned to abduct her."

"When?"

"Don't know the exact date," I reply, "but looking at the diary he kept, it was close."

Cristiano scrubs a hand down his face. "Why didn't you tell me, Benny?"

"That he planned to abduct her? Because I didn't

know he was planning that until we raided his dive of an apartment."

"And the stalking?"

"Because I had it handled."

"How?"

I arch a brow like he really needs to ask me that.

"The barbershop…" he says quietly. "That's why you set up the business?"

I lean back and brush a hand down my suit lapels. "It's not *why* I set up the business. It's a front. I launder money through it. But it's one of the reasons I chose *that spot*."

When I look up, he's staring at me with unguarded gratitude. "Fuck," he whispers. "Your loyalty will never fail to floor me." He steps forward and wraps an arm around my neck before giving me a kiss on the cheek. "Thank you, Benito. I had no idea she was in any danger, but you're right, she's still young and she doesn't appreciate the risks of being connected with us. Please continue to watch her. My fiancée's sister needs to be kept safe."

He releases me and I go back to straightening my lapels. "I'll do anything you need me to. You're my family."

He frowns. "Does she know that's why you set up shop there?"

"She doesn't know that's why I chose that spot for the barbershop, no. Doesn't matter anyway. The brat hates me."

Cristiano tries to cover his smirk with a curled fist. "She hates you? Why?"

A kernel of irritation sends out tendrils from the pit of my stomach to the surface of my skin. "Fuck if I know. Anyway, you don't need to be worrying about her—you've got more important things to worry about. I'll do it."

"So, you're going to spy on her from the barber's chair?" His eyes are practically dancing with amusement.

I can't help the sadistic grin pulling at my scarred cheek. "No, no. I've gone one better than that. I'm leasing the office above her studio. I'll be there every day."

He lowers his fist and pushes it into his pocket, then tips his head back a little and runs his tongue along his teeth thoughtfully. "Wow, you were taking this task seriously before I officially asked you to."

I glare at him, confused. He should be happy I'm taking the brat off his hands.

"Well, this was enlightening," he says with a grin before turning his back and heading toward the door.

I don't like the feeling he's leaving me with. I go to speak but my phone rings and I recognize the number straight away. It's one of my most loyal soldiers.

"Wait. I have to take this," I say and Cristiano stops. I press the phone to my ear. "Yeah?"

Donnie's words tumble out of him at a million miles an hour and I stare back at Cristiano as I listen. The kernel inside me explodes with an intensity I wasn't expecting. When eventually I hang up, I crush the burner into a few hundred pieces.

Cristiano turns his whole body to face me and his features darken.

I clear my throat.

"Someone's burned down my house."

CHAPTER TEN

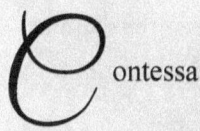ontessa

I finish my stretches, reach into my gym bag and lift a bottle of water to my lips. In the corner of my eye I can see Antonio looking all animated as he gushes over Kelly's performance just now.

"They're fucking." Paige, one of the other dance students, glares sideways at them as she collapses back against the wall. "It's so obvious."

I almost spit out my water. "I thought he was gay."

"Bi," she clarifies. "I've been stalking his socials."

I chuckle quietly. I like Paige. She didn't go to the same high school as me and therefore knows nothing of my family history and the fact I lost my mama a few years ago. She's always been friendly and I've begun to enjoy having a bit of banter with a female who isn't blood-related.

I drop the bottle into my bag and pull a sweater over my leotard. "You have way too much time on your hands."

"True." She grins then her gaze drops to where I'm unstrapping the silver heels on my feet. "I don't understand how you manage to wear those, let alone dance in them."

I wiggle my toes and relish the feeling of freedom as I pack the heels in question into my bag. "Years of practice. And also, the unadulterated fear of breaking an ankle," I smile. "That works a treat."

"Well, you seem to be getting better at the routine." She sighs and stretches out her legs. "Meanwhile, I believe it's secretly trying to kill me."

"So, channel your inner zombie," I say with a giggle. "You've already got the moaning down."

She scowls and playfully smacks me on the arm, then her gaze diverts over my shoulder and she straightens. "Ooh look, new neighbors," she says, nodding to the window. I turn to see what she's looking at and sure enough, there's a U-Haul truck outside and a couple of guys passing boxes between them. I refrain from rolling my eyes. I guess Bernadi was serious when he said he was going to use the space upstairs as his office.

"Wait…" Paige rests a hand on my arm. "They're going upstairs… with a bed…"

What? I spin around to confirm that the men really are carrying a bed. And a clothes rail. And several boxes that have the words 'kitchen' and 'bathroom' written across them.

"I thought the space upstairs was just an office," Paige says, tilting her chin upward at the faint sound of male voices.

"Yeah." I think back to the last time I was up there —with Fed. It was a sparse and barren unit—definitely not apartment material. "Me too."

"You think it's got anything to do with the barbershop over there?" Paige says.

My chest contracts in tandem with my heart sinking. Bernadi's barbershop. Yes, I do. Not least because upstairs is where Bernadi he's planning on stationing himself—with the sole aim of becoming a major irritant in my life.

"Possibly," I reply.

Paige gets to her feet. "I might head out later. My friend's just started working at some cool bar in the city. Do you want to join me?"

She turns away to pick up her bag and I stare at her back wide-eyed. It takes me a second or two to process the fact I've just been invited to something that isn't a wedding, funeral or other family gathering. The invitation has come as such a surprise, my instant reaction is to decline. I knit my lips together. "I'd love to but I promised I'd do some stuff with my aunt. Maybe next time."

She sighs and shrugs. "Yeah, okay. Well, I need to run. I'll catch you in a couple days?"

"Definitely. Night Paige."

As I watch her leave, something twists inside my chest, making me feel oddly sick. I would have loved to go out with a friend, but friendships for me simply don't last. In fact, in my experience, friendships leave nothing but scars.

The 'friends' I had at school dropped me the second I lost my mom and became 'different,' and the 'friend' I later grew to rely on, took my virginity then fled, never to be heard from again. I've only ever been burned by 'friends' and I'm simply not willing to take my chances on them again.

So, it's with this resolution in mind I finish packing my own bag and silently leave.

I wait around the corner until the removals truck has rolled past and the street is quiet but for the indiscreet presence of black vehicles with faceless drivers spaced down one side. I walk back toward the studio. I tried to fight against the idea but an inexplicable need to know if and why Benito Bernadi has actually *moved into* the office upstairs, drives me on.

He said it was just going to be an office. There was a WC up there, so that would explain the box of bathroom items, and maybe he needs a few plates and cups for lunches and drinks throughout the day, so 'kitchen' items would make sense too. But a clothes rail? A *bed*?

I push through the door then bypass the second door to my right—the one I'd normally take into the studio—

and head on up the stairs. At the top is a third door and I rap my knuckles sharply against it.

Heavy footsteps sound on the other side and I hold my breath, suddenly unsure of why I'm even standing here. When the door draws inwards and I come face-to-face with Benito Bernadi, the man I resolutely despise, I'm even less sure.

His gaze lowers over me like hot latte over ice, melting my outer edges. My lips part as I take in his upper body. He's shirtless, and in stark contrast to his scarred face and sharp facial structure, his shoulders graduate with rounded muscle, his chest is smooth and his skin pristine, even where it is decorated with black ink.

My focus dips to the artwork displayed across his torso. Stunningly intricate depictions of everything barbarian—poisoned thorns, scorpion tails and snake tongues, as though the most lethal of defenses has been painted across his skin.

My shocked breaths pump the air as I try to get my eyeballs under control, but they've never been confronted before by such a brazen display of masculinity. The only other naked chest I've seen on a male belonged to Federico, ironically within about five feet of where I'm standing, but his was the build of a boy. The chest bearing down on me, making me feel more claustrophobic with each passing second, is *all man.*

"Do you have something to say to me Castellano, or are you just going to stand on my doorstep and stare?"

His words send a rupture of fire across my collarbone and flames lick at my face, dousing them in burns.

"I… um, I just came to, um…" Blood rushes into my cheeks and I feel so hot I might faint. I have absolutely no explanation as to why I'm here, other than a shallow desire to nose into Bernadi's private business.

His brow up until now has been furrowed in a half-bemused, half-annoyed kind of way, but when nothing comes out of my mouth apart from useless stutters, it falls away and he looks… concerned.

"Are you okay? Is someone following you?"

I shake my head briskly. "No one's following me. I'm fine." I look back over my shoulder, wishing I hadn't come this far, because I have a foreboding feeling I won't ever be able to turn back. It feels like the bottom just fell out of my foundation and I have no idea why.

He looks past me and down the stairs. Through the glass half of the door at the bottom, I can see that daylight is thinning.

"Come inside. You're shivering."

I look up into deadly serious eyes and hug my arms around myself. He's right—I'm shaking like a leaf. Which is odd because I feel several degrees hotter than normal, not colder.

I follow him inside and almost gasp. The place looks completely different to the last time I saw it, which, admittedly, was three years ago. There's a Turkish rug on the whitewashed floor, a neat office set-up in the corner, a spotless white sofa next to a brass cocktail trolley topped with several bottles of liquor. To my left is a small kitchen and beyond it a shower room, and right in front of me, visible through a partially open door, is a bedroom.

"I thought this was just your office," I say, glancing around.

"Me too. But recent events have required me to rethink my living arrangements. Temporarily, at least."

I side-eye him, not because I'm skeptical of anything he says, because that's a given, but because I feel like facing him will leave a permanent imprint on my irises.

"What recent events?"

"Someone thought it would be a great idea to burn down my house." He punctuates that statement with a shrug, then follows it with, "Would you like some coffee?"

My jaw falls but he doesn't see it because he's walking the short distance to the kitchen and is now fiddling with a coffee machine.

I stay rooted to the spot. "Why did someone burn down your house?"

He pauses briefly, then continues to yank at machine parts like they're not doing as they've been told.

Several minutes pass while I stand here feeling awkward at his lack of reply and his growing frustration with the hunk of obscenely expensive metal on his counter. In the end I sigh and walk up behind him. I try not to brush against him when I reach around his solid back. I pop open the overlooked box of capsules and select something strong, then I flip the lid on the machine, slot the capsule in and press the 'start' button.

"Cup?" I ask, blinking up at him.

"Um, yeah. Here." He keeps his gaze on me as he passes me a plain white cup. I push it beneath the canopy just in time. Bubbles spit from the pipe, then a steady stream of dark liquid pours out, the smell of fresh Brazilian coffee filling the small room. We both stare at the machine until the cup is full, then Bernadi passes it to me. I wave it away. "I don't drink caffeine after midday."

His jaw grinds. Leaning back against the short counter, he wraps his hand around the cup and lets his gaze rest on me with one brow slightly raised.

"When was the last time you had to make yourself coffee?" I say, biting back a smirk.

"About four years ago, right before I got a housekeeper."

"So, where's your housekeeper now?"

"I gave her a few weeks off. This place is too small to justify having help."

I resist rolling my eyes. "How gallant of you."

I step backward until my spine hits the wall and we're standing opposite each other, about six feet between us. "So, who burned down your house?"

His gaze penetrates me as he takes a sip of the scorching hot coffee. He doesn't bat an eyelid. "I don't know the specific individual."

"Does it have anything to do with the blood you were washing off your hands the night before?"

His gaze narrows on me until I feel like I'm the only thing he's seeing. "What do you know about that?" His words sound accusatory but his delivery is soft.

"I saw you," I say, swallowing. "Through a gap in the door."

His gaze drops to the cup in his hand giving me a brief reprieve from the weight of his attention.

"Seems to be a thing of yours," he says, then slowly lifts his lids until I feel like I'm suffocating beneath his scrutiny.

I wonder where my breath's gone. "What does?"

"Watching people through gaps in doors."

"I don't know what you mean."

"Last night wasn't the first time you watched me through a gap in a door, was it?"

My heart thumps erratically as an image of him standing in the dining room of Federico's house flashes through my mind. *He remembers?*

"No," I whisper.

He stares at me until my skin burns so intensely I have to look away.

"I suggest the next time you see me through a gap in a door…" He waits until I look back at him. "You keep walking."

I gulp a mouthful of air. "Why?"

"Because I might start to think you want something."

I blink and his jaw grinds. My chest rises and falls

with labored breaths and it takes some effort to push myself away from the wall. "I think I'd better go."

"There's a car waiting down the street. I'll have him drive you home."

"There no need—" I start but there's a fire in his eyes that stops me.

He places the cup on the counter and I glance around the place one last time. "How long do you think you'll be living here?" I ask, in an attempt to bring the room temperature down.

"As long as it takes to rebuild my house."

"Could be a while then," I mutter, heading for the door.

I hear his grin behind me. "Could be."

"Well you know what you have to do, don't you?" I say, lightly. His bare arm brushes against me and his thick, inked fingers curl around the door handle.

His voice is rough and warm across the nape of my neck. "What's that?"

The door opens and I step onto the staircase and say cheerily, "Make like a vacuum and suck it up."

I practically hear his eyebrows shoot up, though I can't see them. I turn just in time to watch his response leave his lips.

"You're such a brat."

Something warm and liquid oozes from my head to my toes and I skip down the rest of the stairs.

When I look back over my shoulder he's filling his doorway, bending slightly so it accommodates his height. His hands are now shoved into his pockets and he's wearing an expression I can't read. All I see is a lowered brow, hooded dark eyes and a bottom lip caught between his teeth.

I give him one last, timid, smile and let myself out onto the street. Sure enough, there's a black car waiting, its headlamps illuminating the sidewalk. As I make my way toward it, his words play on repeat.

They should have felt condescending, disrespectful… Rude, even. They could have implied that I was juvenile—a child. They should have sent me reeling back to when Mama died and I was suddenly treated like the baby of the family—something I've worked hard to shake ever since.

He called me the one name I would normally have hated more than anything.

You're such a brat.

But he said it with a smile. And I liked it.

CHAPTER ELEVEN

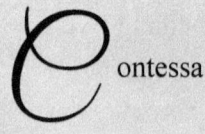

*C*ontessa

As if my dark demons can sense my mind softening toward Bernadi, fate delivers a package that only reaffirms my hatred for the assassin upstairs.

When I toss my keys onto the hall stand, they don't clink like they normally do; they thunk. I look down to see they've landed on a brown paper-wrapped package addressed to me. I pick it up and inspect it for a sender's address, but the only address I can see is mine.

I take it straight to my room and sit on the edge of the bed to carefully open it. I never get mail, but instead of feeling excited at the prospect, my pulse is skittering with apprehension.

When all the paper is in a pile at my feet, I'm left holding a plain white box. I tear off the tape and open it, then my heart *breaks.*

Inside is a pile of envelopes, tied together with string. My own handwriting stares back at me. I don't need to count through the envelopes to know there are thirty-six of them, stacked in order of the date they were sent. Almost one letter for each month Fed has been gone.

My eyes are hot and dry when I blink. They ran out of tears a long time ago.

I take one end of the string and pull, releasing the bow that binds them all together. When they slide apart, I notice they've been opened. Whether Fed received these letters or not, *someone* has read them.

I pick up the top envelope and pull out the letter. Even though it was written over three years ago, my handwriting hasn't changed, and I know what I wrote, word for word, because I've played it back constantly, wondering if I'd said the wrong thing. I unfold the white paper and read.

Dear Fed,

It's only been a few weeks since you left but I already miss you so much. I hope you and your parents have found somewhere nice to settle. Have you started at a new school?

Sorry if I was a bit weird when we said goodbye. I was in shock, I think. Losing my virginity was different to what

> I'd expected and I'm still trying to make sense of it. I need you to know that I love you as a friend, but I don't think I'm ready for anything more right now. I guess with the distance between us now, being anything more than friends is pretty impossible, but I think that's good. I really hope saying this doesn't hurt your feelings. I would never want to hurt you, Fed. I'm really glad we experienced our first time together, as friends.
>
> I can't wait to hear from you. I want to know you're safe and I wish you all the happiness in the world.
>
> Your best friend, Tess xxx

My fingers tremble slightly as I fold the note and place it back inside the envelope, then I take out the one beneath it.

> Dearest Fed,
>
> I really hope you're ok. It's been two months now and I haven't heard from you. I hope I haven't upset you by saying I wanted to be just friends. I think I just

freaked out a bit. It felt like a big deal losing my virginity, but I'm so glad it was to you.

I'm sure that with a bit of time I'll make good girlfriend material, lol. You know what a headcase I am—maybe I don't feel ready, or like I'd be any good at it. If you can be patient with me, I'll try to get there.

I'm so sorry if I made you think it was an impossibility. I think I just need some time, that's all.

Please forgive me for being an idiot, and write me back!

All my love, Tess xxx

P.S. It's official - Kelly Richards is dating Seth Turner, the quarterback. That's all the gossip I know though, I'm afraid. I'll listen out for more just for you!

A knock sounds at the door, making me jump.

"Yeah?" I try to hide the irritation in my voice.

The door opens and Allegra, my aunt, pops her face through it. Just as she opens her mouth to speak, her gaze drops to the box in my lap.

"Ah, I was just coming to let you know a package had arrived for you, but you've found it. Anything interesting?"

When I don't reply, she steps into the room, seeing a response on my face anyway. "What is it, Tess? Is everything okay?"

I shrug and place the second note back in its envelope. "Everything's fine," I say in a monotone voice.

She walks over and sits beside me on the bed. "Do you want to talk about it?"

I shake my head but answer anyway. "They're all the letters I sent to Federico."

She peers over my shoulder. "They've been opened."

I sigh heavily. "Yeah."

"That's weird," she says slowly. "Normally, mail is returned *un*opened. Why would Fed read the letters then send them back?"

"Maybe it wasn't Fed who read them."

She purses her lips in thought.

"Don't worry, there's nothing incriminating in them," I assure her.

She nudges me with her elbow. "I didn't think there would be. But I do think it's odd that someone would hold onto them for this long, read them and then send all of them back at once. I mean, you haven't actually heard from Federico since he left, have you?"

"No," I whisper, sadly.

"When did you send the last letter?"

I sift through the envelopes until I land on the very bottom one, and look at the postmark. "One month ago exactly."

"Did you say anything in the letter that would give him a reason to send everything back?"

"I don't know. Maybe…" I frown and stare at the wall.

"Listen…" Allegra gets to her feet and places a hand on my shoulder. "I'll give you a moment but you know where I am if you want to talk about it. But, for what it's worth, Tess, I think you held out for that boy long enough. If he was going to write you at all, it would have been within the first few weeks. I don't think he's going to come through. I know you're hurting over him, but he's not worth your tears."

"Oh don't worry," I huff. "I haven't cried for him at all."

She smiles. "Good." Then she walks back to the door. "Besides, he was just a friend at the end of the day. Friends come and go and you'll always make new ones."

"Yeah, I know." I force a smile and bite back the words I really want to say: he was more than a friend and he always will be.

He was my first.

The pain of his rejection after what I gave to him cuts deep.

I wait until the door has closed before I take out the

last letter I sent him. My lids scratch against my eyeballs as I read.

> Hey Fed,
> It's been three years and I haven't heard from you once. I know what you're thinking: take a hint, Tess! Well, finally, I have. This is the last letter I'm going to send.
>
> This is so bittersweet. I've never had many friends, as you know, and so this habit of writing to you, well, it's been kinda nice. I'm going to miss sending you gossip from school and complaining to you about Antonio. (I doubt you'll miss that though, huh?)
>
> I don't have many other people to talk to beside my sisters and my aunt. There is a girl at dance class I talk to a little. Her name's Paige and she's kinda sweet, but she isn't you. You knew me better than anyone, and I miss that.
>
> I sometimes wonder if you've changed much. I hope you've found some friends, maybe a girlfriend. I hope you're happy.
> Things are changing around here

anyway. I have a recital coming up and my sister is engaged, so there will be wedding preparations to keep me busy. I have a horrible feeling that despite being allergic to it, I'm going to have to wear pink to the wedding *eyeroll* Apparently, wearing black as a bridesmaid is a bit of a faux pas.

Well, this is it Federico. I have no idea if you've read any of my letters, so if this is the only one you see, please know that I love you so much and miss you every day.
Take good care of yourself.
Yours always, Tess xxx

I close the box and place it on the bed, then I roll onto my stomach and bury my face in the comforter. I feel humiliated. The PO Box I sent the letters to belonged to a friend of Mrs. Falconi. If that had changed, why weren't the letters returned to sender, unopened? I know in my bones that Fed received and read them. He simply chose not to reply. He chose to send them back, making it clear he'd read them all but didn't think me important enough to put pen to paper for.

He betrayed me. After taking one of the most precious things a girl has to give, he then abandoned me. He lied.

Clarity slips through the haze of shame. Fed had coerced me into giving him my V card, by confessing his love for me, and promising we'd be together one day.

I know without a shadow of doubt Federico Falconi used me. He's an asshole. But I can't help but feel heartbroken at his rejection.

My jaw aches with bitterness and another face flashes into front of my lids. It's the same face I saw when Federico took my virginity. Benito Bernadi. Fresh hatred floods my veins and I roll onto my back and stare at the ceiling.

God, I want to hurt Bernadi. It's his fault Federico left. At least if Federico was still here, I could have confronted him on his asshole behavior. Or, I wouldn't have felt obliged to sleep with him in the first place.

The worst part about this is, I can't tell anyone. People still ask me what happened to Federico and his family, but I dare not speak a word of it. I only told Trilby I lost my virginity because she coaxed it out of me after revealing a shocking truth of her own. There's no way I could tell Sera—she would shake her head at me and tut a lot. I couldn't tell Bambi—she'd think it was disgusting. I couldn't tell Allegra—she'd have heart failure. And there's no way in hell I could tell Papa—he feels indebted to Cristiano for saving Trilby and would only want our family to be held in high regard now we're so at the center of the Di Santo empire—he'd be ashamed to hear one of his Italian daughters was no longer pure.

I suddenly feel very tired. Lifting my knee, I point my foot at the box then shove it off the end of the bed. I hear the envelopes scatter across my bedroom floor. Then I close my eyes and drift off into a restless, weary sleep.

CHAPTER TWELVE

*B*enito

Nicolò is already sitting opposite Cristiano when I enter the office and settle in one of the four leather armchairs. A week has passed since I saw Contessa Castellano swim naked in the pool, and the sight is permanently etched on my eyeballs.

Cristiano looks across his desk at me. "Any word on who burned down your house?"

"Nothing," I reply. "I even talked to Joe Bigelow…"

"The Marchesi associate?" Nicolò asks.

"Yeah. He says the Marchesi's are keeping their cards close to their chests."

Cristiano pulls a handful of cell phones out of a drawer in his desk. "Interesting. So, we don't know if this is their way of retaliating after the drug bust?"

I shrug. "I doubt it is. It's not Fury's style. He prefers calculated theatrics over petty arson."

"Your house going up in flames like that?" Nicolò arches a brow. "I'd say that was pretty theatrical."

Cristiano drops the phones on his desk. "He has a point."

"What other enemies do you have beside the Marchesi's?" Nicolò asks.

Cristiano smirks. "How long have you got?"

I slump back in the chair and cross an ankle over my other knee. "I'll find out who it was sooner or later. I've got some feds on it."

Nicolò's eyes narrow. "You don't seem too concerned, Benny. I'd be knocking down doors and threatening lives if someone burned down my house."

I don't like my conviction being questioned. "Yeah, well you don't need to worry about that, do you? Still living at home with your mama."

"Ouch." Cristiano shakes his head.

"Fuck you Benny. Just means I have more money to spend on women," he replies with a sneer.

"You mean shoes," I counter, glancing down at what appears to be another new pair of Saint Lauren Derby's on his feet.

Cristiano pushes the phones across the desk. "To replace the burner you crushed."

He glances sideways out of his window to the terrace—the sun is beating down and I expect his fiancée is enjoying the pool. A smile tugs at the corner of his mouth. "I have a feeling you'll need several."

I frown at his comment. It's not like I crush burners between my fingers on a regular basis. "Thanks."

"So, what do we know about Fury's successor?" Nicolò probes. "Did your mole have any insights on that front?"

Cristiano sits back and watches me as he rubs two fingers back and forth across his lips.

I uncross my legs, lean forward and rest my forearms on my knees, looking both of them directly in the eye. "It hasn't been announced yet, but Bigelow seems to think Fury's nephews are in the running to take over the clan."

"Nephews?" Nicolò squints. "As in plural?"

I turn to him. "Yeah. Three. Lorenzo, Matteo and Luca. Lorenzo's the eldest and the one with the more… shall we say… *colorful* history."

"Meaning?" Cristiano rests his elbows on his desk.

"He was made at thirteen and killed his first capo six months later. Hasn't stopped since. His brothers took a little longer to warm up. They're power hungry but not much between the eyes. They get off on eliminating people—the bloodier the better—as opposed to building longstanding relationships that might ultimately give them control of a city."

"So they're loose cannons?" Cristiano rests his chin on two pointed fingers, brows raised.

"Yeah. At the very least."

"So, what's your recommendation Benny? Where's their preferred heartland? Do we strengthen our numbers in Newark?"

I consider his question. "We could definitely strengthen our numbers there. Losing Newark to us was the biggest blow they've suffered in years—there's always a chance they'll try to take it back. But, last I heard, Fury wanted to focus his efforts on Connecticut. Maybe we let 'em have it for now while we get a feel for the new don."

"Or *dons*." There's a warning note in Nicolò's words.

Cristiano nods slowly. "Fine. Let's lay low and keep a watching brief. Get some more men in Jersey."

I click my tongue. "Consider it done."

Leaving Nicolò in Cristiano's office I head outside to make a few calls. As I reach the exit to the terrace, Contessa Castellano appears in the doorway. I didn't know she was here, so I'm not prepared for the sight of her creamy white body pouring out of a tiny black two-piece and barely-there sarong, full lips parted in surprise, nor the way her eyes widen as she processes the fact I'm blocking her entrance.

Heated annoyance fills out my chest. There are men in the house and she's dressed like *this*?

"Don't you have any clothes?" I snap.

She sucks in a breath through those plump, pink lips, annoying me even more.

"Well, hello to you too," she says with a thin smile and ticked off eyes. She thrusts a hip to one side and props a hand on it, making it almost impossible not to dip my gaze. "What brings you here again so soon? Someone burn down your new apartment?"

"I think you'd know about it if they had, seeing as your dance studio is beneath it."

She chews on her lip before replying. "I wouldn't mind too much. It would solve a few problems."

I fold my arms and lean against the doorframe. "What kind of problems?"

"Like having to run into you on a daily basis, or having to educate a spoiled grown man on how to use a coffee machine."

"Spoiled?" I chew on the word.

"You haven't needed to make yourself a coffee in four years, Bernadi. I would describe that as spoiled."

My jaw stiffens. "I would describe it as 'busy,'" I say with a sneer. "But you wouldn't know about that, would you?"

Her lips purse into a petulant pout which sends an un-planned-for shot of blood to my cock.

"I need you to do something for me," I say, curtly.

Her eyes *roll*. "Oh you need me to do something for you? Consider me at your service… not."

"You'll do as you're told, brat."

Her lids ping open.

"There are grown men in this house. It is not appropriate for you to be walking around in next to nothing. Do you understand? Go and put some fucking clothes on."

"Oh, I'm sorry. For a second there I thought you were my father. But…" She tilts her head to one side, "seems I need to remind you, you're not."

She reaches for the knot at her side and deftly

loosens it, letting the tiny slip of sarong fall to the floor. Her two-piece sits high on her hips and I just know that the string disappears into the round cheeks of her ass.

"I think we might need a little lesson in semantics here," she says in a voice like poisoned silk. She lifts one foot at a time and slips off her patent black sandals, one by one.

"You see, the word 'next' usually means the thing that comes immediately before or after the present thing."

She reaches up and pulls the band from her hair, drops it to the floor and shakes her long black hair out until it cascades over her shoulders and face.

What the fuck is she doing?

"So, in the saying 'next to nothing'," she continues, snapping open the clasp on her watch and holding it up by the strap, letting it dangle between us, "the 'nothing' means exactly that, and the 'next to' means the thing that comes immediately before it."

She drops the watch and I lift my palm just in time to catch it.

Then she reaches her hands behind her back. My pulse thickens, filling my ears.

"Note how I used singular, not plural." She lifts her brows. "Thing. Not *things*."

I note she's wearing two things right now. Two-piece top and bottom. My chest fills out and my arms drop to my sides, fingers flexing and curling.

She turns her head sideways slightly and looks at me from beneath an arched brow and dark lashes. "So, if I really was wearing next to nothing, there would only be one thing between 'clothed' and 'nothing', right?"

Her tongue nips forward and brushes along her top lip, wetting it.

Then she releases her hands to her sides and the bikini top falls to the floor.

"This, Bernadi, is 'next to nothing.'"

My gaze falls, uncontrollably, to her bare tits. They're perfect. Beautiful handfuls of porcelain flesh, pink pebbling around diamond sharp nipples. My cock stiffens and I don't even care. I lick my lips and swallow, unable to tear my eyes away. My hands ache to cup her flesh; my mouth dries at the thought of sucking on those mesmerizing peaks. My head spins at the thought.

"And…"

I drag my gaze back to hers and see she's watching me, each puff of breath lifting the strands of hair that have fallen over her eyes. She's standing defiant on the step but her gaze has softened, which only makes her next words sting.

"…you don't get to tell me what I can and can't wear. I can wear whatever I want. Even 'next to nothing.'"

She turns slowly and walks back out to the terrace, her slim hips swaying. I was right about her ass. It's *devouring* the piece of cotton between her cheeks.

I can't do anything but stand and stare after her, hoping that whatever lava is brewing in my belly settles before I tear this fucking place apart.

CHAPTER THIRTEEN

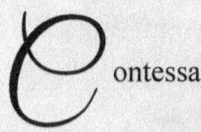

*C*ontessa

I lay back on the lounger, my heart beating through the wall of my chest. Adrenaline is raging through my veins, through my bones. I can't believe I just spoke to Bernadi that way. I can't believe I just stripped off my bikini top in front of him. If Cristiano saw me doing that he'd probably banish me from the house. I'd be branded a slut, especially when everyone discovers I'm not the virgin they all assume I am.

After five years of being helicopter-parented, told I can't do this, can't do that, and being chaperoned everywhere, I've grown somewhat allergic to being told what to do. Sure, I apply some flexibility to Papa and Allegra, but not my sisters anymore, nor my tutors to a reasonable extent, and certainly not consiglieres to mafia bosses who seem to think they own me. And even though a week has passed, the humiliation of Fed's rejection still burns, and seeing as he's not here for me to direct all my shame-filled fury at, Bernadi is going to be on the receiving end instead.

The sun to my right is suddenly blocked out and I look up just as a fluffy towel and my Cartier watch is dropped onto my stomach.

Bernadi is standing over me, fists curled, face like thunder.

"What's your problem?" he growls.

My heart thumps at the base of my throat. I thought I'd had the last word, or at least shocked him enough to keep him at arm's length for a little while. I hadn't expected him to follow me out to the terrace.

I'm about to yank off the towel when his tone thaws. "Leave it… Just while we speak."

I realize he doesn't want the distraction of my naked breasts and I flush. But I'm not thawing that easily.

"You," I snap, feeling an untethered thread of anger wind its way up my throat. "*You're* my problem."

"Fine." He holds his hands up. "Wear whatever the hell you want. See what Cristiano has to say about it."

"It's not about the clothes." I turn and glare at the pool, heaving out hard breaths and feeling a tide of pent-up outrage swelling inside my chest.

"I'm not moving out of the office," he warns.

"I don't care about your damn office." My voice has thinned like a blade. He's done it. The man has managed to wind me up until I can't hold back the truth anymore.

He needs to know why I hate him. Then, maybe, he'll leave me the fuck alone.

"Then what is it, Castellano? Because I can't take any more of your petulance." He spits out the 'p' and that does it.

I leap to my feet and the towel falls to the floor. "You want to know what my problem is? I lost my *virginity* because of you!" I yell.

He steps backward, his solid legs sending the lounger behind him flying across the terrace.

His eyes blacken slowly and he releases a growled whisper. "What?"

I take a step toward him with gritted teeth. "You shut down the Falconis," I say, seething behind a clenched jaw. "You *ruined* them…"

"What does your virginity have to do with the Falconis?"

"They took their son to the other side of America." I take another step forward but he stands his ground, only seeming to solidify more. "He was my best friend and you forced him away."

He goes to speak but I cut him off. "You asked me what my problem is, Bernadi. My problem is I felt so sorry for Federico that when he asked me to sleep with him, I obliged. You forced him out of his home and I *pitied* him."

I shrug my arms to the side. "And now here I am, part of the damn Italian mafia, in which the only currency a woman has is her virginity, and I no longer have it to give." I lean in to him and jab his chest, hard, with a pointed finger. "Because of *you*."

His features darken like thunder and I retreat, wrapping my arms around my chest. Baring the truth has made me feel more naked than losing my top.

When he speaks again, there's a darkness in his low whisper. "What makes you think I forced him away?"

Hi eyes search my face then widen for a fraction of a second,

"You saw me. Through a gap in the door. At the Falconis'."

My lips purse angrily. "Right before you shot Federico's uncle."

Bernadi frowns. "I didn't shoot his uncle. Augie did. But it was justified. The guy had a gun pointed at his head."

I take a step back, feeling suddenly drained. "I don't care," I say weakly. "The damage has been done, and they've gone. You did what you had to do. Just know that, whatever happens to me now, *you* are to blame."

Then I turn around, pick the towel up off the floor, wrap it around myself, and walk back into the house. And this time, he doesn't follow.

CHAPTER FOURTEEN

enito

For the second time in ten fucking minutes I find myself standing on Cristiano's terrace, speechless.

Red tinges the outline of my irises as the realization someone took Contessa Castellano's virginity permeates my brain. Contessa isn't a virgin. Contessa has been with another man. Contessa *blames me*.

In the distance I hear a door slam. I turn to one of the loungers and slowly lower onto it. I stare at the pool water as a shadow stretches across it. Looking up, I see a black cloud pass in front of the sun, then a crack of thunder echoes through the palms.

Usually, I quite like a summer storm—it feels poetic, like it mirrors the darkness in my soul that even the warmth of a sunny day can't conceal. But today it feels like a full stop on a sentence I haven't even spoken.

Heavy raindrops start to clatter around me, turning the pool from a once calm oasis into a choppy, turbulent reservoir. Moisture seeps through the cotton of my suit to my skin, and streaks of water slide down my forehead and drip from my lashes.

Something sharp and unwanted jabs at my shell. I pride myself at not feeling empathy for anyone. Loyalty I can feel—for Cristiano, for the Di Santo family, my comrades. But loyalty and empathy are two different things. Loyalty requires action, whereas empathy requires me to feel. The last time I felt anything, the sensation slid away from me just as all the love I once had for my father evaporated into nothing.

Empathy is an unnecessary emotion. It complicates things. Makes it hard to eliminate people. Not having it is a superpower.

I'm not feeling all that powerful right now.

I'm putting myself in Castellano's shoes and imagining how it must have felt to give away something that our noble culture treasures, for better or for worse.

I'm wondering what her father would say if he knew he had one less bargaining tool, should he ever need it.

I'm forcing myself to confront what it might feel like for a woman to give something so personal away because she felt *obliged*.

And I'm feeling sick to my goddamn stomach.

I know for a fact the Falconis' haven't been back here for three years. Has Contessa been in touch with

Federico in that time? The wall of my chest thickens. Did she love him? Something turns at the base of my throat but I ignore it. It shouldn't matter to me—her feelings for him are irrelevant.

But my feelings for her… I drop my face into wet palms as confusion rides over me.

Nothing has changed, I tell myself. She's a liability —that's the only reason I'm keeping a close eye on her. She's just proved again why she needs someone to watch her every damn move. She's right about being worthless in this culture without purity. No man is going to want her if he can't prove he broke in his own woman. It's shit but it's true.

My eyes open and take in the pools of water collecting across the terrace. An unfamiliar sensation tugs at the very center of me. I feel sadness for Contessa. As big of a brat as she is, she doesn't deserve to be discarded by the men of this family because of a mistake she made when she was too young to know any better.

A thought that could only have been borne of insanity crosses my mind. If she were to be my wife, I wouldn't care if she were a virgin or not. But only because I don't care for any wife. I'm not marriage material. I'm too ruthless. Too lethal. I'd probably kill a woman in my sleep without even fucking knowing it. But the thought of anyone rejecting her for that reason alone makes my blood *rage*.

It wasn't my fault that the Falconi's left, but I played a part. Still, I don't want Contessa to go on with her life believing I'm the evil villain she seems to think I am. At least it all makes sense now—the hateful glares I couldn't decipher, the sharp put-downs she flung at me for no reason, this weird obsession with me shutting things down. She thought I'd ruined her life by sending her childhood sweetheart to the other side of the country.

I don't really care what she thinks of me, and I shake my head before any thought to the contrary can open its mouth. But, it is time she knew the truth.

CHAPTER FIFTEEN

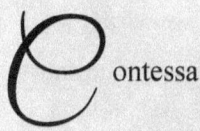
ontessa

As I fling three days-worth of clothes into a bag, I know I've stayed here too long. Trilby would have me move in permanently if she could, but as much as I thought I'd be able to handle seeing Bernadi occasionally, I can't. Especially now I've told him the truth about why I can't bear to be around him.

I open the Lyft app on my phone and watch the cab icon slowly making its way to the Di Santo residence. *Ten minutes away.*

I cast a final glance around the room, taking in the heavy raindrops as they splash off the sill, then someone knocks at the door and I freeze.

"Contessa…" It's Bernadi.

"Go away."

"Just give me one minute, then I'll stay out of your way… for good."

I stand facing the door but rooted to the spot. I feel a strange pull like I want to yank the door open and see his face, but I can also feel the touch of Federico's fingers between my thighs—wanted, yet unwanted at the same time—and the resentment burns inside my chest.

"Then you'll leave me alone?" I glance at my phone. *Nine minutes away.*

"I promise."

My feet feel like lead weights as I walk to the door. I flick the lock, take a deep breath and open it. Bernadi has an arm leaned up against the door frame and his chest alone blocks out all the light from the landing. I dare not look up into his eyes so I skirt around them, taking in the taut shape of his mouth, the normally full lips pulled into an anguished line. His scar seems more prominent in shadow, dancing with each grind of his jaw.

He's completely drenched and my gaze drops to where water pools at his feet.

"What?" I'm aiming for a tone with bite but it sounds more weary than anything.

"Can I come in?" His deep timbre reaches into the room and fills it.

I turn my back to him and walk to the center of the room. The door closes behind me with a soft click.

"You're right, Contessa. I am the reason the Falconis left."

A long, exhausted breath rolls out of my lungs.

"But I didn't *drive* them away. They didn't *flee*. I sent them away for their own good."

I shake my head. "What does that even mean?"

Silence crawls around the walls uncomfortably.

"Enzo Falconi stole from us."

"That's not true." I can't keep the irritation out of my voice. "He missed one lease payment."

"That's probably what he told his son."

I turn around to see Bernadi pinching the bridge of his nose, his eyes closed. I feel safer looking at him when he isn't looking back. If he wasn't such an asshole, he'd be beautiful. His whole frame looks to be carved from granite—all lines and labyrinthine angles. His jacket has been discarded, the sleeves of his button-up are rolled to the elbows and delicate black lines and shapes trip in the light as his muscles tense. I follow them to the curve of his wrist and the thick, inked fingers. The skin is calloused, the nails sharp and neatly trimmed—not jagged and filled with dried blood as I'd expect from a gangster.

I feel lightheaded as I whisper, "What did he steal?"

Bernadi sighs and drops his hand. Before I can look away, his lids pop open and his eyes catch mine. A strange heat floods my chest.

"He stole systematically from us over two years, to the tune of sixteen million dollars."

I gasp and fall a little deeper into the iron grip of his gaze.

"We gave him breaks on fuel, power, equipment; we

funneled contracts away from other businesses for him. We thought he delivered the best. It was only after he left we discovered the extent of his neglect. There were firms his people hadn't visited in months. They were too busy vacationing in the Florida Keys and driving around in brand new Maserati's."

I hang disbelievingly on to his words.

"He skimmed everything he owed us and we gave him repeated warnings. When he started gambling our money, we broke his fingers."

A faint memory slides across my lids. I was sitting in the Falconis' kitchen and Fed was helping me with my math project. I remember his papa entering the kitchen with an enormous bandage wrapped around his hand. When Fed asked about it, Mr. Falconi blamed it on some heavy equipment falling on him in the warehouse. At the time I found it odd that whatever landed on him only got his hand, but I didn't give it any further thought.

"Finally, after failing to pay the lease for three months, we went to the house."

Three months? Federico said it was only one. But if what Bernadi is saying is correct, there was clearly a lot Fed didn't know.

"We came to close down his business. We planned to sell all his assets and make back the money he lost us. It wasn't our intention to kill anyone. But then Mario walked in…"

He sighs and finally averts his eyes. I collapse as

I'm released from steel clutches and land on the edge of the bed. My packed bag slides to the floor.

"He was the worst of all of them—he didn't have just one new car, he had three, and to be quite honest, that was the first time I'd seen him in a year because he'd spent most of that time in his second home down on the Jersey shore. God knows, he probably had mistresses he was propping up with our money. He knew we were there to shut them down and clear them out and he panicked. The second that gun went to Augie's head I grabbed Mario, but before I could calm him down, Augie shot him."

I can feel the warm air of the room touch my eyeballs as I stare back at Bernadi wide-eyed.

"Oh God—" My gaze falls to the carpet.

"After Augie and Beppe had left the room, I hung back and told Enzo to get himself and his family as far away from New York as he could within the next twenty-four hours. If Gianni had found out exactly what Enzo Falconi had done, he'd have killed the entire family."

My brain swims as I try to piece everything together. That's why Federico was insistent on us sleeping together so quickly. It all makes sense now. There's just one thing I can't quite get my head around.

"If Enzo had betrayed the Di Santo's so badly, why did you help them out by giving them a warning? They meant nothing to you."

Bernadi rubs his right hand up and down his left

bicep, inadvertently drawing my gaze to its firm swell. He looks… *uncomfortable*.

He sighs and turns his gaze to the pouring rain. "There was a time when Enzo made us a lot of money and took very little. We made him work for it. Then one of his senior managers was shot dead in a drive-by. It affected him badly. That's when he started the skimming. And it escalated from there. Once he got a taste for cheating us and getting away with it, he couldn't help himself."

Bernadi turns his head, and once again, I'm ensnared in the grip of his gaze.

"I'm not condoning or excusing the stupid shit he's done over the years, but… I don't blame him for how it all started."

I don't know what unnerves me the most—the fact Federico paid for his father's greed by having his life uprooted to start over several thousand miles away, or the fact Bernadi apparently has a heart.

I sigh heavily and frown at the carpet, my head buzzing with new information, rearranging everything I once thought I knew.

When I look up, Bernadi is crouching in front of me. His face is so close to mine I can see every inch of scar tissue down his left cheek, and wide pupils in burnt bronze eyes that are slightly narrowed as he searches my face for something.

A warm flare licks at my insides and I swallow.

"I'm sorry for what happened after that," he says, softly. "I didn't even know you and Enzo's son were…"

He trails off before licking his tongue over his bottom lip.

"We weren't." My dried-out voice cracks a little when I speak. "I didn't know that was something… he wanted."

I drop my gaze back to the floor. Four days ago, no one knew about that night or my loss of impurity. Now, two people do: the sister I felt most estranged from growing up, and the consigliere to New York's biggest mafia family. Not a scenario I'd have conjured up in my wildest dreams.

He reaches up and takes my chin between his thumb and fingers so gently I have to fight the urge to give in to his touch. "What about what *you* wanted?"

I flick my gaze to his and swallow against a desert-dry throat as the truth silently alarms me. "I didn't think that mattered."

Seconds are consumed by uncomfortable silence, then something flips behind Bernadi's eyes.

I watch his expression shift from gently concerned to confused.

"Wait… You don't believe what you want in life *matters*?"

The fact I don't know how to answer that question renders me silent. I mean, of course I know what I want, right? I'm not just doing this whole dance thing because I went a few times as a kid and was pretty good at it, right? Not because Mama always said she loved to watch me dance… *right*?

I used to want to travel to Asia, to work in France, to

study in London… I harbored those dreams for as long as I can remember. But after Mama died, Papa's propensity to worry about all of us reached new and unfathomable heights. He tried to hide the stress of raising four young daughters from us, but the evidence was there in the creases around his eyes, in the lines on his brow and the downward turn of his mouth.

We all watched Trilby's mental health deteriorate even after moving into the apartment. We all knew she hardly slept. No one questioned why she dyed her hair platinum blond, but we all knew… She had her own way of coping with Mama's death.

Sera threw herself into tarot cards, astrology books, placing all her faith and fortune in the stars above. She disappeared into a shell we were all so desperate to see her re-emerge from that Papa didn't argue at all when she announced she wanted to do an internship away from home.

Bambi was only ten when Mama died. She didn't understand it then and I'm not sure she even understands it now, but Allegra watches her like a hawk, knows her inside and out, and will do anything to shield our precious baby sister from the evils of the world.

As for me, I'm just Tess. As long I keep dancing, no one need worry about me. I don't *want* anyone to worry about me. Like I tell myself every morning when I open my eyes and realize all over again that it's not a very bad dream, I'm *fine*.

"You don't, do you?" Bernadi's eyes narrow and he

sits back on his heels like the life has just been knocked out of him.

I can't seem to do anything other than blink.

"Contessa…" He closes his eyes and shakes his head slowly, then lifts his lids, showering darkness and disappointment over me. "You told me to stay away from you," he says in a low voice I'm sure only the devil can hear. "But do you think I'm going to leave you alone in a world that would take advantage of you without batting a fucking eyelid?"

I shift backward on the bed because the truth feels a sharp blade against sore skin.

"I mean it, Contessa. Someone has to protect you, because I don't trust that you will."

"I don't need protection," I say firmly.

He looks twice at me, like he can't believe I just said that. "If I hadn't shot that cretin, he'd have abducted you. You know that, don't you?"

I straighten my spine and lower my lashes defiantly. "He followed me for three years and didn't lay a finger on my body. Stop trying to scare me."

He scrubs a hand down his face and stares out the window disbelievingly. "Oh my God, you're so stubborn."

"I resent that," I say in a trembled whisper. "You don't know me."

He laughs darkly. "I don't need to." He lets those words linger as he shoves himself up to standing. His lip curls as though he's disgusted with me. "I just need to keep you alive."

He turns and stalks back to the door while I shout after his departing back. "I'm not your responsibility, Bernadi."

He turns slowly, and there's a strange fire in his eyes accompanied by venom I can almost taste. "No, you're not. You're Cristiano's. And he has more pressing things to deal with than protecting a woman who refuses to have a mind of her own. So… you've got me."

And with that, he yanks open the door, walks through it, then slams it so hard the wall shudders.

CHAPTER SIXTEEN

enito

The average person might wonder why a bell is needed above the door of a twenty square foot barbershop with a window that gives an unobscured view of the road. But the average person probably doesn't expect there to be a darkened office out back filled with safety deposit boxes, loaded firearms and a small round table that plays host to some of the less salubrious conversations this city has seen.

My height makes it difficult to avoid shop door bells so I have to duck to avoid the tinny ring. The manager stops midway through a beard trim and opens his arms.

"Signor Bernadi... *Bello vederti*."

I let him kiss me on each cheek before nodding toward his client.

"Ciao Gaspare. It's good to see you too. *Rasatura bagnata*? When you've finished up with this gentleman, of course." Sure, I had a different business opportunity in mind when I opened this place, but that's no reason not to build a decent client base for this little outfit. No paying customer should have their service cut short, not even for me.

"*Si, si. Assolutamente*. Please, take a seat."

There are three barber chairs in the shop and each one is full, along with most of the waiting area seats. I recognize most of the men here—they're each involved in Di Santo business in some shape or form. And they've each been trained to only speak to me if I speak to them first. I never intended to become that kind of boss, especially since I'm not even a *capo*—I'm an *advisor*—but my reputation for being a fast aim and taking zero shit from anyone must have preceded me.

Slowly, conversation returns to a semi-normal pace and volume but the topics are tame. Normally the walls are ringing with banter. I don't doubt they're watching their words because I'm in the room.

I scroll through my emails until I've read everything, then glance sideways out the window. The dance studio is lit from inside but, as always, a thin veil of netting conceals anything beyond the window from the eyes of passersby. All I can see are shadows moving about.

A group of girls leaves the studio. My breath hitches as I scan them in search of a familiar, dark-haired brat.

She's due to leave about now, which is a large part of the reason I'm sitting in this chair right opposite, but there's no sign of her.

After her little confession at Cristiano's and her stubborn refusal to see that her life is worth anything, I'm more determined than ever to keep a close eye on Contessa Castellano. She's slipped through the net too many times. She cares more about other people than she does herself, and it makes me so furious I can barely speak.

I'm about to call Nicolò and order him to track her down when a truck pulls up a few yards along from the dance studio.

It looks like it's delivering groceries to the store two doors down, but that's not what grabs my attention. Somehow, the position of the truck is reflecting light into the studio, making the netting almost transparent. There's one person left in the empty space. One person with legs that go on for days, dark hair tied in a severe knot at her crown, and a skin-colored latex outfit that shows every lethal curve and line.

My throat feels suddenly dry so I get up to grab a glass of water, then realize every single punter in the shop is staring at the studio, watching the very same thing I was half a second ago: Contessa Castellano.

I have an inexplicable urge to slit the throat of every one of them.

Even Gaspare.

I push down the urge and splash water haphazardly

into a crystal tumbler before gulping it down, then I slam the tumbler to the table, just to break everyone's trance. It works because the glass shatters, sending tiny diamond-like shards across the tile.

That draws eyes away from the window. The tension tightening the room doesn't dissipate as Gaspare's boy sets to work clearing up the broken glass. Each sweep of his brush only intensifies the discomfort.

I sit back down and return my gaze to the studio and the sight I'm met with takes my breath away. Contessa is dancing with such strength and grace I can't look away. I'm no dance expert but I'm pretty sure she isn't performing a ballet. Nor does it appear to be a street-style dance. It's somewhere in between. It's slow and flowing, dramatic, yet soft. But underlying it all is a fierceness that is indescribable.

Her arms float above her head like angel wings, her back arches into a bow, a leg rises up behind her. She spins and spins and drops and curls. She lowers to her hands and kicks her feet into the air, flipping upright with little effort as though she's an Olympic gymnast, not a dancer. It's dark, it's wild, it's easily the most beautiful thing I've ever seen.

I manage to drag my gaze from the window to Gaspare and he's stopped what he's doing. The entire shop has fallen silent—all eyes are back on Contessa. My blood heats like a fireball about to erupt.

"Avert your eyes," I demand of the room, my growl hitting the walls.

All eyes cast downward to the floor. There's a volcanic edge to my tone.

I pan back to the studio and watch, mesmerized, as she seamlessly twists and turns, controlling her body like a musician controls sound.

Like an unwanted intruder, the memory of Federico Falconi cowering on the landing of his father's home casts a shadow over my view. I didn't know anything about him, other than the fact he was the son of a cheat. He couldn't have been more than seventeen when his family left. Just a boy. Yet he took the most important gift Contessa Castellano had to give, and all he had to do was ask once.

I find it hard to believe she wasn't in love with him. Otherwise, how could it have been so easy? That thought alone fills me with the kind of hatred I usually reserve for the Savero's of this world—despicable human beings who don't even deserve that title. Yet, Federico Falconi was innocent. All he did was take Contessa's virginity. So, why do I feel like I want to tear his fucking eyeballs out and crush them between my fingers?

A movement to my right drags my attention back to the room. One of the men has risen to his feet and walked to the window where he's now resting a scrawny hand on the glass. He looks like he's in a trance, unable to take his eyes off Contessa.

"Did you not fucking hear me?" I don't recognize my own voice.

Gaspare coughs, trying to get this guy's attention, but he's somewhere else. My gaze drops to his pants and a film of red coats my eyelids. He's so hard his dick is sticking out at a right angle, almost brushing the window. My fingers curl around the metal I hadn't even realized I'd pulled out of my waistband, and without giving it a second thought, I aim the gun at the guy's head and pull the trigger.

I stare ahead at my reflection in the mirror. It is now splattered with blood and particles of skull, all sliding down the glass. I lower my gaze to the body on the floor. He still has a fucking hard on. I aim the gun at his crotch and shoot again.

The dick falls limp and my sigh of satisfaction fills the otherwise silent shop. Then Gaspare coughs again, drawing my attention back to him. He gestures to the empty chair. Seems I just shot his current client.

Well, that's one way to get speedier service.

I nod and get to my feet as he studies the shaving blade in his hand.

"*Ne prenderò uno nuovo.*" *I'll get a fresh one.*

Slowly, the room fills with more chatter, and there I was thinking this could get awkward. At least no one's looking out the window anymore.

I turn my head back to the road just in time to see the truck driving off, casting the studio in the veil of a net curtain once more. My stomach hollows out knowing what's beyond that window while also knowing she'd show me again over her dead body. I flip the safety catch on my gun before I can do any more damage because this feeling of sickness that just came over me is unusual. Unpredictable. Un-fucking-agreeable.

I sigh heavily and turn to face my reflection in the mirror. Then the truth slaps me square in the face.

I think I might have a problem.

CHAPTER SEVENTEEN

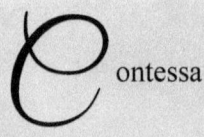
ontessa

Thirty minutes earlier

"You sure you don't want to come for pizza?" The rest of the girls are already on the street but Paige pops her head around the door.

"I'm sure, really. I just want to get this sequence right." And also, I'm pretty certain my movements will be tracked by one of Bernadi's men and there's nothing like a dark faceless shadow following one around to make one look conspicuous.

Paige looks over her shoulder and seeing the coast is clear she steps back inside the room. She dips her chin and gives me a serious look with a lowered voice.

"You know why he's hard on you, right?" My thoughts are drawn from one overbearing man to another: Antonio.

I turn back to my reflection in the mirror and instantly my focus is drawn to not-straight-enough legs, not-relaxed-enough shoulders, not-loose-enough limbs.

"Yeah. I'm not good enough."

She groans and closes the gap between us.

I'm about to get into position to start the routine again but her arms wrap around my middle and her head tucks under my armpit like a cat.

"You're better than all of us," she says, squeezing me tightly.

I lift my gaze to the ceiling. "That's not true."

"Tess, he's harder on you because he knows you can take it."

I squeeze my eyes closed to stop any emotion from dripping down my cheeks. I've never felt so close to letting the wall collapse and the act fall away. I've spent years inside this armor, strengthening it piece by piece. I don't know why but the last few weeks have drained me of the energy I usually reserve for maintaining this iron-clad front. It began with the death of my stalker and the realization he almost raped and killed me and I was completely oblivious to the risk.

I feel her face tilt upward. "Give yourself a break, Tess. You can do this routine in your sleep. Come and get pizza with us."

I gently unwrap her hands and plant a small kiss on

her knuckles. "You are very sweet for inviting me," I say, with a lopsided smile. "But whether I'm good at this or not, I need to keep practicing for my own peace of mind."

She looks back at me with sad eyes and shakes her head. "Okay. Whatever you need to do. But listen, call me if you want to join us later. Kelly's uncle is opening a new bar tonight in the village. You should come."

I nod with a tight smile. "I'll let you know."

Paige sighs and cocks her head to one side. She knows I won't. As she turns to leave I feel a sudden sense of panic. "Paige?"

She spins around with a hopeful expression on her face.

"Thank you."

"For what?"

"For not giving up on me."

She frowns, unsure of what I'm talking about, but winks anyway before skipping out of the studio in pursuit of the other girls.

I follow them past the window then as my gaze pans back they catch on a familiar pair of eyes *hooked* on me from across the street.

I know for a fact the netting in front of the window is opaque. No one can see inside the studio, which is a good thing, because half the time we're almost naked when we dance. Sometimes it's the only way we can truly connect with our bodies—when they're not obscured by cumbersome clothing.

I stand still and stare back. It's strangely liberating and indulgently voyeuristic being able to look at Benito Bernadi knowing he can't see me. Even more strangely, despite that fact, I feel the touch of his gaze like a warm beam of sunlight caressing my skin.

I click the button in my hand then slide it along the floor to the wall. The orchestral score to my favorite movie of all time trickles through the speakers. I hate Antonio and until four weeks ago I was convinced he hated me back. But when he chose Craig Armstrong's *Hotel Sayre* as the starting music for my recital I had to wait until I was sitting alone in my car before I let the tears fall. It reminds me of my mama and papa. It speaks to my heart in a way no human being will ever be able to.

I close my eyes and lift my arms, feeling the air beneath them, floating them upwards. My body weight disappears and I rise to the balls of my feet effortlessly. I can feel Bernadi's gaze burning through me and realize I have a choice. I can choose to feel the weight of it pull me to the floor, or I can allow the strength of it to lift me up. I choose strength.

I know Bernadi can't really see me but part of me wishes he could. The familiar smugness tugs at me—the longing to show him what he ruined—but something else is squashing it down. Since he told me his version of the story, I find it harder to conjure up the same depth of hatred I've fermented him in over the years. And that's further compounded by the touch of his gaze on my breasts when I stripped off my bikini top. As if remembering it too, my nipples tingle beneath my leotard as I twirl slowly, my calf muscles solidifying to keep my movements soft.

My collarbone warms with the recollection of his devilish breath skating across it when I left his apartment. My thighs clench at the thought of his bare chest with it's beautiful curves and angles, the oppressive art that danced with every movement. I keep my eyes closed as the score ends and Florence and the Machine begins, driving a faster, more aggressive tempo. Then I lose myself completely.

Antonio makes no secret of the fact he can't understand how I can keep dancing with my eyes closed. So much of our balance relies on sight. But confronting reality has the opposite effect on me—it knocks me off balance until I don't know which way is up. When I dance with my eyes closed, the only thing guiding me, anchoring me, is gravity.

But tonight, as the music washes me away and the heat of a certain consigliere's gaze is scorching my skin, I don't even feel that. I'm airborne, and for the first time in my life, unafraid. My limbs unfurl and my spine uncurls. My hips take on a life of their own. My breasts seem to swell with every movement. Heavy and loose.

My hands trail up my throat to the tight knot at my crown, loosening the band, letting the length fall.

I lost my virginity three years ago but this is the first time I've ever felt like *a woman*. Feminine… sexual… and simply *hot* all over.

I dance like no one is watching and even though I can't see myself I know it's the best I've ever danced. I can feel it in the marrow of my bones. As the song draws to its conclusion I slow my movements, then just as I'm about to bring the dance to a choreographed dramatic close, a *pop* nearby knocks me to the floor.

My eyes open and focus on the mirrored wall. I'm sprawled on the floor of the studio staring back at myself. White as a sheet and trembling. Without moving my body, my gaze darts around checking every corner of the studio until I feel certain the gunshot didn't come from inside. It was definitely outside.

The barbershop.

Bernadi.

I jump to my feet feeling an irrational sense of need. I need to know he's still alive. I don't know why, and I don't have the capacity to wonder a whole lot about it right now, but I need to know Bernadi isn't hurt.

I walk tentatively to the window, reaching it just as another gunshot shatters the silent neighborhood. Through the netting I can see Bernadi inside the barbershop. He's seated, slowly withdrawing his arm. The sunlight catches on metal as he pushes something into his waistband, then he stands and walks away from the window.

I swallow and take a step backward.

I don't understand what just happened. That dance felt like a dream. I let go of every single inhibition. I was guided purely by the music, by gravity, and by the illusion of Bernadi's gaze. He couldn't even see me, yet

I just performed the dance of my life. I wipe a hand around the back of my neck and feel the sweat dripping down my leotard.

He couldn't even see me.

So, *why* did I just perform the dance of my life?

CHAPTER EIGHTEEN

enito

Gaspare drags the blade smoothly up my neck as two of the men waiting their turn carry the body out back. Gaspare dips the razor into his metal bowl, rinses off the soap, then brings it back to my throat.

"Beautiful day, sir," he murmurs through a furrowed brow.

My thoughts are still on Contessa. I can't shake the image of her lithe form gliding across the room.

"It is," I concede.

"Plans for this evening?"

Standard barbershop talk. Gaspare knows that even if I do have plans, I probably won't divulge them. In reality, I had planned on visiting Augie and bringing him up to speed on some developments in Newark. Since Cristiano fought the Marchesi's out of the place, some loose cannons remain and they're stirring up shit for our soldiers on the ground. But, with the recent burning of my primary residence, and the situation with a certain Castellano girl, I don't have the capacity to deal with Newark too.

My reaction to seeing Contessa dance—and importantly, seeing *other men* watch her dance—has annoyed the fuck out of me. I didn't know I had the gun in my hand for Christ's sake.

I wouldn't normally shoot a guy's dick off—dead or not. For the injured—or deceased—party, it's just one insult too far and I always thought I was above that.

I hate the idea that I might have a problem. That implies I've lost control—of my emotions, my physical reactions. And for a consigliere-come-assassin-come-second-in-command, that worries me.

So, as a priority, I need to get the vision of Contessa dancing like a fucking angel out of my head, the rhythm of her feet sending ripples through her thighs away from my damned dick. I need to be reminded of what I actually want: a *real* woman. Not a young girl—a brat—who's made no secret of the fact she can't stand to breathe the same air as me.

For once, I decide to tell Gaspare the truth.

"I'm seeing a lady friend this evening, Gaspare."

He nods approvingly. "Taking her somewhere nice, sir?"

My gaze flicks to the apartment above the dance studio. "I believe so, yes. Small, bijoux. Exclusive. *Exceptional* personal service."

"She's a very lucky lady, sir."

She damn well will be, after I've paid several thousand dollars for her time and her discretion. One night should do it. A brazen fuck to get that brat out of my head.

I inspect my clean shaven skin in the mirror. "Perfect, Gaspare. Grazie."

I stand and pull a roll of notes from my pocket.

"No, boss." Gaspare looks horrified. "It is on the house."

I tilt my head and smile, making sure it doesn't quite reach my eyes. "How is this place ever going to stand on its own two feet if we start giving service away?"

He looks like he's just been spanked so I pat his cheek with a genuine smile. "You're doing a good job, my friend. Don't sell yourself short."

I have no idea if Contessa is still in the studio as I cross the street, and I force myself not to care. My interest in that brat has gone far enough. To distract myself completely, I pull out my phone and hit a number I haven't used in a while. I place my order, confirm the hour and address, and by the time I've unlocked the apartment door, I have a date for the night and a surefire solution to the problem downstairs.

I throw my keys and cell onto the counter and walk into the bathroom. I've stripped off everything but my boxers when the doorbell rings.

Well, fuck, she's prompt.

I run a hand through my newly trimmed hair, no doubt roughing it up, as I go to open the door, then a sight I was not expecting makes the vision I'm trying to banish swell tenfold in my mind until I'm resting a well-placed hand about pelvis-level. Just in case.

"Miss Castellano. What can I do for you?"

She stands there for a few seconds, nothing coming out of her mouth. Her eyes are wide as though she's trying desperately to keep them focused on my face. She's succeeding to the point of looking slightly unhinged. Maybe terrifying.

I try again. "Contessa? Do you need something?"

"I… um… I—"

Normally, the sight of someone as taken aback and flustered as this makes me feel like a fucking winner. It means I've got the upper hand; I've caught them off guard. But seeing Castellano red-faced and tongue-tied only makes me feel fucking *hot* all over. Exactly the opposite of what I'm trying to achieve. With her anyway.

"Yes?"

She swallows and almost chokes. "I just came to check you were okay," she rushes out. "I heard gunshots earlier, and… Well, I know you were in the barbershop and that's where the shots seemed to come from…" Her cheeks flush.

"Have you been watching me?" I say in a deep, low voice, deliberately ignoring the sheer hypocrisy lining my words.

"No!" She flushes even deeper. "I was dancing, and…"

As she struggles to speak I can feel myself committing the exact same sin my victim committed earlier. My dick is filling to the brim with blood.

"I just heard gunshots, that's all." She straightens her shoulders, collecting herself. "I just came to check you were okay." Finally, her gaze drops to my torso, then my boxers and my naked thighs. Then she shakes her head and shrugs, dramatically. "And, clearly, you're fine. So, everything's good. I'll let you get back to… Well, whatever you were doing."

She turns her back to me, almost stumbling down the steps but then she stops abruptly. Her gaze narrows when she sees something at the foot of the stairwell.

I don't miss the way her knuckles pale as she curls her fingers round the handrail. I lean round the doorframe and see exactly what's stopped Castellano in her tracks.

My call girl.

Castellano spins around to face me, her features taut. "Clearly, you are just *fine*."

I can't help but smile. "Thanks for checking on me."

She dips her gaze and tentatively makes her way down the steps.

Karina looks up at me with an arched brow. It wouldn't be the first time she followed a warm-up act, if only that's what this was. I look past her to the darkened street.

"It's late," I say to Castellano's back. "I have a driver outside. He'll take you home."

Then, Castellano surprises me.

"Oh," she says brightly, spinning around and disarming me with a broad, devastating grin. "I'm not going home." She looks at Karina, then back at me. "You two have a good night now."

She unlocks the door to the studio, drawing a small frown from my brow. It's almost seven pm... Surely she's finished training for the day? Unless, she's going back inside to get ready to go somewhere else... The thought scratches at something in my brain. The other girls who left earlier were dressed like, well, fair game, if you ask me. They were going *out*-out.

Karina approaches, dousing me in a cloud of Opium perfume. "Good evening, Mr. Bernadi," she purrs in a deep, throaty voice, then kisses my cheek, lingering until the warmth pulls me back to where I'm meant to be.

She threads her fingers through mine and pulls me into the apartment, kicking the door closed. I glance at the open door to the bathroom with slight longing. I probably have blood splatters on my face and fingers. But Karina has seen it all before. Made men are discreet when it matters, but when it comes to their sexual exploits, they may as well believe they're Rupert fucking Murdoch. I know I'm not the only mafioso Karina has entertained. The woman has earned her yacht.

I kick the door to the bathroom closed too. I'll shower in the morning.

Exactly one hour later and I'm experiencing yet another first. I'm apologizing to a hooker because I can't get it up.

And now I'm cursing the fact she's a bit too well-connected for my liking.

"I'm not taking your money, baby," she drawls, as she turns to let me do up the zipper on the back of her dress.

I glare at her. "Yes you are, because nothing untoward happened here, okay? I fucked you. I paid you. Alright?"

Her brow twitches. "Benito…" She bends at the knees and brings her face to mine. "Who was that girl?"

Her Russian accent is thick as gelatin.

I roll my shoulders back. "What girl?"

"The girl who was here when I arrived."

I feign a frown. "There was no girl here when you arrived."

She tilts her head to one side. If there's one thing a man will never get past a call girl, it's relationship bullshit, which irritates me because I'm not even in a fucking relationship.

I sigh impatiently and force a note of boredom into my tone. "If you mean the girl who came to check I was still alive after hearing gunshots, that was my boss's future sister-in-law who happens to study dance at the studio below this apartment."

Karina's head tips backward and she eyes me from beneath long, flawless lashes. "She came to check on you." She smiles. "How sweet."

I stand, leaving Karina crouched low. "She is not sweet. She's a brat."

"Milaya…" *Darling*… She straightens and meets me, eye to eye. "A brat is a teenager. The 'brat' who came to check on you this evening was no teenage girl." She stands flush against me and brings her lips to my throat. "She was *all woman*." She lifts her lashes slowly until they graze my jawline. "And your dick knows it."

I squeeze my eyes closed. I don't need to hear this. I uncurl another roll of notes. "Here's a tip."

Her eyes pop at the five hundred I just gifted her for nothing.

"This conversation is closed."

She slides the notes into the pocket of her Vivienne Westwood trench. "What conversation?" she asks with a wicked glint in her eye. "From what I recall of our hour together Benito, there was *no* conversation."

I plant a slow kiss on her cheek. "And that's why you're the best in the business, Karina."

Her smile, for once, is authentic and only intensified when she clasps her fingers around my chin, channeling my focus on what she says next. "I've known you a long time, Benito. You like this woman…"

I'm about to open my mouth to argue but she slams a hand over it. I wouldn't permit that from anyone but her. "So stop fucking around and do something about it."

I roll my eyes. She doesn't understand mafia family dynamics, but she even slays that thinking to a pulp. "I don't care whose fucking sister-in-law's niece's auntie's next-door-neighbor-but-twelve she is. I've never seen you *feel* before. So it doesn't matter who she is, only that she's yours."

Before I can assert that Contessa Castellano is *not* mine, and in fact, that would be her worst nightmare realized, Karina is heading out the door and down the steps. I stand at the top, wearing the same pair of boxers and an unbuttoned shirt, watching her departing back.

"Stay safe," I call after her. She turns and jangles a set of keys, and the Tesla logo glimmers in the fluorescent light. That woman knows exactly what she's doing and who she's playing.

The second the door closes behind her, another one opens and in a matter of seconds I'm staring at a completely different set of long, flawless lashes—only these are a hundred percent natural.

"That was a short date," Contessa says, a smirk lifting one corner of her mouth.

A thread of annoyance winds itself around my brain. "Who says it was a date?"

"You mean you didn't even offer to cook dinner?" Her jaw falls in mock horror.

"You've seen my apartment," I say, shrugging one shoulder. "I barely have enough room to make coffee."

Her cheeks turn pink and I know she's remembering

how she had to come to my aid in operating the coffee machine. But something sobers behind her eyes. Possibly the realization that I did indeed only intend to fuck the woman that just left.

"Well, goodnight Bernadi."

She pulls the door of the studio closed and is about to open the door to the street when something sharp drives through my chest.

"I didn't sleep with her," I blurt out.

She stops dead still and I hold my breath.

Slowly, her head turns, her dark hair falling over her face. "That's none of my business," she whispers.

Whatever sharp thing is in my chest twists painfully. I'm suddenly lost for words.

I find myself, for the first time in my life, feeling weak. Bernadis never admit weakness. Weakness means death, and I will not die for anyone.

I remember the car on the corner. I resume my dry, soulless tone. "My driver will take you home." She opens her mouth to object but I beat her to it. "Cristiano's orders."

Her mouth snaps shut and she opens the door. Karina's words ring in my ears no matter how hard I try to push them away. *She's yours*.

Contessa Castellano will never be mine, so there's no point in imagining anything else.

CHAPTER NINETEEN

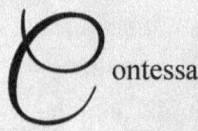ontessa

"I've got something for you."

I'm lying face down on a lounger beside Cristiano's pool when the sound of Trilby's voice makes me jump. I've unwittingly made this place my second home, purely because it affords me an escape from the ever-watchful eyes of my aunt and Papa. At least that's what I keep reassuring myself. Not because I'm half-hoping a certain bronze-eyed, gun-wielding consigliere happens to frequent it too.

I roll onto my side and shade my eyes from the sun. Trilby is holding something that looks like a box.

Is that what I think it is?

I sit up and rub my eyes, hoping it will make me focus better.

"I know you always wanted it," she adds in a soft voice.

I realize what it is before my vision adjusts and I hold out my hands to take it from her. The weight of the box fills me with warm memories. And knowing my way around it like the back of my hand, I pop open the lid. A beautiful ballerina sits proudly on a pedestal, just waiting to be wound up.

I feel my way to the handle at the back and twist it. Music heavily tinted by the sound of vintage carousels echoes around the terrace and tears fill my eyes.

We both watch in silence, each of us remembering Mama in our own way. The music slows to a clink clunk, so I wind the handle all the way and watch the beautiful little figurine spin in her pink lace tutu. I touch the sparkling gems on the bodice of her dress.

"Those are real, by the way," Trilby says.

"What?" My voice feels ethereal as I watch the stones glisten in the sunlight.

"They're diamonds."

I watch the little figure spin with renewed awe. "But, there's like twenty of them."

"It was a wedding present to Mama from Great Aunt Chiara."

No further explanation is needed. Great Aunt Chiara is legendary in our family and I'm sad I never got the chance to meet her. She married into old world money at just seventeen. She and Great Uncle Guiseppe never had children, and so Mama, being the only daughter in the family, became the beneficiary of all the gifts Chiara would have bought her own daughter if she'd had one.

"I had no idea."

I always thought this was a cheap bargain basement jewelry box, but nevertheless, I craved it like every other kid my age craved candy. But now, my feelings are spinning like the diamond-encrusted ballerina.

The sun shifts behind Trilby, casting a shadow over the box and me.

"Is there a reason you're giving this to me now?"

She sits down opposite me. "You look like you're in a bit of a funk."

I lie on my back and rest the music box on my stomach. "I'm fine."

"Yeah. That's what you always say," Trilby says, not unkindly. "Believe it or not, we speak the same language, Tess."

I release a long breath.

"Is Antonio still giving you a hard time?"

I close my eyes. "Yeah, but that's nothing new."

Silence stretches before Trilby asks, "So, what is new?"

It's a good question, and one I don't have the answer for. All I know is, lately, my feelings seem to have intensified, and I don't know why. I just seem to feel everything more. Like the sunrise. I used to always take it for granted, the fact I was up with the larks, stretching my limbs beneath the deep pink rays before anyone else awoke. These days I pause. I stare at the damn thing like it's a miracle. I notice the sound of birds, for crying out loud. I no longer view them as vermin, primed to shit on me from a great height, but as gifts from God—things that make the most captivating music of all.

And… I cry. This is new. Until recently, I hadn't shed a tear since Mama died, but now, show me a pet food commercial and I'm crying a damned river.

"I don't know, Trilby." It's the truth. "Maybe it's hormones…" Though I *hate* blaming anything on hormones. "Maybe it's the stress of not knowing what's going to happen after this recital, whether Papa will let me continue to study dance, or whether he'll marry me off like he did with you…"

"Oh Tess…" Trilby wraps her arms around me and it's nice. She and I were never close growing up. She moved out straight after Mama died, when I was only thirteen. She always had a wall built up around her. I guess we all did, in a way, but Trilby's involved an *actual* wall because she physically moved into the apartment next door.

"You know…" she presses her lips to my hair. "I don't think Papa has any plans to marry you off. You should talk to him… Tell him what you *want* to do. You have a rare talent, Tess. You're a beautiful dancer—we can all see it."

I hug her back, tentatively.

"Look at Sera…" she continues. "Papa let her move to the Hamptons so she could train in hospitality. If anyone was going to be set up for marriage next, it would be her, but there've been no signs of that. You only have to see how involved Papa is in our wedding plans to know how proud he is that Sera is organizing everything at the other end."

I can't argue with that. Trilby and Cristiano are holding their wedding at the hotel Sera is interning at, and Papa, despite being extremely busy with the port, is always the first to visit the location to vet things, try things, inspect the place. There are literally zero signs that he's unhappy about Sera's career choice or future.

"Talk to him," she says, pulling back. "It might help you feel better."

I nod. "Yeah, okay. I will."

"And why don't you go out some? Let your hair down. You're always training—you need to find time to have fun too."

I cast my eyes downward. I'm not a social creature —never have been. I reserve all my extroversion for dance. The rest of the time, I like to be alone, recuperating. Expressing myself through dance takes *a lot* of energy.

She releases me and pats my arm. "Think about it, yeah? You're too damn hot to hide yourself away on this terrace. As Allegra always says, you won't be lean and luscious forever, so make the most of it while you can."

I can't help but smile at Allegra's view of life. "Fine," I reply, rolling my eyes. "I'll go out. Just give me a few months to get used to the idea."

Trilby pushes me playfully then gets to her feet. "I'm heading over to the gallery. You want to join me?"

I think about it. The gallery is Trilby's dream and

Cristiano has given it to her. He'd initially said she could work in any gallery she wanted as long as it was in a part of the city he ruled, but then he surprised her on her birthday with a space of her own, right in the heart of Williamsburg. The only concession she's had to make is to hire a team Cristiano has personally vetted, and keep security with her at all times. It's a small price to pay.

But the gallery is indoors, and the sun is outdoors, so… "Thanks but I'll stay here if that's okay?"

"Of course it is. And last I looked, Benny wasn't here so you're safe." She winks and leans over to plant a kiss on my cheek.

I feel a strange sinking sensation in my chest.

"Will you be staying for dinner?" she asks, ruffling her bleached blond hair.

Hunger. That must have been why I feel so weird all of a sudden. "I don't know. Probably not. I need to show my face at home. But are there any snacks I can help myself to?"

"Yeah, loads. Just have a rummage around the kitchen."

I call out my thanks as she's almost halfway back to the house, then I wind up the ballerina again and watch her twirl.

Ten minutes later and I'm definitely feeling hungry so I rest the jewelry box by the lounger and go off in search of snacks. I bite into a protein bar while I chop up some fruit into a small salad, then carry it out to the terrace. I'm about to sit at one of the small tables and pull out my Kindle when I hear male voices coming from a concealed corner. I stand still and listen, hoping I don't overhear something not intended for my ears.

I suddenly wish Trilby was still here. Without her I'm just a young girl hanging out alone at a mafia don's house. I swallow back a laugh at how absurd that sounds. A year ago, I had no idea how closely involved with the Di Santos my father was. Now, we're all as central to the family as it's possible to get. I'm one of *them*.

That thought doesn't make me feel any more comfortable though, especially when I hear someone talking about "another" hit on the Marchesis. I slowly lower my bowl to the table and slide onto a chair.

"They're hiding it from us, but there's definitely someone else involved," one of the voices says.

"Someone who isn't related by blood," another voice says.

"But they're made?" The third voice makes me sit up and my heart pump fast. Bernadi is here.

"Must be."

"That was fast. I thought we knew all of Marchesi's wise guys."

Another voice chimes in. "With Fury stepping down and our hit the other night, they're panicking. They've yet to announce the nephews at the helm and they need a strong man at the top, if only for the optics. This one, whoever he is, could be the answer."

"We need to find out exactly who this guy is," Bernadi says. "If he's a made man, he's probably been around a while. Get some of Augie's men on it."

"Will do, boss."

Hearing someone call Bernadi 'boss' makes something regrettable flutter below my waistline.

Footsteps crunch on gravel and I hastily put my pods in my ears and focus all my attention on my Kindle. Three men appear around the corner and stop when they see me. Some parting words are muttered and two of the men disperse—one inside the house and the other across the lawns to the security gates. Bernadi doesn't move and I feel his gaze pressing on me like a branding iron.

I glance sideways at him, and his feet take slow, measured steps in my direction. I remove the ear pods one by one, expecting some sharp put down to fly out of his mouth but he walks straight past me, his jacket sleeves brushing the hairs on my arm.

He walks right to the edge of the terrace and stands with his feet braced looking out over the ocean drop.

"Good afternoon to you too," I say, snarkily.

I know he heard because he gives his head a small, exasperated shake.

But, for all intents and purposes, Benito Bernadi is *ignoring* me. And I realize I like that even less than when he's shooting people in the head without giving me any warning.

No doubt to Bernadi's relief, Cristiano walks out onto the terrace. "Hey, Tess."

Cristiano's greeting makes Bernadi look round and his gaze caresses my skin for just a second longer than is comfortable. Warm blood rises up my collarbone into my cheeks and I look down at the salad wondering where my appetite has gone.

"Hey, bro'," I reply, biting back a grin, then I push back the chair and return to my lounger by the pool. The atmosphere on the terrace feels prickly. I want to stay, for reasons I don't understand, but I also don't like this feeling of being snubbed. I hesitate briefly before typing a quick text to Paige. She's always inviting me out and I never go. It will be just my luck—and everything I deserve—if she's not doing anything I can join in on right now.

While I await her reply, I take one of the pool towels and wrap it around the jewelry box. I love my car but it's a vintage convertible Camaro that hasn't had nearly enough TLC, so I want to make sure this beautiful box is as safe and secure as possible when I drive it home.

Quicker than I'd expected, Paige replies.

"Hey there Dancing Queen. So great to hear from you. Sure. At a pool party. Come IMMEDIATELY."

I look down at my outfit—a tiny black two-piece, fitted top and a black skater skirt. I think it's pool-party-esque. A second text arrives with the address of the party and a photo of Paige and two girls I don't recognize all pouting at the camera. My stomach fills with anxious butterflies but I force myself to type a message back.

"Great! On my way!" I'm so not an exclamation mark kind of girl but I figure this is how sociable types communicate, and when in Roma…

I put the wrapped box into my tote and return to the table to collect my bowl just as Cristiano heads back my way. My gaze darts timidly in Bernadi's direction but he's resumed his moody perusal of the landscape.

"You heading out?" Cristiano nods to my bag as we walk back inside the house.

"Yeah. Pool party."

"Nice. Whose pool?"

I arch a brow. "You really want to know?"

He smiles and pushes the door open. "I think I probably should, don't you?"

I manage to not roll my eyes though it takes some effort. "I doubt there will be any mafiosos there, but if you insist…"

I give him the address and he nods thoughtfully.

"Do I have a curfew?"

Cristiano frowns. "Does your father give you one?"

A laugh bursts out of me. "Not usually, no. But then again, I rarely go out-out."

The frown deepens—he's not amused. "Then yes. Midnight, Cinderella."

Something glistens behind his eyes and the penny drops. "You're going to have me followed, aren't you?"

A corner of his mouth ticks up. "No. But I do have a

couple of guys in that area who'll be given the heads-up you're there."

I force a smile and grit my teeth. "Great!" I'm getting good at this whole exclamation thing.

"Have a nice time," he calls after me and I wave a hand overhead before pulling the door behind me a little too hard.

CHAPTER TWENTY

$\mathcal{B}$enito

With Beppe and Nicolò on their way out, I decide to take a moment on the terrace. I have real issues to solve on a legal front but there's nothing that fires me up more than seeking revenge on an enemy.

For a long time, the Marchesis were that enemy, but in all honesty, they've gotten boring. Predictable. We've pushed them out of New York almost completely, leaving us entirely in control of the city.

We now have multiple possible moves in front of us —we could take Philly, or Jersey, maybe even Florida, but with the New York officials in our pockets and the officials of most other states in theirs, we wouldn't be up against much friction.

The suggestion that the Marchesis have a wild card

yet to play turns me on a little, I have to admit. Well, it's either that or the scene laid out in front of me.

Contessa damn Castellano is draped over a chair in the center of the terrace, seemingly oblivious to all other human life. One leg is curled beneath her while the other is stretched out an unfairly long way. Her alabaster skin is showed off to perfection in a barely-there black two-piece that doesn't seem to be much more than a few pieces of string tied together. The only thing covering her ass cheeks is a tight black belt—oh wait, my mistake. *Skirt.*

Good Lord Almighty, I am just about done with this.

Back at the barbershop, I thought I had a problem. And now, three days later, I *know* I have a problem. Hiring Karina was nothing but an expensive research exercise that didn't yield the results I'd hoped for. I silently thank God that only I can see through the façade. When it comes to Contessa Castellano, I'm nothing more than a borderline alcoholic abstaining for a weekend just to prove something to myself, then failing miserably.

I hired a call girl to prove I can still get it on with other women and… turns out I can't.

Ever since the day I saw her dancing, I haven't been able to get her out of my head. Actually, make that since the day she confessed she's no longer a virgin. Actually, who the fuck am I kidding? It's since Gianni's fucking funeral. Contessa Castellano has taken up permanent residence in my head. And I just know, the crazed, single-minded masochist I am, if nothing changes, this will turn into some unhinged obsession that can only lead to danger. I fought hard to become consigliere to this family and nothing—not even Contessa Castellano—is going to threaten that. I cannot and will not allow it. If I lose my focus, my edge, my *grip*, everyone will suffer. Not just Contessa but the entire Di Santo family. The only way through this nonsense is to take a good, hard step back.

I hesitate, my gaze drawn to her like an irrational obsession, and that gives me even more ammunition.

It's for the best.

I feel her eyes flick my way as I walk straight past her. I don't trust myself right now to hold a conversation that doesn't end with the words "bend the fuck over."

I stand at the edge of the terrace and drag in some long breaths. I should have gone straight into the house as soon as I saw her, but I needed *air*.

"Good afternoon to you too."

Her words carry on the light breeze but her tone is loaded with spite. I've pissed her off. Well, *good*.

Maybe she's halfway to knowing how I feel just having to be in the general vicinity of those damned legs.

Cristiano joins me and we both feign interest in the view while discussing business in hushed tones.

At the same time he walks away, Tess gathers her things and follows him into the house. I can't help my gaze narrowing as I watch her disappear from view. Instinctively, I want to follow. But rationally I know I can't. This has to stop.

I wait for Cristiano to come back outside, but it takes an *age*. My fingers ache from curling and flexing and I can feel blood in my palms from where my nails have dug in deep. I'm looking at one of the most beautiful views New York has to offer, yet all I can see is black. Black hair, black skirt, black lashes. They blur into more black. The black room that held hundreds of pictures of her, black painted carpet and windows. The black dress she wore to Gianni's funeral with the long, sexy split up the side—the only thing distracting me from the black hatred in her eyes.

Black, black, *black*.

"You okay?" Cristiano's voice slides into my ears. "You look like you're about to kill someone."

I rub a hand down my face, dragging the visions with it.

"Not today," I reply.

His brows hitch and he looks sideways at me. "What's bothering you?"

"I need someone else to watch her, Cristiano."

"Who? Tess?" He sounds surprised.

I shove my hands deep in my pockets to hide the blood. "Yeah."

"Why?" He draws the word out slowly, as though he's relishing the change in topic.

"I have too much on and… I know how important she is to the family. I can't protect her properly right now—my head is in a million other places. We need to find someone else."

Cristiano's gaze pans to the horizon. "But you're the best, Benito. And I don't trust many other people."

My chest feels so tight I worry it might explode.

"Nicolò can do it."

"I've just given him the lower east side."

Fuck. "I'll take it."

"Benny, it was kind of a promotion for him."

I groan. Something tells me I'm not getting out of this. "Fine. Maybe we can split our time with her. I'll keep an eye on her when she's in the studio…" *When she's a floor below and I can't see her.* "And Nicolò can watch her at your place."

"Okay, sure. I'll let you talk to him." Cristiano's lip twitches as he delivers the next blow. "Either way, you should both know she's headed to a party right now."

I do a double take. "What?"

"Pool party, about ten miles east of here."

"But she doesn't do parties."

Cristiano shrugs and I can almost sense glee rolling off his shoulders. "She does now."

An unpleasant taste fills my mouth. Something is amiss here. The whole time I've been watching her, Contessa has never been to a pool party, nor a social event for that matter. What the fuck is she playing at? Maybe she's seeing someone, in secret. That could solve the problem of having to turn down an arranged marriage because of a lack of innocence.

"You let her go?" I can't help the growl at the base of my throat. Cristiano pans an innocent gaze in my direction. "Dressed in—" I'm about to say 'next to nothing' but think better of it, "a *two-piece*?"

A small smile dances across his face. "She's a grown woman, Benny. She can wear whatever she likes. And as far as I know, her father hasn't promised her to anyone—yet, so she can come and go as she pleases. Our remit is only to make sure she's safe."

Yet. Something dark and inhuman explodes behind my eyes.

"She's *not* safe," I say, my voice dropping to inhuman depths.

Cristiano steps to one side and I take that as my cue to leave. I scrub my bloodied hand down my pants as I stride across the terrace and over the lawns. When I'm sure I'm out of sight, I break into a run. As soon as I'm sitting in the driver seat of my car, the gates open, as though the world knows exactly what my game plan is.

Only…. I didn't finish my sentence.

Contessa Castellano *is not safe*.

From me.

CHAPTER TWENTY-ONE

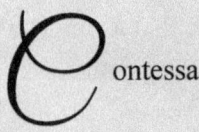
Contessa

The freeway passes in a blur of Fleetwood Mac and Chanel Mademoiselle as the wind whips up my hair.

I allow my senses to tune out my neurotic thoughts. It's helping to cover up the guilt I feel at leaving Cristiano's for a pool party instead of accompanying Trilby to her gallery. And, handily, it's softening the urge to scream the words "I fucking hate you, Bernadi" at the top of my lungs.

How *dare* he? He insists on following me around when I never asked him to, and I hate that he's doing it under the guise of defending me from myself. He looks at me like he hasn't eaten any solid food for days and is prepared to try human for the first time. Then he just goes ahead and ignores me, like I don't even exist.

I shake the image of his burnt bronze eyes from my

head and my gaze catches in the rearview, and something—*someone*—is driving like an absolute lunatic, seemingly in pursuit of my car. I glance at the road ahead. Thankfully it's clear. Looking in my rearview again, I see a black BMW getting closer, faster. Whoever's behind the wheel must be driving at a hundred forty miles per hour, at least.

I look straight ahead and press my foot to the accelerator. My hair whips around my face and I wipe it away with a shaking hand. I suddenly wish Bernadi *was* following me.

I jab at the dash, trying to locate a number to call. Papa, Cristiano, Trilby... *anyone*.

In the corner of my eye, I see the car closing in. It's too close now. My foot is flat to the floor but the BMW has power that my car simply doesn't. It sails past and pulls in front of me. Then it slows right down.

I jam my foot on the brake and the rear wheels skid to the side. I scream, my hair rushing forward and obscuring my view of the road.

I'm a dead woman.

In seconds, my car finally screeches to a halt. Through my beating heart and hazed vision I can just about form an image of a man stepping out of the BMW and running towards me.

Mentally, I surrender. He's got me, whoever he is. There's no way I can get out of this vehicle and walk, let alone run. I'm a mass of shaking limbs and lightheadedness.

The door to the driver's seat is yanked open and a

strong hand wraps around my neck, hauling me out of the car, pressing my back against the black metal.

I'm half-panting, half-sobbing when a face rams up against mine and I almost faint with relief.

"What the *FUCK* was that?" Bernadi yells, his saliva hitting my cheek.

The relief is so immense, my chest feels too light. So light that I laugh. I *laugh*. In Bernadi's face. I can't help myself.

If I thought I'd seen darkness, I was mistaken. Bernadi's glare thickens like molasses and a growl rolls out from somewhere deep within him.

"I swear to God, Contessa, if you don't shut the hell up now, I'm going to either slap you or fuck you."

My mouth snaps closed.

I search his eyes for some suggestion he's spoken out of turn, that he's said something wildly inappropriate to his boss's sister-in-law—something he absolutely has to retract, but his gaze only thickens. That's when I realize… he might be a paid consigliere but he answers to no one. If he wants to slap me, he will, and not even Cristiano can stop him. And if he wants to fuck me… I swallow.

He shoves his hips into me, pressing me flat against the car. Something hard presses into my pelvic bone. The thought of what it might be tears breath from my lungs. The pain of the pressure is quickly overtaken though by an intense heat that crawls over my clit and up through my core. If he wasn't pressing me into the car, I might've crumbled to the ground.

"You wouldn't," I whisper, my hoarse throat aching with the effort.

He slips a hand into my hair and fists it at the follicles, taking a never-ending breath that expands his chest until my mine feels like it's about to collapse under the force.

When he speaks, it's as though his voice has been taken over by wolves. "Try. Me."

My thighs tremble and I become distantly aware that my panties are starting to feel damp. I should be cold with fear but I'm burning hot… *everywhere*.

"Wh—" My throat feels scratchy when I swallow. "Why are you here?"

His gaze drops to my lips where I've just wet them with my tongue and he rolls his shoulders as though he's holding himself back.

"I'm taking you home."

That's all I need to hear to be reminded of why I hate him. "I'm not going home. I'm going to a party."

For a few seconds, he stares at me, and his dead expression fools me into thinking no thought is going on behind it. I play my trump card, even though I hate it. "Cristiano said I could go."

I'm still stunned when he takes a step back and says, "Fine."

I heave in a breath now that his chest isn't pressing the life out of me. "Fine?"

He shrugs but there's a glint in his eye I don't trust. "Sure. Go to the party. Just know that every single man who lays his eyes on your ass in that skirt will get his head blown off."

I drop my gaze to the gun I hadn't realized he'd been holding by his side. When he cocks it, I physically jump. I dart my gaze back to his and know, unequivocally, he isn't bluffing.

His voice carries an innocent lilt as his brows hitch. "You don't want that on your conscience do you? I mean, you seem to care so much about *other* people…"

I clamp a hand over my mouth and squeeze my eyes shut. Emotions rise up my body like a wave, threatening to engulf me.

"I hate you." The words slide weakly through my fingers.

I refuse to open my eyes, letting the tears fall through cracks as I surrender to the fact that he's right. If anyone were to be hurt because of me, I wouldn't be able to live with myself.

A warm hand presses to my cheek and I retreat into myself. He can do whatever he wants but if I make myself small enough, insignificant enough, nothing will touch me.

"I know."

My insides shatter with those two words. He's just going to accept it? He doesn't care that someone in this world hates him? What does that say about the life he's had?

My racing thoughts are only interrupted by the searing touch of his palm on my skin. I try my hardest not to admit how strangely exquisite it feels, but my body has other ideas.

My head turns to the side and his pinky brushes against my lips. He doesn't move it away as I linger there, hearing only labored breaths and heavy heartbeats. The skin covering my entire body comes alive and my lips part, a quiet moan escaping on a long exhale.

The pulse in my ears quickens and Bernadi's pinky curls inwards, the tip gliding along my bottom lip. Keeping my eyes closed, I let my tongue inch outward to taste his finger. I hear a sharp intake of breath which urges me on. He dips the tip into my mouth and I wrap my lips around it and suck.

Oh God, what am I doing?

"Tess..." His voice cracks as he says my name.

My mind fills with a black stare through the gap in a door, the sound of a gunshot, Mrs. Falconi's scream. Heat floods through my veins and prickles my skin. My teeth graze along his calloused skin as I chase them with my tongue. The humidity wraps around me like a hot, damp sheet.

I suck his finger deeper into my mouth, then I release my hands from behind my back and grip onto his jacket lapels, pulling him toward me.

"Tess..." he says again, this time withdrawing his finger.

My lids pop open and I don't know what he sees in my eyes but it makes him pause. His pupils cover the whole of his eyes—black with burnt bronze edges.

He starts to shake his head and my heart flutters in a panic.

I tighten my grip around his jacket.

His hands reach up to cover mine, gently easing my grip. My heart skydives at the rejection.

"You started this," I whisper, accusingly.

He holds both my hands inside one of his inhumanly large ones, and passes the fingers of his other hand through my hair. His gaze strokes my ear.

"I don't know what you're talking about."

Embarrassment floods my throat, my cheeks, and I yank my hands away, balling them into fists at my side.

"Get in the car," he says, calmly but firmly.

I curl my fingers around the handle and pull the car door open but he shakes his head once and pushes it closed. "Other side. I'm driving you home."

"And your car's going to get itself home is it?" I snap, turning away so I don't ever have to lay eyes on this man again.

Instead of answering, he turns me toward the back of the car, clamps his hands to my upper arms and chaperones me around the vehicle as if I'm a small child. As soon as I'm clear of the trunk I shrug him off. The feel of his skin against mine is searing.

We each close our doors at the same time and he puts my vintage Camaro into gear. Just before he pulls out he stops and stares straight out the windshield.

"Contessa…"

"What?" I snap.

"Don't ever put your mouth on me again."

My breath rushes out and I pan my gaze to him. His jaw grinds slowly like he's chewing on bone.

"Why?" I whisper.

"Because you'll start something I won't be able to stop. And that's a promise."

CHAPTER TWENTY-TWO

enito

My entire body is vibrating, and not just because this ancient piece of tin has the suspension of a feather. I can still feel her soft, warm lips wrapped tight around my pinky, licking and sucking like it's a piece of candy. My cock is plastered against my thigh, dying to jerk upward to make itself known, but I need to keep my head on straight.

This is Contessa Castellano. She's barely twenty—six years younger than me. She's the sister of my boss's fiancée. And the biggest brat I've ever met.

When I look at her, I don't just see the creamy legs that go on *forever*, the long dark hair begging to be wrapped several times around my fist, or the pink pouty lips that I ache to kiss—and not just to shut her up, but because they look like they might taste like Satan's temptation.

I see a young woman who doesn't even realize how broken she is. Someone who feels like her life spiraled out of control the day her mom died, and she's too small to make it count. Someone whose only way out of the mess in her head is to lose herself in dance.

I could have let her lips suck on my finger for days, but a voice in my head is asking why—why would she do that when she hates me so much?

A note of smugness unravels across my chest. I didn't ask her to do that. She took my finger between her lips because she wanted to. Federico had to ask her for her affection; I didn't. But this can't change a thing. I can't lose my grip around her, because if that happens, there's a very real chance I'll lose my grip on *everything*. I just need to take her home.

Her chest rises and falls in my peripheral vision and her tongue keeps reaching out to wet her lips. It's doing nothing to quell the hard-on threatening to rival the length and girth of my leg.

"I don't want to go home," she says, almost breathless, and as if she can read my damn thoughts.

I don't respond. We still have a few miles of this stretch before we're even off the freeway.

"I'm serious, Bernadi. Please… can we go somewhere else?"

I dart my gaze to her. "Like where?"

"Anywhere." She grips the sides of her seat. "The ocean."

"Why don't you want to go home?"

There's a long pause. "It's stifling," she says, quietly.

I flick my gaze her way then back to the road, and swallow. "I can take you back to Cristiano's."

She barks out a bitter laugh. "Yeah. So I can be ogled by *grown men*, have my outfit choice judged at will, then be chased down the freeway because my choice of destination isn't to your taste either."

I grind my teeth. She makes several fair points. "Ocean it is."

She's quiet as I come off at the next exit. I take some of the backroads to a secluded bay just east of Washington Port. It's not exactly the closest ocean point but it's the one least likely to be littered with tourists at this time of year.

I pull into a small parking area and shut off the engine. Ahead of us is a sandy clearing, with a few swaying palms, and the sea.

"There," I say, fixing my gaze on the view through the windshield. "The ocean."

She pushes open the passenger door, then steps outside, straightening her long legs like a cat. I watch curiously as she walks the short distance from the car to the water's edge where she stretches her arms up and over her head, drawing the hem of her top high up her back until it skims a small tattoo. It must have been covered by her hair when she swam in the pool because I haven't seen it before. And even though I can't see what it is, the fact some man has had his inked needle that close to her makes me rigid with tension.

She shakes her hair down her back, blocking the view of the tattoo, and bends down to slip off her sandals. A small gust of wind flips up the skirt of nightmares and gives me a perfect view of her rounded cheeks, a black thong disappearing between them. I lift a curled fist to my mouth and bite down on it, leaving red teeth marks on a white knuckle. Jesus H Christ, what I wouldn't do to feed my fingers beneath that cotton and grab a handful of her ass.

With her back still turned toward the car, she folds her arms across her middle then pulls the top over her head. Then she reaches behind her back and pulls at the delicate string holding her modesty together. That joins the top on the sand.

I try to blink away because if she turned around, this could signal the end of days for me. If Cristiano were to ever find out that I've seen his sister-in-law up close and practically naked, not once, but twice, I'm pretty sure he'd kill me. But, like a man seeing the Aurora Borealis for the first time, I can't tear my eyes from her.

Seconds pass as she looks out at the ocean, topless, and I hold my breath in anticipation of what's coming next. My body moves on autopilot and I step out of the car, my gaze glued to her. She hooks her fingers over the waistband of her skirt, then pushes it, and the entirely ineffective thong over her *outlawed* ass and steps out of them before tossing both to the side.

My jaw unhinges as she walks like some fucking Greek goddess into the waves without looking back. The scene takes me back to when I watched her swim naked in Cristiano's pool. She had never looked more authentic, more free. My frown dips. Maybe this is how she copes with all the shit life throws at her.

I swallow. I just became some of that shit. But, I remind myself, I have to be. It's the only way to assure her safety.

She disappears beneath the waves and, for a second, my heart stops. It only seems to beat again when she pops back up, her jet black hair glistening.

My gaze tracks her for several minutes then I'm forced to avert it when she starts striding out of the water. It's agony to not look her way. I just know that decadent droplets of water are running over her fucking perfect breasts, dripping off the peaked tips of her nipples, leaving tracks down her stomach, pooling between her legs. I'm suddenly ravenous and thirsty and *aching*, and my dick is so fucking hard I'm not sure I can walk back to the car.

I can feel her green gaze on my face as she walks slowly toward me, *naked*. I tip my chin, my hands stuffed into my pockets, training my focus on the swaying branches of tall palms. My voice is croaky and foreign. "Are you trying to get me fired?"

"I'm not trying to get you *anything*," she replies, her voice lusty and all kinds of tempting. I keep my gaze averted and let out a breath of relief as she walks straight past me.

When I hear the creak of the car's suspension, I turn around. She's lying across the hood of her car, arms resting languidly over the top of the windshield, one knee propped up. Her black-painted toenails gleam in the sunlight, her long limbs taut with stamina and muscle.

Fucking fuck me.

"What do you want, Contessa?" My words come out on a long exhale.

There's a long pause filled with breaths that float on the breeze.

"I don't like being ignored. I want you to look at me."

What the actual? I *always* look at her. Even when she's not there, the vision of her is front and center of my mind. It won't fucking leave.

With her permission, I allow my gaze to *ravage* her. Those taut, honed limbs, criminal curves, felonious tits, gorgeous hips flattened on the metal hood. I don't need to starve myself anymore—I can fucking ogle her like a dirty old man in a trench coat.

Her eyelashes are framed with droplets of saltwater, her lips scandalously plump and parted, waiting.

"I thought you hated me," I say, my voice soft but with a surprisingly bottomless depth.

I notice her breaths becoming shorter the longer my gaze devours every inch of her.

"I do."

Fuck. My dick is screaming at me. "How much?" I challenge, in a sunken baritone.

Several seconds pass with nothing between us but rasping breaths.

Her voice cracks. "So much I could cry."

I take a step toward her and wipe the back of my hand across my mouth. My timbre is rough.

"You wanna cry?"

She hesitates, her eyes widening a fraction. I am *not* bluffing.

She wets her lips.

Swallows.

Whispers.

"Yes."

I take another step toward her. I'm so close I could reach out and coast my fingers across her pussy. Her breaths are erratic.

We've been talking in code. I know what she really wants, and dear God, I want it too, like a man on death row wants redemption. I want to bury myself inside her, feel her insides fucking *eclipse* me. I don't care that she's not a virgin. In fact, it's better that she isn't. I want her to feel everything, without any pain. I want to watch those green eyes roll back in her head and hear my name whimpered from the lips that have spouted so much fucking hate.

"How about if I made you cry my name? At the top of your fucking lungs?"

Her limbs tremble and her fingers curl into her palms.

I take one final step toward her and gently lift her other leg so her foot is resting alongside the other on the hood of the car. The feel of her soft skin is *addicting*.

"How would you feel about me then? Would you still hate me?"

Her breaths stutter and I hear her swallow several times before she replies. "I'd hate you even more."

I gently press my weight on her knees and coax her knees apart. She resists but I'm strong. I keep pushing until her hips are flattened and her bare, shaved pussy is open for me and I can count every single one of her swollen folds. I'm staring at the doors to fucking Heaven. I lick my lips and swallow.

"I'm going to make you hate me with every inch of your soul."

Her eyelids pop and she sucks in a panicked breath, then I lower my face between her legs. Hovering over her pussy I inhale deeply. Mother *fuck*. Her scent penetrates every fucking pore. I *need* to taste her.

I inch my tongue forward, torturously slow. This may be the only time she allows me this close. I need to savor it, commit it to memory, embed it in my flesh.

The tip of my tongue makes contact with the edge of her pussy. She almost jumps off the hood, pushing me backward. We stare at each other and my mouth *floods* with saliva. I am gone. Frozen. She's the sweetest thing to ever touch my taste buds.

Her hands curl around my neck, pulling me forward.

Then, like a rabid dog who's just been given flesh to sink its teeth into, I bury my face between her thighs. I push my tongue between her folds and lick the length of her, feeling the bud of her clit swell instantly. Wrapping my lips around it, I pull it into my mouth, suckling on her sweetness. She gasps and it turns me on so much my head spins. With undiluted focus, I alternate between softly sucking her clit and licking through her folds, tasting every damn inch of her.

As the haze of insanity thins, I settle in, resting my elbows on the hood. My tongue and mouth find a torturous rhythm, and *my God*, she tastes so fucking sweet I might die.

Contessa *moans*, making my dick swell even thicker. Her head flips to the side and she sobs my actual name.

I swirl my tongue around her clit, then lap at it gently like it's a rare delicacy. Letting my lids drift closed, I let the scent of her arousal draw my mouth to her opening. I wet my thumb in her juices and massage her clit while I stare greedily at her cunt.

Her fingers wind through my hair and the words, "I fucking hate you so much," are purred from her lips.

"I fucking hate you too," I groan. Then I press a hand to her stomach and tease my tongue around her opening, tasting the new territory.

The desperation it invokes in my chest shocks me and I remember why we're here. She hates me, despite knowing the truth about the Falconi's. She taunts me like this is a game. This isn't a fucking game. This is war, and she started it.

She releases a battle cry and I know I'm winning. Her thighs shake against my shoulders and I press my hand more firmly onto her stomach, preventing her hips from pushing up toward my mouth.

Oh no, Contessa. If you hate me, you're my enemy. And this is what I do to my enemies. I annihilate them.

I tease her entrance with my tongue, feeling every

sob and whimper in my pants. If this is killing her, it's sure as hell finishing me off too. Bit by bit, I push my tongue inside, letting her sweetness wrap around my taste buds. Then I fuck her, slowly, curling the tip of my tongue with each thrust, in the exact spot I know will *end* her.

"Oh *God*…" she weeps.

Her fingers release my hair, making me glance upwards. After dwelling in the darkness of her core, the sunlight almost blinds me, but then what I see challenges every urge I have to unzip my pants and push myself right in, up to her damned cervix. She's holding her breasts and pumping them softly. They look heavy and swollen, the nipples peaked painfully.

Shit.

I withdraw my tongue, making her head jerk upward, then I lean over her body, ignoring the frenzied look in her eyes, and hold her hands above her head. Then I lower my mouth to her right nipple, sucking the sharp diamond into my mouth. She breathes out a languid sigh, chased by a delirious moan. It takes no time at all for me to get lost in the sound of her helplessness, but I'm half-aware that her hips are moving, rubbing her clit against the bulge in my pants.

I remember the other breast and continue to massage the right as I transfer my mouth to the left. Her moans sail into the trees, getting louder and more frustrated. Her soft skin feels like butter, melting beneath my fingers and lips.

"Please Bernadi…" she whispers. "I need—"

I smile around her nipple. "What do you need, Contessa?"

"I need to come."

"You want me to *let* you come?"

"Yes," she whimpers. "Please..."

"You come. I win," I growl, gently.

"I don't care," she pants. "Just please finish me."

"Do you still hate me?"

She bends her neck to glare at me. "With every fiber of my being."

"Good." I smile and dip my face back between her legs, then I hold her down and fuck her pussy until she can't convulse anymore.

CHAPTER TWENTY-THREE

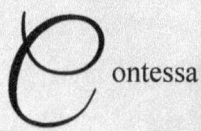

Contessa

I come around to the heat of the sun on the side of my face and the feel of someone's fingers teasing my hair behind my ear. I open my eyes and see Benito Bernadi hovering over me with a look of concern on his face.

"Still alive then." His furrowed brow doesn't ease up.

"I'm sure you can do many things Bernadi, but don't add 'death by orgasm' to your repertoire just yet." I push myself up to my elbows and note that at least he had the decency to close my legs.

"Damn." His lips break a smile and he holds out my two-piece and skirt.

I slowly sit up and slide off the hood of the car. Bernadi turns away while I dress, which seems a little counterintuitive now I have no modesty left to protect.

"Done," I say in a slightly shy voice. I avert my gaze as he turns back around. Setting eyes on him, even after what we just did, makes me feel weak.

Though I'm not looking directly at him, I know his feet are braced on the sand but his stance is relaxed. I know his jacket was discarded long ago and his sleeves rolled up before he opened my legs. I know his hair is mussed up from where I grabbed at it.

"You ready to go home now?"

And I know his voice has never sounded so soft.

I nod because I don't feel confident enough to open my mouth.

He tips his head toward my car. "Let's go."

I buckle myself into the passenger seat and lift the towel-wrapped jewelry box onto my lap, then fix my gaze straight ahead as we drive back along the freeway. Every now and then, I can't help my gaze from drifting to the side. The muscles beneath his forearm dance each time he turns the wheel and his thumb taps against it to a beat I can't hear. On anyone else it would look like a nervous tic, but I'm pretty certain Benito Bernadi doesn't do nerves.

My gaze slides upward and I get a glimpse of inked chest through the button holes of his shirt. Up some more and I take in his jawline. It's so angled and precise, jutting occasionally as his thumb taps the wheel. I can't see his scar from this side but the rest of his face is untouched and frighteningly beautiful. His eyes glisten bronze beneath unreasonably perfect, thick lashes and his dark hair cut close to the nape, longer on top, gives him a tense, controlling edge.

"What is that?" His voice makes me startle.

I follow his brief glance to the bundle on my knees and I carefully unwrap the towel. Once free, I lift up the box and inspect it from every angle, hoping it didn't acquire any bumps when I hit the brakes earlier.

"It's a jewelry box."

"It looks special," he says, glancing at it again before focusing his gaze back on the road.

"It is. It belonged to my mother. I always wanted it, but I never told her and she gave it to Trilby."

Bernadi doesn't respond and I don't feel any judgement coming from him, so I feel safe to continue.

"I couldn't ask her for it. Not after everything she went through."

When the car slows and the wind dies down, I can hear Bernadi's breathing, It soothes me, so I hold onto each breath I hear.

"So, why do you have it now?" Bernadi asks, quietly.

"Trilby gave it to me this morning. I guess she feels she doesn't need all those things anymore. Not now she has Cristiano and a full life ahead of her to look forward to. And she knew how much this box means to me. It's what inspired me to dance in the first place."

He turns his head briefly. "You were inspired by a box?"

I'm about to give him a piece of my mind when I realize he has no idea what's inside it, so I lift the lid and wind up the handle at the back. Music fills the car and I watch as the little ballerina spins on her pedestal, the diamonds flickering in the sunlight.

"Ah. Makes sense now."

I let the ballerina dance until she winds down then I close the lid. "What about you? Do you have anything sentimental from when you were growing up?"

The light smile falls from his face and his jaw clenches. After several seconds of silence I turn to look ahead. I don't know why but whenever I find myself in an awkward situation I have to make a joke. It's a character flaw, I know.

"You probably don't remember. I mean, it was likely *decades* ago."

To my dismay, he doesn't even quirk a grin.

Silence fills the car and my skin starts to itch with discomfort. I hate long silences. Normally, I try to fill them with sarcastic nonsense but this one feels unfillable.

I try again. "Or, anything sentimental from the modern era?"

He grinds his teeth and pulls the car off the freeway. We're not far from my home but I don't want to end the conversation here. It feels unfinished and as though the second he leaves he won't want to speak to me ever again.

I remind myself that wouldn't be a bad thing, because I hate him, right?

"I don't believe in sentimental value," he says, finally.

I open my mouth to challenge his claim but see his clenched jaw and snap my lips shut. Why would someone not believe in sentimental value? Perhaps if they'd never been the recipient of something worthy of being sentimental? The idea that Bernadi might not have experienced that makes me feel sad to my bones, and that shocks me. I've always been an empath but I've never felt sadness for someone else so deep in my core.

Something ill-advised but tenacious makes me probe him further.

"Didn't your parents ever give you anything meaningful?"

He *swings* the car round a corner. "I don't have parents." I can see our driveway looming ahead, getting closer as Bernadi puts his foot to the floor.

Disbelief unhinges my jaw. "Then, who raised you?"

The tires of my car screech against the sidewalk and Bernadi pulls up hard and cuts the engine. When his gaze pans to me, he looks tired.

"If I answer that, can we consider this conversation closed?"

I hesitate, then I nod.

We both get out of the car and shut the doors, staring at each other over the top of my convertible. Then he tosses me the keys and replies, "I raised myself."

The retort is out of my mouth before I can stop it. "Then no wonder you're such an asshole."

A devastating smile picks up the corners of his eyes.

"Get your butt in the house, Castellano." He takes a few steps backward, in the direction of the main street.

"And where are you going?" I ask. "You know, your car is still parked on the freeway."

"No it isn't," he says, a note of smugness on the tip of his tongue. "It's at Cristiano's."

I roll my eyes. "Oh right, you had your men collect it?"

He doesn't reply.

"You need a ride to Cristiano's?" I kind of don't want him to leave.

He shakes his head, his steps taking him further away.

"Your men are coming to collect you, aren't they?"

His lips twitch but his expression gives nothing else away.

"Do you still hate me, Contessa?"

Time seems to stop as the growing distance between us heats up. His feet pause and he pulls one hand out of his pocket to wipe a thumb across his mouth. His focus on my response is unwavering.

I wet my dry lips then swallow. "With every fiber of my being, Bernadi."

My heartbeat fills the next few seconds and just as the fire licking at my skin becomes too much, Bernadi tips his head back with a smile, spins on one foot and walks away.

I stand at the side of my car and watch him reach the street where a black car pulls up right on cue. He gets in without looking back and drives away, leaving me with a sentimental old music box and a head full of questions.

CHAPTER TWENTY-FOUR

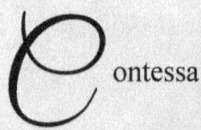
Contessa

I've clearly forgotten about the pool party when I turn up to the studio the next morning, but Paige puts that right in less than ten seconds.

"What happened to you?" she squeals before the door has even closed behind me. "I've been so worried! You didn't answer any of my calls or texts… I thought you'd been kidnapped or something."

I resist the temptation to roll my eyes, then remember how close I actually came to being abducted and possibly raped by my stalker. "I'm sorry, Paige. I—."

A few other girls are stretching their limbs, readying themselves for rehearsal, and clearly eavesdropping on our conversation, so Paige pulls me to one corner. "What happened?" she hisses in a stage whisper.

"My car broke down." I almost kick myself at the lame excuse but I figure it's less interrogate-able than 'my new brother-in-law's consigliere chased me down, threatened to murder anyone who looked at me, then gave me multiple orgasms on the hood of my car.'

Her eyes widen. "And your phone? Did that break down too?"

"I had to call home to get someone to pick me up and then my phone died. I'm so sorry, Paige. I really am."

She straightens and folds her arms. "You never come out and I was so stoked you finally wanted to join us."

God, now I feel like a real ass.

"I know. I promise if anything like that happens again, I'll call." I bite the inside of my lip. "That's if you invite me again. I won't blame you if you don't."

She blinks a few times then shrugs her arms back to her sides. "Oh, Tess, of course I'll invite you again. You're like my bestie in this place. Be nice if we could be besties outside of it too."

She wraps her arms around my neck and I hug her back. Having a bestie is a slightly unsavory notion to me now. The only bestie I've ever had was Federico. I understood that he had to leave. I never expected him to completely abandon me, but he did. And for a long time, especially after I'd trusted him with my virginity, that hurt. So, naturally, I've grown a little averse to the idea of having a best friend.

My response is cut short by the arrival of Antonio.

He barks at us all to get into position and we obey. As the music starts my eyes drift closed and a darkness wraps itself around me. A gap in a doorway, a spinning ballerina, the graze of unshaved skin along the inside of my thigh.

Then I dance.

"That was spectacular." Antonio's words halt me as I'm halfway through the door. Most other girls have already left and those remaining are pulling on shoes and jackets, chatting amongst themselves.

I turn timidly. "I'm sorry?"

"Your dancing this afternoon. It was spectacular."

I swallow and hold the door open, not sure if I should stay or leave.

"You've always been a good dancer—I don't always tell you. But, I've never seen you dance like that before."

I let the door close and hug my arms around myself. I'm kind of stunned. Antonio never gives me compliments; he only ever makes me feel as though I'm not good enough.

He looks around as if trying to find the words. "It's like you're dancing from here." He presses his palms to his chest. "From your soul. Instinctive. Innate. Like… you're not even trying."

He stares at me, waiting for a response, but I'm at a loss because I can't explain it myself. But I've noticed a change in my dancing too—in my ability to feel the music, to become one with it, to lose myself in a certain darkness. It began the day I heard gunshots across the street.

He sighs. "Well, whatever is making you dance this way, don't lose it. Keep dancing like that and you will go wherever your heart desires."

I nod once and open the door, only breathing again when I'm on the other side of it. I stare at the opposite wall and try to believe what just happened. Then I hear a faint noise coming from the top of the stairs.

Before I know it, I'm standing at Bernadi's door, tapping my knuckles against it. When it opens, my stomach almost bottoms out. Is it possible for someone to get even more beautiful not twenty-four hours since I last saw them?

He's wearing dark jeans and a black T-shirt that accentuates the bronze flecks in his eyes. The cotton wraps around his torso like a glove, rippling over his abs and revealing the barbed wire ink curling round his bicep.

He wordlessly takes a step backward and I walk into his apartment. Once I'm inside he closes the door.

He looks down at me through heavy lashes. Both of us are waiting for the other to speak, but neither of us does.

My pulse is thundering through my ears as adrenaline skitters across my nerve endings. Looking up into his thoughtful gaze, I know exactly what is making me dance better than I've ever danced before.

It's *him*.

It's Bernadi. He's unlocked something in me that makes it a little easier to live with myself. His darkness somehow makes mine okay.

I step forward until my chest is brushing against his. He doesn't move. He doesn't do anything. My pounding heart makes me feel lightheaded and I'm conscious of the hate I've professed to feeling for him for so long slipping away, out of my grasp. It makes me feel untethered and at sea.

Instead of feeling angry at him, I feel a strange pull that I can't explain. My stomach warms like liquid and my skin prickles with anticipation, remembering how good he made me feel. How can someone I hate make me feel so *treasured*?

I tilt my chin and without thinking pull my bottom lip between my teeth. His jaw grinds but his expression doesn't move. His body seems to have solidified, watching me with narrowed, beautiful eyes.

I reach up onto my tiptoes and let my lips part. My lids fall and something presses against my mouth. It isn't his.

My eyelids pop open only to see his finger pressed against my lips. His voice is gravelly. "What did I say about putting your mouth on me, Contessa?"

I lower my heels to the floor, feeling some of the wind knocked out of me.

His voice lowers to a deep, haunting whisper. "I won't be able to stop." He lets those words sink in, then finishes with, "And that's a promise."

I freeze, my inexperience hurtling toward me at a million miles per hour. I got lucky on the hood of my car. He could've walked away and completely shattered my self-esteem. In reality, I have no idea how to play this game.

I feel a guttural need to thank him in some way for releasing some of my inhibitions. It's too big of a coincidence that my dancing took on an even greater life of its own almost to the minute he showed up on the sidewalk.

His body heat is burning me up and he's just said, in a roundabout way, he wants me. I mean, I'm reading between the lines here, but I think that's what he meant.

Relief and something akin to want makes me curl my trembling fingers over the waistband of his jeans. I almost *die* at the sound of his sharp intake of breath.

The buttons pop out effortlessly and when I look down I see why. His cock is straining against the fabric. Even through the cotton of his designer boxers, I can see it's as big as my forearm.

"Take it out." The bite in his tone makes me startle and my heart shoots up to the base of my throat.

My whole hands are shaking but I force them to work apart the opening in his boxers. I hold my breath and feed my hand through, then I feel the taut, soft, *hot* skin of his cock and my brain melts. It takes no effort to pull him out, but I'm stunned when confronted with exactly how well-endowed he is, and what he's waiting for.

"Look at me."

I'm grateful for the command. I feel slightly drunk trying to lift lids that have grown heavy with lust. He takes my chin between a finger and thumb and gently lifts it until my gaze meets his. His voice is a whisper. "*Look* at me."

I swallow, painfully aware my hand is holding his throbbing cock.

"You've never done this before."

I'm about to shake my head in agreement, but he applies pressure to my chin, holding it in place. "It's not a question."

He lifts his gaze to the ceiling for a second, then drops it back to mine. "You sure you want to do this?"

Oh *God*. No? Yes? I want—I *need*—to do something.

I nod. "Tell me what to do."

His other hand is still in his pocket, his cock jutting into my stomach, regardless of my grip around it.

His jaw unlocks. "Hold it firmly," he orders. "Then stroke me from the base to the tip. Slowly."

I do as he asks, and each time I try to look down to check I'm doing it right, he pinches my chin.

After a few strokes, a hoarse groan feeds its way out of his throat. The place he stroked with his tongue the day before starts to throb but I drag my focus back to his cock. It's growing longer, thicker and so much firmer in my hand.

"Come closer," he says.

I have to aim his cock upwards so I can step into

him. My hand grazes his T-shirt and mine as I rub him up and down.

My head tips back even further as I maintain eye contact, like he told me to. Both our lips are parted and our breaths mingle, growing heavier and deeper.

His eyes close and he hums an untethered moan, then his lips form a word. "Contessa."

My thighs part instinctively, and my panties feel soaked. Oh God, am I going to come from just doing this to him?

My mind flashes back to the point at which I was desperate for him to finish me and the little devil in me takes over. I pause the movement of my hand and watch his lids pop open. "Do you hate me, Benito?" I ask innocently.

His lips part and a tight breath escapes them. "Yes, my little brat. I hate you."

Oh *God*.

I tighten my grip and stroke him harder. I love how these simple movements are unraveling him. And I love how he can't seem to control his response to me. I have him literally in the palm of my hand and I've never felt so powerful.

His eyes close again and he clamps his hands to each side of my face, then he pulls me toward him and presses his left cheek to mine. His breaths pump into my ear, long and tortured.

Then he starts to whisper.

"That's it, honey… Just a little harder… *Un*… Perfect…"

My legs shake. He called me 'honey' and now I think it might be my favorite word.

"That's my little brat… Oh Jesus… *Contessa*…"

Hearing my name on a note of desperation makes everything below my waist swell. I press my cheek into his, and his fingers caress a trail from my nape to my shoulder blades.

"Lift up your shirt," he whispers softly.

I do as he asks. I guide his cock beneath the fabric and press it against my breasts.

"I'm going to come all over you, little brat," he says, his voice cracking like ice falling into warm whiskey.

I tug at him once, twice… On the third stroke he groans and grips my face so hard it hurts. I feel his hot semen flood into the canal between my breasts. His body shakes as it expels every last bit and he seems heavier against me, panting from the exertion.

Quietly, I dip my fingers into the pool of come and pull a trail of it over my breasts. His breaths slow and his cheek releases from mine with a gentle pull on my skin.

He raises his head and releases his grip on my face, then he lifts my T-shirt and sees what I've done. My breasts are coated in his come. For a second, he stares at me, like he can't believe I would do something like that.

Then his gaze darkens like a deathly shadow just fell over him and he quickly shoves himself back inside his pants and buttons up the fly.

"I guess we're even now."

I step back at his sharp tone.

"What?" I whisper.

"You won this one, but I won the last."

"Do you think this is a game?" I ask, my voice pitching higher.

His teeth grind together. "Not so much of a game, more of a stand-off."

Something inside my chest hardens. He just let me do all that to him so he could get *even*? For a moment there, I thought we were playing at this game of hate, but, as he's just clarified, this is no game. He really does hate me.

And how do I feel?

Mortified. Embarrassed. Exploited.

Hate is too small a word.

And words are too generous a form of communication.

We're still standing by the door so I feel for the handle without taking my eyes off his, then I pull the door open and step outside, leaving him with nothing but a sneer for company.

CHAPTER TWENTY-FIVE

*C*ontessa

I run down the steps, ignoring his instruction to have his damn driver take me home. Then I slam the door to the street and march to the subway, fighting back tears.

The night is closing in and there's a chill in the air as I run underground to get my train. When I emerge at Grand Central I dig out my phone to call Allegra to see if she can give me a ride. For once I don't want someone's 'men' to collect me from the station in Port Washington; I just want people who are real and won't lie to me because I'm a pawn in some chess game.

I swipe the screen and a half dozen notifications pop up. Text messages, phonecalls and VMs—all from Paige. Instead of reading and listening I hit the green button and wait for her to answer.

"There you are! I've been trying to get ahold of you

since class." I thank the good lord she can't see the blush flood my cheeks at the memory of where I've been, or the scowl that chases it.

"Sorry Paige, my cell was at the bottom of my purse and I just got off the subway."

"I was calling to see if you wanted to come out this evening. My friend has just started working at a cool bar in the city and he can get me and one other onto the guest list. This is your chance to redeem yourself after standing me up the other day." She finishes on a giggle.

"Okay… Um, maybe."

"Where are you?" Her voice is threaded with excitement and it's infectious.

"Grand Central."

"Shoot. Can you get to Brooklyn College? I could collect you and bring you back here and we can get ready together. What do you think?"

My initial reaction is to say no, because just the thought of socializing with people I barely know tires me out, but the sting of Bernadi's rejection is still so acute I can feel it across every inch of my flesh. I want to be rid of it, and what more satisfying a way to do that than by spending a night out dressed in *next to nothing*—something I now know Bernadi would hate.

"What about my clothes and make-up? I don't have anything with me."

Her voice dips. "Babe, I have enough for both of us, and half the street."

"Then, that sounds amazing," I reply. "Only if

you're sure, though? I don't want you to have to go out of your way—I can probably hail a—"

"On my way!" I hear a set of keys jangle and a door bang shut. "I'm not far from that station at all—I'll see you there."

I'm practically hopping from foot to foot with nerves when I see Paige parked outside the station. But, as I'm beginning to understand, nerves don't have to hold me back from doing anything. Look at what I did to Bernadi, and I was *crapping* myself.

She leans over the seats of her truck and pushes the passenger door. "Get in!"

I slide onto the seat. "Where's the belt?"

"Isn't one," she replies, spinning the car across the street to head in the opposite direction. "So, hang on."

When we reach her apartment I estimate I've lost half a stone in sweat. The girl drives like she has nine lives. Me on the other hand? I think I'm down to seven, and after today, maybe six.

We climb the steps to her place and I ask if I can use her bathroom. I can still feel Benito's come across my chest and need to be rid of it. When I return, Paige immediately furnishes me with a margarita that is so strong it burns my throat. But after the afternoon I've had, I don't care. I drink half in one gulp and relish the citrussy zing as it takes a layer off my esophagus.

"I've dreamed about this day, you know." She guides me toward her closet.

"What do you mean?" The fuzziness in my head relaxes me and I take in her apartment. It's dressed up like an extra from Moulin Rouge. Everywhere I turn there's a corner filled with bright feather boas, and sequined jackets flung over velvet button-backed chairs.

"I love the whole Wednesday aesthetic you've got going on but I would kill to be able to do you over in some color."

I follow her into the master and the first thing I see, aside from a bed with makeshift four posts embellished with vintage lace piano shawls, is a stunning fifties-style dressing table—all cream and gold and completed with a light bulb studded mirror. It's decorated with enormous old glass jars filled with golden perfumes and cloud-like cotton balls.

It is far from tidy, but that's what I love. It's messy and lived-in and filled with heart. There are clothes lines hanging in a crisscross formation below the high ceilings, peppered with lace underwear and chiffon babydoll dresses. She catches me staring and tips her head to one side. "I do burlesque," she says with a shrug. "To pay the rent."

All I can utter is, "*Wow*." Because never in a million years would Allegra or Papa let me step foot inside a burlesque club, never mind on the stage. "I'm kinda envious."

She grins at me and clamps a hand over a door handle. "If you're envious of that, just wait till you see this…"

With true dramatic flair she pulls open two doors, revealing what I can only describe as the closet of dreams.

"Pick whatever you like," she says brightly, then skips past me to refill our glasses. I stare at the one she just took from me. No idea when I'd emptied that.

I gently draw items of clothing along the rails, inspecting each one, then I find the perfect garment.

It's a short satin babydoll dress in midnight blue that nips in slightly below the bust and flares out just above the knee. The skirt is somehow weighted down and the hem decorated with feathers. I've never seen anything like it before, but the shade is just a touch darker than my eyes.

"I would have picked that one out for you too," Paige says, reappearing with a refilled glass. "I'd love to see you wear it."

I take a long sip of the margarita then place it on the dressing table. I strip down to my underwear then step into the dress. It fits like a glove.

"Wow," Paige says, turning me to face a mirror. "You look stunning. And I haven't even done your hair and makeup yet."

I wasn't expecting her to do my hair and makeup but I don't say anything because I'm speechless. This dress makes my legs go on for *days*. Normally I'm embarrassed by how pale-skinned I am but this dress is a celebration of my porcelain, almost blue-toned hue.

"Are you sure I can wear this?"

"Wear it? You can have it. Now that I've seen what it looks like on you, I'll never be able to do that thing justice again. It was made for you, Tess."

"I can't take this," I say.

She laughs. "You already did. Now, sit. The least you can do in exchange for that dress is let me give you a makeover."

I bite my lip and glance at her in the dressing table mirror. I don't usually wear makeup, and the most I do to my hair is wind it into a ponytail, so the idea of being made over is a little disconcerting.

"You look petrified," she says, giggling. "Don't worry, I know what I'm doing."

Thirty minutes later, I'm no longer bothering to pick my jaw up off the dressing table. I have no shame. Paige really does know what she's doing. She's lifted my hair at the roots and curled the ends so that it bounces when I move my head. She's put various creams on my face to make my skin appear dewy and fair, and she's applied make-up so expertly, it looks though I'm hardly wearing any, but my face is flawless, my lashes thick and long, my lips full and moist.

I manage to tear my eyes from my reflection and glance up at her. "Can I keep you?"

She puts her arms around my neck from behind and gives me a light squeeze, being careful not to smudge or ruffle any of her work. "I thought you'd never ask."

She straightens and I turn my head this way and that, taking in all the details while she changes into a short pinafore dress over a chiffon T-shirt and Mary Janes.

My lips curls. "I only have my sneakers."

"You can borrow these," she says, then she reaches into her closet and pulls out a pair of soft brown leather thigh-high boots.

I almost choke.

She senses my trepidation. "You won't look like a hooker. Trust me. These are Cristian Dior. Got them at a super high-end flea. Researched them and they sold full price for nine hundred dollars."

I'm in awe as I take them from her.

"You're a seven, right?"

I nod, bend over and slip my feet into the boots then unfold as I zip them up all the way to my mid-thighs.

Well, Christ on a cracker.

"Come on, a Lyft's on its way. We should get going."

I quickly text Allegra to say I'm hanging out with a friend from dance class, so she doesn't worry that I'm not home for dinner, take one last look at myself in the mirror, then follow Paige out the door.

"What is this place?" I crane my neck to look up at the building. There's no sign on the walls to tell us what we're lining up to get into.

"It's called Arena. It's kind of exclusive—not many people know about it. Only the ones who matter if you know what I mean?"

"And we matter?" I raise a skeptical eyebrow.

She returns a wink. "We do to my friend who works behind the bar."

"Good answer." I grin and pan my gaze along the people in front. I count three Fendis, a real mink and some exceedingly expensive looking shoes. There's a lot of money in this line.

We reach the front and the guy at the door appraises us. His gaze flicks to me and hovers, making me look back over my shoulder to see the more interesting person behind me. There's no one.

"It's Paige Thorp. I'm a friend of Cassian's."

The guy's focus slides down my body then he looks at the list in his hand.

"You can go right on in, Miss Thorp, and Miss…"

His gaze flicks back to me.

"Castellano," I reply.

"Miss Castellano." My name rolls approvingly off his tongue and I flush. I don't have time to become too flustered though because Paige grabs my hand and pulls me through the ropes into the club.

We head straight for the bar and Paige introduces me to Cassian who clearly only has eyes for Paige because he barely registers my existence. Then, furnished with brand new margaritas we find a booth near the dance floor.

"So, you and Cassian…"

Paige takes a sip of her drink, then throws her head back and laughs.

"Me and Cassian… we're not a thing, although he's tried his luck a few times." She leans across the table and points her finger discreetly across the dancefloor to another set of booths. "But *him*… Now *he's* a different story."

I slowly turn my gaze to follow her finger and the scene I arrive at turns me cold. She's pointing to a table filled with suits. Sharp, black *Italian* suits, complete with expensive watches, leather brogues and—just guessing here—gunmetal beneath their jackets.

"Looks like a scene from Goodfellas, doesn't it?" she giggles.

"Yeah," I reply, my tone flat.

"But, isn't he just beautiful?"

I know who she's referring to. There's four of them sitting in a curved booth. Three are older, maybe forties, fifties. One is more like late twenties and a dead ringer for a young Marlon Brando. His lids lift and lock on mine and something about them is a little too familiar. He's one of Cristiano's men, I'm sure of it.

My heart sinks low in my ribcage. It doesn't matter where I go in New York, I can't escape them. The Di Santos are *everywhere*.

My breath feels severe when I inhale. "Hey. Where's the restroom?"

Paige doesn't tear her eyes from the poorly disguised mafioso across the room when she answers. "Back toward the bar, second door on the right."

"Great. I'll be back in five."

I stand and walk to the restroom feeling more fucked off with each step I take. It's not enough that my sister's marrying into this family, I have to go and do brazen, sexual things with the second in command, who then humiliates me by tossing me to one side after I've bared everything to him but my soul. And when I try to get away, to have a night on my own with a friend, their presence hangs over me.

Each step I take feels angrier, so that by the time I've reached the restroom, I'm questioning my sanity. I stand in front of a floor length mirror on the far wall. I look like a queen but it's wasted on men. It's wasted on *him*.

I think back to the way he held my face, like he was struggling to hold back. The way he jerked into my hand, coating my skin. It was so raw and vulnerable for both of us. His gaze was so gentle when he lifted my shirt, then it turned to stone. After what he'd done to me, coming over my breasts like that, I did not expect him to shut down after seeing that I'd stroked his semen across my skin. It doesn't make any sense.

Because I won't stop. And that's a promise.

Those were his words when he told me not to put my mouth on him again. Those are not the words of someone who isn't attracted to me, surely.

The space between my thighs starts to throb at the memory and I feel an unhinged desire to show him what he's missing. It hurts to admit it to myself but my hatred for him is only skin deep. I know there's more beneath the surface and I need to see it.

I take a few pictures of myself in the floor-length mirror, then I hold my middle finger up and snap.

That's the one.

I don't bother adding a message—I just text the photo straight to Bernadi's phone. Then I smile triumphantly to myself, slip the phone into my purse then head back out to the club. Our booth is empty when I return, and when I look around I see Paige cosying up with the guy I'm pretty sure is one of the soldiers working the upper west side.

She looks up and nods as I signal to her that I'm going to have a little explore. I walk around the edge of the dancefloor sipping my margarita. This place is hot. And lavish. Coated in textures of satin, leather and velvet, with reds and blacks dominating the color scheme. The booths aren't overcrowded and the ice buckets are laden with European wines.

The bartenders move like shadows in a dance, their techniques a blur, their creations brighter than stars.

I'm completely absorbed in this decadent scene when a figure appears at my side.

"Miss Castellano…"

"Yes?" I look up into dark eyes I don't recognize.

"Your presence has been requested in the VIP lounge. Can I escort you there now?"

I look across the dance floor toward Paige. She and the soldier are deep in conversation, their feet entwined beneath the table. She won't miss me for a few minutes.

"Um, of course." I follow the large-boned, intimidatingly tall man to the back of the floor into an elevator. Once inside, he presses a button and the doors open again almost immediately.

"Make yourself at home, Miss Castellano," he says and I step out into another darkened room.

I turn around. "Who asked—" I want to know who's

requested my company back here but the elevator doors close, concealing the man inside, and in another second, I'm completely alone.

CHAPTER TWENTY-SIX

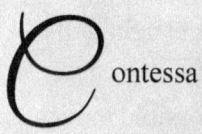ontessa

Well, this is weird.

I'm standing in a circular room, furnished with two small, curved sofas and one long, low glass table. It looks luxurious and exclusive but… there's no one here.

I sigh out a long breath. As much as I wanted to escape the day I've had, the thought of being with other people and making small talk, even with Paige, makes me so tired. I need time to process what happened earlier—the dancing, the completely out of character compliment I got from Antonio and the surreal moment I shared with Bernadi. And, of course, the rejection.

I walk into the room and look around. It feels as snug as it appears. Velvet drapes line every wall but it sounds as though the far wall isn't a wall at all. I walk towards it and pull back one of the drapes. Immediately, the dance floor below appears. This room is on the first floor looking down on everyone in the club below. There isn't a corner of the club that's concealed from this balcony. It's the perfect place to spy on every patron.

Something feels off. Do all clubs have a voyeuristic control tower like this one? I doubt it.

My skin prickles as though someone's watching me and I let the curtain slowly fall, closing off the view. I turn around, about to walk over to one of the sofas when a figure in the center of the small room makes me freeze. I would scream but my breath is caught at the base of my throat.

The angle of the light makes it impossible to pick up facial features but I don't need them to know who's standing in front of me. His silhouette is, annoyingly, etched on my brain.

Benito Bernadi.

It doesn't make any sense. He can't be here because of the message I sent him. I sent it less than six minutes ago, and it surely couldn't have been obvious from the photo where I am.

I can't restrain the contempt in my tone. "What are *you* doing here?"

He steps forward and the lights illuminate his scowl, along with the moody cut of his jaw and too-beautiful hooded eyes. "I should be asking you the same thing."

"I'm here with a friend. Not that it's any of your business."

"Where you go and who you're with is *all* of my business."

Anger singes my skin. "Do you know what? I don't want you anywhere near me, Bernadi. I don't care what Cristiano says. I am not your responsibility and I don't need to be chaperoned wherever I go."

"I don't care what you think."

I force out a laugh. "If you don't care, why are you here?"

"That photo you sent me… What did you expect would happen? You think I'm just gonna let that go?"

I jerk backward with a frown. "Let it *go*?"

"Like it or not Contessa, I'm responsible for your safety. I cannot let you be somewhere—anywhere—dressed like this, without someone looking out for you."

"But this isn't *next to nothing*. I'm wearing actual clothes and quite a few of them too, as a matter of fact."

"That dress is too…"

I'm so sick and tired of him telling me what to do, and the rejection still burns. I stamp my foot in frustration. "Too what? Too blue? Too pretty? Too flattering?"

He stares at me like he can't find the words.

"Come on, Bernadi, what exactly is it? What's wrong with what I'm wearing?"

His jaw is clenched and I see his fingers flexing by his side.

"Come on," I goad, spitefully. "What's *wrong* with it?"

He explodes. "It's too fucking *hot*, Contessa," he

shouts. "And *no one* gets to see you looking like that but me."

I gasp and stagger backward. "What?"

"You heard me."

My brain scrambles to make sense of his words. "But... this is just a game to you."

He chuckles, darkly. Takes a step toward me. I take one back. "This is no game, Contessa."

I wonder how far the drop is from the balcony to the dancefloor below because I'm certain the only safe way out from under his predatory stare is to jump.

"I'm tired of your behavior Contessa. You need to be taught a lesson."

"What do you mean 'my behavior'? What lesson? I haven't done anything wrong."

"You think? Where do I start? How about dressing like fucking catnip for every man in the city? How about wandering around a nightclub filled to the brim with firearms, on your own?"

I swallow.

"How about taking a photograph of yourself giving the bird dressed like that and sending it to me? And if all that wasn't enough, you don't even question why someone might want to see you in a VIP room, you just follow a stranger into an elevator? Contessa, you're about to become a part of the Di Santo family and you are a *fucking liability*. You need to learn a few things, and fast."

"So, you're going to 'punish' me?" I hook my fingers into quote marks.

He steps right up to me, flooding my senses with the scent of his aftershave.

His face is like thunder but his caress on the side of my face is soft.

"Yes, brat."

His neck bends, bringing his face down, closing in on me. Everything goes dark as if he personally controls the lighting in this room.

I grip my purse defensively but still feel an unbridled urge to confront him. "Tell me, how did you get here so quickly? I only sent that message ten minutes ago. You were here within five."

"I was in the basement having a business meeting."

I blink. My instincts were right, this place is riddled with mafia.

"And it's *my* club."

A shiver coasts across my shoulders. "You own a club?"

His mouth ticks up. "I own several. This one's the best."

"The other ones must be pretty poor."

My sarcasm earns me a painful tug on my hair, and it's only then I realize he's grabbed a handful of it with one hand while now holding both my hands behind my back with his other. My purse has fallen to the floor.

"I was going to go easy on you, Castellano, but you just sealed your fate."

I frown, not having a clue what he's talking about and my head spinning from having him stand so close.

His face is still lowered over mine. It's despairingly

beautiful. Without thinking, I rise up to my tiptoes and press my lips to his. At first, he's like stone—solid and unyielding. I breathe against his mouth, willing it to open. I want to taste the bitterness on the edge of his tongue.

It happens slowly. His lips part and the tip of his tongue ventures forward on a moan. He gently sucks my bottom lip between his teeth.

Then he bites it.

I yelp and try to pull back but he's holding me so tightly I can't move.

"What did I say about putting your mouth on me, Contessa?" I can hardly make out the words because he *growls* them, like an animal.

The room starts to spin as his words fly at me. *I won't ever stop, and that's a promise.*

A frightening sense of foreboding creeps beneath my skin and his gaze devours the terror in my face.

The room stills as if awaiting his next move.

"There's one thing you need to know about me, brat," he says, his voice deep and otherworldly. "I don't break promises."

His mouth slams down on me so hard I can't breathe. The force bends me backward and only his firm grip of my hands keep me from collapsing. He plunders my mouth, swiping his tongue across my mine with relentless force. His pelvis grinds against me, shocking me to my core.

"I warned you," he snarls, and suddenly he's carrying me across the room, his mouth melded to mine.

I'm lowered to something hard and cold and his body presses down on me so I can't move. His kiss alone is punishing, giving me no room to breathe. He kisses me like he's been starved of oxygen and I'm his last breath. It's disorienting and the force of it is tearing me apart.

When he releases the pressure on my ribs and stands, I still can't move and it takes my brain a few seconds to realize I'm trapped. Somehow, while kissing the absolute life out of me, he's managed to tie my wrists and ankles to the legs of a long glass coffee table. No wonder he's so lethal in his line of work—nothing and no one can get past him.

"What are you doing?" My voice trembles.

His gaze rolls slowly from my wild eyes, down my body to my strapped feet, and a smile dances across his mouth. Then just as quickly, his brow falls into shadow and the smile is wiped away with an inked knuckle.

"You need to learn a lesson, brat."

I blink up at him, confused.

"I want you to feel the way I feel every single fucking day. How I've felt since I saw you at Gianni's funeral."

"What do you mean?" My voice trembles.

His chest concaves and he suddenly slams his fists into the table, bringing his face close to mine. "Fucking *needy*."

My chest thumps with the echo of a frantically beating heart. He strokes an inked finger down my forehead, making my skin burn. "I need to know what's going on in here."

He slides his finger down my throat to my collarbone and then between my breasts. "I need to know what you feel in here."

His finger trails a line of fire down my stomach over the satin dress and rests on the spot between my thighs. "I need to taste *this*."

I inhale sharply, but the sudden throbbing between my legs takes that breath away.

"You already did," I whisper.

He glares at me, his bronze eyes now black. Then he grunts. "It wasn't *fucking* enough."

He straightens to his full, intimidating height, then walks around to my feet and bends at the knees.

I lift my head off the table so I can see him.

His gaze holds mine and his voice drops low. "Was it enough for you?"

My entire body heats and I give a small shake of my head.

"What would be enough?"

His question makes me shiver. I haven't dared ask it of myself but now I'm confronted with it, the answer makes me feel weak and vulnerable. So I don't reply.

He places his large hands either side of me on the coffee table and lifts himself a fraction. "Would my mouth on yours be enough?"

I hesitate. My answer should be yes. That should be enough. But I know with haunting clarity it isn't. I shake my head slowly.

He straightens his legs and hovers over my thighs. "Would my mouth on your pussy be enough?"

I squirm under his scrutiny, the need for friction becoming close to unbearable. I shake my head.

He moves higher up my body and grazes his nose along the channel between my breasts. It pushes the blue satin further up my thighs until the conditioned air is lapping at my underwear, sizzling against my hot skin.

"Would my mouth on your perfect tits be enough?"

My mouth falls open and a tainted moan escapes it. I shake my head.

He walks his hands up the table until they're either side of my breasts. He lowers himself, his biceps bulging through his shirt, until the hairs along his top lip are brushing the corner of my mouth. I'm so turned on I could cry.

"Do you want me *inside* you, Contessa?" he breathes heavily.

He nuzzles against my mouth then slowly lifts his head and looks hard into my eyes. "Would *that* be enough?"

I swallow.

"Take your time," he says softly. He lowers his hips and rubs his stiffened cock over my clit. I push up into it, relieved for some friction. "I already know the answer but I want to hear it from your lips."

I throw my head to one side. I don't recognize myself. I hate this man. He's the reason I gave my virginity away too soon. He humiliated me in his apartment. He sleeps with other women. He said he didn't that one time, but I don't believe him. Bernadi's been toying with me. He thinks I'm *his* for crying out loud. My stomach drops with the weight of inevitability. There's no getting away from it. I *want* this.

"Look at me Contessa."

I do as he says, clawing my gaze back to his.

"Do you want to feel my thick cock inside you? Do you want me to fuck you, deep and slow, hard and fast, until you're screaming for me to make you come?"

My breaths are coming out short and fast.

"Honey, your body is answering for you, but I still need to hear it from your mouth. Tell me brat, do you want me inside you?"

Oh *God*.

"Yes."

He lifts his eyes to the ceiling, closes them and releases a triumphant sigh. A second stretches like a held breath, then his lips draw into a wicked smile. "Then you're going to have to be patient like a good little girl."

What? I glare at him, my eyes hollowed as desperately as his.

He stands and lifts the hem of my dress, pushing it up to my collarbone. The feathers tickle my nipples. He draws in long heavy breaths, and thoughtfully peruses my body. It only burns me up more, making me squirm.

He then straightens and walks to the bar. He returns with an ice bucket and places it on the floor beside me. He dips his hand into the bucket and lifts out a cube of ice. He holds it over me and tightens his fist around it. Liquid appears through the cracks in his fingers and a large drop of water collects at the base. I hold my breath when it drips onto my stomach, then gasp at the shock of freezing water rolling over my burning skin.

Bernadi smirks and holds his fist over my breasts. More drips make me jump and squirm even harder.

He opens his hand and places the ice cube on my chest. I stare it, panting.

"I'm going to make you feel so good, Contessa." I'm surprised at the gentleness of his voice. "Do you trust me?"

I nod.

"Words, Contessa," he says, as though he has all the time in the world.

Weirdly, I don't need to think about my answer—I know what it is. What I don't know is how to feel about it.

"Yes, I trust you."

"Good girl."

He lightens his hold on the ice and pulls it down between my breasts. The melting liquid runs down my sides making my teeth grit. My thighs are shaking and I feel so exposed.

He draws circles with the ice around the circumference of my breasts pulling a moan from my chest, then narrows the circle until it's touching the dimpled edges of my nipples. I anchor my gaze on them and watch them sharpen under Bernadi's touch. He's commanding my body like a puppet master.

My lips grow taut and I dart my tongue out to lick them.

"Your body is begging for this," he says with a dry throat.

My hips ache to push up toward him, demanding attention, but I manage to solicit a bit of self-respect from somewhere and keep them pressed into the table.

Too slowly, he strokes the ice down my stomach, letting the water pool in my belly button. He lowers his mouth to the small crevice, dips his warm tongue inside and sucks the water out. With a soft, "mm" he urges the ice further down, pushing my panties to one side, until it's rested just inches from my clit.

"Breathe," he whispers through a smile. I didn't realize I'd been holding my breath but a gush comes out then is sucked straight back in again when he draws a circle with the ice around my hardened clit.

I've never felt anything like it. Hot blood rushing to my core, swelling my flesh, priming it for arousal. Then sharp, cool ice nipping at the skin, sending spasms of shock along my nerves.

The ice is melting quickly against my opening. Bernadi just holds it there watching it turn to liquid against my pussy. When there's nothing left between his fingers and my flesh, he leans down and sucks up the water with a soft lick of my pussy. A faint moan sails out of my mouth.

He looks up and inhales deeply, his shoulders rounded with tension. His face is taut with the expression of someone who's waging an internal war.

Keeping his gaze on mine, he reaches into the bucket and pulls out another cube of ice. He brings that to my opening, the frigid temperature making me jump again. Then, without warning, he pushes it inside.

Icy tentacles spread out from my core to every inch of my skin and I start to hyperventilate. My body doesn't know which way is up. It's burning with anticipation and now freezing cold from the inside out.

Bernadi pushes a hand up to my neck. "Slow down," he orders. "Slow your breathing."

I do as he asks, anchoring my gaze on his.

"Good girl."

He shifts to my feet and looks at his handiwork. I feel sopping wet, as though the cube is melting faster than a polar icecap in the blazing sun. "*Thirsty* girl." His praise makes my toes curl. Then he rocks forward on his knees and holds my thighs apart with his thick hands. He leans in and licks me from my back opening to my clit, sucking up the liquid as it spills out of me.

A delirious moan works its way from the base of my chest.

Again.

His tongue is perfection. I don't need to ask as just one lick has him obsessed. He laps at me furiously, his fingers digging craters in my thighs. He suckles on my clit while squeezing fistfuls of my leg. It's painful and delicious and in seconds I'm moaning like a wild animal.

He goes back to licking and uses his fingers to move the ice around inside me. It's almost completely melted now and my panties are soaked through. I'm starting to lose sense of where I am and grind against his mouth, drawing a growl from his throat. Thankfully, he doesn't let up. In fact, his efforts become more single-minded and he focuses them on my clit, licking and sucking me into a frenzy.

"Benito... I'm going to come."

He hums his approval into my flesh and I buck up to him letting him feast even harder, then a white light explodes behind my eyes and my awareness narrows to the sensations between my legs and nothing more. I convulse madly as he finishes me off, not letting up even as I jerk sensitively under his mouth.

Finally, his licks soften and he looks up, wiping the back of his hand across his mouth. We stare at each other, both of us short of breath. Then his gaze darkens again.

"On your knees."

Through the haze of post-orgasm, I wonder how he can be so optimistic. Has he forgotten he's tied me to the table?

I try to lift my arms and apart from the fact they feel heavy having been restrained, they do actually move—they're no longer tethered. I sit up and watch him back up towards the curtain-covered balcony, his eyes following me the whole way. "On. Your. Knees."

He can't be serious. I glare at him, wondering if it's appropriate or not to laugh, but he levels me with a dark look. "Contessa, if you want me to fuck you, you have to show me how much you want it. Now *crawl*."

There are a million sharp retorts on the tip of my tongue but they won't come out. Because even though the idea of crawling to a man makes my blood run cold and challenges my feminist ideologies, I want to do this. I want to please him. And, if the way he moves his dick is anything like the way he orchestrates his tongue, by God I want him to fuck me.

I drop to my knees and his Adam's apple moves in a dry swallow. He strokes a hand down his tie then shoves both hands into his pockets. He leans back against the concealed balcony and watches me.

I pull my dress down over my bottom, timidly, then place my hands on the floor. When I look up, I can see a huge bulge in his pants which is all I need to see to drive me forward. I crawl slowly towards him. Though my legs and arms are shaking, every inch makes me feel bolder. About three feet from his shoes I give my hips a slight wiggle and hear a string of Italian curses leave his mouth on a long, tight breath. I love what this is doing to him. He deserves to feel as out of control as I do.

When my nose is touching his slacks I lift my head. He's looking down at me with a wild, rabid look in his eye. I slowly rise up to my knees, then keeping my eyes on his, I lean in and lick his dry pants, right over his cock. It jumps beneath my tongue and I can't help a smile light up my face.

"Get up." His voice is strained.

I get to my feet and lift my lashes to look up at him.

"That was the single most sexy thing I've ever seen in my life," he says, softly. He draws one hand out of a pocket and pulls back the curtain overlooking the club. I suddenly flush, feeling completely exposed, then realize I'm not actually naked; I only *feel* naked.

He steps to one side. "Rest your arms on the edge."

I do as he asks and lean over the balcony. The height means my ass is canted out, the hem of my dress barely skimming my hips. Ice water still drips down the insides of my thighs and my panties need to find a trash can somewhere.

Bernadi moves to stand behind me then rubs a palm over the small of my back, then he places his hands on each of my hips and positions me level with his cock. My breath hitches and my mouth dries out, anticipating what's about to happen.

One of his hands leaves my hip and I hear the faint sound of a zipper being lowered amidst the chaotic blur of music and hundreds of voices fighting to be heard over the top of it. When the crown of his cock slides between my thighs, my head drops forward, hair falling across my face as my lungs empty. I look out across the club with heavy lids. Everything below waist height is hidden from the room below. No one would have any idea the owner of the club was pushing my panties to one side and guiding his cock between my legs.

Bernadi leans forward and rests his arms outside mine, his hard chest bearing down on my back. Our positions would look innocent enough to anyone who might care to look up. He slowly pumps his cock in and out of the gap between my thighs. When I pull my legs together tightly, he hisses in my ear.

"Let me in, honey."

I *melt*.

One of his hands leaves the edge of the balcony and he works it between my legs, coating his fingers in a combination of my arousal and the water from the ice. He rims my entrance, readying me, then guides the crown of his cock to my opening. "Do you want me to go easy on you, Contessa?"

I turn my head slightly and murmur, "No. I don't want easy."

In one smooth, controlling movement, Bernadi curls his hips upward and shoves himself deep inside me. I clamp a hand over my mouth because I don't trust myself not to scream.

I'm not a virgin anymore but it's been three years since the one time I slept with someone. Bernadi's cock is thicker and longer than Federico's. Three years ago was barely anything more than a heavy make-out session. Now, I feel like I've just been broken in.

Bernadi's breaths pump in and out of my ear and a groan rolls through him into my bones. "Jesus, Contessa. You feel incredible. You're so fucking tight."

I can't seem to process anything. Only the hard fact that Benito Bernadi is *inside me*. He's inside me, and aside from feeling as though I've been torn, I'm on fire. My skin is sizzling with desire and my stomach is hot to the touch. I just want to close my eyes so I can focus on the feel of his thick length pushing against my soft walls, and nothing else.

I whimper into my hand and nod. I don't want him to know I'm shocked to the core.

"Let's just pause a minute," he whispers. "Let you get used to me being inside you."

His words melt my nerve endings. They're dirty but beautiful. I don't remember needing such a moment even when Fed took my virginity. It wasn't like this—completely overwhelming.

Images flash before my eyes. A gap in a door, a man in black, a dark stare. A tall ask and a gift given. A different pair of eyes when I came undone.

I suck in a sharp breath and my eyes ping open. It wasn't Federico I saw when I came during my first time; it was Bernadi. And since then, my shadows have grown fuller, my sanity less tethered.

This is why I'm dark.

This is why I'm wild.

It's because of the man behind me. Inside me. All around me.

Stark realizations come hurtling toward me. I was running from who I was because I terrified myself. There's never been a model in my life for how to make my wildness 'work'—it has always been something to be feared. *Bernadi* was something to be feared.

But I don't fear him. What I feel for him runs deeper than that.

"That's it, my beautiful little brat. You're relaxing so well, so soft." His praise does things to me and I turn my head.

"I'm okay, Bernadi. You're not going to hurt me."

He drops his forehead to my shoulder. "Damn," he whispers. Then he moves.

He's slow at first, pinning my hips with his fingers. He buries his head into the crook of my neck, releasing muffled animal groans as he slides in and out of my soft entrance.

I tip my head back onto his shoulder and moan freely, knowing no one can hear but Bernadi. His cock is perfect and I grip it snugly, feeling every ridge moving through me. I find it hard in this moment to ever understand why I hated him so much.

I lift a hand and run it up his neck into his hair.

"Don't—" he starts, but all that comes out of his mouth next is another moan when I shift my hips, taking him deeper.

I tug at his hair while his strokes become harder, firmer, faster. Neither of us care anymore what this might look like from below. I can't see anything beyond this overwhelm.

"Oh shit," he pants. "Condom."

"No—" I grip him tightly. I don't want to stop now. "It's okay—I just had my period."

He melts into me and keeps thrusting, even harder now. I'm bouncing against the balcony rail with each of his staggering thrusts.

"God, I'm right there Tess."

I almost collapse at the sound of him using my abbreviated name. So, for the first time, I use his. "I am too, Benito," I gasp.

He pauses for a second as though acknowledging that whether we like it later or not, by using each other's first names in such an intimate way, we've crossed a line.

He lifts my right leg and rests it on a ledge then feeds his fingers through my folds. He tugs at my clit and I explode into a million little pieces. I'm vaguely aware that he's growling into my ear, shoving his length to my very edge and emptying himself deep inside me.

When I come around I'm half hanging over the edge of the balcony with Benito's weight across my back. I lift my heavy lids and see a couple of faces turned our way. Neither of them I recognize.

Benito pulls out, still hard, and his semen runs down my thighs. I'm too exhausted to move, so I don't attempt to, even when he disappears and returns a few seconds later with a warm cloth. I hear him drop to his knees, then he wipes the cloth up and down my legs, paying extra attention to my sensitive opening.

He helps me step out of my panties and balls them up with the cloth. Both are tossed into a trash can behind the bar. I'm now naked beneath this napkin masquerading as a dress.

His thick hands grab the tops of my legs and turn me around until I'm facing him. I'm struck with emotion when I look into his eyes.

"Are you okay?" he asks softly.

I nod again. "I'm fine."

"Do you think you'll regret it?"

I step into him, pulling his head into my chest, then I whisper into his hair. "No."

CHAPTER TWENTY-SEVEN

enito

I've never felt more free in my life. It feels as though I've been holding on to something so tightly my bones ache, but being inside this woman has released my grip. I feel free but I don't feel safe.

Until this point, the understanding that she hated me, that nothing could ever come of my infatuation, prevented me from falling. That barrier is now gone. I have no balcony ledge. There's no parachute and there's definitely no soft landing. Contessa Castellano doesn't hate me anymore, and that frightens the life out of me.

The beginning of the end was that very moment when she spread my semen across her chest. *What the fuck?* Everything that came before it was fair game. I loved taking her hate the way I love killing my enemies.

I could wallow in the dark thrill of her loathing the same way I thrive in the sound of my rivals' breaking bones.

She clutches my head to her chest and her heartbeat races through my ear canal. Since I saw her at Gianni's funeral, I haven't been able to get her out of my head. It wasn't just the never-ending legs that made my mouth water, or sleek glossy hair that made my fist ache, it was the scowl, the sass, the unknown reason why she wanted me to go to hell that makes me *so damn hard*. I've spent the last six months trying to piss her off, just so I can get a glimpse of that hatred.

The day she walked into me outside the barbershop, that was the day my intrigue turned into something more. She was so close I could smell the soap she'd used that morning, the detergent her outfit had been washed with. She was so clean, so fresh and so damn perfect. Even her scowl was perfect and I felt it against my thigh when my dick grew a couple inches.

I had no idea the guy was stalking her. He intruded on that moment and that's why I killed him. I wanted more of her sneers and eyerolls—they made me feel so fucking alive—and he was in the way.

Discovering his true motivations was like hitting the fucking jackpot. I had every possible excuse then to stay close to her. No one questioned me when I took the office above the studio; no one arched a brow when I moved in to it full time so that I could be wherever she was—either at Cristiano's or the studio.

And no one would ever suspect I burned down my own house to make that happen.

I stand and lift her up, resting her legs over one arm. She looks softly into my eyes.

"What are you doing?"

"I'm getting you out of here."

"But, what about Paige…"

"She's with Donnie. I'll make sure he takes care of her."

She smiles into my cheek. "I think she'll like that very much."

I carry her to the elevator then select the button for the basement floor. I don't want anyone setting eyes on Contessa when she's wearing no panties, regardless of whether that's visible or not.

"You don't have to carry me," she says. Normally her words would be laced with something deliciously spiteful, but they're warm when they brush my skin.

"I know I don't." The elevator doors open and I carry her into a dark corridor. All the doors to the offices are thankfully closed but I can hear voices continuing the meeting without me, as instructed, behind them. "I want to."

She buries her face into my neck.

"Are you tired?"

"A little."

Her stomach groans and I remember how she seems to live for food. "You're hungry."

She nods timidly.

In that case, I'm taking her to the best restaurant in the city.

We pull up to the loading bay of New York's most discreet and exclusive hotel. I called ahead so I'm pleased to see they've heeded my warning to clear the entire ground floor kitchen so we can pass through unseen.

A back elevator takes us to the penthouse. A doorman is waiting for us, his eyes averted, as briefed. He holds open the door to the penthouse and I slip a hundred into his palm before carrying Contessa over the threshold. I won't ever marry so this is the closest I'll get to carrying my bride into our new life together. Because, little does she know it, but Contessa is mine now, and this is just the beginning.

I lower her feet to the thick pile carpet and she stretches her arms overhead like a cat. I watch her, my knuckle pressed to my lips. She's the most beautiful thing I've ever seen.

She turns to face the dining table in the center of the room and her mouth drops open.

"Is that all for us?"

I walk over to the table and lift silver cloches off the trays. "For you. I already ate."

"I can't eat all of this."

I chuckle darkly. "I don't expect you to, but I didn't know what you'd want so I ordered everything on the menu."

Her eyebrows shoot up her forehead, but she still lifts a plate and helps herself to a bowl of pasta, several helpings of coq au vin and an entire bowl of green salad.

I pull out a chair opposite and rest my arms on each side.

"So, what other clubs do you own?" she says, between mouthfuls.

"I have four. Arena, which you know, Kiki's on the upper east side, The Sawmill in Brooklyn and Cairo's in the East Village."

"Are they all fronts for mafia meeting places?" She flicks a glance my way.

"They're not fronts for mafia meeting places," I reply, a lazy smirk crossing my lips. "They're fronts for other things, actually. But each venue has meeting rooms and we do occasionally host business discussions to which members of the family are invited."

She continues eating, unfazed.

"And you have the barbershop…"

"Yes."

"Do you own any other frontages—sorry, businesses?"

I narrow my eyes considering how I can make her pay for that later, then my face softens. "There is one other business I own, which isn't a front for anything. It's a genuine family business. It was given to me by a friend of Gianni's. It has nothing to do with mafia business, and it means a lot to me."

That gets her attention.

"Oh? What is it?"

"A restaurant in Little Italy. La Trattoria. It's tiny,

and the chef is old-school—barely speaks a word of English—but he's a genius in the kitchen."

Her brow furrows into a frown and her gaze disappears for a second. "I think I know it."

"Yeah?"

"I think Cristiano took us there once."

I cross an ankle over my knee. "Entirely possible. He likes it there." I let my gaze roam her and feel my chest brace. "Did you?"

She's just shoveled a forkful of lettuce into her mouth. "Mm?"

"Did you like my restaurant?"

She stops chewing and lowers her fork. Then she wipes her mouth with a napkin and swallows. Her lashes lift, shyly. "I loved it."

My chest expands so much I have to cough. "Great. I'll take you back there one day."

She coasts a gaze across the remaining food. "I can't eat anymore, but I can't bear to waste all this food."

"It's nothing," I say, waving a hand. "Hotels like this get rid of all that and more every night."

Her eyelids pop open. "That's appalling!"

"You think all these wealthy, skinny people eat everything they're served?" I bite back a grin. "Half of them are filling up in the restroom on lines of coke."

My quip doesn't have the desired result.

"That's even worse!"

She looks around at all the beautiful dishes. "I can't just leave all of this. I wouldn't be able to live with myself."

I lower my leg and drop my elbows onto my knees while I study her. "So what do you want to do?"

She inhales deeply then puffs out a breath. "Can we have the kitchen pack everything up and give it to the homeless guys a few blocks over?"

I'm not sure I heard correctly. "You want to give all this food to the homeless guys down the street?"

She frowns as though she's second-guessing herself. "It's the right thing to do."

"Okay…" I say, slowly. "I'll just make a call."

Three minutes later, a waiter is delivering some cardboard food containers to the room and helping us portion up whole meals. Tess commandeers the entire operation while I stand back and watch. I'd always assumed that because her daddy owned the big port Savero was obsessed with, she and her sisters didn't want for anything. I suppose I assumed she was spoiled.

Fucking hot and fucking annoying, but a little bit spoiled.

How wrong I've been.

"Okay, I think that's all of it." She looks up at me with a timid smile. "Um…" Her gaze darts between me and the waiter. "How will we get this to them? I can't go out dressed like this."

My gaze drops to the thin stain of her dress. She's damn right. I'm not *letting* her go out like that. For a start, she'll freeze. But mostly, she'll be inadvertently responsible for the death of any pedestrian we encounter along the way who dares look at her bare, beautiful legs in that dress.

I tap two fingers against my lips while my focus drags over her body. My voice turns gruff. "I'll have one of my men take it for you."

"Are you sure? I don't want to inconvenience anyone—"

I bite the inside of my cheek. "You're not inconveniencing anyone. Every second they're standing outside this hotel doing nothing, they're getting paid handsomely."

She flashes a shy glance toward the waiter who feigns interest in the wall. "They're not doing *nothing*, Benito. They're looking out for you."

Something expands inside my chest. "And you," I correct her. Then I step forward and take her chin between my finger and thumb, tilting her gaze to mine. "But here's the thing…" I dip my face until her breaths brush my nose. "I'm more than capable of looking out for the both of us, baby."

Her pupils bloom and her cheeks flush. I can tell my words traveled to a sensitive part of her. I turn to the waiter. "Give these bags to one of my men and tell them I sent you. Explain exactly where the food is to be delivered. And then bring me an outfit Miss Castellano can change into. Anything you've got." *Anything to replace that scrap of fabric that leaves nothing to the imagination.* "And make it a size four."

The waiter stands to attention. "Yes sir, I'll do it right now."

I release her chin and she swallows as the door closes. Her bottom lip shivers before she bites down on it with her teeth. "I guess you know women's bodies pretty well."

I stroke my hand around her nape and push my fingers through her sleek, dark hair, tugging her toward me. "I know yours."

She scowls. "You've only had your hands on it twice—the time in your apartment doesn't count. *Twice*, Benito."

I fist a handful of her hair and smile. "Yeah, but I've watched you for *six months*. I know what fucking size you are."

I hold her stare, daring her to argue but she doesn't. She just lifts herself onto her toes and presses her sweet little mouth to mine. Oh God, this simple soft touch *undoes* me, and I have to force myself to pull away.

Only a minute or two later, the waiter returns with a bag containing a pair of gray sweatpants and a t-shirt. Luckily for him, he's left by the time we've opened it and discovered the contents. I might have wrung his fucking neck. My phone rings before I can go after him. It's Beppe with a report on the rogue soldiers in Newark.

I keep it short, not wanting anything to cut into this time I have with Tess. When I locate her in the bedroom, she's already changed into the outfit from hell—or, more likely, the outfit from the depths of some lost and found laundry bin. Fresh hate for the cretin who thought this would be acceptable fills my mouth. Without saying a word, I turn and leave the room.

"Where are you going?" she calls after me, and I

don't miss the thread of fear in her tone. I must look ready to kill someone.

"To run you a bath."

"Why? Do I smell?"

I walk back to her wiping a smile from my face with a calloused thumb. When she tilts her face up toward me I have to fight to keep my lips from *consuming* her.

"Tess," I say, with gentle seriousness, "I made you crawl across a floor. I fucked you over a balcony and filled you with my come. I managed to get you dressed in some cheap sweats that belong to someone else and possibly haven't been washed..."

Her eyes round, her lips part and her pupils widen. Each time she blinks, a shot of hot blood is mainlined to my dick.

"You deserve perfection. Let me give it to you."

I leave her standing, speechless, in the center of the room while I run her a bath, then I lead her to it, help her undress and leave her to soak while I make a few calls.

First up, Cristiano.

"Hey…" No capacity for pleasantries because I know where they'll lead and I'm not in the mood for being teased over a girl. "Is Trilby with you?"

Cristiano: "Yeah."

"Can I talk to her?"

"Everything okay?"

"Everything's fine, but I have a message to pass on."

Trilby takes the phone. "Benny? What's going on? Have you seen Tess?"

I hear Cristiano groan in the background.

"Yes. She's with me. She's safe. Can you let your father know?"

"Of course. Where are you?"

"The city," I reply. If Cristiano finds out I've booked us into the most expensive hotel in Manhattan—into the penthouse no less—I'll never hear the end of it. "She'll be home Monday."

"In *three days*?"

"Yeah." That's how long I'm keeping her. "Anyway, that was all. Thanks Tril."

I hang up before she can interrogate me any further. Next up, the hotel concierge.

"Signor Bernadi, what can I do for you?"

"You can do a damn sight better than some tatty sweats for my girlfriend," I bite out. "Get me twenty *stunning* outfits for a woman—all designer, all size four. By morning." I remember Contessa's palette of choice. "And make them all black."

I hang up and stare at the phone. Did I just say *girlfriend*? The fuck?

Why?

My back thuds against the wall as I try to decipher how I feel about what I just called her. I've never had a girlfriend before. I've never *wanted* one, for God's sake. Aren't people supposed to have conversations about that kind of thing? Come to a mutual agreement? How the hell do I know?

My breaths slow as I taste the word on my tongue. It's not all that bad. It's not *pungent*. Then I imagine if

Tess weren't my girlfriend. That would make her a free agent—available. And she is not available. She's mine.

I bite down on a silent growl. She's fucking *mine*.

When I return to the bathroom, my breath escapes me. Contessa is sitting up, covered in a mass of bubbles, shaving her legs with a razor. Screw the crawling. *This* is possibly the sexiest thing I've ever seen. I stare at her, unable to tear my eyes from her soapy skin and slippery curves.

"Where did you find that?" I rasp, nodding to the razor.

She doesn't look up, which means she knows I've been standing in the doorway watching her for a full minute. "Cabinet," she smiles. It's then I notice wet footprints across the carpet.

"Thought I told you to relax."

She lifts her lashes slowly. "I want to look nice for you."

My chest expands and my jaw unhinges. "You always look nice." I kneel down by the tub. "I don't care if you have hair on your legs."

She purses her lips. "I do."

She drags the blade up her soft skin one last time, rinses it in the water then rests it on a soap dish. Then she faces me, a blush crawling up her cheeks. "Can I get out now?"

"One second." I stand and pull a fluffy towel from the rail and hold it out for her to step into, then I gently pat her dry, all over. There's a guest robe hanging in the closet so I fetch that and wrap it around her.

I notice her glance toward a tray of oils and lotions.

"Can I choose one for you?" I ask.

"Um…" she looks unsure. "Okay."

"Go into the master suite and sit on the bed."

She does as I say while I peruse the various bottles and creams. I uncork a few and smell the fragrances, settling on one that promises to seduce the senses – a heady mix of Rose, Jasmine and Neroli. I carry it to the bedroom and try not to react at the way she's draped herself over the comforter, the robe splayed to the sides, showing off her flawless skin and lean limbs.

"Are you trying to ruin me, Contessa?"

She shakes her head slowly. "I want *you* to ruin *me*."

Okay, so my dick just swelled to twice its size.

I'm still fully clothed as I prowl up the bed and straddle her with my knees. Her eyes sparkle with challenge.

"You're hardly wearing this, brat," I say, giving a cursory glance to the bathrobe. "Let's just take the whole thing off, shall we?"

She hooks her eyes on me and wiggles out of the bathrobe, tossing it to the side of the bed. "We're back to 'brat' I see."

I tip some of the liquid into my hand and rub my palms together to warm it. "Well, if the shoe fits…" I smirk. "Now lay back."

She lays flat on the bed and I place my oiled hands on her shoulders. A long languid sigh rolls off her tongue and her lids close. I stroke the oil down her arms, kneading her tight muscles. She must be dehydrated because her skin is soaking up the oil faster than I can apply it. I move my fingers to her collarbone and massage the taut chest muscles, then—fuck it—I just dribble the oil across her breasts and stomach. She hums her approval so I set to work. I rub the oil gently into her breasts, quickly learning how she likes them to be handled—what movements earn a sharp intake of breath or an exquisite sigh.

I then move to her stomach feeling the curve of her ribs and the dip of her muscles. I bypass her pelvic area, placing a chaste kiss on the small mound of hair, then work the oil into her legs. Only once I've coated her front completely do I order her to roll onto her stomach. She obliges, then turns to look over her shoulder.

"I think I prefer 'girlfriend'," she says.

My entire body stills, my hands paused on her shoulder blades. "You heard me."

"Yes," she says in a whisper. "I liked it."

My cocks grinds against her ass and relief fills me. "You want to be my girlfriend?"

"I think I'd prefer it to being your brat."

I bite my lip and rub myself up against her. "You'll always be my brat, Tess."

She smiles then buries her head into the comforter. *Well, I guess that's the mutual agreement box ticked.*

I coat her in the oil and massage it into her skin, but I don't take my time about it. My cock knows where it wants to be, and I don't want to waste another minute. I unzip my slacks, part her thighs with my knee and push myself inside her. She releases a long, heavy whimper and her walls clamp around my dick, tightening my balls.

She lifts her bottom, taking my cock deeper, and a warmth drenches me in tingles. I lower my stomach to her back and settle in, driving into her slow and deep until she's begging me with her breaths.

I flex my hips, hitting that tender spot inside her over and over until she screams into the pillow. Then I shove forward one last time, spilling myself into her thoroughly. I rest my forehead between her shoulder blades and release a blissed-out moan. "Yeah, you're my girlfriend."

The words come out hoarse and fractured and foreign, but they taste fucking pretty on my tongue.

CHAPTER TWENTY-EIGHT

ontessa

Four of us walk through the security gate into the Di Santo residence, dressed in our Sunday best, but each for very different reasons. Papa is heading to a business meeting straight after lunch; Allegra is determined to outshine Cristiano's late mother's second cousin; and Bambi has discovered fashion magazines and the teenage affliction that is raging hormones and rollercoaster self-esteem, which of course, can only be tempered by Abercrombie & Fitch.

I'm wearing my usual palette of black, the dress McQueen and the heels vintage Chanel, but the reasons for my efforts are different again.

These days, black feels authentic. I don't feel like I'm dressing a part; this is genuinely me. I'm pretty dark, apparently. But I'm not in my daily American

Apparel uniform; I'm wearing designer because I want to look sexy and I want to impress a certain consigliere.

I hold back behind Allegra and Bambi, only half-listening to Allegra's monologue about Cristiano's hostile yet strangely charismatic family, because Papa's work call is also infiltrating my consciousness. Ever since Trilby told me his business is only safe now because of Cristiano, my interest in it feels weightier.

But, the real reason I'm hiding behind my aunt and sister is because I know Bernadi is going to be here and I have no idea how to be around him in public. No one knows we're having a thing and I don't particularly want word getting out just yet. If Papa and Cristiano found out Benito and I had slept together, they'd force us to marry, and I don't want anyone to be put in that position. After I was put in the position of feeling obliged to give my virginity up, I know how that feels and the resentment it can cause.

Cristiano has arranged a get-together with his family and ours, to encourage us to "get to know one another" but after the car crash that was the party for Trilby's engagement to Cristiano's late brother, Savero, I don't have high hopes for this lunch.

The sound of exuberant female voices reaches us before we round the corner to the terrace.

Allegra mutters something under her breath.

"Now, remember, we're doing this for Trilby," I remind our aunt.

We walk along the footpath crossing the lawn and I search frantically for Trilby or Cristiano. Aunt Allegra isn't best known for her patience or tact, and both have the power to derail Trilby's relationship with her soon-to-be in-laws.

Unfortunately, my view is restricted to that of three exuberantly curved olive-skinned women with bleached yellow hair—one around Aunt Allegra's age, the other two late-thirties perhaps—a rotund man with a glistening sheen on his forehead and a large scotch in his hand, and two younger men I don't remember seeing before. They're both dark-haired, of Italian blood and as sworn in as the man whose house we're gathering at. It's obvious in the way they stand, the way their eyes dance over our bodies as Bambi and I approach, and the way one hand nurses a single malt in a lowball, while the other rests casually in their pockets, shielding any .45s from view.

Nervousness skitters down my spine at the thought of Benito seeing that look in their eyes. While the last three days have suggested many things to me regarding our relationship, the most prominent is that I'm not anyone else's for the taking.

We didn't leave the hotel room once. We slept, we talked, we ate, but mostly, we explored each other.

The more time I spent with Bernadi's naked body, the more I learned about him. I learned that his cut muscles and defined form are a result of daily workouts, usually in his own house but while it's under reconstruction, Cristiano's. I learned that trailing my fingers down the side of his ribs earns me a sharp spank, while pressing my lips to his neck sends him into a mindless frenzy.

I learned that he hates eggs but eats three every day for protein. And that he loves chips so much I have to hide them so he doesn't inhale the entire bag.

I learned that he can, and seemingly does, manage to function on four hours sleep, and that he can hold three phone calls at once discussing a varied mix of topics including architectural engineering, the legal ramifications of bribing government officials, and the intricacies of vehicle maintenance—specifically *my* vehicle and my particular brand of maintenance, which is basically none at all.

I learned that once he's made a decision about something, or someone, he doesn't retract it easily, my car being a case in point. The second he decided it was now his problem, my protests fell on completely deaf ears as he orchestrated an army of people to fetch it, fix it, upgrade it and not let me anywhere near it until the former three stages were complete.

Despite everything I did learn, there are still things I didn't learn, and not for a lack of trying. When I asked him how he became the consigliere to the Di Santo family, his gaze darkened and he changed the subject. He spoke fondly about Gianni, Cristiano's late father and former don, but shut down the conversation when I asked him how they first met. And when I asked why he'd inked his entire chest with defensive depictions of electric fencing, snake bites and poison ivy, he threw on a T-shirt. I pouted like an actual spoiled child. So, naturally, I'm not going to ask *that* question again.

What I absolutely do know, however, is it is entirely possible to fall head over heels in total lust with an enemy within seventy-two hours, and discover erogenous zones I never knew I had. I don't have much to compare him to, but he knew his way around me like he had a secret map, and his focus over the three days was squarely on discovering how many ways and how many times he could make me come. I was so exhausted when he returned me home, I skipped two dance classes and didn't leave my room for a further three days.

The five of them form a human barrier between the lawn and the terrace. But, fortunately, Trilby delicately pushes her way through to envelope each of us in a warm, relieved hug.

"I'm so glad you're here," she murmurs into my ear.

"I didn't expect there to be so many people." The terrace is thick with the scent of expensive perfume and cologne.

She pulls back and rolls her eyes toward Allegra. "*Big* extended family," she says through a smile.

Just as Trilby wraps her arms around our aunt, two of the women approach us.

"Trilby?"

My sister looks around and beams politely at the older woman. "Yes?"

"I'm Bianca, Cristiano's aunt—his mother's side."

"Oh!" Trilby gives Bianca's hand a soft shake. "It's

wonderful to finally meet you. Cristiano has told me lots about you and your family. Is Isabella h—"

"Hi!" The younger woman, who looks a little closer to Trilby's age, steps forward. "I'm Isabella. We've connected on Insta but, wow, you're even prettier in the flesh."

I glance sideways just in time to see a soft blush creep up my sister's cheeks. "Thank you. And so are you," she smiles.

"How are the wedding plans coming along? I hear the hotel is absolutely gorgeous."

"Oh it is," Trilby gushes. "Our sister Sera is doing her hospitality training there. I hear your wedding to Augie's nephew was beautiful. I was hoping to get a few tips from you."

While Trilby and Isabella talk weddings, Allegra turns to Cristiano's aunt. It seems the good natured banter stopped at Trilby and Cristiano's cousin—the atmosphere that has suddenly descended over the two aunts is decidedly frosty.

I make an excuse about needing a glass of water and leave them to their differences.

After Bambi and I have dissected the outfit choices of nearly every guest, Bambi heads off to find Allegra and Trilby takes her place.

"Who's that?" I ask, nodding toward a woman who seems to have caught Papa's attention. She's around Allegra's age with long dark hair softly curled and a beautiful figure wrapped in a conservatively tailored dress.

Trilby's gaze narrows. "That's Nicolò's mother."

"She and Papa seem to be getting along." My voice is flat because I don't know how to feel about the idea of Papa 'getting along' with any woman after Mama. "Is she married?"

"She's widowed," Trilby enunciates carefully.

We both watch as Nicolò's mother says something that must be funny because Papa's face lights up and he shakes his head. My chest aches as I grapple with the turmoil of emotions the sight has stirred up in me.

Trilby turns back to me with a sigh and slides her fingers around my hand. "It's nice that someone can make him smile."

I swallow and give a brief nod. Of course I want Papa to be happy—I just wasn't expecting another woman to come on the scene. I know I'm getting ahead of myself; they've only just met. I shake the concern from my shoulders and straighten.

"I'm going to go freshen up."

"Sure," she smiles. "Come find me when you're done."

I arch a brow. "Isn't this your opportunity to get to know your new in-laws?"

She chews on her bottom lip. "Fine. Then come *rescue* me in thirty."

"Gotcha." I give her a wink and wind my way through various relatives-to-be and into the house.

My mind must be someplace else because as I walk through the double doors to the entrance hall, I don't see a figure coming the other way until I've crashed against its chest.

A deep, rasping voice wraps around my ears. "I thought looking through gaps in doors was your thing, Castellano. How did you not see me coming?"

My gaze crawls upward, taking in a snug-fitting black shirt, thick and tan neck, and a jawline so sharp it could cut a steak. My breath escapes as I reach his eyes. They're black from this angle and weighted down with the promise of possession.

"I wasn't looking where I was going," I reply, breathily. "I was thinking about other things."

Benito doesn't budge and his hands remain firmly settled in the pockets of his slacks.

"What 'other things'?"

The intensity in his eyes makes me blink away but that doesn't stop a full flush of heat from crawling up my throat.

"Oh, you know…" I shrug. "*Ice*." I could kick myself because that isn't the word I had in my head.

I flick my gaze back to him nervously, and he's chewing the inside of his cheek.

He lifts a curled fist to his lips. "Ice?"

I nod. "Mm-hm."

"You like *ice*?"

"I do," I reply.

"Interesting." A glimmer of something squeezes through his narrowed eyes. "*How* do you like your ice?"

I blink. "What do you mean?"

He pulls his bottom lip between his teeth, his gaze all sexy and distracting. He lifts a shoulder. "Do you like it crushed? Cubed? Or just, you know, as it comes?"

I swallow. My mouth and throat are so dry I'll take any form of ice right now.

"Melting," I say. "I like my ice melting."

His eyes widen a fraction, then he nods. "Noted."

My skin feels like a livewire, getting more charged the longer I stand here, so I smile and go to walk past him, but long fingers curl around my wrist pulling me to a halt at his shoulder.

His chin dips but his gaze remains on something in the distance. His voice rolls like a tropical thunderstorm. "You look like a *fucking* goddess. Stay where I can see you."

My entire body vibrates with his compliment, chased by the electric current of his command. I can't find the words to respond so I simply nod once and feel his fingers slip from my skin.

As I walk to the restroom I have to cradle that hand in my other, purely to convince myself the skin he grazed wasn't singed by the contact. My heart is fluttering so wildly that when I reach the restroom, lock the door and stare back at my reflection, I can't remember why I'm standing over the faucet.

I cool my palms beneath the running water and press my fingertips to my temples. My pulse is racing and the base of my glistening collarbone rises and falls with every breath.

After a couple of minutes I walk back out to the terrace, allowing my gaze to search only for my family. When it settles on Allegra's clenched brow I sigh with relief.

"Everything okay?" I ask her. "You look like you just swallowed detergent."

"A large measure, I'd say," Bambi mutters under her breath.

Allegra's gaze darts to Cristiano's second cousin Giulia and I pan my eyes toward Bambi.

"She just came over here asking what we think of her family residence," Allegra hisses between pursed lips. "This place isn't hers; it's Cristiano's."

"Well, technically, it's the Di Santo residence…" I start, clearly unappreciative of the nuances at play.

"Exactly. Which she *isn't*."

"Isn't she Cristiano's cousin?" Bambi asks in a newly adopted, not unlikeable bored tone.

"*Second* cousin," Allegra corrects. "She's barely even related. So to come over here acting as though she's the lady of the manor… Well, it's rude. And besides, this place is as good as Trilby's," Allegra finishes, rolling back her shoulders and throwing a glare in the cousin's direction.

"Trilby and *Cristiano*'s," I clarify.

Allegra sips her wine and resumes her glaring with a distracted "hmm."

I turn to Bambi who gives a rundown on everyone who has and hasn't yet introduced themselves, but I don't register a thing because my body has heated like a furnace. The hair across the nape of my neck prickles. My skin dances like I have a fever.

When I turn my head, Benito is standing at the opposite end of the terrace, not even looking my way. He has his back turned, his focus on a conversation with Cristiano's underboss, Augie. He looks relaxed with a hand resting in the pocket of his slacks and the other cradling a whiskey, which he sips in between nods and spoken words.

"At least he isn't staring at you." Bambi's voice cuts through my reverie like an ice pick.

"What?"

"Bernadi." She nods toward him. "Last time we were all here he was staring at you from across the table, remember?"

"Oh, um, yeah." My head is spinning, not from the recollection but because my feelings for him now are a world away from what they were then, but I've no idea how to tell that to Bambi.

"And you hate him because he sent Federico's family away," she continues.

I swallow, searching for words, but her expression seems to retreat.

"Actually, wait…" She pops open her purse and pulls out an envelope. "This arrived at the house for you. The postmark says California. Isn't that where Federico moved to?"

"Yes." My voice sounds like it's been drained of moisture as I take the envelope and turn it in my fingers.

When I recognize the handwriting, my heartbeat rises up to the base of my throat.

"Do you know anyone else in that part of the country?" she presses.

"No," I reply, breathless. I rip open the envelope. "No one."

With one hand pressed flat against my chest, I read.

> Dear Tess,
>
> I'm sorry it's taken me so long to reply. I read every single one of your letters, but I didn't want to reply until I had something of substance to say. I sent them all back because I'd started to lose hope, but I have it now.
>
> I promised you I would ruin Bernadi, and I've finally found a way. He had no right to threaten my father the way he did, or ruin the years of work my family put into our business. He will get what he deserves, I can assure you. Soon he'll know how it feels to lose everything dear to him. I know what his Achilles heel is, Tess, and I'm going to ruin it.
>
> I just have to confess to one thing, and you won't like it. I know you hate the Marchesi's for what they did to your

mother, but they are still the most formidable force against the Di Santo's. For me to end Bernadi for good, I need to work with his enemy. I hope you can forgive me for associating with them. The Di Santos are the ones who've kept us apart, Tess. They need to pay.

I'll be in touch again very soon, but in the meantime, know that I love you, Tess, and I want you back in my arms where you belong. Yes, we are friends, but we are also more than that. You said so yourself in your letters. I'm coming home to get you.

Fed x

It's Federico. After all these years and all those unanswered letters, he's finally written back. My chest releases a heaviness I've been carrying around for too long. All my thoughts about him have been dark and foreboding. Either he doesn't want me anymore, or he's dead. Neither of those things are true and I can't wrap my head around it.

It's clear my earlier letters haven't offended him, and the relief is immense, but then it's quickly replaced by guilt, because I meant what I said: I only ever saw him as a friend.

My head throbs as confused thoughts collide behind my eyes.

I read the note several times but still the words don't sink in. The handwriting is definitely his but matured. The tone and inflections are all him. Little things I'd forgotten but now come flying back at me. All I know is they're weighty with promises I no longer want him to keep.

I look up and feel reassured that Benito's back is still turned. I didn't bring a purse with me so I slide the folded note beneath the collar of my dress and into my bra, and plan to read it later when I'm alone. Maybe I can write him back, somehow explain my change of heart. It doesn't sound like he knows who Trilby is engaged to or that I'm practically a part of the Di Santo's already.

I don't have the capacity to think about it now. Not when another relative of Cristiano's is making a beeline in our direction. And not when I glance away briefly, only to be met by a renewed presence and a stare that is loaded, heated and so unbearably electric it takes my breath away.

I politely shake the hands of yet another Di Santo cousin, who seems perfectly nice and welcoming, before excusing myself to get a drink. My throat is parched despite the gallons of water I drink every day.

Waiting in line, my nape tingles as a hot breath lowers onto it. "There's a wine cellar just inside the entrance. Get your sweet ass down the steps right now." Then the heat vanishes, leaving only a shiver of anticipation in its wake. Then the taste of panic glides across my tongue. I didn't even know this place *had* a wine cellar.

I inhale a whole glass of water then cast my gaze to the ground, avoiding any eye contact as I make my way back inside. The evening is starting to close in, casting the house in shadows, so I push the note further inside my bra as I follow a warm glow through the entrance hall toward the back of the house.

Behind the staircase is a door, slightly ajar, a shard of light seeping through the gap. I look left and right to make sure no one has seen me, then I open it and step through onto a small set of stairs. The door closes softly and I take extra care walking in my tall heels down the steps, landing at the bottom on a concrete floor.

I'm standing in a reasonably large room, surrounded by columns and rows of dark bottles, all encased behind glass doors. A figure steps out of the shadows and my heart races like I just injected a bunch of steroids into it. "Come here, goddess."

I take three steps toward Benito then he closes the gap impatiently, slamming his lips onto mine with an urgency that shocks me to the bones. His tongue swipes across mine, tasting every line and curve of my mouth. I'm bent backwards, the air squeezed from my lungs. A beautiful, addictive pain radiates from my chest where he's crushing against me.

When a small note of desperation curls up my throat, he pulls back for a brief moment, mutters something about need, then crashes down on me again.

I'm ushered backward until my spine hits glass and a large hand grabs a handful of thigh and kneads its way up until it reaches my underwear.

Feeling how blood-scorchingly *soaked* it is, a growl rolls through his chest and tunnels into my body.

He roars between clenched teeth, "I told you I wouldn't be able to stop."

His rage sounds bottomless, and hot with terror. Yet, I can't pull away. I nip at his lips and claw at his shirt like a naughty kitten, needing his heat on my tongue and trembling muscles beneath my paws.

One hand mauls the neckline of my dress, dragging it over one breast. My heart stutters. Fed's letter… I'm about to protest when Benito's other hand tears my panties clean off. He shoves them roughly into his pocket then returns his hand to my heat and only then does he seem to breathe. He kneads my breast and pussy in tandem until my body doesn't know what to rock into so I cling to his lips, nipping them and sucking as he moans low, desperate curses that don't make any sense. The note pales in significance as he overtakes me with a raw passion.

We're wound up tightly in a ball of madness, unraveling with each ground heel of a palm, and with each thrust of a thigh against his erection.

I rub my leg into him mindlessly until he bites my jaw drawing a yelp. "Stop it. You'll make me come."

My eyelids shiver, faintly.

"I want you to. Fuck me… please," I whimper.

He slides three thick fingers inside me, tearing breaths from my lungs.

"Not here," he growls, returning his tongue to my mouth.

I lick it ravenously, my focus scattered, my senses overstimulated and burning.

My back slams against the glass with each hard fuck of his hand and I cry into his mouth, helplessly on the edge. The sound of rattling glass and slickened flesh drives me to the end of sanity and I orgasm with unbridled force around his knuckles.

He continues to fuck me with his fingers and swallow my gasps while he presses my vibrating body between his chest and the glass wine cabinet. Only when I've stopped trembling does he remove his hand and his mouth from my two plundered openings. He gently rights my dress, easing out any creases with calloused fingertips.

He stands back and drags his gaze over my quivering body.

"Fuck, yeah," he drawls. "Only *I* get to make a dirty wet mess of my goddess."

I almost pass out at his words. I love the possessiveness in his slow, lazy gaze, and the helplessness in his solid cock, obvious beneath the clipped lines of his slacks.

I'm addicted to this man, this *feeling*.

Then his tone turns sharp.

"Get up the stairs, Contessa, before I commit a fucking crime."

My breath feels heavy and languid. I rise up to my tiptoes and brush my lips across his. "I didn't think you cared about crime. You certainly kill enough people to make me question your... *conviction*."

He doesn't blink. He doesn't breathe. He just parts his lips and speaks in a low monotone growl.

"Get up those stairs before my cock gets any damned harder and I fuck you *to death*."

CHAPTER TWENTY-NINE

enito

She blinks once, inhales sharply, then *runs* up those wooden steps. And thank God she does because I'm *this* close to taking her and pulling her apart whether she consents or not.

I rest my damp palm against a glass door and breathe heavily until my pulse slows. Then I allow my eye to be drawn to the folded note on the floor. I reach down and pick it up, confirming it is the note I saw her stuff into her bra when she didn't think I was watching.

Of course I was watching.

I watch her all the fucking time.

Seeing her press the piece of paper to her breasts like that just gave me one more reason to get her down here. There was no way I was going to last much longer without feeling her skin against mine.

I unfold the note, lean a shoulder against the glass, and read.

At first the sentences swim and I put it down to the fact my body is trying to absorb the unused come my balls had readied to plough into Contessa. But the more I read the same lines, the clearer they become, until all the blood that has drained from my cock has flooded my eyeballs.

I force myself to stay in the cellar for another thirty minutes. I need to calm down before I see her again.

She's in contact with Federico Falconi. The boy who took her virginity. The same virginity she blames *me* for having lost. And they're plotting to ruin me?

A small voice in the back of my head sings "I told you so," but I physically try to shake the words away. My arms twitch with the urge to smash my curled fists into the coolers but I dig my fingernails into my palms to distract myself.

It can't be true. Contessa wouldn't do that to me. She *wants* me. I can still smell and taste the proof on my fingers. And even if it is all an act—an incredibly fucking convincing one—and she is pretending to be into me while colluding with Falconi to bring me down somehow, she surely wouldn't drag her sister's fiancé into it, would she?

My bones are solidly against this one. They know this doesn't make any sense, but my muscles—and more importantly, the ones shaped and forever stained by memory—are itchy with doubt.

The closeness we've cultivated over the past couple

of weeks means nothing. I've been betrayed by people I was closer to for a hell of a lot longer.

I swallow repeatedly as the extent of my foolishness sinks in. *She lied to me*. Not only did she blame me for losing her virginity—something she willingly gave away—but she's been in contact with Falconi all along. And all this despite me telling her the truth about his father. She's chosen to believe *him* over *me*.

I don't register anything as I leave the wine cellar—not the change in temperature as I emerge into the cool summer air, nor the descent of nightfall drawing shadows from the foliage. I don't register the words of friends and colleagues as I make my way to the gates. When I'm over the other side, a fence separating me from the woman I was falling hard and fast for, I take out my burner.

A few calls to associates in California and one to an informant for the Marchesi's confirms Federico *is* coming to town and that he has indeed been in contact with the Marchesi's. But, unusually for the rival mob, the Marchesi's are keeping a few things close to their chests. Still, it's enough to convince me of the authenticity of Tess and Falconi's correspondence.

I ignore the dull ache in the pit of my stomach that seems to be growing with each new realization and make one last call, then I return to the apartment above the dance studio. And I wait.

Exactly twenty-four hours after I found the note on the floor of the wine cellar, a familiar figure emerges from the studio below. I saw her enter two hours ago and I've been sitting at the window, watching, waiting and counting the minutes ever since.

My gaze glides across the room slowly until it lands on the bottle I collected in the early hours of this morning. I stand and unwrap the cloth that came with it, and squeeze several drops of the liquid into the fabric. Then, grabbing my keys, I close the door behind me and make my way down to the street.

I feast my eyes on her from the back, torn between needing to do this and wanting to grab her ass in both hands, spin her around and kiss the living daylights out of her. The fact I'm even thinking of the latter makes me pick up the pace, my silent footsteps closing in faster.

It's dusk so the dark hasn't quite settled and I can tell she's jumpy. When a car alarm sets off over the other side of the street, she goes to turn. In a beat I have the cloth pressed to her face, my other hand holding the back of her head. Her arms fly out, flailing ineffectively as I hold her firm. As she starts to wilt, I remove my hand from her head and catch her just before she hits the ground. Then I scoop her up, slide her into the back of the waiting car and climb into the front.

The driver doesn't blink an eye.

"Where to, sir?"

I interlock my fingers and stretch out my knuckles, relishing the cracks. "The club."

CHAPTER THIRTY

Contessa

My head is pounding. Blood is coursing through my veins, chased by adrenaline, making me feel delirious. I can only open my eyes a fraction, and when I do get a glimpse beyond my lids, everywhere is black as night. And I have no idea if it is indeed night time because I don't know how long I've been knocked out for.

My awareness comes back in fragments. First, of my limited sight; second of my restricted movement. My hands are tied behind my back. When I try to move them, sharp ties bite into the skin. I don't know how long I've been restrained like this but my shoulders already ache painfully from the unnatural position. My feet are tied, not together, but to a chair—two separate chair legs. And my mouth is immobile because something has been taped over it.

I realize with encroaching dread, I've been kidnapped, to be used no doubt for leverage with the Di Santo family. Why else would anyone want me? Even my stalker didn't have a good reason for wanting to abduct me—he was simply insane.

My heart is banging against my ribcage because as much as I naturally try to make light of every situation, there really is no more doomed a situation than this one. The mafia don't make friends or do deals. They make threats and do lasting damage, of the homicide variety. I won't make it out of whatever place this is alive. The blood I did have running through me sinks to my toes, making me lightheaded. Then I hear a door close and long, firm footsteps heading toward me.

I start to hyperventilate. Knowing something of my fate is one thing, but not being able to see it coming is a torture unto itself.

I squeeze my eyes closed and pray for Benito to find me. When he finds out someone has drugged me and tied me up in some damp, disgusting basement... I shudder. He will kill them.

All my awareness is tunneled through my ears—they're the only reliable sense I have right now. Something wooden is dragged across the floor and placed in front of me. Then I feel warmth at the side of my face as someone tugs at the knot in the blindfold.

I have to blink repeatedly to get used to the change in light, but it doesn't take me long to recognize the person sitting in front of me. It's the one person I've been more intimate with than anyone else in my life. It's the man who only a few days ago called me his *girlfriend*. But now, as he glares at me like he'll hate me until my dying breath, it's the one person I suddenly feel most afraid of in the world.

A tide of confusion swells and ebbs in my stomach. *Is this a joke?* I search his face for some suggestion he's still playing some weird game, but I draw a blank.

His eyes are black. *So black.* And ice cold. His brow is furrowed, casting the whole of his face in shadow. Even though he's sitting calmly, his knees apart and his forearms resting on them, his spine is straight, his breaths steady, the movement of his fingers as he cracks his knuckles, impeccably controlled. There's no warmth to him at all. In fact, his presence makes me feel as though I've been dropped into a tub of ice and held under while I gasp for air.

I suck a terrified breath in through my nose and try to shuffle the chair backward. Benito watches my repeated poor effort at moving out of his space, then he leans forward, grasps the seat between each of my thighs, and pulls me back to him as though I weigh nothing more than a rose petal.

I try to cry out in the hopes he gives up this horrible act, but the thick tape across my mouth pins my lips together making my words senseless.

He gives a small shake of head. "Scream all you want. We're thirty feet below the ground. No one will hear you."

Then he reaches forward and pulls the tape off my mouth. The soft skin of my lips *burns*.

I clench my teeth together. "Then why bother taping my mouth at all?"

He tips his head back slightly and regards me. "I don't know how much of that stuff you breathed in so it's possible you could have come round while I was getting you here."

"And where's 'here'?"

His lips quirk into a cruel smile. "Oh Tess, you know I can't tell you that. It would spoil all the fun."

"If this is your idea of fun, there's no wonder you're single." I'm shaking with fear but I can't stop the smart comments coming out of my mouth.

He wipes his smile away with a curled fist.

I glance around the space. It's a large room, empty but for a few boxes stacked in one corner. I try to read the logos to see if they'll give me any clue as to where I am, but they're too far away and it's too dark to see clearly. What I can see, though, is a dark, crimson stain on the floor about six feet away. I almost wretch. This must be where Cristiano's men bring their victims to torture confessions out of.

"This isn't funny, Benito. I don't want to play this game."

He tips his head to one side and his eyes dance with morbid amusement. "Game? This isn't a game, Contessa. At least, not one that I would have started."

I narrow my eyes as if that might help me make sense of his riddle. "At what point do you bring me up to speed on why I'm here?" I sigh heavily, hoping for dramatic, but the air shivers too much as I breathe it out.

"I was wondering when you might ask that." He stands and walks around the back of the chair. Despite his air of calm control, his fists are clenched and his jaw ticks as he grinds down on his teeth.

"But first, can I just say…" He uncurls his fists and turns his body to face mine, then brings his palms together in a slow *clap… clap… clap.* "Congratulations, Contessa."

I frown and gulp down damp, frigid air.

He laughs bitterly and clasps his hands together. "You had me completely fooled."

What?

He shakes his head again. "I even thought your feelings for me were genuine, but I was wrong, wasn't I?"

He rests his forearms on the back of his chair and glares at me.

"What are you talking about?" I whisper. I feel a tsunami of dread fill up my core. I don't think he's playing around.

"You and Federico…" His tone cuts through the words like glass. The mention of my childhood best friend doesn't feel right in this stark, empty room.

"You had me believe it was just some teenage crush on his part, that my actions forced you to sleep with him, and if you could turn back time, you wouldn't have given him your virginity."

"It's t—"

He cuts me off. "But that's not *exactly* how it happened, is it?"

My pulse races through my eardrums. I've no idea what Benito is getting at but his weighted stare and aggressive stance are scaring me.

"You don't regret that night at all. You would have slept with him even if he hadn't asked."

I start to shake my head but he *bellows* at me. "It's NOT a question."

I jump with fright, my eyes so wide they hurt. I don't understand what's going on. I've never seen this side of Benito before and I'm *terrified*.

He straightens and starts pacing the floor. My gaze follows him side-to-side until he stops and looks over his shoulder at me. "You loved him."

I want to scream that I didn't but his temper is bristling over his entire body like a livewire.

"You still do."

I'm too afraid to defend myself so I just let my lids close. Even when he's burning up with bitterness and anger, Benito Bernadi is still the most beautiful man I've ever laid eyes on, and the pain of seeing him hate me so much for reasons unknown to me is unbearable.

"Do you know how much that hurts?" His voice carries a softer note but I dare not look up. "To know that you've been lying to me? You had me think it was all my fault, when you'd wanted it all along. I suppose you were a little bit honest in the beginning… You said you hated me for having the Falconis sent away. Well, now it's time for me to be a little bit honest with you. I can live with you hating me for that. What I can't live with is knowing you've hated me *all along*, that you've been playing me this whole time to help Federico get his revenge…"

I look up sharply. His summary is so far from the truth it's laughable. "What?"

He opens his jacket and pulls out a folded note. I recognize it immediately. It's the note Bambi passed to me at the lunch. My stomach drops as I try to remember everything Federico wrote. I wasn't able to take in or process a whole lot in because my mind and body were so preoccupied with being in the vicinity of *this* man.

"You've been writing to him," he states.

"No, I—"

He points to the note. "It's here, Tess. In black and white. 'I'm sorry it's taken me so long to reply'. Reply, to what, Tess?"

"I—" Shit. I haven't written to Federico in a few months but I kept it up for a long time. Still, it was before I became close to Benito. I haven't anything wrong. "My letters. I write to him every month."

His eyes narrow. "So, you knew his address?"

"No! I had a PO Box number. I have no idea where he lives."

He ignores my defense and ploughs on. "You've been discussing ways to get revenge on me."

My breaths are short and tight. "We never discussed that…" My gaze darts about, frantically. He talked about it before he left, but it was one sentence, Benito! I didn't take him seriously. And I haven't heard back from him at all… until now."

"Until now?"

He walks around the chair and holds the note up in front of me. "Don't you mean two months ago?" He points to the date in the top corner and my heart plummets into the base of my stomach. The note is dated March, not long before I saw Benito that first time at Cristiano's house. That day was the first time I ever spoke to Benito and I wasn't polite to say the least. I look up into his eyes. They're sad and hostile at the same time. "Interesting timing, wouldn't you agree?"

I rewind back to that afternoon, trying to piece together the chronology of events. "Bambi gave it to me after lunch. I read it once but I was too preoccupied to process it so I put it in my bra to read properly later."

A sadistic slant crosses his face as he straightens. Then he laughs. "You expect me to believe that? The timing is too perfect, Contessa. You've hated me for three long years, then you show up at Cristiano's and suddenly your childhood sweetheart is 'replying' to your letters explaining in some detail how he's planning to exact his revenge on me. It's too much of a coincidence."

My heart is rocketing around making me feel nauseous. "Benito—"

His jaw grinds, then he holds up three fingers. "You were thinking about *him* when I ate you out on the hood of your car," he rasps, ticking off one finger. "You were thinking about *him* when you came to my apartment and jerked me off." Second finger. "You were thinking about *him* when you *crawled* to me." Third finger.

I shake my head frantically. "That's not true!"

"What do you know about the Marchesis?" he shouts, spit landing on the damp floor.

My hands curl into fists behind the chair. "They killed my mother!"

"And?"

Tears start to well in my eyes. I can't believe this is happening. "What do you mean 'and'? Isn't that enough? They took away the most important person in my life."

Damp air licks at the streaks on my face as tears course down it and drip to my knees.

Benito pauses for a second, then inhales deeply. "What is Federico's involvement with them?"

I sniff, unable to wipe my nose, and look up through watery eyes. "I don't know, Benito. I haven't spoken to Federico in three years. I promise you, I don't know anything."

He folds his arms, continuing to regard me with real, venomous suspicion. I have a terrifying feeling I'm not getting through to him. He doesn't believe me.

His voice dips even lower. "When is he coming here?"

"What?" I hiccup through a sob.

"Federico," he repeats. "When is he coming here to 'ruin' me?"

I shake my head and don't reply. There's no point when he doesn't believe a word that comes out of my mouth.

Seconds pass that are only filled by the sound of my soft cries.

"When Cristiano finds out you've tied me up in some basement…" I choke out.

"He knows."

That stops my tears instantly.

"And Trilby?"

Benito waves a hand like it's irrelevant. "That depends on how much he tells her."

I feel a small nugget of hope in my belly. There's no way in this world Trilby would allow Benito to hold me hostage like this. It's unbelievable.

"You're colluding with someone who is affiliated with the Marchesi's, Contessa. And as you said, they killed your mother. And Trilby should know… She was there."

He leaves those words to penetrate my brain. If Trilby believes this, then the rest of my family could too. The thought makes me feel hollow and helpless.

"I'll leave you to think about that, Contessa."

"No—" I glance up sharply. "You can't leave me here."

"You need some time to reflect, I think."

"No, Benito, please…" More tears pour from my eyeballs. I had just started to care for this man, but the first suggestion that I might be keeping the truth from him, he gives the benefit of the doubt to Federico, not me.

He's about to walk out of the room when he stops and turns to look at me over his shoulder. "Federico was right about one thing though…"

I hold his gaze, seeking the warmth I once found there but finding none.

"He does know my Achilles heel." He feeds his hands into his pockets and regards me one last time. "It's *you*. And he's done what he set out to do. He's ruined it."

Then he spins back around and walks to the far end of the room. He pulls open a door and exits, leaving me alone, in tears and feeling so utterly helpless I could die.

CHAPTER THIRTY-ONE

*B*enito

Only Cristiano looks up when I return to the VIP room. "Sorry about that. Update on the renovations."

Beppe glances at me briefly before downing half a bottle of beer. "Are you any closer to finding out who did it?"

"No. Fingerprint scans were lost. My guys are searching through more security footage."

I reach for my glass and inhale a large mouthful of whiskey, feeling Cristiano's narrowed gaze on the side of my face.

The image of Tess tied to a chair in the basement settles across my lids, stubbornly refusing to abate. I won't be able to hold out much longer. While she's destroyed any chance of us being anything more than a three-day-hotel fling, and loose relations through mafia ties, I can't simply switch off the way she makes my balls ache whenever I look at her, or the way she makes my cock stiffen with a gentle laugh. I also won't get away with keeping her in the basement forever. The clock's ticking and I need to make the most of my little captive whore while I can.

"They're looking into something for me now so I'll have to duck out again shortly."

"Anything I can help with?" Cristiano asks, his gaze still narrowed.

I suck my bottom lip into my mouth while seeming to consider his offer, then shake my head. "I'll let you know."

Beppe and Nicolò have resumed a conversation so Cristiano pulls me to one side. "I just got an update on the Marchesi situation," he says. Normally, *this* would make me hard but it's taking all my effort to focus squarely on the topic at hand.

"Go on."

"Fury's definitely handing the reins to his nephews."

I nod while digesting what I'd suspected Fury would do all along. "The three brothers?"

"All three. Two had already been sworn in. The third is being sworn in as we speak."

I wipe a bemused smile from my face. "Too green. All of them."

"Don't assume green to mean ineffective," Cristiano warns. "They're hungry and bitter. Sometimes, that's all you need along with a good fucking aim."

Cristiano's gaze falls to my scar, reminding me that

those were the same three qualities I brought to Gianni's table sixteen years ago. He took a chance on me and now I'm the best arsenal the Di Santo's have.

My thoughts turn back to Falconi. "Do we have a list of everyone they've made?"

His gaze diverts for a second. "No, but to my knowledge they've slowed right down. Haven't made anyone in the last year."

Federico's note stated he's "associating" with them, and it was written only a few months ago. Sure, he wouldn't broadcast the fact he's a made man in a letter if that was actually the case, but he'd have worded it differently, because a made man is a hell of a lot more formidable than a mere associate. Still, his father knew our business inside out. He could give them useful information if it came down to it. Federico Falconi could be a viable threat.

"We've always been rivals," Cristiano continues, "for as long as I can remember. But bringing down the Mexicans my brother was cavorting with, and the group behind Gio's murder started a war, you know that."

"Yeah, which we won when we took Newark."

"And then we twisted the knife with the drug bust."

"They were on our turf," I argue.

"Fair point, but we're goading them. *You're* goading them. The drug bust was your idea. We didn't need to do it."

I inhale a long breath. "Cristiano, you hire me as your advisor. For what? To help us plateau? We're not just a bunch of fucking gangsters, we're *businessmen*.

We're in this to make *money*. If we let others encroach on our space, we send the message we can be fucked in the ass. If you ask me, we need to be taking what little they have left. Letting everyone on the east coast know we mean fucking business. We have all the right people in our pockets—the world is our goddamn oyster. What are we waiting for?"

Cristiano sits back in his leather chair and rests his gaze on me thoughtfully.

"Okay. What are you suggesting?"

I don't even need to think about it. Not after Contessa's betrayal. "We ruin the Marchesi's. Then, we take Boston."

"I'll need more captains."

"Leave that with me." I know exactly which of our soldiers are ready for promotion and which ones need a discreet shove off the Brooklyn Bridge.

"Alright." Cristiano leans forward, his gaze trailing once again over my scar. He's only three years older than me but it's moments like this he reminds me so much of his father, Gianni. "We'll take the Marchesi's. Organize a crew to replace any of Fury's soldiers who fall, then come back to me with a plan."

I nod, feeling the embers catch light in my stomach once again. This is what gives me life—having a purpose, someone's trust, and free rein to annihilate anyone who declares themselves my enemy. In this moment I feel a small, itchy need to celebrate, and I know exactly who I want to do that with.

"Ah, almost forgot," I say, getting to my feet. "Need to make that call."

Cristiano sits back again and watches me as he brings the whiskey glass to his lips. "Take all the time you need."

Her head is resting to one side and her hair has fallen across her face.

"So?" I bark at her.

She doesn't move.

I pick up the chair that is still facing her and slam it to the floor. She jumps, a terrified look widening her eyes. Immediately, she starts trembling and tries to scoot backward but I grab the seat of her chair again. My fingers accidentally brush the soft flesh of her thigh and even though I couldn't be more furious with this woman, my cock startles awake.

I look up and her lips have parted, her hair blowing from her face with each puff of her breath. Despite the fact I've got her tied up and believing her whole family distrusts her, she's still affected by me, and that thought alone is making me painfully hard.

"I said, 'so'?"

"So what?" she answers, croakily.

"You were reflecting."

She swallows and licks her lips which pushes my self-control to a new limit. "I have nothing to reflect on, Benito. I only got that letter the other day and I have no idea what Federico's involvement with the Marchesi's is."

I settle on the opposite chair and stroke a hand down my tie, then I smile at her.

"Contessa… Usually, when I capture someone and ask them to reflect on their story, they do it, and then they tell me the truth. If they need a little more persuasion, I torture them."

It's true and she knows it. She's seen me wash the blood off my hands.

Her head falls forward and she gazes up at me through thick, damp lashes. The sight of it does nothing to soften the erection growing beneath my slacks.

"Benito, I have nothing more to tell you. Please believe me."

Cristiano's permission rings loud in my ears. We're going to ruin the Marchesi's. If Federico is in contact with them, I need to get *something* out of Contessa. She's a damn good liar. She's had me fooled up to this point, but that ship has definitely sailed.

"Which Marchesi is he talking to?" I bite out.

She sighs heavily and drops her gaze to the ground. "I don't know."

"In what capacity does he associate with them?"

Her head shakes softly. "I don't know."

I try a different tactic. "He's in New York."

Her head jerks upwards and alarm flashes across her features. "Federico?"

Hearing his name on her lips feels like a sharp knife is being driven through my chest.

"Where would he go?" I press.

She shakes her head and pins her lips together.

Something inside me snaps. "I've had enough of this shit."

I push the hem of her skirt up to her hips and drop my gaze to the pink panties covering her pussy.

Her thighs tense and her voice trembles. "What are you doing?"

I don't answer because I'm completely focused on the mesmerizing vision between her legs. I hate that I know how she tastes and I hate that it's so fucking *sweet*. I curl a thick thumb around the edge of her panties and drag them to one side.

Her breath hitches and her shoulders brace.

"Benito…"

Oh *God*. Her beautiful pink clit is becoming engorged. It's swelling before my eyes. Federico might be the one she loves but I'm the one who turns her on, whether she likes it or not. I press my thumb to the gorgeous nub and soak up the moan that it pulls from her throat.

"Please, Benito. Don't…"

"Don't what?" I smile, unable to tear my gaze from her pussy. It's leaking with her arousal, making her flesh glisten. I use my other thumb to drag her wetness through her folds and lubricate the swollen bud as I circle it softly.

"I don't want to do this," she says, her breaths short and erratic.

"Your body doesn't agree with that statement."

"You don't believe me. You *hate* me," she pants. "Why would you do this?"

I finally lift my lids until they catch on her long lashes and delirious gaze. "Because I want to show Federico what his little whore gets up to when he's not around."

She swallows, hard.

I jerk my head toward a camera set up in the top corner of the room above the door. "Yeah. He's going to see all of this. He's going to see exactly what I can do to his little sweetheart."

"No," she gasps. "Please Benito."

I rub small circles around her clit and watch as her breasts lift brazenly, her stomach rolling with the effort of not letting this affect her.

"Oh God, Benito, please—"

I smile at the sight of her falling apart. "Are you begging for me to stop or continue?"

"S—stop." She rotates her hips, pushing her pussy toward me, while her eyes roll back. "Please…"

"Is this what you want, brat?"

I slam to my knees and give her pussy a long, deep lick.

"Fuck!" she cries out. "Oh God, please stop."

She's trembling so hard, the chair legs are shaking. And my cock is so thick, kneeling on the floor is fucking painful. But I can't not taste this sweet pussy one more time.

I bend down again, wrap my lips around her nub and suck softly, swirling my tongue around it. She bucks up against me, reckless moans flying out of her mouth.

"Please… Oh *God*…"

I keep the sodden panties pulled to one side and lick her rhythmically, curling my tongue into her heat. She's sobbing now because she's on the edge.

"Benito… Oh *fuck*. I'm going to come."

I pause for a second and look over my shoulder at the camera. I wasn't lying. That thing is recording on a loop and I absolutely plan to chop out this coverage and send it to Federico on a fucking platter.

"You hear that, Falconi? Your little sweetheart is going to come on my tongue. And do you know what?" I give the camera a slow wink. "She's fucking delicious."

I twist back to see she's turned solid, her gaze wild and desperate. I smirk and dip back between her legs, and wrap my whole mouth around her pussy.

"Oh *God!*" She starts to jerk frantically. "Benito, I'm coming…"

I slide a finger inside her and ignite a whole new set of convulsions until she's literally coming apart on the chair.

I feast on her arousal until she's a dry, quivering mess, then I get to my feet.

Her head has fallen over the back of the chair. Eventually, she drunkenly lifts it. She looks depleted of everything and so goddamn beautiful. Her eyes dart sideways as I stroke her hair behind her ear.

"I'm going upstairs," I say, firmly. "I want you to

try again, at *reflecting*. If you don't have anything further to tell me about your boyfriend's involvement with the Marchesi's, I will fuck you senseless for him to see."

I hold her stare as I bend down and brush my lip across hers. Then I steal her last breath as it gushes from her chest and leave.

"That was a long call," Cristiano says, the second I return. "How many houses are you building?"

I ignore Cristiano's remark and instead flash Federico's note in front of his face. I have his attention immediately.

"What is this?"

"It seems your future sister-in-law is aligning herself with an associate of the Marchesi's."

He takes the note in his fingers. They're not inked like mine, but they've been in a few eye sockets since he took over as don, so they're just as lethal.

"Federico Falconi. Why does that name sound familiar?"

"His father cheated your father. The guy earned us a lot of money once upon time, but then he turned crooked. I sent his family away before Gianni could execute them all."

Cristiano looks sideways at me with an arched brow and it's in this very moment I wonder if he really has become as ruthless as his father was. For what I'm about to tell him, I hope he has.

"Seems Federico has a chip on his shoulder," Cristiano says.

I stroke my chin. "Yes it does. And like it or not, Contessa is involved."

Cristiano sits back and assesses me. Probably to see how insane I really am. Funny, usually in our line of work it's seen as a strength.

"Where is she?" He takes a long slug of whiskey then regards me.

I cut to the chase. "Tied to a chair in the basement."

And just like that, my suit is covered in whiskey.

I let Cristiano compose himself while making a mental note to send him the dry cleaning bill.

"How long has she been down there?" His eyes are rimmed red from the burn of single malt flying out of his nose.

"Just a few hours. I'm questioning her."

"That's where you've been? You were down there a while…"

He leans in toward me, takes a sniff then chews away a smile. "You're fucking crazy."

Irritation scratches at my patience. "She's sleeping with the *enemy*."

He swallows a mouthful of whiskey then glances at me with a smirk. "That she is."

"Cristiano, look at the damned note. She received this months ago and she's kept it from me."

He shakes his head. "I don't know, Benny. I saw the way she was looking at you over lunch. I don't think she's playing you. And all the sisters are downright *allergic* to what we do. I really don't see her voluntarily getting involved with something like this. When did she get the letter?"

I chew on my lip. I don't like to be proven wrong. "I don't know exactly. She says Bambi gave it to her at the lunch, but that doesn't explain the date. The date says she got this *months* ago."

"Cristiano whips out his cell and dials a number. "Hi Allegra… Yeah, all good… Is Bambi there? Okay great, thanks…"

He looks at me out of the corner of his eye. He's just a smirk waiting to happen. "Hey Bambi, you gave Tess a note at lunch the other day, right?" There's a long pause. "No, it's okay, she's not in any trouble, but… do you know when the note arrived?" After another long pause, Cristiano signs off, hangs up and looks at me.

"The letter only arrived at the house Saturday, she said. It was sent to the wrong house originally, unopened and sent back to the mail depot. The first Tess saw it was at the lunch."

My jaw drops and a swarm of emotions collide inside my lungs. I struggle to breathe. I didn't believe her. All it took was one misunderstanding and I jumped to the conclusion she was lying. I assumed she was playing me. I was born paranoid and it hasn't left me. Not even becoming consigliere to the most notorious mafia family on the east coast protects me from it.

When I gasp for air, an enormous sense of relief drapes over me. Tess hadn't lied to me after all. Maybe she really isn't like the others. In this world, finding people you can trust—men and women—is like finding your way out of a maze in the darkness, blindfolded.

Maybe my instinct was right all along—maybe Tess is different. Maybe the one thing I fear more than anything—finding that one person who matches me wild for wild, crazy for crazy, heartbeat for heartbeat—has been standing right in front of me all along. I hadn't dared imagine anyone out there could possibly be perfect for a dark soul like me, but not only has that impossibility become possible, but I might have lost it before I even knew it was found.

"I guess you have some apologizing to do?"

I grind my jaw and slowly get to my feet. "Something like that."

"Don't let me keep you," he says, a sly smile curling the side of his mouth.

I scowl at him. "Don't wait up."

"Oh I won't."

CHAPTER THIRTY-TWO

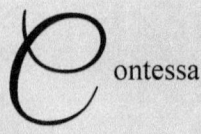ontessa

I feel disgusting.

My panties are soaked through and it's starting to get pretty cold down here. I can still feel Bernadi's head between my thighs and I'm still *throbbing*. I hate myself right now. I haven't done anything wrong yet I'm being punished in the most despicable way.

I've never been more turned on than when he licked me despite my protests. When he turned to the camera and said I was delicious, I almost came right then.

How has this happened? I've let Satan himself lick me to an orgasm as punishment for something I know nothing about. And dear God, I *loved it*.

My thoughts are interrupted when the door opens again and a blush floods my cheeks. I feel like I'm on show—a brazen hussy—with my hands tied behind my back, my legs parted and my skirt pushed up to my hips.

Bernadi strolls into the room looking as cocky as ever and I have to stop my chest from ballooning. I hate what this man does to me.

"Okay, let's shake things up a little."

My heart flutters when it should be quivering.

He gets down on his hands and knees but it's too dark for me to see what he's doing.

"Cristiano says hi, by the way," he says, glancing up before returning his focus to the ties around my ankles.

I suck in a breath. "He's here? In this building?"

He doesn't answer.

"Does he care that you've got me tied up in some basement, freezing to death with no food or water?"

He looks up and strokes his chin. "I don't know actually. I didn't ask."

"It doesn't matter what I say, does it?" My voice trembles. It seems fear and anticipation are two sides of the same coin. "You'll never believe me."

He continues to pull and tug at my ankles while I've given up showing an interest in what exactly it is that I'm tied to.

He's still a scary son of a bitch but something about his manner has softened so I try a different approach. "I was starting to like you a bit, you know?"

I feel his fingers close around one ankle, moving my foot backward. It's deceptively gentle. "Then it's a good thing I showed you my true colors before you started to like me a lot."

"Yeah." I swallow. "It is."

"Did you reflect? Like I asked you to?"

A shiver slices across my spine. "I have nothing to reflect on. I don't know anything about Federico other than this letter, which is the first I've heard from him in three years. But it's pointless me repeating this, because you've already made up your mind that I'm lying."

Something clicks behind my eyes and I narrow them. "Why are you so determined to believe I'm a liar, Benito?"

He sits back on his heels but doesn't look at me, then moves to my right foot, unstrapping it from the chair and re-strapping it to my left.

"It's written on the note right here," he says again, but there's not as much bite in his tone now. In the short time he's been gone, something's changed, I can feel it.

He unties my wrists but the blood has drained from them so they merely flop to my sides instead of lashing out like they should do.

"That note is as much about me as it is about you," he says, calmly bringing my hands together on my lap and strapping a tie around them again. "And you hid it from me."

"I didn't hide any—"

"In fact, you hardly spoke to me before I got you in the wine cellar," he snaps, yanking the tie hard.

"I was nervous!" I say in a high pitch. His eyes dart to mine.

"You were nervous? Why?"

I swallow and stare wide-eyed at him. How does he

not know? "You'd just declared me your girlfriend, and my entire family was at that lunch. For God's sake, Benito, I was trying to figure out how to tell my papa and my aunt and sisters that I didn't hate you anymore and that I, in fact, felt quite the opposite. I was nervous because… well… you make me nervous. And I was nervous because I didn't want to fuck it up."

His face ticks to one side like he's doing a double take. "Fuck what up?"

"Ugh!" I tilt my gaze to the ceiling because I can hardly shrug my arms when my wrists are tied. "Me and you." I drop my head and glare at him accusingly. "This." I start to shake my head, feeling an hysterical laugh climb its way up my throat when he stands, pulls me off the chair and flips me onto all fours.

"What are you doing?" The laugh turns to a shocked gasp.

"I can't do this." Benito's tone frightens me. It's sharp and unhinged.

A fly rips behind me and I hear him fumbling with his boxers.

"Do what?" I breathe, panicked.

"I know you're not lying, Tess. I honestly thought you were at first, but Cristiano called Bambi…"

My chest deflates with relief but my heart is hammering. Is he going to drive into me now? Without my consent? Licking me when my body was arching into him is one thing, but to penetrate me dry while I'm tied up and at his mercy is a whole other thing.

"Benito, what are you doing?" Panic infuses my voice and I start to tremble from head to toe.

He crouches down behind me then slowly lowers his chest over my back. Seconds pass and his heat warms me through until a damp sweat sticks to my skin.

"I would never hurt you," he whispers.

I choke out a held breath.

"If you know I'm telling you the truth, why don't you let me go?"

He rests his cheek on my shoulder blade. "Because you like this, Tess," he says softly. "And so do I."

A cool draft blows between my legs making them flutter. When I don't deny his words, he lifts a hand to my hip and smooths it down over the round of my bottom and feeds it between my thighs.

"Jesus Christ," he breathes. "You're soaking."

I grind myself against his fingers and whimper.

He gently cups his hands beneath my arms and lifts me up until I'm resting back against his chest. He dips his fingers between my folds and rubs my arousal into my breasts.

"You remember when I came beneath your T-shirt?" he rasps.

"Mm," I roll my head back against his pectoral muscles.

"You spreading my come across your chest…"

I stop moving and open my eyes.

"That ended me, Tess. I knew that if I touched you after that, I'd go fucking crazy. And I have."

"Is that why you pushed me away?" I ask quietly.

He shifts slightly and threads his hand back between my legs. "Yes. I'm sorry."

I pull at the tie holding my wrists together and groan.

He chuckles into my ear. "I'm not untying you. You touch me when I say you can touch me. Do you understand?"

My body hums at his words but my brain is fighting against them. "This is fucked up," I whisper. "*You* are fucked up."

He lifts a finger to his lips and sucks it slowly. Then he returns it to my heat. "I'm not fucked up, Tess. I'm *obsessed*. There's a difference."

My back arches and my knees spread involuntarily.

"That's my little brat."

He parts my ass cheeks and feeds his cock between them. Then I gasp as he pulls me down hard.

He stills, letting my walls relax while panting heavy breaths in my ear. "Oh fuck, you feel so good Tess."

My brain is reeling. I've never felt so helpless in all my life. I've never felt so afraid. I've never *yearned* for someone this much.

Part of me wants to surrender to him, to this. Part of me wants to run far, far away. But, not only am I restrained, my body is *melting*. All this man has to do is brush me with a finger and my skin *burns*.

He starts to move and my lids fall. His cock travels through my core, expanding me and filling me with his madness, and all the while he breathes harsh curses and sweet promises into my ear.

And I surrender.

The *snap* of a pocket knife makes my eyes pop open. Benito feeds a blade between my wrists and slices through the plastic ties, then he reaches behind us and cuts the ties around my ankles too. He helps me to my feet and pulls my skirt back down over my hips. He places thick hands on the dip of my waist and turns me around, then I look into his eyes one last time.

They're deep and dark and almost impossible not to fall into. I make myself hold onto them while I wait for the blood to return to my hands and feet.

His thumb brushes across the dent in my wrist. "Beautiful," he murmurs.

When sensations return to my fingers, my eyes fill with tears. "Is the door unlocked?" I whisper.

The smile falls from his face. "Yes, it is."

One tear makes a track down my cheek and I wipe it away with the back of my hand. "Goodbye Benito."

I turn around and run for the door. My fingers shake as I curl them around the handle, but he was telling the truth—it's open. I have to blink as I step into a brightly lit corridor. I look left and right and see an elevator a few yards down. I run to it and press the button repeatedly until the doors open with a ping. I step inside the empty cavity and search for more buttons. They look vaguely familiar. I search for one that looks like it might be the ground floor and press it. Then I face the doors, my shoulders heaving as I hyperventilate.

The corridor I've left behind is empty. If Benito had planned to stop me, he could have done so easily, but he hasn't. Still, my lungs empty with bitter relief when the doors slide closed and the elevator starts to rise.

I squeeze myself through the doors, not waiting for them to open fully, and run into a sleek black lobby. I'm struck by the realization I know where I am. *Arena.* I recognize this lobby from when I came here with Paige. I run towards the main exit and my heart sinks as two suited and probably armed men step out of the shadows. One lifts a radio and mutters something into it. I don't slow down—I need to get through those doors. As I pass, I hear a familiar voice come through the radio. *Let her go.*

I stop mid-stride and glance at the man. He punches a button on the wall behind him and the doors hiss apart.

I pause outside but only for a second, to drag in a lungful of clean air, then I look up and down the street. Predictably, there's a couple of black cars parked up. I run to the nearest and wait for the window to wind down.

"You drive for the Di Santos?" I ask, hurriedly.

"I do, Miss Castellano."

I do a double take; I don't recall seeing this man before, but he knows who I am.

"Where can I take you, Miss?"

My heart thumps. "Home," I whisper. "I want to go home."

CHAPTER THIRTY-THREE

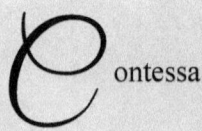ontessa

A knock at the door makes my lids pop open. "Who is it?"

"It's me." *Bambi.*

I push myself up to my elbows and try to ignore the crap scattered all over my bedroom floor. "Come in."

The door opens and her brows shoot up. "You're not packed yet?"

"We're not leaving for a couple of hours," I say with a sigh.

Her eyes are wide as they roam the dumping ground that is the floor. "I fear you might need longer than that. Do you want some help?"

I lay back down with a thump and close my eyes. How has it come to this? My little sister offering to help me get my act together for a stay in a luxury hotel in the

Hamptons? I should have been ready hours ago but all I've managed to do is shower.

I know what's putting me off—it's the thought of seeing Bernadi when I get there. Unfortunately, it's inevitable—he's Cristiano's best man.

Shame floods through my ribcage at the thought I've worked hard every day to banish, though it still creeps back beneath my skin when I drop my guard.

I haven't told a soul about the day in the nightclub basement, because I'm so ashamed at how I feel about it. Despite the terror his cold gaze and sharp tone provoked in me, I knew deep down he wouldn't truly hurt me. But the most shameful thing about it was, Benito was right. I liked it. I liked being tied up and at his mercy. I liked him 'punishing' me with his tongue. I loved his dirty words and the way insanity seemed to infuse his conviction and blind him to everything but my body, my pleas. The only truth either of us were able to confront in that deep dark room was the undeniable chemistry that crackled and combusted beneath every touch.

The sound of his murmurs still fills my ears, the vibration of his anger as his fingers coasted up my skin still touches my nerves. My helplessness as I trembled beneath them still empties my lungs.

Even as I lie here on my bed, delaying the inevitable, I'm short of breath.

Then the sound of a suitcase being slid out of the closet makes me jump. "Do you know when Trilby's getting there?" Bambi asks.

My throat is dry and scratchy when I swallow. "No idea. I haven't seen her in a while." Three weeks to be exact.

"Aren't you guys pretty close now? At one point I thought you'd actually moved into the Di Santo residence." I hear a zipper and the suitcase cover hits my leg.

I huff out a sigh and sit up. There's no getting away from it. I have to pack. "Yeah, I guess. I've just been busy."

"When's the recital? It's got to be soon. Feels like you've been rehearsing for years."

Just the thought of my upcoming show fills me with the kind of dread that stops someone eating for several days. And that's without the underlying anxiety I'm experiencing because my dancing has taken a total nosedive since Benito had me tied up in the basement of his club. "A week after the wedding."

"So this should be the perfect distraction," Bambi says, with a happy lilt.

I reply with a faint smile that fades the second she looks away.

Since I fled Arena three weeks ago, my life has become unrecognizably dull. I go to the studio. I don't hang around. I come straight home. I eat. I stare at the ceiling. I sleep.

I haven't looked out of the studio window once; I haven't glanced up the stairs to the apartment above; I've avoided Cristiano's house completely. But that doesn't mean I haven't seen anything of Bernadi. He's there, on the back of my lids, when I go to sleep, when I dream at night, when I wake up, when I dance. His jet black hair, his scarred left cheek and those dark bronze eyes that *glisten* when I come undone. He's there in all of it, making me warm and weak. Embodying the beautiful things he said to me while I curled around his body in the hotel bed.

But he's nothing but an empty promise wrapped in a dark suit.

All it took was one unvalidated suggestion I might have corresponded with my old best friend and he jumped to the conclusion I was betraying him. He didn't give me any benefit of the doubt—he immediately accused me of lying, and no declarations of truth would change his assumption. It wasn't even me who got him to see sense—it was Cristiano.

The hurt in his eyes when I ran away tugs at my weakened bones, but I can't return to a man who doesn't trust me. And Benito doesn't trust me as far as he can spit. And after the way he treated me, as though I was heartless betrayal personified, I don't trust *him*—with my body, my mind, or my heart.

I wished I still hated him—things were much easier then—but in the last few weeks he's molded me into someone I barely recognize. I was closer than I've ever been with my older sister; I was dancing better than I'd ever done before. I'd begun to feel more comfortable in my own skin—at ease with my wildness. And my darkness—or so I thought.

I've never felt more dark than I did when Benito had

my wrists and ankles bound together as he slid his full length into me on the cold concrete floor. I *loved* it.

I hate that I loved it.

It *scares* me that I loved it.

"Are you even listening?"

I blink back to my youngest sister who's neatly folding clothes and placing them in my suitcase.

"Sorry," I mutter. "Thinking about the recital. What were you saying?"

"Did you reply to Federico?"

The temperature in the room seems to drop at the mention of his name.

"No. I'm not sure I will."

Bambi folds a short black bandage dress over her arm and scrunches her nose. "I thought he was your best friend?"

"Three years ago," I say, lying back down on the bed and covering my eyes with the palms of both hands. "Not anymore. This was the first I'd heard from him in all that time. He could've been dead for all I knew."

"What did he say in his letter? Is he coming back?"

I slide my palms down my face and stare at the stark white ceiling. "I don't know."

He said in his letter he was returning to New York, but he didn't say when, how, who with. And remembering what I can of my old friend, what Federico said and what Federico did were often two very different things.

Bambi's voice dips. "Would you like him to come back?"

I swallow, my gaze still glued to the shards of light stretched above my head. Truly, I don't know what I want. I want for Federico never to have written the letter; I want for Benito to never have doubted me so quickly. I want to turn back time so I can forget the heat of his lips on my throat, the scorching trail of fire his fingertips left on my thighs.

But I also want to know Federico is okay, and that Benito sending his family away didn't hurt them too badly.

I recall the bite in his words and know one thing for sure: The Falconis *were* hurt by Benito's actions—enough that Fed seems determined to get his revenge. The only problem is, he still believes I want revenge too, but I don't. I know Benito now, and I know in my bones he was telling the truth when he said he'd sent the family away for their own protection.

I worry for Federico if he does choose to return. If Benito can turn on me at the mere suggestion I was plotting against him, I'm frightened for what he'll do to Federico knowing my old friend really is seeking revenge—it was written in his letter; it was there in black and white.

With that in mind, I reply with a fervent, "No. There is nothing he can gain from coming back here."

"Not even your heart?" If Bambi's own heart wasn't so sweet, I might have snapped, but she knows nothing of my history with Federico, nor my past and present with Benito.

I lift my head and let out a soft sigh. "No, Bambi. That ship has sailed."

An hour and significant effort on Bambi's part later, I drop my suitcase into the trunk of the car and ignore Allegra's scowl as I slide in behind her.

"Honestly," she mutters. "You girls will be late for your own funerals."

"I was on time!" Bambi shoots back. "Besides, not planning on dying any time soon."

I look across to see her inspecting her newly painted nails. "Well, if you do, you can rest assured our aunt will get you to the burial on time."

"Not if I go before you," Allegra snaps.

"We've got an hour's drive ahead of us," Papa grumbles from the driver's seat. "Can we pick a more optimistic topic?"

I chew the inside of my cheek and drift my gaze out of the window. The grey of the roads eventually gives way to expanses of green, trimmed lawns warming under a cloudless sky.

I feel like I'm on the edge of exhaling a long breath, emptying me of the tightness that has allowed me to function over the last three weeks. But the knowledge of what awaits me keeps the iron fist closed around my heart.

I want to feel everything for Trilby—this will be the happiest day of her life. But I can't and won't be vulnerable. I'll watch the proceedings with a detached eye, I'll hold a tissue to dry cheeks and I'll make my apologies at the earliest opportunity. If I stay around just a second longer than I have to, I'll risk being drawn back into darkness and that scares the life out of me.

For now, darkness recedes as the view ahead fills with bright white architectural splendor.

"Oh, it's gorgeous," Allegra says, fanning herself with a magazine.

"It's even nicer than the pictures on the website," Bambi adds.

I step out of the car and take a deep breath. My chest releases a little. Somehow, I know he isn't here yet.

The wedding isn't for another three days but we've arrived early to help Trilby with preparations, hold the most epic bachelorette party for her, and of course, spend some time with Sera, our second eldest sister.

A doorman hurries down the steps towards us and Papa tosses his keys to a valet. We unload the trunk and leave the suitcases with the doorman as we climb the steps to a picture-perfect country club-esque hotel.

"How did Sera land this gig?" Bambi asks in a voice full of wonder.

"I never asked," I reply, "but I expect Cristiano had something to do with it."

Just as we reach the doors, a flurry of dark auburn hair rushes toward us. I recognize Sera immediately and she barrels straight into me and Bambi for a hug.

"It's so good to see you all," she squeals. "I can't

wait to show you around. Trilby and Cristiano got here an hour ago…"

My chest tightens again. "Where are they?"

"They were in the lounge last time I looked but they might be in their cottage unpacking."

"Cottage?" My eyes pop.

Sera beams proudly. "Yeah, we have four cottages on the grounds as well as all the suites in the main house. It's perfect for their wedding night."

Bambi's nose scrunches. "Isn't it bad luck to see the bride though, on the day or even the night before?"

Sera turns and guides us inside to where Papa and Allegra have already sunk into deep chairs in the reception area. "Cristiano will be staying in Benito's room the night before…"

My lungs constrict and suddenly I'm finding it hard to breathe.

"Besides," Sera continues, "we'll be rooming in a suite with Trilby for two nights. Bride's request."

I thump a fist against my chest in the hopes it will kickstart my lungs' ability to operate.

"You okay?" Sera shoots me a concerned glance.

"Yeah," I squeeze out. "Just… swallowed a bug I think."

"What?" She looks horrified. "There shouldn't be bugs in here! Wait here and Sergei will get you all checked in. I'll meet you on the veranda for lunch in thirty minutes."

Bambi and I watch Sera scurry away to locate some

no doubt toxic chemical to eradicate the place of non-existent insects and wander out onto the patio.

"Wow…" Bambi twirls around, taking in the immaculate white building with its sash windows and manicured foliage. "I feel like we could be in England."

I resist the pull to open my heart to the place. As gorgeous as it is, I dare not let my guard down. It's challenge enough taming the butterflies coursing around my belly—they don't understand that the man I'm so nervous about seeing is no good for me.

She takes out her phone and starts snapping photos while I wander off the patio to the lawns. Two of the cottages are set to the side—beautiful miniature versions of the big white country house, surrounded by small picket fences and flowers. Trilby will be in heaven.

I sit on a bench beside the lawn and listen to the waves in the distance. In seconds I'm lying on the hood of my car by the ocean looking into Bernadi's glittering bronze eyes before he throws my legs apart.

Heat spirals down to my core knocking me off my axis and whipping away my breath.

The view ahead of me spins and suddenly I feel completely out of control. I have no agency over my visions and emotions. How am I going to get through the next few days if I can't even get him out of my head, let alone my direct eyeline?

My heart sinks as I realize the only way I can stay afloat is to go back home. My heart sinks even further knowing Papa would have an aneurism if I even suggested it.

I drop my face into my hands and will the time to pass quickly. Then a warmth beside me draws my gaze to the right.

"What's wrong, Tess?"

As my eyes get used to the light again, I feel some relief to see Trilby settled on the bench.

"How long have you been sitting there?"

"Couple minutes." She strokes a hand down my back. "Tell me what's wrong."

"It's nothing," I say but a taut sigh follows the words. "Headache, that's all."

Her brow dips into a small frown. "Sera said you swallowed a fly back there. Are the two connected?" She arches a brow like she knows neither of those excuses are authentic.

I exhale slowly and turn to look out toward the ocean. When I don't speak again, she continues. "You haven't been to the house in a while. Does it have anything to do with Benny?"

A shiver curls its way down my spine and I'm sure she notices, but she doesn't say anything.

"No. Why would it?"

She clicks her tongue. "Because he's looked like shit for the last three weeks, which is roughly when I last saw you at Cristiano's place."

I turn slowly back to face her.

"Cristiano told me Benny was getting a little touchy about you. Has something been going on? I won't judge you, Tess. I know you hated him—and for good reason—but I also know that feelings can change."

I drop my gaze to the ground and notice my hands are shaking. Just talking about Benito has whipped me up into a frenzy.

"Has he really been looking like shit?" I ask in barely a whisper.

"Yeah. Well, as shit as someone blessed with the skin of a supermodel and the jawline of a steak knife can look, sure."

A smile pulls at my lips but I'm too shaken to give in to it.

She breathes out and rests her hand on mine. "You don't have to tell me, but if you're worried about seeing him, I can ask Cristiano to give him stuff to do that keeps him out of your way for the next few days. Obviously, the day of the wedding won't be easy—you'll be in the same room all day, but—"

"He tied me up in a basement, Tril."

Trilby sucks in a breath, removes her hand from mine and clamps it over her mouth. I don't bother looking up. I see enough judgement in the mirror—I don't need to see it from my sister too.

From what I can tell, she may in fact have *stopped* breathing, so I figure she deserves the full story.

"We've been having a thing since… well, since the day you gave me the music box."

I eventually glance across to see her eyes widen further.

"But things got a little more serious when I went to Arena with my friend Paige."

Trilby nods. So she knows about Arena.

"Benito was there. We went to a hotel, we stayed there for three days. He called me his girlfriend…"

A choke begins to work its way up my throat but I swallow it down because I refuse to cry any more tears over a man. Federico had my tears three years ago and look at what came of that…

"I was going to tell you at the lunch Cristiano hosted at his house, but…"

Trilby's hand slides from her face and concern shrouds her features. "But what?"

"He found a note Federico had sent me. It arrived completely out of the blue and Bambi had only given it to me that day. But in it Fed talked about wanting to get his revenge on Benito for sending his family away. He said something about knowing his Achilles Heel and working with the Marchesi's—"

"The Marchesi's? Are you serious?" She says, a little too loudly.

"Sshhh," I hiss, knowing the patio is filling up not far behind us. "They're empty threats, Trilby. I know Federico, and he isn't like that. The note was written a few months ago. If he was going to appear and cause trouble, I'm confident he would have done so by now. That's if he was going to do it, anyway, but he was always good at talking the talk—not so good at putting his words into action."

That seems to settle Trilby slightly, then her frown sharpens. "Why did Benny tie you up in a basement?"

I take a long breath in. "He found the letter, believed I was working with Federico to avenge what Benito did to the Falconi's. What hurt the most was, he didn't even question it. Despite everything that had happened between us, he couldn't find it in himself to trust me."

Trilby rubs her eyes in my peripheral and mutters, "What the *fuck*, Benny?" Then she looks up suddenly. "Did he hurt you?"

Heaviness seems to engulf me until I can barely lift my head. "No. He didn't hurt me. Not physically anyway."

"So, what happened? How did you get away?"

"He released me eventually. But only after Cristiano confirmed the letter was old and Bambi had only just given it to me."

"So Cristiano *knew*?"

Oh *shit*. They're getting married in three days and I might have just got Cristiano into a bit of hot water.

"According to Benito, yes."

I can hear her teeth grinding beside me. After a few long moments, she huffs out a tight breath. "Well, that certainly explains why you haven't been around to the house and I don't blame you one little bit."

I look up and she's shaking her head, vehemently. When she stops, her gaze is hard. "Are you okay, Tess? Answer me honestly."

"I'm fine, really. I just don't want to see him. At least, I don't think I do… It's complicated."

"I wish you'd told me sooner," she says through thinned lips. "I'm so angry with both of them."

"I wish I hadn't told you at all," I murmur. "This is your moment and I really don't want to ruin it for you."

Trilby wraps an arm around my shoulders. "You won't. I'm glad you told me. I'm going to be looking out for you better from now on, Tess. I promise. I'm never going to let anything bad happen to you again, okay?" She hugs me into her side but I don't reply. It's a sweet and honorable sentiment, but contrary to most peoples' opinions, I wasn't born yesterday. As much as Cristiano loves my sister, he's still a mob man, and her influence can only stretch so far.

"Come on," she says, pulling me to my feet. "Let's go and get you some food."

We turn and walk back toward the patio. From the sound and volume of voices, it seems our family and a large proportion of Cristiano's have now arrived. We duck around some foliage framing the eating area, then my heart stops and the blood drains from the crown of my head to the tips of my toes.

Trilby is whispering something in my ear but I can't seem to hear her. My gaze is caught like a rabbit in a snare. Benito Bernadi is standing at the doors to the patio and even though twenty people are chattering and moving around between us, it feels as though a tattooed calloused hand is sliding around my naked waist, hot breath coasting over my shoulder.

His eyes have darkened and even from this short distance I notice his jaw moving from side to side. One hand rests in his slacks while the other holds a lowball of whiskey. Whenever the light catches the dancing golden liquid, I'm reminded of the glisten in his eyes when he's pulling me apart with his bare hands.

They're not glistening now though. They're opaque, and black.

Eventually, Trilby's words cut through the haze. "Do you want me to get rid of him? Or we can take a walk. Whatever you want to do Tess. I'm right here."

I give my head a small shake, my gaze still captured in his. "I'm fine."

I'm *not* fine.

My stomach has liquified and the butterflies are careening about within like they've been electrocuted. And a stone-cold heaviness pulls me downward, as though something inside me is trying to keep my feet on the ground.

The movements between us slow down until I'm painfully aware that people are watching us as we stare at each other. All I can hear now are my heart beats—hard, short and filled with heavy emotion.

"Benito!" Cristiano's bark cuts through the tension across the patio and makes me draw in a breath. Benito doesn't look away. He holds my stare a few seconds longer, making it subtly but crystal clear he will do as Cristiano asks eventually, but only because he *wants* to. Just like there are a million other things he could do, if he *wanted* to.

When he glacially pans his gaze to Cristiano, the chattering across the patio slowly picks up again and I release my breath.

"Get some food," Trilby says, in clipped tones. "I'll be right back."

She marches across the patio, around various

members of the two families, and follows Cristiano and Benito into the hotel. I can't help the little ball of guilt that forms in my chest at the thought I've muddied what should have been Cristiano and Trilby's idyllic and problem-free wedding event.

"There you are!" Sera bounds over with a plate. "Come on, the food here is so amazing. And I sprayed the whole lobby. There won't be any more irritating bugs, I promise you."

I take the plate and follow her to the buffet table, marveling a little at how much Sera has come out of her shell. She was always the quietest of the four of us but she seems far more excitable and exuberant than she used to be. Usually, she keeps herself to herself and her astrology charts and tarot cards, but she seems lighter now, somehow.

"This place suits you, Sera," I say, helping myself to a pizza slice and some salad.

"Does it?" She beams at me. "Well, I do like it here."

"How's the job? Are you enjoying the work?" I take a large bite of the pizza and resist swooning because it really is delicious.

Sera's gaze softens, wistfully. "It's good. It's hard, I mean, the place is fully booked all of the time, so we don't get many breaks but… the guests are fantastic, which makes it all worth it."

"What kind of guests do you have here?" I've always been curious about how the other half lives. As a family, we're not exactly poor, but we're not uber rich like some.

She smooths down her dress and it's only then I notice how amazing she looks. Her figure has filled out in all the right places, the hem of her skirt is just short enough to reveal the bottom of her slim thigh. Her auburn hair bounces joyfully around her face and her skin is *glowing*.

"We get a real mixed bag. Wall Street financiers, actors, New York society of course, and also just regular, nice people."

"Celebrities?" I ask, shoveling the rest of the pizza into my mouth.

"Sometimes, yes. But we don't get to see them a lot. They often stay in the cottages and we're given strict instructions not to bother or approach them." Sera lets out a soft breath. "Doesn't matter though. I think ordinary people are far more interesting."

My gaze narrows. Something about Sera is different, but I can't put my finger on what it is.

"So, what's the plan for the next few days?" I ask. Forewarned is forearmed and all that.

"So, tonight we're having a dinner with all the guests…"

My heart sinks.

"Tomorrow is Trilby's bachelorette party. I have the day off so we're going down to the beach then up to one of the suites for a girly pampering session."

"That sounds fun," I force out, though I'm still

mentally figuring out how I can either get out of or survive the family dinner.

"The following day is for final preparations and the rehearsal, then the next is the wedding!" She squeals and bunches her hands into fists, clapping them together excitedly. "In fact, you should probably try on your bridesmaid dress—Bambi too—as it's been a while since your last fitting. We have a dressmaker on site who can make any last-minute alterations."

Perfect excuse to get away. "Great! I'll do it now. Where is it?"

"In your room. I'll take you there now if you like?"

She takes my plate and hands it to a passing waiter who gives her a huge grin in return.

"How much longer do you plan to stay here?" I ask as we walk through the lounge to the main staircase. I glance around nervously, with half an ear listening for the sound of Benito's voice.

"My placement is for twelve months, and I'm halfway through that now."

She looks back over her shoulder at me as we climb the softly carpeted staircase. "I really love it here. I'm hoping they offer me a permanent job. If they don't, I guess I'll come home and figure out what next."

Her shrug speaks of regret but her shoulders are light. The prospect of not getting what she wants doesn't seem to bother her all that much. Then it occurs to me...

"Are you seeing someone?" I blurt out.

She doesn't turn back around but I'd spot the immediate flush in her cheeks a mile away.

"You are, aren't you?" I tease.

"No," she replies quickly. "Not really."

"Not really? You either are or you aren't."

We reach the top of the stairs and she takes a sharp right away from me. "Then it's a no. I'm not *officially* seeing someone."

"But you like someone," I muse behind her. "And you speak so highly of the guests…"

She stops suddenly and spins around. "Here's your room," she says brightly, the flush still evident in the apples of her cheeks. "Your dress is inside, and your luggage has been put in there too."

"Why are you being weird?" I frown. "So you like someone, it's no big deal."

"It's nothing." She shakes her head, bouncing her hair about, but it doesn't shake the smile from her eyes. "So drop it, Tess, please?"

There's something slightly pleading in her voice and I instantly empathize. I wouldn't want anyone prying into the 'thing' I have with Benito, even if that 'thing' no longer exists.

"Sure, no worries. And thanks for bringing me to my room. Will you be at the dinner too? Or will you be working?"

She wraps her warm hands around mine as if to say a silent thank you for not pushing her. "I'll be at the dinner," she says with a smile. "I wouldn't miss it for the world."

Then she walks past me and heads back downstairs leaving me to ponder the very real possibility I actually *would* miss it for the world.

CHAPTER THIRTY-FOUR

*B*enito

I chew my lip while Cristiano gets it off his chest. It's only slightly annoying that he knew I'd had Tess tied up in the basement all along—the reason he's giving me shit is because he kept it from Trilby. That was his choice not mine.

"I'm getting married in *three* days, for fuck's sake, Benny," he groans, rubbing his eyes. "And she thinks I'm keeping secrets from her."

I don't say anything. I know if I open my mouth, declarations of my innocence in that regard would come flying out, and this is neither the time nor place for the don of New York to hear some key home truths.

"What can I do?" I ask instead. "Do you want me to talk to Trilby?"

Cristiano barks out a bitter laugh. "Good luck with

that. She'll grind your balls off the mood she's in right now."

I narrow my eyes at the thought.

"Just… promise me you won't tie any more of her sisters up in a basement again, okay?"

I ignore the urge to shrug nonchalantly. "I won't."

What I don't say is, Tess has only told Trilby the half of it. She clearly hasn't told Trilby that, regardless of the way she left, Tess enjoyed every single thing I did to her in that basement. I can still taste her come on my tongue and feel her peaked nipples on the tips of my fingers. Her soft skin still ripples beneath mine whenever I close my eyes. Her tight little pussy still grips my cock possessively whenever I let my mind wander back to that moment.

"The Federico thing," Cristiano says with a begrudging sigh. "Do I need to worry?"

My chest bristles at the sound of his name and I hate that it has infiltrated first my relationship with Tess and now the equilibrium I've worked hard to maintain with Cristiano.

"No," I reply. The last three weeks have been preoccupied with getting eyes on him and monitoring every move he makes, every breath he takes, every wipe of his ass. Which reminds me, I haven't heard from Nino in a few days, the guy I sent out to California to do just that. I make a mental note to check my phone and follow up the second Cristiano finishes telling me off.

"He's just a kid anyway. A bitter kid who can't accept the truth." Assuming his papa actually gave him the truth. Enzo was always a good guy before he wasn't. Maybe I overestimated him.

"Okay, fine." Cristiano settles a weary pair of eyes on me. "Listen, keep your distance from Tess. I don't care how much you might want to speak to her, if Trilby sees you anywhere her sister, she'll bust a blood vessel, and I can't have that so close to the wedding."

One of my vital organs thuds into the bowels of my belly. I was planning on trying to talk to Tess, to talk some fucking sense into her, but that's off the table now.

"I will," I concede, reluctantly. "Anything else?"

"Figure out where the Marchesi's are. They've gone awfully fucking quiet. They know what's happening this weekend and I don't want them bursting in here and fucking up my wife's day."

I nod.

"In fact, get more security around the perimeter and double check all the staff IDs. I don't want there to be any cracks for these bastards to fall through."

"I'm on it."

I get to my feet and re-button my jacket.

"Benny…"

The change in Cristiano's tone makes me pause. "I know you like Tess."

I don't look up for fear he might see something in my eyes resembling vulnerability.

"You have to talk to her eventually—I can't watch you walk around looking like shit forever. But not yet. Give her some space and do it after the wedding."

I straighten and inhale a long breath then look him directly in the eye. "Sure, boss."

My blood is boiling as I walk out of the business suite, and that won't do. I didn't get to this point in my life by being a hot mess. I step outside and breathe in the warm air then take out my phone.

I notice a few missed calls from a burner, which I ignore in favor of calling Nino. He answers on the second ring and sounds out of breath.

"What's going on? I haven't heard from you in two days."

"He's gone," Nino says, panting down the phone. "The fucker tricked me. He must have known I was following him—he waited until I was in the restroom of a diner then bailed before his food even arrived."

"Fuck," I spit. "When was that?"

"Tuesday, five in the afternoon."

"So, exactly two days ago. Why the fuck didn't you tell me?"

"I was on his tail. I almost got him twice. I only lost him for good this morning."

My muscles brace and harden. "Where?"

"LAX."

"You didn't see which flight he was boarding?"

"I'm so sorry, Benito. I lost him."

"What about the airport staff?" Tension grips my

chest like an iron fist. "Couldn't you have threatened someone? Got access to all the flight logs?"

"And alert the authorities over here? This isn't New York, Benito. They'd have thrown me in jail and I'd be of no use to you there."

I yell down the phone. "FUCK!"

"He's coming to New York, Benito," Nino says calmly. "We don't need to be tailing him to know that. The most we can do is be ready for him."

I inhale slowly, straighten my shoulders and smooth a hand down my tie. "Is he armed?"

A beat passes before Nino responds. "He wasn't when he left, but there's something else you should know."

Irritation presses against my spine. "What's that?"

"I got hold of his call history. There's one number he's been in contact with a lot. And it's the last one he called before he left."

"Whose number?"

"Well, that's the concerning thing. There's no owner data available. Nothing to say where it was purchased or when. It belongs to someone who knows exactly how to work the system."

"It's a burner," I say.

"Has to be."

"Where is this burner located? Where are the calls going to?"

From the length of Nino's pause, I know the answer before he opens his mouth. "New York."

I hang up and call Beppe immediately.

"We need eyes on JFK and Newark," I bark before he has a chance to speak.

"How many?" he shoots back, reminding me of why I value him so much. He doesn't ask fucking useless questions—he just gets on with it.

"As many as you can spare."

"What about the hotel?"

"Covered. I'll get a few more of Augie's men here."

"Who are we looking for?"

I shake my head. "You won't fucking believe this," I sigh. "Federico Falconi."

"Enzo's kid?" The upward lilt of Beppe's question only confirms the ridiculousness of the situation—I'm rallying the troops to fend off a teenager. Well, he's early twenties now I reckon, but still, Beppe's right—he's a kid. I might still be in my twenties myself, but I've lived a whole life in the underworld. He's merely a tourist.

"He's coming back here with a motive. But, it's not what *he*'s capable of that worries me." I pinch the bridge of my nose between a thumb and forefinger. "He's in touch with an unknown entity. That's a risk."

"Understood," Beppe replies. "I'll put a call out now, get a recent photograph and we'll make sure he doesn't leave whatever airport he arrives into."

I'm about to hang up when Beppe says my name, and the way he says it makes clear he's bearing bad news.

"What is it?"

"Our contact is dead."

It takes me a second to figure out who he's talking about. "The Marchesi associate? Bigelow?"

"Yes. Him."

I scrub a clammy palm down my face. There goes our upper hand. "How?"

"The nephews got to him. Slit his throat, threw his body on a boat and let him bleed out all over it while floating down the Connecticut River."

"They're sending a message."

I can hear Beppe nodding. "We got away with it for a year."

"And now?"

"We have no idea what they're planning but I have a bad feeling about this Benito. The nephews have moved fast. They haven't officially taken over as the leading members of the family, but no one seems to give a shit. They've taken the drug bust real personal. My guy didn't say this outright but he may as well have done: They're coming after us."

Not yet, I hope silently. "I need to call Augie and make sure nothing is getting into the Hamptons. You'll keep me posted on any sightings?"

"I will."

"And you'll head over here for the wedding?"

"Absolutely."

"Thanks Beppe." I hang up and stare out at the green and blue view, seeing nothing but slit throats, black lashes and parted lips.

I refuse the second refill of wine and cut into the steak. Blood oozes across the plate and I stare at it as I chew. I know if I look up my gaze will be drawn ahead and to the left, to where Contessa Castellano is sitting with her own eyes averted. I find myself yearning for the days when she would glare at me across a table, the hatred spewing forth from beneath a dark brow. She's doing her best to angle her bare shoulders away from me but the close-knit seating plan is working against her.

"Someone cut off your tongue?"

I pan my gaze to my right and shoot a glare of my own at Nicolò. "What?"

"You're not usually this quiet. I assumed there'd be a medical reason for it."

"I'm preoccupied," I snap.

"Don't worry." He waves a relaxed hand. "We've got this place locked down. No Marchesi's are getting in here. I went through all the IDs myself and Augie has got a whole army surrounding the place."

That does make me feel a little better.

"Good. I need to make a call." I stand and push my chair back, which makes a loud enough noise that the whole room looks up. Her gaze burns my skin. I don't need to make a call but I do need to get out of this room.

I can still feel the sting of her stare as I head outside and light a cigarette. I'm not a regular smoker but I need something to calm my agitated nerves. If only I had just Tess to worry about—now I have Federico fucking Falconi and the Marchesi's-on-a-mission to contend with too.

I smoke half a pack before I eventually go back inside. Darkness has fallen but it gives me some sense of relief to see shadows in every corner. I know they're Augie's men watching the perimeter of the hotel.

The lights inside have been dimmed too and most of the guests have moved into the bar area. I can't bear to see her apathy, knowing there's fuck-all I can do about it until after the wedding, so I dip my eyes as I work my way through the designer dresses and tailored suits. My cell feels hot in my pocket as I wait for a call from Beppe. If it doesn't come, I can only hope the Falconi kid has flown someplace else.

Just as I reach the bar, a small figure turns around, not looking where she's going, and walks right into me, sloshing the contents of four champagne flutes over my suit. My teeth grit until I realize who it is.

"Oh gosh!" Tess gasps, then averts her eyes faster than a rat flying up a fucking drainpipe. "I'm so sorry. Can I get you a towel?"

Her question sends me right back to when she stripped down to 'next to nothing' and I practically threw a towel over her. "I'm not naked," I say, then bite the shit out of my tongue.

Her cheeks flush so hard I want to lick them, and all kinds of things are happening south of my belt. And if that wasn't unfortunate enough, I feel Cristiano's eyes on the back of my neck, watching me doing exactly what he told me not to.

"That's not what I meant," she says quietly, looking at the floor.

"I know. Sorry." I rub a hand round the back of my neck trying to erase the sensation of Cristiano's glare. "I'll replace those."

I nod to the bartender who quickly pours out four more flutes of champagne while I unbutton my jacket and shrug it off my shoulders. I hang it on a hook beneath the bar and roll up my sleeves. It's a reflex but I'd do it a million times over just to see her gaze flit to my forearms and the flush creep a little higher up her cheeks.

God, there's nothing I want more than to reach out, take her pretty chin between my fingers and press my lips onto hers, but the sensation on the back of my neck is only growing hotter.

I place a few notes on the bar then speak to the thickly perfumed air above her head. "Enjoy your evening," I force out. Then I turn around and walk away.

CHAPTER THIRTY-FIVE

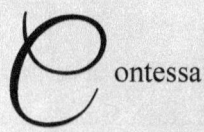
ontessa

"Pink or silver?" Bambi waits, wide-eyed for my verdict.

I have to drag my attention from the cool, calm sea outside, back to the room. "Pink or silver what?"

"Crystals," she replies, frowning. I drop my gaze to her nails. They've been painted a bright bubblegum pink and she's now sitting, tweezers in hand, poised to embellish them with sparkling gems.

"Silver."

I turn to see Sera with her hands full of Trilby's bleached blond hair. She looks like she's taken on Kate Bush in a battle of the blow-dryer and she isn't winning.

I glance at my empty flute and go to refill my glass but nothing comes out.

"I think this is the last of the champagne." I hold the

bottle upside down and inspect the mouth for drips. "I'll call room service."

"No!" Sera says, her mouth full of hair pins. "They'll just give us the house stuff. I put a couple of the expensive bottles to one side for us."

"I don't mind going to get them," I offer.

"Okay, great. Yeah, I might be a while." She jerks her head toward Trilby and it does appear Sera underestimated how long the hair preparation would take.

I get to my feet, grateful for an opportunity to stretch my legs. "Where do I go?"

Sera takes the pins out of her mouth. "Go out of this room, turn right, down the hall, past the staircase. At the end is an elevator—it's the staff elevator. Go down to the basement…"

Trilby's gaze flashes in my direction and I swallow.

"Basement. No problem."

Sera, unaware of my recent experience with basements, continues. "When you step out, there are two doors on the left. One is the dry food store—ignore that one. The second is a cleaning closet. I put a couple of bottles on the floor just inside the door."

"What if someone sees me?"

"Just tell them I sent you. I haven't done anything wrong, I just forgot to bring the bottles upstairs."

"Okay then." I twist the door handle. "I'll be back in a little while."

The rest of the hotel seems quiet but we are on the top floor and the acoustics are well-contained with all the thick pile carpets and soft furnishings. My pulse quickens as I near the end of the landing. I'm imagining the basement to be dark, damp and eerie, just like the one in Arena. My hands feel clammy just thinking about it.

My mind flashes back to when I was sitting on the chair in Arena's basement, pleading with Benito to believe me. I remember the warm glow in his eyes when he dropped his gaze to between my thighs, and in seconds I'm *hot* all over.

I go through the motions of pressing the elevator call button and waiting for its arrival, all the while holding my thighs together, trying to find friction I can use to ease this building pressure. When the elevator arrives I step into it. The face of the person looking back at me through the mirrored wall looks untethered. Full, parted lips, large eyes rimmed with long black lashes, damp from crying with laughter most of the night.

When the doors open again, I step out automatically, then feel a huge sense of relief to see the basement is just another corridor, albeit wider than those upstairs—dry and brightly lit. I can also hear voices, so I'm thankful I'm not alone. The doors are clearly labeled, the first one I see signposted 'Dry Store'. I'm almost right past it when I have an idea. We ate a gorgeous but very light dinner, and Trilby needs to keep her strength up the next couple of days. We could all probably do with some more food inside us. I open the door to the dry store and flick the light switch on the inside wall.

My eyes widen at the sight of dozens upon dozens

of shelves holding tins of sauces, bags of dried beans, every type of flour and sugar imaginable, and—the thing I'm really looking for—stacked boxes of chips. I make a beeline straight for them and a mental note to pay for it all in the morning. I grab some barbecue chips, popcorn and pretzels, then flick the switch and pull the door closed.

When I reach the cleaning closet, the door is slightly ajar. I open it fully and peer inside, but I don't see any bottles. I look around both sides of the door and there's nothing. My pulse quickens, my nerves jumping to the conclusion something is off, but I shove them down into the base of my stomach. I was nervous about coming down here and everything has been fine. I have to remind myself, this is the Harbor's Edge in the Hamptons—it isn't the seedy basement of a mafia-run nightclub.

Just the peripheral thought of Arena heats my skin again. Simply knowing that the place belongs to Benito makes me ache to return, even though the sensible part of my brain—and Trilby's voice in the back of my head—says that is the last thing I should do.

I flick the switch. I'm surprised to see the room is quite large. More shelves are lined with cleaning products and vacuum cleaners. Mops and brooms of all sizes are stacked in two corners. I inspect both sides of the door again but don't see any champagne bottles.

"Where did you put them, Sera?" I whisper under my breath, taking a few steps into the room. Maybe someone came in, saw the bottles close to the door and put them on a shelf so they wouldn't be kicked over by accident.

I walk to the nearest shelf but before I reach it, the sound of the light switch shutting off fills the room and I'm cast in complete darkness.

I spin around quickly, not that it helps—I can't see a thing, not even a sliver of light from where I'd left the door ajar. It isn't ajar anymore.

My heart beats at the base of my throat and my head feels light. "Hello?" I call out, my voice empty and trembling.

I shiver in the cool basement air and the hairs covering my whole body stand on end. I wrap my arms around myself and take a nervous step toward the door. I can sense someone is in the room with me. The presence of warmth makes my head tingle—it's the sensation I often have right before I pass out.

"Please…" I say, but the word sticks to my dry lips. I have to force out the rest. "Who's there?"

The sight of my stalker collapsed on the street with blood running from his mouth fills my vision and nausea crawls up my throat. Why do I keep doing these foolish things—letting a crazy person follow me around for three years, and now walking blindly into a basement room without checking it was completely safe to do so. Benito was right—I do need protecting from myself.

A fragile slice of light is visible beneath the door, alerting me to where it is. I don't take a breath before bolting toward it, but before I can reach the handle, a giant hand whips out and wraps around my face, turns me around and pushes me up against a wall.

My scream is muffled against calloused skin and my heart is silenced by a burning heat against my back. The shape of it, the severity of the burn, is familiar. But the fact my captor isn't speaking makes me doubt my judgement.

I pant against the unyielding palm, tears rolling down my cheeks and over the man's fingers. Then his weight is pressed against me—clear, defined lines, curves and ridges. I almost faint with relief. It's Benito, I'm sure of it. But, the brute force he's using to hold me still and the unemotive lingering while I cry is *terrifying*.

The removal of my sight only makes room for my other senses to soar. His heavy, masculine scent floods my nostrils and the nerve endings across my skin dance like electrical currents. He passes a hand under my arm and up through the middle of my chest and uses it to keep me still while he softens his hold on my face. Then, with a gentle thumb, he wipes away my tears.

After several minutes have passed, my breaths lengthen and my shivers ease. With his hand still covering my mouth, he slides the other one down the middle of my body. The satin ripples around it, chasing its path to my navel. A ball of heat unfurls behind my belly button and slides down to my core, where it sits heavily between my thighs.

The breaths at my back are ragged, his chest pressing against my spine with each inhale. He's undeniably turned on, which only fuels the aching pull around my opening.

Up to now, my hands had been fisted at my sides, but slowly, they uncurl. I place one hand on the wall to ground myself and reach the other behind me tentatively. My fingers graze familiar Italian cotton and my lids flutter shut.

His flattened palm inches further downward until it's pressing softly against my pelvic bone. Slowly and torturously, he walks his fingers to drag the remaining fabric up my thighs, each inch of flesh uncovered sending sparks of fire to my clit. When the final inch of fabric is in his grip, his fingers venture inwards and find me.

I release a long-held breath and it's chased by an entirely uncontrolled moan. Instead of taking that as permission to continue, he pauses as if soaking up the moment, absorbing it into his being. The seconds drag until it is all close to unbearable. Without thinking, I lick the palm of his hand. He rewards me by stroking his fingers over my clit. It is achingly slow, as if he's memorizing my sex from every angle.

I shift my hips forward until I'm pressing into his hand. He responds by thickening his grip on my mouth, but then gives me what I want and pushes two long, thick fingers inside my heat. I tighten around him, ensuring I can feel every stroke and glide of the tips, and his touch lights me up everywhere.

The air in the room is thick with arousal—his and mine—and it dawns on me what he's doing. He knows I hate the reason he imprisoned me in the basement of Arena, but he also knows that what he did to me down there... I *loved it*. And he knows I don't know how to feel about that. I feel ashamed to have enjoyed it, but I yearn for him to take that control again. He knows I *should* be avoiding him, but he also knows I *can't*. This is why he's here. He's giving me no choice, just the way I need it to be.

The rhythm is torturous. His fingers caress me back and forth, then play my clit like an instrument. He pinches it tightly then rubs my arousal around, soothing it until I'm humming for release.

Softly, he removes the hand from my mouth and pulls my hair back over my shoulder tilting my head to the right giving him access to the skin at my nape. He licks it gently then paints a line of hot, wet kisses all the way to my shoulder. A reckless shiver ghosts over my spine.

Knowing I'm now unlikely to scream, he withdraws his hand. In the darkness, the sound of a zipper releasing fills the air and my pulse races. I grind against his fingers giving him silent permission to enter me.

The movement of his fingers doesn't falter once as he pulls himself out of his boxers and drags the head of his cock along the crevice of my bottom. My eyes almost roll back in my head at the prospect of what's to come.

I need him to fill me to the brim. I want him to make me his, in every possible shadowy, shameful and dirty way. I want his darkness. I want his wild.

My head falls forward and I rest it against the wall, still chasing his fingers as they stroke me into a frenzy. I'm on the edge, about to tip over, when his cock slides beneath the fabric of my negligee and into the arousal pooling between my legs. It slips back and forth, stimulating my clit along with his fingers. An untethered moan falls from my lips and my thighs tremble.

Just as I think he might give me what I need, the crown of his cock moves backward and presses against my other opening. My eyelids ping open, seeing nothing but shadows. He dips his fingers into my heat and uses my arousal to lubricate my entrance. I tense, stiffly, but his skilled fingers work my opening until I feel able to relax. Then he angles his cock perfectly and pushes the head inside.

Breath is dragged from my lungs. I've never felt anything like it. He continues to massage my clit and push his fingers inside to caress a spot that splits me apart, but I'm hyper aware of his cock stretching another part of me wide open.

His breaths grow short and heavy, making it clear what this is doing to him. His unwavering control is being challenged. This motivates me to push my ass backward, taking him another inch. A hoarse breath scratches his vocal cords and he presses his lips harshly to my throat. He keeps his right hand between my legs, coaxing me into a state of oblivion while his left finds mine pressed into the wall. Just as the white heat unfurls across my core, he threads his fingers through mine and thrusts a little. The pressure it unravels lights up every cell in my body and I come hard with his fingers deep inside me. The tremors roll right through my bones, tightening the muscles in my ass and tugging at the sensitive skin at his crown. I hear another rasping moan and he jerks into my back opening, flooding me with heat.

His chest molds itself around my back as we convulse for what feels like a full minute. By the end of it, we're both out of breath and sticky with sweat. He glides his lips from the base of my throat to my ear, then sucks the soft lobe between his lips. I want to turn my head and catch his lips in mine but I don't. It would break the spell. It would mean I'd walk out of here knowing with absolute clarity what I've just done, and the shame will engulf me.

The one thing that will save my sanity is the ambiguity. It's easier to live with the thought I just consented to let a stranger fuck me in a darkened room, than the thought that I returned to the man who abducted me, insisted I couldn't be trusted, then made me come against my will.

The truth stings like the whack of a belt. I just gave him a different version of my virginity, and I wouldn't change it for the world.

Deep down, we both know.

We both know we've crossed a line so raw and so intimate, that despite whatever comes next, there is no turning back.

I stagger back along the corridor to the suite in a daze. The same daze I fell into as Benito tore off his shirt and wiped me clean, then stepped back to let me walk past him and out of the room.

I take a deep breath that does nothing to snap me out of the trance I'm in, then open the door. Bambi is playing some game on her phone but Trilby and Sera look up. From the looks of the pins and rollers in Trilby's hair, Sera's work was done a while ago.

"Where've you been?" Sera asks with wide eyes. "France?"

I stare at her, blankly.

"The champagne, Tess," she continues. "Did you get it?"

"I—" My spine trembles, my blood hot, shame creeping across the surface of my skin. The space between my ass cheeks feels like it just went through three rounds in a boxing ring but my clit is *singing*. I have to work hard to drag my focus back to Sera's question. "No. I couldn't find it."

She jumps to her feet and I'm expecting an exasperated huff but instead she beams at me. "Don't worry, I'll go get us a bottle from the bar. Back in a sec!"

As the door closes I pan back to Trilby and notice she has a brow raised.

"Are you okay?" Her tone is doubtful.

"I'm fine," I reply, monotone. "I just couldn't find it."

"Looks like you found other stuff though," she

grins, and it's only then I realize Benito must have picked up the chips I dropped and shoved them into my arms as I left.

"Oh yeah." I stare at the bags like they came from Mars and pass them to Trilby who rips them open and shoves literal handfuls into her mouth.

I sit at the window and watch the sunrise over swaying palms, my negligee pooled around my hips. It's five a.m., the room is cool with conditioned air, and I'm barely clothed, yet I still feel hot all over. I rest my head back against the window frame and close my eyes. I see nothing but a wall of shadows, but I can feel everything. My stomach liquifies as I recall the soft touch of his fingers and his hard penetration of an unfamiliar part of me. And my head reels at the realization that, yet again, I loved it.

I don't understand myself. I always knew I was wild, but this is different. This is dark. I've been tied up against my will and I've been approached in a blacked-out room. I was complicit in the pleasure that was created and received; I fully participated in the actions. And I would do it all again—with him.

A rustle of a comforter lifts my lids.

"What time is it?"

I look over and see Trilby rubbing her eyes. "It's only five o'clock. You should try and get some more sleep. Big day for you—it's the rehearsal."

I smile and feel a combination of excitement and dread flow through my veins.

She sits up and looks around the room. Sera is laid next to her in the king sized bed, fast asleep, and Bambi is equally as dead to the world on a guest bed over the other side of the suite.

"I can never get back to sleep once I've woken up." She stretches her arms over her head then slips her feet into the totally cliched fluffy slippers we bought her as a bachelorette gift.

She softly pads across the carpet and joins me in the window, sitting opposite me on the ledge. "Did you sleep?"

I note she didn't say 'much' or 'well' and figure there isn't a lot I can hide from my big sister. "Not really."

She lowers her voice to a whisper since we're not alone in the room. "Is it because of him?"

I sigh and pan my gaze out the window. "Yes."

"I spoke to Cristiano about… you know, what happened."

I'm about to roll my eyes. "You shouldn't have—"

"I am still annoyed with him," she says in a grave tone.

"As am I with you," I say, levelling her with a glare. "I didn't want this to become a big deal."

She holds up her hands. "And it isn't. I said my piece and he's given strict orders that… *he*… is to stay out of your way, at least until after the wedding."

An unladylike snort shoots out through my nose and I hastily try to cover it up with a cough.

"What's so funny?" Trilby frowns.

"Nothing." I shake my head. "I wasn't laughing."

"You smirked."

"I did not."

"Tess…" her voice carries a warning note.

I close my eyes and sigh out a long breath. "It's just, I don't think Benito listens to anyone. Not even Cristiano."

"What do you mean?" Trilby frowns. "What has he done now?"

I look up at her through my lashes. "Why do you think I took so long trying to find the champagne?"

Trilby sucks in a dramatic breath and clamps a hand over her mouth. "What?" she mumbles. "You ran into him?"

"It's okay—he didn't hurt me or upset me. It was fine."

"So, what? Did you guys talk?"

I swallow and look away, too quickly. "Something like that."

In the corner of my eye I see her slowly lower her hand. "I'm not going to pry, Tess. It's only my business if you want it to be. Just know that if you need anything—anything at all—I'm here, okay?"

I bite my lip and nod, then move off the ledge. "I'm going to go to my room and shower," I say, changing the subject. "You're sure you can't go back to sleep?"

"Are you kidding?" She grins. "Even if I could, I

wouldn't want to. It's the day of the rehearsal! And I'm getting married tomorrow! To Cristiano!"

My smile widens at the flush spreading across her cheeks. Her eyes dance with excitement and her whole body lights up. Without thinking, I throw my arms around her neck.

"Yes you bloody are!" I squeal into her shoulder. "And it's going to be the best wedding ever!"

And as the words leave my lips, I know without a doubt it really is.

CHAPTER THIRTY-SIX

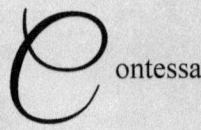

ontessa

I take advantage of my inability to sleep by taking a walk along the beach, relishing the feel of the warm sand between my toes and the soft breeze in my hair. I feel lighter than I have done in a while, and despite the confusion I'm battling around my feelings for Benito, I cannot wait to see Cristiano and Trilby become husband and wife.

For all intents and purposes, this is a mafia marriage, bringing two families together, albeit willingly, for mutual benefit. But from where I'm standing, it's the marriage of two souls who love each other so much it sometimes makes my eyes hurt.

I glance at my watch and realize I have only one hour before I have to join the wedding party and prepare for the rehearsal. I hurry back to my room and change into the bridesmaid dress. Trilby chose a beautiful dusky rose taffeta for all our dresses, which somehow compliments our various skin tones and eye colors. Me with my pale skin, jet black hair and green eyes; Sera with her equally pale skin, auburn hair and blue eyes; and Bambi with her dark hair, olive skin and rich brown eyes.

The styles are all different too. Sera's dress is backless with a halter neckline and empire waist; Bambi's dress is short and light, cut to bounce around her knees as she walks; while mine is strapless and fitted, with a beautiful long slice up the right thigh. It reminds me of the dress I wore to Gianni Di Santo's funeral all those months ago.

As I gaze back at my reflection I have to concede it really is a beautiful dress and the color does highlight my better features. Still, I can't help but feel a little bit itchy that it isn't black.

I pick up the pearl-covered purse that Trilby had specially made for each of us as a bridesmaid gift and make my way down the main staircase. The wedding party is gathering in one of the function rooms on the ground floor, away from the main hall where the ceremony will take place.

I silently curse that an imaginary bug cut short the tour I should have had from Sera when we first arrived because I really don't know where to go. There are signs nailed to the walls, pointing to beautiful room names, but I have no idea which room we are meeting in. I remind myself Cristiano has hired pretty much the entire hotel so it's unlikely I'll go far wrong.

I turn into a corridor and follow the sound of voices. They're coming from a room at the far end, but I'm curious to see what the other rooms look like. I decide to take a sneaky look before the rehearsal gets underway and I become swept up in the mayhem.

The first door to my left is called 'Maine'. The interior is beautifully colonial—lots of white rattan furniture and nautical striped cushions. A large glass-topped table forms the focal point, reflecting the mid-morning sun.

I close the door softly and cross the corridor to another. I push it open and step into the room. 'Manhattan' has a more masculine feel—dark wood paneling, gold picture lights and leather club chairs surrounding a solid wood boardroom table. I decide I much prefer the other one and start to back out of the room. But the door closes sharply and a hand wraps around my face, flattening my cheeks.

My body lights up everywhere, my core smoldering at the memory of last night. Shamefully, I want nothing more than to feel his large hands on my thighs, beneath this beautiful dress, his tongue licking and probing at my lace underwear, my fingers wrapped around his erection… But I'm already late and I'm wearing a bridesmaid dress for heaven's sake.

I go to turn around, mumbling a weak protest into his palm, when the door flies open and Benito steps through it, his face contorting into something *deadly*.

It takes me too long to figure out what's happening. Benito is standing in front of me. So, *who* is holding his hand over my mouth?

Alarmed, I try to scream but it's muffled. The hand squeezes me tighter, then I'm pulled back against a hard chest. Another hand whips out from behind me and points a gun at Benito. I struggle against the chest but whoever has me in a headlock is freakishly strong. I start to hyperventilate, unable to grasp air.

My brain scrambles. Why would anyone here want to kill Benito? Cristiano has this place locked down—anyone who isn't a trusted guest or member of the wedding party is allowed within a two mile radius. Is there a traitor on the inside?

I try to shout "No!" but the word is absorbed by the solid palm.

My gaze darts frantically to Benito. He is eerily calm, as though he's used to people attempting to assassinate him on a fairly regular basis. He even drops his gaze to his *phone*, and types something out before sliding it into his pocket. A soft exhale leaves his lips, then he says, "Put the gun down, Federico."

What??

I somehow find strength I couldn't before—perhaps it's knowing that my childhood friend, my *first*, wouldn't truly hurt me—and I duck out of his grasp, then spin around, my arms outstretched, hands braced.

The air is swiped from my lungs.

It *is* Federico—the boy I lost my virginity to three years ago. The boy I mourned for weeks, months, *years* after he left, who never wrote me back… until a couple of months ago.

"Fed…" I gasp, words forming on my tongue but not quite sailing on the air. "What are you doing?"

"What I promised I would do. Now get back Tess. You don't want to see this."

He cocks the gun and I don't even think. I throw myself at him, knocking him backward into the table. Another click of metal sounds behind me.

"He's right, Tess. Get out of the way." Benito's voice is low and vicious. "In fact, leave the room."

My breath stutters and the room spins. Long fingers wrap around my wrist. "No, Tess. Stay."

"Don't you *dare* tell her what to do," Benito growls. "You're waving a fucking gun about like a child. I don't want her to get hurt."

"A child?" Fed's voice is unrecognizable and his hold on my arm is unyielding. Yes, he was a boy when he left, but he's not a boy anymore. I glance at him through trembling lashes. He's filled out to twice the size and his cheekbones have emerged through a face of carved granite. I swallow, unable to believe the person who coaxed me through my first sexual experience is the same person still wielding a firearm at the infamous Di Santo consigliere.

"I haven't been a *child* since I watched you murder my uncle in cold blood."

My eyes flick to Benito expecting him to deny it, but he doesn't. Somehow I know he wasn't lying when he said Augie killed Mario, not him, but I guess a Di Santo kill is just that—a Di Santo kill. The small matter of who pulled the trigger is irrelevant. "Seeing something that *evil* makes you grow up pretty fast."

"If you think that's evil, why are you working with the Marchesi's?" Benito grits out through a clenched jaw. "Have you forgotten how they killed Tess and Trilby's mother?"

Federico lets go of my wrist, spins me around and pulls my face into his chest. His coarse whisper reaches my ears. "I've got you Tess. Don't listen to him."

I dare not move. I use the wall of flesh to hide away. I don't want to confront any of this. All I know is Benito can do more than hurt me—he can rip out my heart and grind it beneath his foot. I've had a small taste of it and the pain is unbearable.

Fed has already given me his worst—he ignored me for over three years. And now he's back.

Despite the hard lines of his chest, he's still the softer of the two men. He's the one least likely to put me in compromising positions that I enjoy too damn much. He's the one who would listen to Cristiano when he says to keep away, because he's sensible like that. He doesn't need to be prepared to lose everything simply because he *can't* stay away.

I feel Benito's glare on my back but I can't move.

"Fury Marchesi doesn't have anywhere near as much blood on his hands as you do," Fed spits over my shoulder.

"That's because he got his minions to do his dirty work for him," Benito bites back. "And if you still think that's tame, how about the nephews quartering Joe Bigelow and draping his bleeding corpse over a fucking boat and sailing it down the river for everyone—kids included—to see?"

"Fine." Federico is trembling with anger. "If you want to talk kids, what about your former don's child trafficking activities? Weren't you serving him while he was off making deals with the cartel?"

I lift my head at the same time as my stomach drops. *It can't be true.* I knew what Savero had planned—we all did—but only after Cristiano discovered it and killed his own flesh and blood, putting an immediate end to those plans. Had Benito known all along?

"I advised Gianni for seven years," Benito grits out in a voice as low as the devil himself. "I *inherited* Savero. And, not that it's any of your goddamn business, he didn't let anyone in. Not even me."

A shiver of relief ghosts down my spine.

"You haven't answered my question," he continues. "Why are you working with the Marchesi's?"

Fed's breathing steadies, then he says, "I'm not."

I jerk my head up. "But… you said in your letter…"

"I thought I was," Fed says, a look of discomfort eating into the corners of his eyes. "But the man I thought was a Marchesi is someone else."

"Who?" I whisper up at him.

"He isn't connected to either family," Fed says, his glare boring into Benito. "But he's been very helpful to me."

"In what way?" Benito demands.

"Well," Federico flicks the wrist holding the gun to check his watch. "I would say that, any second now, your precious restaurant is going to go up in flames."

"What the fuck are you talking about?" Benito's voice dips to a new low and I genuinely fear for Federico's life.

Fed picks up on Benito's waning restraint and goads him further. "Your Achilles heel, right? La Trattoria?"

Benito's gaze flicks to mine then narrows on Federico.

"No—" I push myself away from Fed, breathless. "No-no-no-no. Please say you're lying, Federico."

Fed drops his gaze to mine. His mouth quirks lazily in one corner. "Why would I lie about it, Tess? I told you in my letter that was my plan."

"Not La Trattoria," I whisper.

"What else?" He frowns. "What else would be his Achilles Heel, Tess?"

My heart jumps into my throat, then a thought occurs to me. "Benito's house… Was it you who burned it down?"

"No." He wipes a hand across his mouth. "But kudos to whoever did."

I'm about to plead with him to stop being so damned cocky when Benito lunges at him from across the room.

I'm knocked to the side, my head cracking against the wall. I slide in my dusky pink dress to the floor in a daze. In my blurred vision, I'm aware of Benito bending over Fed, pummeling the life out of him. I bend my knees and anchor my tall heels against the floor but I can't find purchase. They simply slide away from me. "No, Benito, please," I beg. "Stop."

Fed's gun clatters to the floor and I push my torso away from the wall to kick it completely out of reach. The fewer firearms available to them right now, the better.

The door bangs open and Nicolò appears with Augie right on his tail. "What the fuck?" Nicolò says, shaking his head as he walks into the room.

"Wondered where you'd got to," Augie says, as though Benito isn't holding a guy by his throat with a gun pointing between his eyes. "The rehearsal's about to start. You wanna finish up?"

"There's a call for you." Nicolò puts his cell on speaker and holds it a few feet from where Benito has Federico pinned against the wall.

"Enzo?" Benito says, like he already knows the answer. Then I remember Benito doing something with his phone almost the second he saw Federico.

Fed struggles at the sound of his father's name.

"Benito," Enzo says at the other end. "It's been a long time."

"Yes it has, but I'm not interested in pleasantries. Know where your son is?"

Federico tries to speak but Benito head butts him in the face, putting a stop to any words coming out of his mouth. I wince at the crunch of forehead on teeth. Blood streams from Federico's mouth but Benito seems unharmed. *Unaffected.*

"Not right now," Enzo replies. "He's a grown man—"

"Who deserves to know the truth, don't you think?" Benito replies in an ice-cold tone.

There's a beat of silence before Enzo replies. "Is he there?"

Federico mumbles through a split lip.

"Fed? Are you there with Benito?"

Benito flings him a warning glare. "Yes he is. Came at me with a gun. Burned down my restaurant, so he says. Revenge, apparently, for me shutting down your business and sending you all away."

"Oh God." A resigned moan surfaces through Nicolò's cell into the room.

"It's time to tell him the truth, Enzo."

Federico's gaze flits between me and Benito and the same feeling I had when we parted ways comes back to me in a breathless rush. Right this second, it's crystal clear. I never loved Federico. I liked him, of course—he was my best friend. But the feeling that has confused me ever since, that I haven't been able to put into words until now, is pity. Not love—*pity*.

Federico has just done what Federico always did—barreled headlong into a situation before taking the time to really figure out why. He's still the same, rash, hasty and naive Federico I knew from school. And it doesn't matter how earnest his declarations are, or how convincing his words, my feelings about him haven't changed.

"Benito didn't ruin us, Federico," Enzo says quietly. "It was all my fault."

Fed tries to speak but his injured mouth prevents it.

"Go on," Benito says, urging Enzo to continue.

"I was gambling and got into a lot of debt. I did my best to pay my debtors, but I simply couldn't kick the habit. The more I paid off, the more I gambled. I'm sick, Federico. It's a disease. I couldn't stop gambling and in the end I had to sell off most of our assets. The Di Santo's…"

Benito coughs loudly.

"Benito…" Enzo corrected, "told me to leave and take the family far away. The business couldn't be saved. I let the Di Santo's down and I owe Benito my life."

Fed's stare falters and his grip on Benito's arms loosens. He's just become aware he's unknowingly walked right back into the hornet's nest. Benito lets go of Fed's throat but keeps the gun pointed at his head.

"Papa—" Blood spits from Fed's lips when he says that one word, and his eyes fill with tears.

"Tell him about Mario," Benito barks.

A sigh can be heard down the line and Federico glances to the side, his gaze resting on Augie. "Your uncle took liberties, Federico. I couldn't control him. He hadn't worked for the family business for six months and in the end he only cared about his cars and his mistresses…"

Fed's eyes widen, letting a tear fall to the floor.

"He knew the Di Santo's were paying me a visit and

he panicked. All he could think about was losing the life he'd built up on the money we skimmed from the Di Santo's."

Federico deflates against the wall and Benito removes the gun and takes a step backward.

"I should have told you the truth, but honestly, I feel so ashamed. I didn't want you to think badly of your papa, Federico. I didn't want you to hate me for taking you away from your life, your friends…"

I lower my gaze to the floor. Seeing Federico crumble under the truth is too painful to watch. I only look up when Augie slips a hand under my arm and helps me to my feet.

"Come home, Federico, please," his father begs.

"He will," Benito says, sternly. "My men will escort him until the flight is off the ground."

"Thank you Benito. I truly am sorry."

Nicolò snaps the phone closed, terminating the conversation. "And we *truly* have to go," he says to Benito. I'm pretty certain Cristiano's closest cousin is the only person Benito allows to speak to him in that way.

"Um—" Federico tries to speak. Augie steps forward and offers him a handkerchief. Fed takes it and mops up his mouth as best he can. Several of us avert our eyes. "I, um… I'm sorry about the restaurant."

Benito glances at Nicolò who shakes his head.

"We haven't had reports of it being burned down," Benito says with an arched brow.

Federico swallows. "But, Andreas said—"

"Who's Andreas?" Augie snaps.

"The guy who said he works with the Marchesi's. He said he would organize it." Federico blinks at Benito as though he's expecting another head butt.

"It won't happen," Nicolò says, inspecting his nails. "The place is locked down."

"I… I didn't burn down your house," Fed rushes out.

Benito stares at him with the scariest of poker faces. In this moment I understand why he has such a lethal reputation. It's impossible to know what he's thinking or planning, until it's done.

"I-I promise, Benito. I didn't go anywhere near your house. I promise."

Still Benito stares, not saying a word. The atmosphere in the room recedes to nothing but cold heartbeats and frigid truths.

"Please believe me," Fed begs. I can see the panic in his eyes, the acceptance of certain death. "I didn't burn down your house."

Benito doesn't blink. "I know you didn't." The room falls eerily quiet. "I did."

I dart my gaze to Benito. Augie swings round. Fed lets out an audible breath of relief and Nicolò looks up from his fingernails.

"What?" Augie says with a frown.

"I burned down my house."

Nicolò rolls his eyes. "Now, why would you do that? It's not like you need an insurance payout when we run the damn insurance companies anyway."

"You're right," Benito says, calmly. "That's not why I did it."

His gaze pans softly to mine and I suddenly know. My heart stops beating and the room sways.

With eyes locked on mine, he enlightens us all. "I did it for her."

There's complete silence while Augie, Nicolò and Fed look from Benito to me and back to Benito again, rightly wondering if this is a joke.

"I did it so I'd have a viable reason to move into the apartment above your studio," he says, thinning my breath.

"You didn't need to burn down your ho—" Nicolò starts, but Benito lifts a hand that stops him instantly.

"Come on," Augie says, putting a hand on Nicolò's elbow. "Let's give them a minute."

"Only a minute," Nicolò replies. "Cristiano will slice my dick in two if I don't get them into the function room, stat."

"They won't be long," Augie assures him.

"What about this one?" Nicolò jerks his head toward Federico.

"He's coming with us," Augie says before whipping out a pair of handcuffs and attaching them to Federico's wrists. "Just in case," he winks.

Nicolò looks horrified. "What? You just carry those around? What sort of sick shit do you get up to in your spare time?"

Augie slides past him and through the door, pulling Fed behind him. "Wouldn't you like to know?"

A flush crawls up my throat and I don't know if it's caused by the sight of a pair of handcuffs, Benito's declaration, or the fact I'm suddenly alone in a room with him. I back up into a wall and grip my purse nervously. My gaze flits around, unable to focus on him.

I expect him to walk towards me and tower over me like he usually does, turning me on through sheer intimidation, but he doesn't move. I flick a timid glance his way and notice the lines etched into his brow.

"I'm sorry," he says, quietly.

The intensity of his gaze burns my skin so I escape it by looking down at the floor. "For what?" My mind has gone blank so I'm honestly at a loss as to what he's apologizing for.

"For not believing you."

Oh, *that*.

"Why didn't you?" I look up before I can stop myself and am immediately caught by his bronze eyes reaching into me like tendrils.

He leans back against the table and releases a controlled breath.

"You remember when I told you I raised myself?"

"Yes."

"That was true. But the bit about me not having parents… I did, once upon a time."

It feels as though my heart is crawling up my chest and into my throat, trying to get a better view of this man bearing his truth.

"My mom died when I was four. I might have had a relatively normal childhood up to that point but I don't remember any of it. I don't remember her. My father was a hateful man. He was aggressive and abusive—to me and my brother—"

"You have a *brother*?"

He closes his eyes for a moment, then looks distantly across the room. "I *had* a brother. God knows if he's still alive. Ran away when he was thirteen."

My fingers close tighter around my purse.

"After Leo Jr. left, I survived by being at my father's disposal. He was a petty criminal doing small time jobs for a local gang." He shrugs like it was mere child's play. "I hid stolen goods, lied to the police, provided alibis, that sort of thing. Then one time, he let me in on a big job. I was excited about it—my father letting me work with him and his gangster buddies. He didn't tell me much about it, just told me to follow and do as I was told, so I did. We broke into a warehouse in the Bronx. The plan was to steal a whole bunch of firearms being stored there."

He takes a deep breath and scrubs a hand down his face like he's trying to wipe away the memories.

"When we got inside, while some of the guys loaded up the boxes, my father handed me a gun. I'd never held one before and I just remember thinking it was so much heavier than I'd imagined. He took off the safety clip, then told me to point it at a door which led out the back, and said if anyone was to walk through that door, I was to shoot them."

He chokes out a laugh filled with bitterness. "I wasn't even sure where the trigger was."

My heart thumps and I realize I'm holding my breath.

"It wasn't long before somebody did walk through the door. A security guard who likely had no idea what was in those boxes. But I did what my father had instructed. I aimed the gun at him and pulled back what I assumed was the trigger. The force of it knocked me flat on my back but my aim was perfect. Killed the guy, clean and quick."

The breath leaks from my lungs and I swallow. "How old were you?" I whisper.

He lifts his gaze and I can't see any emotion behind it. "Nine."

My saliva goes down the wrong way and I choke on it. Benito's frown dips in concern but he doesn't move to help me. When the choking subsides I look up. He hasn't moved. He's still completely unaffected.

"Why are you telling me this?" I ask in a scratchy voice.

He hesitates. "I want you to understand me. I want you to know why I am the way I am."

I watch him for some sign of softness but he holds his ground.

"We got busted on the way out anyway," he sighs, his shoulders rounding out. "I was so stunned at what I'd done I couldn't move, so my father left me there and drove off with the goods and the rest of the men."

What?

He slides his hands into his pockets and narrows his

eyes at me. "That was my first lesson in trust—even blood betrays."

"Oh Benito…"

"Don't feel sorry for me." There's a bite in his tone. "That moment changed everything. The people we stole from descended pretty quickly and took me off to some location on the river. I was beaten, drugged and tortured and I still didn't give up any information about my father and his acquaintances. When I didn't break, they tried blackmailing him for the stolen goods, using me as leverage, but he told them to keep me."

Nausea crawls up my throat and I clasp a hand over my mouth.

"That was my second lesson in trust—the only person you're worth anything to is yourself."

I start to shake my head but his dark stare freezes me in place.

"The people who tortured me were so impressed with my ability to keep a secret, they handed me over to Gianni. By the time I was twelve years old I had the most lethal aim in the organization and was on track to be sworn in by my sixteenth birthday. That was my third and final lesson in trust—survival is about transaction. Turn yourself into a valuable weapon and you'll never need to trust anyone again."

I slump back against the wall.

"This is why you didn't trust me?"

"Yes."

"And now?"

He walks toward me in a slow, firm gait, and stops a

couple of feet in front. "I really want to trust you, more than anything."

My chest rises and falls with a quickened tempo and even though his words have scratched against my softness like a sharp blade, I can't help but fall into his tragic, haunting gaze.

"But?"

"It isn't going to happen overnight. You'll need to be patient with me. That is, if you'll have me back."

My heart wants to cry. All I can see standing in front of me is that lonely, helpless little boy forced to fend for himself, trained to not trust a soul.

"Is that what you want?" I whisper.

He reaches up both hands and takes my face in his warm palms. His eyes roam me ravenously. "It's all I want."

When he presses his lips to mine, there's no darkness—only daylight. No wrist ties—only a soft caress. And it's now that I realize none of us perfectly fit into a box. We're all complex. Me? I'm dark, I'm wild, but I'm soft and grounded. Benito? He's dark, he's rough, but his palm is light and his heart is swollen. And that's what makes people so hard to trust—they're fluid and ever-changing. And being vulnerable to that takes a kind of strength that can elude even the most powerful among us.

CHAPTER THIRTY-SEVEN

ontessa

Somehow I manage to get through the wedding rehearsal without letting on to my sisters the fact my life just tilted on its axis and I no longer know which way is up.

As we all leave, I sense Benito watching me closely from the corner of the room. I walk over to him and tilt my gaze to his. He leans back against the paneled wall and looks down at me through thick lashes, his bottom lip pulled between his teeth.

"I need to see him," I say, quietly but firmly.

His gaze searches my face, then he nods slowly. "His flight leaves in two hours."

I press my palm against Benito's chest, feeling his heart pumping hard beneath the flesh. "Take me to him."

He pushes himself off the wall and slides his hands into his pockets, then gestures for me to lead the way through the exit and down the corridor.

His hand touches my shoulder, making me pause and turn around. We've stopped at the door to another room. He knocks twice and it opens from the other side.

A soldier I vaguely recognize steps to one side and Fed's form comes into view. He's sitting on a chair, his back to the door and his hands have been bound to the chair with the handcuffs.

I feel Benito's hand at my back, coaxing me gently into the room. I walk slowly round the outer edge of the room until I'm facing my childhood friend. He lifts his head and his face brightens instantly, despite the blood drying around his mouth.

I look over at Benito and the soldier. "Can I speak with him in private?"

Benito's jaw grinds.

"Please?"

After a painfully long few seconds, he nods and they both leave the room, closing the door behind them.

I tentatively walk to Fed and lower to my knees before him.

"Why did you come back?" I whisper.

He goes to speak but his lips are dry. There's a glass of water on the table beside him. I lift it to his lips so he can drink. After a few sips I place it back on the table and sit back on my heels.

"I promised you I would," he says slowly.

A frown knits my brows. "You promised me you'd write."

He sighs heavily and looks out of the window.

"I couldn't write you until I had something valuable to say. Didn't you get my last letter?"

"Your *only* letter," I correct. "Yes, I did."

His gaze doesn't waver from the window. "I didn't want you to think I was so weak that I couldn't seek revenge for my family."

I reach out to touch his knees, drawing his gaze back to mine. "I never thought you were weak."

"But, you didn't love me."

The hurt in his eyes almost destroys me.

"I wasn't sure," I reply. "I didn't think so, but the more time that passed, the more hurt I felt and the more I wondered if perhaps I did love you."

"Did?" His tone lilts with expectation. "You loved me?"

I blink slowly, trying to keep a semblance of strength in my heart. I can't tell him the truth, not when he's looking at me like this, with so much vulnerability in his eyes.

"Tess…" He shuffles forward on the chair until the handcuffs prevent him from moving any closer. "Tess, what we had was so special. I fucked it up by not writing you, but I thought I would fuck it up more if I told you I hadn't made any progress in getting revenge on these people."

He's rambling but I try my best to keep up.

"When I didn't reply, you started to question your original feelings for me—I could sense it in your words. You even said it yourself, you felt more for me than you realized. I didn't want to stop those feelings from evolving, Tess. I needed to hear you say those things. It reassured me I wasn't going insane. I planned on coming back for you this whole time."

"And now?" My voice is firm. "Now you know the truth about your father and there is no need for revenge, what now?"

He licks his lips and a flush spreads over his cheeks. He looks like a young boy again.

"I still want you, Tess. I never stopped wanting you. I love you."

I swallow. I'm not like him. I can't stay silent and leave him wondering what the hell I'm thinking. "I've moved on, Fed," I say, softly. "My life has changed and I'm happy."

The hope in his eyes falls. "With Benito Bernadi?" There's still a tense bitterness in his words.

"Not just with him," I say, not wanting to twist the knife my words have already driven into his abdomen. "I'm about to become a part of the Di Santo family," I say, slowly.

His eyes widen.

"Did you not know what you were walking into?" I find it hard to believe he didn't know this was a mafia wedding involving my eldest sister.

He shakes his head. "Andreas just told me to come

here and this is where I'd find you. It was my reward for telling him everything I knew about the Di Santo's."

I narrow my eyes, my thoughts stuck briefly on the name Andreas. We still don't know who this man is and what he wants with the Di Santo's. "And you didn't question why I would be here, with the entire Di Santo mafia family?"

"N-no… I just thought perhaps your father was working with them…"

I stare at him, waiting for the penny to drop.

"What do you mean you're about to become a part of the family?"

I sigh. "Trilby is marrying Cristiano tomorrow. The don."

He sucks in a breath, unable to conceal the horror in his features. "The don who killed his own brother in cold blood?"

So, news *does* travel coast to coast. Nevertheless, I don't have the energy to explain why Savero's murder was actually a good thing. "Yes."

Fed pales. "Is that why you're with Bernadi?"

"What do you mean?"

"Are you—?" His arms are shaking behind his back.

"Engaged? No! Bernadi and I are not engaged. But, we are together." I can't believe I'm telling Federico when I haven't even told the rest of my family.

Fed's voice lowers to a whisper. "Is he forcing you to be with him?"

I can't help a smile catch the edges of my lips. "No.

He isn't forcing me. Believe me, I tried to fight it, but I'm helplessly in love."

Fed gasps. "You're in *love*?"

I haven't even spoken those words in my own head, so God knows why I just blurted them out to Federico, but it's true. I'm in love with Benito Bernadi. He made me fall hard and fast, and I'm going to kill him.

"Go back to your family, Federico," I say, smiling.

"You sure you don't want to come with me?" he asks, but the conviction in those hopeful words doesn't appear.

"I don't belong in your world anymore, Fed. And you don't belong in mine." I stroke my palm down the side of his face, remembering our friendship and how much it once meant to me.

"I do love you, Fed. I will always love you. But only as a friend. And that's the honest truth."

He closes his eyes and nods, sadly.

"Please give my love to your parents. I miss them." A memory of Mrs. Falconi warms my chest. "Especially your mom."

His eyes crack open a fraction and I see tears brimming in the corners. "She misses you too. She'll be pleased to hear you're happy."

"I am happy." I stand and let my hand fall back to my side. "And you will be too, Fed. I promise."

I turn around and walk back to the door.

"Tess?"

His fractured tone makes me pause. "Yes?"

"Would you have loved me if *he* hadn't walked into your life?"

I take a sobering breath before I reply. "No, Federico. And he didn't just walk into my life. He *is* my life."

And with that, I open the door and step outside, the air feeling easier to breathe than it has in years.

CHAPTER THIRTY-EIGHT

Contessa

It's the day of the wedding and I'm running late. At least today I know my way around all the rooms and corridors. I make a beeline for the room where the wedding party is gathered.

"Oh my God! There you are!" Trilby's gasp of relief echoes around the small room. "We've been waiting for you."

I ignore Allegra's scowl and run up to Trilby. "I'm so, so sorry, Tril. I really am."

After clasping her hands, I stand back and take her in. She's wearing a forties-style gown with a slash neckline, fitted at the waist and falling to the floor in a delicate train. The back is so low it only just graces the top of her butt cheeks, and it is covered entirely in pearl sequins. It is perfect.

"Oh my word, Trilby. You look stunning."

She smiles and twirls in front of the floor length mirror.

"Way better than the last one," Bambi says, then snaps her mouth shut when we all spin around and glare at her. She shrugs dramatically. "Well, it is."

"That was a beautiful dress, too," Sera says, diplomatically. "But this one is better."

"Cristiano saw me in my last one, so it would have been bad luck anyway," Trilby says, unable to stop smiling at her reflection.

We all nod in agreement and I wipe a tear from my cheek.

The door opens and Papa walks in, then stops abruptly. His eyes take in the four of us and he doesn't say a word.

"Tony—" Allegra hiccups loudly and rushes to his side. "Your girls—"

It's the first time I have *ever* seen our aunt speechless.

Papa sniffs and swallows. "Beautiful," he whispers. "You all look so... *beautiful*."

He swallows again and seems to struggle for the words. "Your ma—"

"Don't say it," Trilby blurts out, holding up a hand.

"Please," Papa says, his eyes watery. "I have to." He takes a long, strengthening breath. "Your mama would be so proud to see you all now." An enormous tear rolls down my cheek and soaks into the carpeted floor. "There's something of her in each of you, and it makes me so proud to see the women you are all becoming. I wish she were here to see it too."

Allegra loops an arm through Papa's and kisses his shoulder through his tux.

"I wish she were here." Sera turns to Trilby, her cheeks wet. "I wish she could see you now. So happy and so radiant." She sniffs and wipes the back of her hand across her cheek. "She'd be fussing around us, remember how she used to do that? Fluttering around like a butterfly, making sure we each had our shoes on, faces washed, teeth brushed."

A hard lump forms in my throat and no matter how much I swallow, it doesn't shift.

"I do." Trilby nods, her gaze liquid.

Allegra sniffs and Papa blows his nose.

I need to do something before this descends into a water bath.

"You should be saving those words for when you get down the aisle." I hope the joke masks my croaky voice. "Come on. We're so late already."

"Quick sister hug?" Trilby spreads her arms and we all pile into them.

With our eyes dried and happier memories touching our lips, Papa opens the door to let us three bridesmaids through. Bambi swishes her skirt around playfully, while Sera smooths down the bodice of her dress, repeatedly. I pass them both, taking care not to let my gown drag on the floor, when my gaze takes in a pair of Italian leather shoes heading towards the function room.

I stop short and look up into bronze irises.

Benito stops too and for a long, delicious second, I see everything in his eyes. Our dark truths colliding, our renewed commitment effervescent in the air around us.

As if time hasn't just stood still, Benito continues toward the function room with my flushed cheeks and addicted gaze watching him go.

Then Sera's face appears in front of me, blocking the view of Benito's solid back disappearing through the door. "Pray tell?" she says, a smirk playing across her lips.

"I'll exchange my truth for yours," I shoot back.

Her face falls. "I walked right into that one, didn't I?"

I take my place behind her, ready for the doors to open. "You sure did."

A few seconds pass and I watch her shoulders rise and fall. "Fine," she acquiesces. "I've been seeing someone."

"I knew it," I grin, smugly. "Who?"

"No one…" She shakes her head softly. "I mean, no one you know."

I tip my head to the left. "Is that important?"

She turns to the side a little, so I can see her flushed jaw and fluttering lashes. "It is to me." She lowers her voice. "He's just a *normal* person. Works in business— not in… well, you know."

My tone dips. "Yeah, I know."

"But he's kind, and sweet, and…"

"Hot?" I ask.

"Oh, extremely."

"Nice. Is he here? In the hotel?"

She turns back around to face the door. "Not today. Said he wants to give me space to spend time with my family. It's definitely too soon for him to meet you all."

I laugh softly. "Yeah, we can be a pretty scary bunch."

Her shoulders shake and I can tell she's laughing, but I don't have a chance to press her further because the doors open with a dramatic flourish and the music begins.

I walk down the aisle staying three paces behind Sera, as I've been instructed, but the joyful anticipation filling the room is distracting. The air is thick with the scent of roses and Italian leather. My heart pounds in my chest as I place one foot in front of the other.

Allegra stands alone on the front row of seats and I can see her tears falling from all the way down the aisle. My gaze pans to the right and takes in Cristiano. He looks taller and broader, like he's about to burst with pride. And he hasn't even *seen* her yet.

The music drifts through my ears, lifting me until I feel like I'm floating. Bronze eyes are the only things keeping me grounded. I let myself be drawn to them, hooking my gaze on Benito as I reach the end of the aisle and stand beside Sera.

The guests, sharply dressed in black tuxedos and

evening gowns, are all staring toward the back of the room.

The music swells—deep and haunting. And then, with her arm threaded through Papa's, she enters.

I can't breathe.

Her dress—an ethereal gown that skims over her curves and falls to the floor in a delicate train of sequined satin—glides across the floor. Her bleached hair is rebelliously loose, curled enough to kiss her shoulders, a few soft strands framing her face.

My sister, the bravest of all of us, the one who'd throw herself into icy waters from dramatic clifftops, the one who buried the trauma of seeing our mother killed and kept it from us all, the one who fearlessly fell for the most dangerous man in New York, is walking down the aisle toward *him*—Cristiano. The Di Santo don, my soon-to-be brother-in-law, and the man who killed his own flesh and blood to protect our family.

I glance sideways to capture his reaction. He's still standing tall and impossibly composed. But there's something in his eyes I don't recall seeing before. I swear his gaze softens just for her, just for a split second, as she approaches. His eyes don't stray as she glides toward him.

I lift my gaze momentarily to the ceiling in a bid to stop the tears from rolling down my freshly powdered cheeks. When I lower it again, Trilby is kissing Papa on the cheek, then she takes Cristiano's hand. I watch his fingers curl possessively around hers, and her lips curve into a softly delirious smile. My cheeks heat from the strain of holding in a happy sob and the sensation of Benito's burning stare.

My gaze flickers beyond the couple to the man whose eyes haven't left my face once. I feel his touch on my skin, his lips on my throat, and my heart skips a beat.

The guests are asked to sit, and the ceremony begins. Words pass through my ears, unheard, as I focus on the expressions on Trilby and Cristiano's faces. I've seen my sister and her fiancé content before, but nothing like this. My chest blooms with happiness for them both.

Halfway through the sermon, a bird flies through an open window and rests on one of the beams overhead.

"Look at that," Sera whispers in my ear. "It's a barn swallow. Isn't it beautiful?"

I nod in agreement. "Do you think it's an omen?"

Knowing how spiritual my sister is, I expect her to agree. When she doesn't reply straight away, I tear my gaze from Trilby, Cristiano and the bird to focus on her.

"No." She shakes her head. "I think it's Mama."

Right at that moment, Trilby gasps and I turn back to see the bird has flown to the front of the room. It is perched on a table just behind the priest, and it's *watching* her.

I feel Sera's soft, warm hand rest on mine while tears roll down my cheeks. I sense Benito's gaze narrow on me, but I can't take my eyes off the bird. It sits there until the end of the sermon, only flying to a window sill when it's time to exchange vows.

The priest's voice cuts through my tears. "Since it is your intention to enter the covenant of Holy Matrimony, join your right hands, and declare your consent before God and his Church."

He nods to Cristiano.

"I, Cristiano, take you, Trilby, for my lawful wife, to have and to hold, from this day forward, for better, for worse, for richer, for poorer, in sickness and in health, until death do us part."

I hold my breath and watch Trilby's lips move as she repeats the words.

My hands tremble as I watch the exchange of rings, and I half-listen to the priest's blessing.

When they are pronounced man and wife and Cristiano is invited to kiss his bride, the room erupts. After sitting through uncharacteristic calm and silence, I'm now reminded that I am actually sitting in a room full of Italians. Whoops and hollers rise up from the chairs and Cristiano presses his lips to Trilby's. A beautiful pink blush creeps up her cheeks and I clap until my hands burn.

When they pull apart, they stare at one another, the roomful of guests falling away to insignificance. My eyes drift to the man behind them and my heart warms. Benito blinks at me slowly, both hands resting in his pockets, then he smiles.

CHAPTER THIRTY-NINE

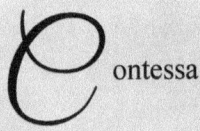ontessa

The topic of watching Trilby walk down the aisle, looking more radiant than a buttercup in full bloom, will never get old. Sera, Allegra, Bambi and I have talked of nothing else, through the champagne and canapés, through photos, and through dinner. And now the lights have dimmed and the band has started to play, we still can't stop marveling at how utterly beautiful she looks and how smitten Cristiano is.

Allegra and Bambi have gone to find Papa, leaving me and Sera to sip our wine and reminisce all over again. When Sera stops mid-sentence, her gaze arrested by something—or someone—behind me, I turn around and my heart expands. Benito is standing with one arm behind his back and the other outstretched toward me. "May I have a dance?"

A nerve crackles through me. "I thought you said you didn't dance."

His brow dips into a frown. "I never said that."

I glance back at Sera and she nods encouragingly.

I turn back around. "Okay, well, sure."

He takes my hand and guides me to the dance floor. I feel the music instantly, as though it's roots are coming up through the floor and entwining around my feet.

Benito lifts my arms and hook my wrists around his neck.

"Jeez, I'm going to get frozen shoulder dancing with my arms at this angle," I moan.

His eyes roll. "Are you always this dramatic when you're dancing?"

I'm about to shoot back a sarcastic quip but the feel of his hands sliding around my waist whips the breath from my lungs.

Seriously, though. He is enormous and my neck is already aching from craning upward.

"Okay, brat," he sighs. "But just this one time."

Before I can ask what he's talking about, he scoots his large hands beneath my arms and lifts me until our faces are level.

Nerves make me glance about, searching for Allegra who may well, if she sees this, come storming over and demand to have him put me down.

He pulls me into his chest then somehow removes his hands from under my arms and wraps them around my back.

His eyes narrow and his full, dangerous lips move.

"What am I going to do with you, Contessa Castellano?"

I pull a lip between my teeth and slowly drag it out until it pops free. Benito watches it, swallowing. I dip toward his ear. "Nothing too extreme," I whisper. "Just yet."

His gaze is soft when I return it. Then he arches a brow. "Handcuffs? I could borrow Augie's?"

I shake my head, fighting a smile.

His eyes narrow further. "Missionary?"

My core *melts*. Just that one, straight-laced, vanilla word has set my blood on fire. A vision of Benito lowering his weight onto me, pressing my thighs apart with just one of his solid legs, the ink on his chest dancing with the tension in his arms, and the feel of his cock sliding into me, makes my eyes glaze over.

"Fuck," he drawls. "That's it, isn't it? Me on top of you. A nice, long, slow fuck."

A rush of blood surfaces all over my skin.

"Take off my tie."

My lids ping open.

"Your hands are already there," he says, casually. "Just take it off and put it around your neck."

My brows knit. "Why?"

"Can you just, for once, do something I ask without giving me the Spanish Inquisition?"

"Careful," I warn. "I could strangle you."

"I thought you didn't want *extreme* just yet," he smirks.

I smack his shoulder playfully. "I won't ever want *that*, Bernadi."

I push the smooth satin through the knot, gently pulling it free. It feels like such a raw, intimate thing to do for a man and a shiver down my spine makes him splay his fingers across my back.

The tie slips from around his neck and he watches me intently as I slide it around mine. I hold his gaze while I tie it into a loose knot beneath my collarbone.

He shakes his head, slowly. "You have no idea how sexy that is."

"What now?"

A smile dances across his lips. "Oh… You're looking for direction?"

My own smile falls. "Yes."

He closes his eyes for a long moment. When he opens them again, they're a little darker.

"Unbutton the top of my shirt."

I suck in a surprised breath. "What? People will see."

"Just the top two buttons. And trust me, no one is watching us."

My fingers shake as I fumble with the buttons and slide them through the holes. My breath stutters when a fragment of his bare chest is revealed.

"You like that, huh?" Bernadi's voice is gruff, like he's barely holding himself together.

I swallow. "Not at all."

"Oh," he replies, leaning forward a little and brushing his top lip against my jawline. "You hate it."

My eyelids flutter shut and I momentarily forget where I am. "With every fiber of my being, Bernadi."

"Ah," he says, amusement tickling the edge of his tongue. He slides one hand down my back and presses me into his rock solid erection.

A fractured gasp leaves my lips.

"That's a relief. I'd hate it if the feeling weren't mutual. I mean, it could get a little awkward."

"I, um… I agree." I can hardly speak, I'm so turned on.

He stops swaying gently and leans forward so his breath brushes the shell of my ear. "Promise you'll hate me forever." His tone is laced with a vulnerable heat that sings in my veins.

"I promise."

"Until death do us part?"

"Until death do us part."

"Any last requests before I lock this down with a kiss in front of your entire family?"

My pulse *thumps*. He knows that if we're seen kissing in public, both our families—the Castellano one and the Di Santo one—will insist on marriage. Maybe not yet, but eventually. And this is what he's asking.

I smile into the cut of his jaw. "No more basements."

"Got it. No more basements."

Well, that was easy.

"No shooting people a foot away from my head."

"Um, nope. Can't promise that."

Okay then. "No abductions."

"No abductions—of you anyway."

I have no response to that and an eye roll doesn't feel appropriate.

"Okay, my turn," he says. "No more having my men deliver Michelin-starred food to the homeless."

"Oh come on," I pull back to look accusingly into his eyes. "There has to be a Good Samaritan in there somewhere."

His response is a glare and a raised brow that says, "Do you not know what I do for a living?"

"Okay, fine. But then no more ordering ridiculous amounts of food you know I'm not going to eat."

He rolls his eyes in response.

"I have another one. No assuming I could find it *remotely* possible to lie to you."

He stares at me, eyes roaming my face, then he nods. Just when I think he's about to kiss me, he whispers, "I love you."

I kick my head back and laugh. "No you don't—you hate me."

A sharp tug on my ponytail cuts my breath. "That previous condition applies to you too."

I dip my lips toward him, brushing my breath across his. "You know what they say—love and hate are just two sides of the same coin."

He cups the back of my head in one hand. "Then it's a good job I'm fucking rich. Now shut the fuck up little brat, and give me your mouth."

Then he pulls my lips onto his and kisses me in front of the whole room.

CHAPTER FORTY

enito

I can feel the widened eyes of Tess's family as I brazenly devour her mouth in front of them all. Fuck it. She's mine now.

I pull back only when I'm ready to and she stares at me with liquid eyes and swollen lips, utterly breathless and fucking beautiful. I drop her to her feet and take her by the hand. Before she can object, I'm tugging her toward the exit.

"Where are we going?" she says.

I grin at my own ingenious idea. "The beach."

"Why?"

Why? Because it's where she comes alive. It's where she loses all her inhibitions. It's where she becomes herself. And I want her to be herself in this moment. We just, for better or for worse, showed the Castellanos and the Di Santo's that we're together. I want her to really feel this, without the expectations or judgements of others weighing on her.

I could tell her all this, but I decide to tell her another truth.

"I want you all to my-fucking-self."

We reach the terrace and I pick her up in my arms. She squeals as I stride down the lawns to the beach. The crashing waves reach our ears, drowning out the sound of music from inside the hotel. Figures watch from the shadows but I know they'll avert their gazes when it matters.

When I'm certain we're out of view of the hotel and its surrounding gardens, I lay her on the soft sand, then rest my weight over her, bringing my lips heavily onto hers.

She releases a tender moan into my throat and I savor it with my tongue. Searching her mouth and lips for more sweetness, I bury myself in her warmth, only pulling away for a second at a time to let her breathe.

My God, I'm in so deep I can't see anymore. I want this girl like I've never wanted anything before in my life. I yearn for her like I used to yearn for my next kill. Her skin beneath my fingers feels like something I've never experienced but instinctively know exists. It feels like *home*.

I nudge my knee between her legs, feeling her dress part at the traitorous slit running from her thigh to the floor. The heat of her pussy greets me like a wet kiss.

She blindly fumbles with my fly, releasing my cock

with a languid sigh. Then she pulls her panties to one side, moaning a soft plea into my lips. I don't even need to hold my cock and angle it to where it needs to be. It fucking knows.

I coax her thighs further apart and press my hips forward. I slide into her with a smooth ease that only reaffirms my conviction that she was made for me. Our lips rest against each other as I move slowly, in and out of her.

I don't want dark this time. I want vanilla. Just as she asked for. Only, there's fucking *nothing* vanilla about this. I'm *dying* of need. I don't want this to ever end. If someone held a gun to my head right now, I'd let them shoot, because they'll never find me in a happier place, deep inside my girl, feeling her tremble around me.

"I love you," she whispers into my mouth.

I inhale her words. "I love you too," I reply, re-angling myself so my cock strokes a different part of her.

"I'm going to come any second," she says, gasping.

"I've got you." I run my fingers through her hair and dip my tongue into her mouth. Her pussy tightens around me and I drive deeper, rolling through her climax and swallowing every whimper and every moan. I slow as she comes down, but I don't stop. I shift my angle again and in seconds, she's panting and quivering beneath me.

"God, you're ending me with these cute little noises," I whisper.

"I can't think straight," she gasps.

"You shouldn't be thinking at all," I say, softly, tugging on her hair and fucking her slowly. My cock thickens. I'm so close I feel delirious. The waves crash behind us and her thighs pool around mine. It takes all my strength—and I pride myself on typically having an inhuman amount— just to hold my orgasm back. This evening, I want to devour her pleasure, tremor by tremor. I want to feast on it. I want to feel her body beneath me, fragile yet forceful. Trapped but with all the power to bring me down should she ever wish to.

Her pussy tightens again, bringing me home. I force myself to keep pace. I want to draw her out so long she forgets her own name.

"Benito…" Her gasp floods my ears and she clamps down, milking all the come from my cock. It floods out of me and into her, where it belongs. My vision disappears and heat flushes through my chest. I feel *fucking* invincible.

I push myself so deep I can feel her edge as she shakes beneath me. I jerk one more time then press my lips to her damp throat.

Unable to see straight, I keep my eyes closed and breathe one single word. "Fuck."

To my surprise, she giggles.

"What's so funny?" I groan.

"You say 'fuck' an awful lot."

"It's versatile," I say, lacking the energy to frown.

"Is that right?"

"Sure. It can communicate surprise, commiseration, confusion… rage."

I can sense her smiling even though my head is buried in her neck.

"And sometimes it's the only word that carries the gravitas I need in a particular situation."

"Like now?"

I lift my head and almost drown in her green eyes. They seem to embody the deep ocean that laps at the shore just feet away from where we lie.

"Yeah. Sometimes, the right words simply don't exist."

Before she can question me any further, I push myself up to my knees and pull her with me, then to our feet.

"God, I must look a mess," she says, brushing sand out of her hair.

"You look stunning," I reply. I move around her, putting strands of hair back into place, brushing creases from her dress, then I do the same to my suit. Then I take her hand and we walk back to our families.

CHAPTER FORTY-ONE

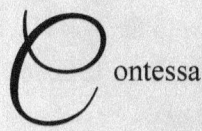ontessa

"You and *Bernadi*?" Bambi is standing next to me, having followed me into the restroom, with her jaw on the floor and a particularly judgmental scowl on her face. "I thought you hated him."

I run a finger under my eyes wiping away some of the smudged mascara and apply another slick of gloss. "I did."

"And now?"

I glance sideways at her, unable to contain a grin. "I don't anymore."

She turns around and leans back against the vanity, folding her arms. "I don't ever want to be interested in men," she huffs, pouting. "The whole thing looks woefully confusing."

"Well, yeah…" I snap my purse closed. "It can be. But it's worth it."

I rinse my hands under the faucet.

"Hopefully Sera will stay single so I don't have to die alone."

A laugh bursts out of me as I dry off with a towel. "That's morbid. Besides, give it a couple years and I guarantee you'll feel differently."

She pushes off the vanity to follow me out. "I highly doubt that."

When we re-enter the function room, the dancing is in full-swing. Trilby seems to be in the middle of it all, twirling circles in her beautiful gown, her train fastened into a bustle at her waist. Sera is dancing beside her and her enormous smile makes me smile. All four girls under one roof, celebrating our older sister—I didn't think it would make me feel as happy as it does. Though, of course, a certain bronze-eyed consigliere might also be to thank for my deliriously happy state.

"Who's Papa talking to?"

I look across the room to see who Bambi's referring to. "Um, that's Nicolò's mother," I reply, recognizing the tall, lithe figure and black, softly curled hair. She's a beautiful woman.

"They were talking earlier too," Bambi says, and there's a cool edge to her tone.

I put a hand on her arm to reassure her. "I think they get along. It's nice that he can talk to someone other than Aunt Allegra."

Bambi turns to me with a frown. "He has other friends."

I take a breath and shrug. "I know it's painful, Bambi. But Mama has been gone five years. I don't think we should stand in the way of Papa finding happiness again. Besides, their friendship might be completely innocent—we don't know."

My gaze is drawn to Benito as though magnets have been sewn into my eyes. He's standing at the far end of the room, watching me with something indecipherable in his darkened expression. It sends a bolt of fire traveling down my core only to rest, sizzling, between my legs.

I'm about to leave my little sister pouting beside a large planter when shadows move swiftly in my peripheral vision and a voice cries out from the corner of the room.

"*DOWN!*"

Screams ring out everywhere.

The *pop, pop, pop* of gunfire slams into my ears.

Something large and heavy knocks me to the floor and covers me completely.

More cries of, "*Get down! Down!*" chorus through the air, cut only by the whistle of bullets overhead.

Through the bedlam I think I can hear Sera, and my only thought is, *she's alive. If I can hear her scream, she's alive.*

"Augie!" A male voice yells. "Augie, that way…"

Another one calls out. "Cristiano!"

The form on top of me shifts and a loud pop sounds close to my head, almost deafening me.

Oh God. I'm going to die.

"Don't fucking move…" Benito's voice carries above my head and my heart crawls to a stop at the sound of his voice. He's alive.

Through the ringing in my ears I hear more shouts, more commands, the helpless cries of terrified women.

Trilby…

I try to lift my head but the weight above me is pinning me down. My breasts are flattened against the cold floor and my cheek is pressed painfully into the tile.

The gunshots recede but the crying doesn't.

When the weight shifts a little I peel my cheek off the floor and look up. Benito's hand is pressed into the floor above my head, the rest of his length pinning me to the ground. I crane my neck further and see his other arm outstretched. The pulsing veins in his taut muscles lead me to his hand. I follow the aim of his gun and freeze in terror.

Cristiano, Augie and Nicolò are upright, their arms outstretched, guns pointing at three men I've never seen before. The looks on the strangers' faces are menacing, like they've waited their whole lives for this moment, and that makes my insides crumble. But then, Cristiano and his men stand inches above them, with everything of value to them scattered about on the floor.

Cristiano, still wearing his tuxedo with a crisp white

shirt, his bowtie falling to the side, has his pistol pointed unwaveringly at what appears to be the leader of the other men. His face is unreadable, but his eyes, dark and calculating, never stray from the man across from him.

Augie's jacket has been discarded and shirt sleeves rolled up revealing thick, corded muscles primed for standoff.

Nicolò looks bored, his raised arm and cocked brow the only parts of his body seemingly engaged with the scene in front of him.

One of the other men draws his lips into a sneer. "I almost forgot. Congratulations." He nods toward the floor and I follow his gaze to a pool of white. *Trilby*. The urge to run to my sister instantly eats up my insides but I know Benito won't let me move. Her body is shaking beneath that of another man who is shielding her from the gunfire while Cristiano protects the entire family. I can't see who it is.

When her new husband speaks, his voice is thin, icy, loaded with the kind of hatred only reserved for the devil himself. "I don't recall inviting the Marchesi's."

I glance back at the three strange men, and *true* hatred, like nothing I've ever felt, rises up my torso.

The target of Cristiano's aim is a cocky-looking man with a hook nose that seems too large for his face. Either side of him stand two younger versions, both equally nauseating in their arrogant stance and calculating smirks. The thinner one on the left has his gun aimed directly at Augie's chest. The one on the right, a broad-shouldered man with a rough jaw, has his eyes locked and gun trained on Nicolò.

Silence hangs between them like a thick fog. Only the faint echo of strained breaths and leaked sobs taints the edges of their standoff. The sound of one of their voices tightens my chest like a wound spring and a small voice in the back of my head asks, "Is that the same voice my mama heard?"

"No invitation was necessary, Cristiano. We were coming whether we were invited or not. And the perimeter was wide open."

The three Di Santos standing don't move a muscle, though I know this is news to them.

"The place was surrounded," Cristiano grits out. "How many have you killed?"

Augie cocks the trigger on his gun. They were *his* men surrounding the hotel estate.

"Lost count." The man in the middle sneers.

A helpless wail rises from the floor. Guests are strewn everywhere, face down on the cold tile.

Cristiano's chest expands while Benito's hold on me tightens. "So, to what do we owe this pleasure?"

"You *owe* us our fucking money." Spittle flies from the middle guy's mouth, landing on the floor by Cristiano's wedding shoes. "That shipment would've made us three million and you fucked it over. For what? Just to piss us off?"

Benito's breathing is alarmingly steady.

"You were on our streets," Cristiano replies. "We

had every right to bust you. We re-drew territories after Newark and you crossed the boundaries."

"No—*you* re-drew territories. We never agreed to them."

"That part of the city was ALWAYS OURS." Cristiano's roar ricochets around the walls, making my ears ring.

I feel Benito's thighs tense beside me, as though he's getting ready to pounce.

"You're confronting a family that's been running this city longer than you've been alive." Augie takes over since Cristiano looks like the next sound out of his mouth might be nuclear warfare itself.

"I don't doubt that, Zanotti. You certainly look like you're older than the hills and it's about time we had a new style of leadership in this city."

Nicolò coughs out a bitter laugh. "Like you'd know what that looks like, Lorenzo. You and your brothers are barely out of diapers."

The middle guy—Lorenzo—flexes his fingers around his gun, glee dancing on his thin lips. I hold my breath, knowing the smallest twitch could result in many of us being killed.

"Give us Manhattan and we'll leave right now, no more bodies," the eldest Marchesi drawls.

"Not happening," Nicolò almost chuckles. "Santa only gives presents to the nice kids."

Lorenzo's top lip curls. "I wasn't asking you, *asshole*."

Cristiano's response starts as a low rumble, the words initially difficult to make out, but they become way clearer with context. "You murdered Gio, my late father's best capo. Then you took my brother's driver, while my *wife* was in the back seat of the *fucking* car." His jaw is steady but I've never seen a body so tense it could slice through an iceberg. "You took our informant, skinned him alive and left his corpse to weep blood all over the Connecticut River. You took our underworld *above ground* you fucking *imbecile*."

The air thickens with bated breaths.

"*That's* why we took Newark," Cristiano says, with a sharp tip of his head. "Because you can't be fucking trusted with it."

"Nice speech," Lorenzo grits out. "Shame it isn't going to save you and your new family."

Everything happens slowly but then again, too quickly for me to keep up.

"Fuck this," Benito mutters under his breath. Then, before I realize what he's doing, he's pressing a hand into my back. "Stay down," he growls.

One of the guns swings toward him as he straightens up, but Benito's too fast. His bullet flies through the air and pierces the chest of the Marchesi closest to us.

The man falls to the ground, then hell descends.

For the second time today, a gun spins toward me—it has slipped from Benito's victim's grip—and this time my shaking hands don't hesitate to reach out and grab it. The threat in the room now is far worse than the threat of Federico. Fed wouldn't have killed me, but these guys would *relish* it.

In the corner of my eye, Bambi flies toward me, crouching behind my back as I extend my arms. I rise to my knees and lift one leg so I have a foot on the ground.

Cristiano fires a bullet toward his target but Lorenzo is too fast and ducks out of the way. Another bullet sails past Cristiano and screams ring out from the edge of the room. Augie's aim catches the other brother on the shoulder, then more bullets rain into the room from the terrace.

There's more of them?

My heart hitches as Benito runs to the doors, arms outstretched, right into the middle of the chaos.

My instinct to turn my head to the side is strong but I have as much blood in this game as he does, so I keep my focus, and the borrowed pistol, trained on the doors.

More bullets fall like snowflakes through the terrace doors and Benito ducks them like it's a dance he's been performing since kindergarten. My heart expands like a balloon when I remember that he *has* been doing this shit since he was a kid.

Bambi screams in my ear and grabs my dress in her small fists. "Tess, we gotta go. Tess, come *on*."

"I'm not leaving him," I say firmly.

"What?" Her voice is breathy with terror.

"I'm not leaving Benito."

Cristiano has thrown his gun to one side and is head-to-head with Lorenzo, their hands around each other's throats. It's clear from their drawn faces and whitened knuckles, this conflict goes back *years*.

Benito is firing bullets onto the terrace with Nicolò at his back, the remaining Marchesi brother is running, his gun held aloft defensively.

Then a scream drags everyone's attention back to the hustle in the center of the room.

Lorenzo Marchesi has a gun driven into Cristiano's jaw, his finger poised on the trigger, an eerily satisfied smirk on the summit of his lips.

"No…" Trilby's whisper shakes the room.

Benito spins around, having terminated whatever risk existed on the terrace, and his jaw falls open.

The room is deathly silent—everyone awaiting the click of the Marchesi's trigger, ending the life of his rival don, my sister's new husband.

I feel Benito's gaze land on me and the gun in my hands feels heavy and lethal. I have it aimed right at Lorenzo's head. The implication in my boyfriend's eyes is unequivocal. I have the aim. I don't need to move. I could kill. All I need to do is pull the trigger.

The gun shakes as I extend my finger then press it gently into the thin, curved strip of metal. My head feels light, as though I haven't taken a breath in *days*. I've never fired a gun in my life. And the one time I have the opportunity, a man associated with my mama's murder just happens to be the target. It couldn't be more serendipitous. Yet, I can't quite go all the way.

My eyes flick to Benito. His gaze is warm and filled

with love and… something else. Faith. He believes in me. He believes I can do this.

Lorenzo doesn't seem to know I'm aiming his brother's gun at his head, so I have the upper hand.

Then, footsteps, quick and firm, arrive in the doorway to the terrace.

In a blind panic, I draw my finger toward me. The force of the bullet flying from its chamber knocks me onto the floor. Firing a gun is fucking harder than it looks.

Lorenzo squeals in pain and another pop rings through the air.

Then another.

All I can think is my panic has set off a chain reaction and now we're all going to die.

Bambi's arm curls around my neck, muffling at least some of the shouts and screams.

In mere seconds, everything stops.

"Holy crap." Bambi's gasp of disbelief makes me unfurl from her embrace and twist to face the room. My gaze immediately searches for Benito. When it finds him, his gaze is still on me, as though he never looked away.

Terrified, I pan my focus to Cristiano. Relief floods through my body when I see he's still standing. And unharmed.

Lorenzo is lying at his feet, blood running from his skull.

Vomit crawls up my esophagus. I did that to him. I killed him.

In a second, and somehow without me even seeing him move, Benito has me in his arms. "It wasn't you," he says rocking me into his chest.

"I-I don't understand."

Benito presses his mouth to my hair. "You got him in the ribs. It knocked him off balance. You did good, baby."

Silent tears stream from my wide-open eyes.

I hear voices, distantly.

Luca's down.

Matteo ran.

Where?

Out the gates.

Gone.

Motherfucker.

"Doesn't matter." Cristiano's voice cuts through the murmurings, with earth-shattering heat. "Lorenzo Marchesi is fucking dead."

I somehow focus my gaze enough to watch Cristiano kick the corpse laying at his feet. Then he lifts his head and turns toward the door.

It's only then I realize another stranger has entered the room. He doesn't seem to be a Marchesi, since the gun at his side is still cocked and primed to shoot again if he has to. But neither is he a Di Santo. And I can also tell from his attire—dark jeans, black tee and leather jacket—he's *definitely* not a wedding guest.

"You gonna introduce yourself?" Cristiano barks.

Everyone's gaze coasts toward the man whose frame is filling the doorway. So far, he's nothing but a lethal silhouette with a sawn-off shotgun adorning his right hand.

Then, from the floor where she lays sheltered by a hulking body, Trilby makes a sound like a dying animal. Nicolò rushes over and pulls the dead weight from my sister's body. Then he shouts out two words. Two words that change everything.

"Beppe's dead."

CHAPTER FORTY-TWO

enito

I feel like I've been rammed in the chest by a wrecking ball. The only things anchoring me are the feel of Tess's shaking hand wrapped around my arm, and the guttural roar of Cristiano as he grips his head between two hands and *growls*. Then he strides directly across the dance floor, stepping over motionless bodies, with eyes trained on Trilby. Only when he's scooped her into his arms and pulled her face into his chest does he turn his gaze to Beppe.

His expression contorts with each second that passes and I know, without a doubt, if the missing Marchesi were to walk in here now, he'll be carved up and buried alive.

The room is silent but for the sound of Trilby's cries. Her dress is stained with Beppe's blood from where he protected her from the gunfire. If it weren't for him, she'd be dead.

A hard shudder rolls down my spine at the thought of losing Tess. There is no law, no vow—not even a Cosa Nostra oath—that would stop me from mowing down every single person remotely connected.

When it becomes too uncomfortable to watch Cristiano and Trilby rocking together on the floor, I pan my gaze across the room. All the men are standing, apart from those lying motionless on the ground. Most of the women have staggered to their feet. Everyone looks stunned.

The man in the doorway hasn't moved. The fact he is the one who killed Lorenzo doesn't fully reassure me. He isn't an invited guest, and therefore, he isn't one of us. He isn't to be trusted.

"Who are you?" I demand. With my girl in my arms, my voice rolls along the ground like an avalanche.

The stranger doesn't reply. He just steps into the room, letting it bathe him in light like some Christ-like figure. My breath escapes me at the familiar features. There's something about him that warms my blood, yet I know for a fact I've never met him before.

Through the deathly silence, one woman's whisper rises through the haze.

"Andrew?"

My gaze whips to Sera. She's risen to her feet and has one hand pressed to her chest. Her focus hovers unwaveringly on the stranger.

"Who the fuck are you?" Augie barks, his gun primed at his shoulder.

The man drags his gaze from Cristiano to Augie, bypassing Sera completely. "Andreas Corlioni." His voice is deep and confident. I feel admiration and an unwelcome sense of camaraderie settle somewhere in my veins.

"That means nothing to me." Augie's gun doesn't move.

"I just took New Haven," the stranger says, like that explains everything. And actually, to me, the consigliere with an eye constantly on the next prize, it does.

"The Marchesi's wanted that," I say, rising to my feet.

"I know." A corner of his lip curls when he looks at me and a strange warmth runs through my torso. I don't like it.

"What does that have to do with us?" Augie says. The tension in his tone makes it clear to me he's losing his patience.

Beats pass. Andreas doesn't move his eyes from mine. It's like he's trying to communicate something without words. But I don't speak gaze. I speak Tess, sex and bullets.

"I want Boston."

My brows hitch and Augie inhales slowly.

The stranger continues before we can emphasize our stake in the ground.

"I know you do too."

"You think killing Lorenzo means we're just going

to hand the next phase of our growth over to you? A fucking stranger?" I bite out.

His pause drags until I'm almost so done I consider killing *him*. Then his cryptic response sends waves down my spine.

"I *think* blood is thick."

"Depends whose blood you're talking about." Nicolò is back in play.

"*Bernadi* blood is thick," the stranger drawls. Suddenly, the eyes of the Di Santo family are on me.

"How the fuck would you know?" I curl my fingers tightly around my gun, even though something in my bones is holding me back.

"You don't recognize me," Andreas says, his tone lightening, his gaze resting heavily on me.

I watch his lips part, time slowing to a low, grumbling tempo as he finishes his sentence. "Brother."

I hear Tess smack a hand over her mouth, while my world spins. I focus on my feet anchored into the floor.

I knew it. As soon as he stepped into the room, I knew. But it was such a surreal thought, an impossibility, my brain wouldn't entertain it for a second. But my body knew. My bones, my flesh, my blood. It knew my brother was in the room.

If he's expecting an open-armed welcome, a celebratory clink of two lowballs and a cozy catch-up by the fire, he is sorely mistaken. My comrade has just been shot, my girl has just fired a gun for the first time in her life and my boss's wedding has just been *ruined*.

And as for his quip about blood being thick, I share

blood with my downbeat ass of a father. *That* blood means fuck-all to me.

"My blood is all Di Santo," I grit. Ever since Gianni made me, it's been running through my veins. "And that's where my loyalty lies."

"I respect that." Andreas drags a thumb across his bottom lip as he watches my reaction. "But I still want Boston."

Cristiano is back on his feet, holding Trilby into his side. "The Marchesi's barely had a hold on it, and now Lorenzo is gone it could be anyone's for the taking. You don't need our permission."

Unease makes me twitch. "But we will fight you for it."

Andreas—or Leo Jr as I once knew him—drops his hand, his eyes sliding from me to Cristiano and back. "I don't want to fight, if I can help it."

"So then we have quite the conundrum." Cristiano holds Trilby tighter.

Several seconds of silence stretch, then Andreas tips his chin upward. "Let me join you."

"We don't know you." Cristiano's eyes narrow.

Andreas pushes his gun into the back of his pants. "That can be fixed. Make me a part of your family."

I almost choke. Five minutes ago, I didn't know my brother was alive, and now he's here asking to be part of the family I made for myself?

"Why did you change your name?" I snarl, feeling Cristiano's swing back to me.

My brother smiles but it's bitter. "If you think I'm

going to keep the name that deadbeat ass of a father gave me, just so it could live on after his death, you're not the bright spark you used to be."

I work my jaw side to side. I'd purposely forgotten that I was always the one hiding behind books, even at that young age, while Leo was the brawn our father used to drag around on his jobs.

He sighs impatiently. "I'm taking Boston whether you like it or not. Wouldn't you prefer to keep it in the family?"

My brow dips. "So you'd take control of Boston, then share it with us? It doesn't make sense. What would you get out of it?" I'm done with cryptic and I'm impatient for answers. "What *exactly* do you want?"

Silence falls over the room like a blanket, all eyes trained on Andreas—my brother. His gaze doesn't shift from mine as he raises an arm to the right and points to where Sera is standing with a hand still pressed to her chest, her lips parted, short breaths blowing the strands of auburn hair that have fallen across her face.

"I want *her*."

The end - for now.

ABOUT THE AUTHOR

Victoria Holliday is a contemporary romance author who writes dangerously delicious romance. When she isn't daydreaming about her husband or dirty dons and hot heroines, she can be found running around after either a) a small child b) a dog with slippers in his mouth c) one of three flighty chickens, or d) all of the above.

- instagram.com/victoriahollidaywrites
- tiktok.com/@victoriahollidaywrites

www.ingramcontent.com/pod-product-compliance
Lightning Source LLC
LaVergne TN
LVHW041616060526
838200LV00040B/1310